A WORLD FORMED BY DRAGONS ...

The Age of Dragons was a time of wonders. This was the age of the Three Dragons, the first and greatest of all dragonkind—Siberys, Eberron, and Khyber. In those most ancient of days, Siberys and Khyber fought one another. The powers wielded by these progenitor wyrms brought the world to ruin. Great Siberys, wounded and torn, became the Great Ring that surrounds the world. Khyber, the great Dragon Below, was sealed within the world. Eberron took his place between the rivals, healing the desolated world by becoming one with it.

But there are those whose thirst for power leads them to seek the power of the Dragon Below. Time and again they have risen to corrupt the world, and time and again heroes have risen to oppose them. . . .

THE
DRAGON BELOW

THE BINDING STONE

The
DRAGON BELOW
BOOK I

DON BASSINGTHWAITE

THE BINDING STONE

The Dragon Below · Book I

©2005 Wizards of the Coast, Inc.

Distributed in the United States by Holtzbrinck Publishing. Distributed in Canada by Fenn Ltd.

Distributed to the hobby, toy, and comic trade in the United States and Canada by regional distributors.

Distributed worldwide by Wizards of the Coast, Inc. and regional distributors.

Printed in the U.S.A.

Cover art by Michael Komarck
Map by Dennis Kauth
First Printing: August 2005
Library of Congress Catalog Card Number: 2004116876

9 8 7 6 5 4 3 2 1

ISBN-10: 0-7869-3784-X
ISBN-13: 978-0-7869-3784-4
620-96929000-001-EN

U.S., CANADA,
ASIA, PACIFIC, & LATIN AMERICA
Wizards of the Coast, Inc.
P.O. Box 707
Renton, WA 98057-0707
+1-800-324-6496

EUROPEAN HEADQUARTERS
Hasbro UK Ltd
Caswell Way
Newport, Gwent NP9 0YH
GREAT BRITAIN
Please keep this address for your records.

Visit our web site at www.wizards.com

For Ole

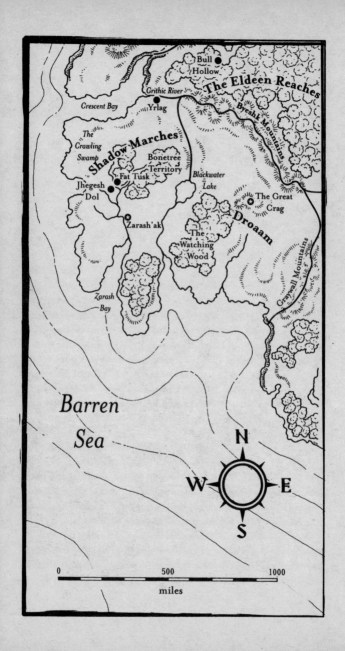

PROLOGUE

Screams, thin and high, shivered the night air.

In the camp that spread out at the foot of the ancestor mound, men, women, and even the smallest children of the clan touched their fingers to lips and forehead in a sign of obedience and respect to the great powers that dwelled beneath them—then went back to whatever they had been doing. Stitching clothes from leather or rough cloth taken in raids from neighboring tribes. Pounding pale yellow flour from the pith of dark gold reeds. Sitting by fires, telling stories beneath the light of Eberron's moons and the glowing streak of the Ring of Siberys. In the case of the children, sleeping in knotted piles with brothers and sisters and cousins and such dogs as were allowed into the clan's shelters.

In the case of Ner, leader of the Bonetree hunters, running a whetstone up and down the length of his sword until the metal sang. The ancient blade was the best weapon among the clan. When Ner paused and looked up as the screams continued, Ashi glanced away before he could see the envy in her eyes. *"Che Harana shialo betgri jun,"* she said. *The Revered was praying late tonight.*

"An shial todo'o mogri bet kei an tohushenr andgri'imo," added Breff. He lounged on the far side of the fire, a bowl of beer in one hand. His other was held gingerly against his body. The fresh black of a new tattoo stroked his forearm.

1

Ashi smiled and the thin bone hoops that pierced either side of her lower lips pressed against her teeth. The Revered had prayed late every night since he returned from his most recent trip downstream. The three outclanners he had brought back with him must have been tougher than they looked. *"Eches duskavs eva an toklavito itri taos pareis kto ans kritaos!"*

"Eches toch krii ches duskavsit ahines," Ner said. His face was turned toward the dark silhouette that the mound made against the winking lights of the sky. Ashi realized that he looked worried. The thin screams ended abruptly. She set her own bowl down and twisted around to follow Ner's gaze.

She was just in time to see strange white flames flare in the mound's mouth. *"Rond betch!"* she choked.

Her cry brought Breff upright, his beer slopping across his chest as he whirled around to stare as well. Across the camp, dozens more voices were raised in wonder and fear.

A long fluting call came drifting down from the mound. Instinct closed every mouth so that the hunters could hear the signal—even though this call was one that every member of the clan knew by heart.

Help! Danger!

Ashi recognized the warble in the call. *"Eche Gig!"* she said. The hunter had been standing honor watch outside the mound.

Ner was already on his feet, his sword sheathed so that his hands were free to cup his mouth and let loose a call of his own. *All hunters respond!* As the Bonetree warriors snatched up weapons and tumbled out of shelters in a flurry of reaction, Ner snapped around. *"Ashi! Breff! At sutis!"* he called, leaping away from the fire and racing for the mound.

Ashi grabbed her sword—a crude weapon stolen from orcs—and ran after him. The pale beads woven into her thick hair made a clashing rhythm as she stretched her legs. At her side, Breff matched her stride for stride. Downstream from the mound, the ground turned wet and mucky until it was overwhelmed by the water and became marsh. Bonetree territory was much drier, the footing solid.

Long strides on solid ground ate distance quickly. The hunters reached the mouth of the mound in only moments, but in those moments, Ashi saw flames flare again, this time even brighter, and a hot wind blew against her. By the light of the flame, she could see three figures at the mound's mouth.

Two were Bonetree hunters. Gig, who had given the call, writhed on the ground, his skin burned bright red. Pai, the hunter who had stood honor watch with him, was stretched out, charred black and motionless.

The third figure stood in the very mouth of the mound. White flames seemed to shimmer and cling to it. Ashi put up her hand to shade her eyes. Against the glare of the flame, she could see almost nothing of the figure. It was light and lithe, she could tell that much.

As more hunters swept up to the mound, though, and before Ashi could see any more, the figure crossed its arms over its chest. For a moment, the shimmering flames seemed shot with pale colors. Then the air around the figure seemed to collapse and fold before springing back again.

The figure was gone. The white fire guttered and died. Ashi blinked, trying to clear the glare of it from her eyes. The air was still heavy with heat and the smell of burned flesh. What had just happened? *"Tokrii eche?"* she asked.

"Khyberit gentis," breathed Ner. *"Toch pinde!"*

He knew no more than she did. *"Cheo as andoas tmake?"*

Ner shook his head. *"Breff,"* he said, *"ches broshamas viti. Gig domado kebrono —"*

A cry cut him off. Every eye in the crowd of hunters darted back to the mound's mouth. There was a new light glowing within it, pale and watery, dimmed further by smoke. Three more figures moved against it. One of them was a tall man, his face clear and pale, his hair black, his eyes bright and shining green. He was dressed in robes of fine black leather. Set into the sleeves of the robes, like jewels in a necklace Ashi had once seen around an outclanner's neck, were half a dozen smooth, gently polished stones that glowed a soft red against the black leather. A single smoky crystal that winked deep blue was set at the center of the man's chest. Dragonshards, all of them.

The Bonetree hunters dropped to their knees in unison, their fingers darting to their lips and to their foreheads. Ashi found herself trembling.

"Revered!" Ner gasped. "What has happened?" He spoke the outclanner language that the Revered preferred. Ashi and Breff spoke the language as well, though most of the hunters were ignorant of it.

"Ner, master of my hunters." The Revered's voice was smooth as oil. He held out long, perfect fingers. Ner crept forward on his knees and kissed the man's fingers, then touched them to his forehead. The Revered lifted his hand, gesturing for Ner to stand. "I have lost someone," he said. "Take the best of your hunters. Retrieve her for me."

Ner glanced over his shoulder. "Ashi," he said. "Breff. Hand-wit. Mukur. Dal. Etta. *At dosut kebronos.*" The named hunters shifted with anticipation—Ashi a little bit more for having been named first. She watched as Ner looked back to the Revered.

The tall man raised his eyebrows. "More." As the hunter blinked in surprise, he added, "She is wily and fast, Ner. You will need more hunters."

"No one is faster than the Bonetree hunters," Ner said.

The Revered shook his head. "Don't underestimate her, hunt-master. She escaped from me."

Ner flushed and bent his head. "I can take two dozen and still leave the mound and the clan protected, Revered."

"Do that. You will have other help as well." The Revered motioned, the smallest twitch of his hand, and one of the figures who had accompanied him moved forward. The figure wore a cloak and a deep cowl, but Ashi could tell that underneath it was tall and lean. "Hruucan will accompany you as my Hand," said the Revered. "Address him as you address me. When the time is right, he will summon the children of Khyber to aid you."

"Revered! Hand!" Ner dropped back down to his knees. "You honor us!"

The Revered reached out and rested his hand on Ner's head. "Use every trick and tool you have. I must have her back!"

4

Ecstasy washed over Ner's face at the man's touch. Ashi, however, frowned. "Revered," she said as loudly as she dared, her eyes downcast, "there is something. The woman you want . . . with the fire behind her, we didn't see her. And when we approached, she vanished!"

She felt the weight of the Revered's gaze on her. "Ashi, you are as bright as you are strong. Look up." She did. The Revered favored her with a smile, then looked to the second figure who had come with him out of the mound. "Medala, show them."

As the figure moved out from the Revered's shadow, the gathered hunters fell silent. Dressed in draping robes of fine but soiled green fabric, Medala was a woman with dusky skin and dark hair streaked with gray at an early age. An outclanner. One of the three outclanners the Revered had brought back from his recent journey downstream and taken away into the depths of the ancestor mound.

By all rights, she should have been dead instead of standing at the Revered's side.

For a moment, the woman's gaze swept over the hunters, her face as hard as if she could sense their fear and dislike. Then, with an effort, her face smoothed and she nodded to the Revered. "Of course," she said in a knife-edge voice. She looked back out at the hunters.

Ashi's ears seemed to ring with the sound of a single, pure note and an image leaped into her mind—an image of the woman they sought, as clear as if she had stood before her in broad daylight. Her name poured into Ashi's mind. Her name, what she was, what she was capable of doing. What she had done within the mound—or at least some shadow of it. Ashi gasped out loud, her exclamation part of a chorus that erupted from all the hunters. She clutched at her head. *"Rond betch!"* she cursed. *"Cheo kint?* What kind of magic—"

"Not magic," said Medala. "Psionics. The power of the mind."

"Kint by any name has the same stink," groaned Breff.

Medala's eyes narrowed, but the Revered gave her a sharp glance. "Medala," he said.

5

The green-robed woman flinched as if he had struck her, shrinking back in terror from the rebuke. "Your pardon, Dah'mir."

Her words silenced the hunters more than any actions ever could. The name of the Revered hadn't been spoken aloud among the Bonetree clan in four generations. Ashi held her breath, waiting.

But if the Revered was offended, he didn't show it. "What of her vanishing?"

"She can step short distances across the dimensions of space," said Medala. Confusion must have shown on the face of the hunters because she looked disgusted. "She moved from one place to another," she added, then looked back to the Revered. "She can't manage it more than once a day and she can't go very far. Two hundred paces at most. Enough to break her trail."

"Two hundred paces?" asked Ner. His pride seemed to return. "Nothing. We'll pick her trail up again, Revered." His hand dipped into a pouch at his hip and emerged with a thin bone whistle. He put it to his lips and blew a series of shrill notes.

A moment later, Ashi heard a splash and a rustle from the specially prepared pond close to the village. Wings beat into the sky. "Your birds, Revered," said Ner. "They will see her and guide us to her."

The Revered smiled. "Move fast, Ner. Bring her back to me." He held out a strange band of woven copper wire and clear crystals, folded like a cloth headband and big enough to stretch around someone's head. "Take this. If you need to speak with me, wear it and Medala will hear you."

Ner bowed his head and accepted the device, but not before Ashi saw him throw a look of malice toward Medala. She understood his anger. How could an outclanner claim a favor and trust from the Revered that he barely showed to the Bonetree, a clan he had guided for generations?

The master of the hunters said nothing, however, and Ashi knew he never would. She kept her mouth closed as well.

The Revered raised his hands over them. "Go," he said. "Do my bidding and with it the work of Khyber. The Dragon Below promises glory to the Bonetree!"

The gathered hunters might not have understood the Revered's words, but they understood the blessing. Their voices rose in a roaring response. *"Su Drumas! Su Darasvhir!"*

For the Bonetree! For the Dragon Below!

Ashi mouthed the words, but her eyes were on the Revered and Medala. And Medala's eyes, she saw, were on Dah'mir.

998

YEAR OF THE KINGDOM

CHAPTER

I

The golden light of late afternoon filled the little valley like honey. Insects flashed as they drifted through the still air, lazy now that midsummer's fierce heat had passed from the far west of the Eldeen Reaches. There was a spot Geth knew of, up high on the valley's northern slope, where a slab of bare rock thrust out from the trees. On an afternoon like this, there was nowhere better to lie out and bask in the sun, alone with the sky, the forest, and the stone.

On another afternoon, the shifter thought, but not today. He shook thick, sweat-damp brown hair out of his eyes and growled between sharp teeth, "They're toying with us, Adolan. Three times back and forth across the valley. Are they going to run us all the way to the Shadowcrags?"

Well-worn leather leggings whispered as Adolan paused and looked back along the valley's length. His nose, sharp and pointed as human noses tended to be, crinkled. "If we take a straight path, it's not so far back to Bull Hollow."

Geth stared at his friend, then blinked wide amber eyes. "You'd see the Ring of Siberys in a mud puddle," he grumbled in annoyance.

Adolan's smile broke through his red-brown beard. "What's the matter, Geth?" he asked. "Can't enjoy your fleas when someone's scratching you?"

Geth paused in the act of reaching to scratch at the thick sideburns that grew down a shifter's jaw line. Another low growl rolled up out of his throat. The heavy hair on the back of his neck and on his forearms rose and his lips pulled away from his teeth. "If one of my fleas ever bit your thin skin, Ado, we'd need a needle and thread to sew up the wound!"

"Then it's good thing they like your furry hide better, isn't it?"

"Small-eye human."

"Furball shifter." Adolan held out a flat packet. "Jerky?"

"Tak." Geth plucked a strip of the dried meat from the druid's packet with thick, heavy-nailed fingers. He stuck it in his mouth and sucked at the smoky saltiness for a moment, then said around the meat, "They are toying with us, though."

"They're too bold," Adolan said as he took a piece of jerky for himself. "We're closer to them than they think. We'll catch them soon."

The tall human slid the jerky into his mouth and started walking again, eyes scanning the ground for signs of their quarry. Geth followed him at an easy, loping gait. "Do you think they'll talk?" he asked. "I hate it when they talk."

Adolan's only answer was the slow grind of flat teeth on jerky. Geth snapped at his jerky twice. Sharp teeth tore the hard meat into slivers. "More?" he grunted.

Adolan tossed him the packet.

"There's something in the woods," Sandar had said when he dropped by their cabin that morning. The man who owned the last inn in the Eldeen had somehow appointed himself the mouthpiece of Bull Hollow's elders.

"There are a lot of things in the woods, Sandar," Geth had told him with his usual bluntness.

Blunt words rolled off Sandar like water. "A lot of things," the elder had replied, "don't come prowling around people's farms."

Adolan had stepped in, as he so often did, before things deteriorated too far. "Bull Hollow doesn't have any shortage of hunters, Sandar," he had pointed out.

Sandar had crossed his hands over his belly. "Bull Hollow only has two hunters who can take on whatever dragged Ellio Tuck's biggest breeding sow out of her pen and carried her off toward the high valleys."

Geth and Adolan had been on the trail by mid-morning.

Fortunately, their quarry had been easy to track—and to identify. Two trails of massive cat-like paws traced around Tuck's farm, led to the remains of an enormous sow in the woods, and continued on up into the higher reaches of the forest. Two trails, but with six paws to each trail. Deep scratches had been torn in the wood of the sow's pen and high on tree trunks along the trail, all without any of the twelve paws leaving the ground. Only displacer beasts—six legs and a pair of barbed tentacles sprouting from the shoulders—left spoor like that.

Not even Adolan could argue that the beasts might be passing through on their way to new hunting ground. *Everywhere* was a displacer beast's hunting ground. The monsters were dumb enough to hunt anything they came across—and just smart enough to get away with it.

An uneasy thought made the hair on Geth's arms and neck stand up again. How long had the beasts known they were being followed? Had they been toying with their pursuers even before they reached the valley?

Had the beasts led him and Adolan here deliberately?

The beasts' trail turned back down toward the valley floor. Geth scanned the valley through gaps in the trees. The valley was uninhabited, so no chance of allies. Lots of crags and displaced boulders. Steep sides. A narrow lower mouth that was easily guarded, an upland slope that was steep and more easily descended than climbed. A good place for an ambush.

Suddenly the gentle gold of afternoon light seemed harsh and the lazy hum of insects an annoying drone. "Ado," Geth said, "I think the beasts are trying to turn the hunt on us."

"I know," Adolan answered, "but don't worry." He twitched his head toward the sky. "Breek is watching over us."

Geth glanced up. High above, the black dot of an eagle skimmed against bright blue. Adolan's half-wild bird was on guard. He let out a grunt of relief. Breek's eyes would spot any tricks the displacer beasts might try. Even so, his hands went to his belt and touched the paired, short-hafted axes that hung on either side of his waist.

"How far ahead of us do you think they are?" he asked.

"Not far. They came this way about the same time we were at the top of the slope. They're taking their time, walking slow." Adolan pointed at a patch of fallen leaves and Geth glanced at it as they passed. Paws had pushed the leaves down into the damp earth underneath. The prints were evenly spaced and well formed. The displacer beast that had made them was in no hurry.

He would have rather the beast had been running. He stuffed the packet of jerky into a pouch on his belt and drew one of the axes. Adolan glanced back and raised an eyebrow, but said nothing.

As they reached the valley floor, however, the druid paused. Geth stepped up beside him. "What?" he murmured.

Adolan pointed again. Geth followed his gesture. He hadn't practiced woodcraft to the same degree as Adolan for a long time, but some skills never faded. A stream passed through this part of the valley. All around its soft banks, the grass was crushed as if the beasts had milled around like excited kittens before turning aside from their path across the valley and abandoning their casual pace. Their paws had ripped into the ground as they opened up their stride to follow the stream back down the valley's length.

Geth stepped out into the open and slid up to the stream. Stamped in the soft ground were the marks of shod human—or at the very least, humanoid—feet. "Ado!" he hissed.

Adolan crouched down. "Ring of Siberys," he murmured in surprise. "I think we know what got the displacer beasts excited." He reached down and traced the shape of the footprint. "Sandals. Well-worn. And on the feet of someone light. A woman or maybe an elf. "

"No one lives in this valley." Geth turned and peered upstream. There were traces of passage on the grass. He paced swiftly back alongside the water. More footprints revealed themselves in an unsteady line, some prints deeper and harder than others. He lifted his gaze. In the distance, the water that became the stream spilled over the steep slope at the top of the valley in a fine white cascade. He returned to Adolan's side. "I think they came down out of the hills. They're staggering—probably tired or wounded. They must have come a long way."

"Well, they've staggered right into the path of the worst predators this valley has seen for decades," Adolan said. He reached behind his back and freed the spear that he carried. "I think the displacer beasts have forgotten about us—they have a new toy. We need to hurry."

Geth tightened his grip on his axe and flexed the thick muscles of his arms and shoulders. "Cousin Bear, finally!"

Adolan winced. "You don't have to sound so eager."

"We've been tracking all day. I want a fight!"

"And shifters wonder why other races feel uncomfortable around them."

"My ancestors were predators," Geth replied, baring his teeth.

"You've argued the point for me," said Adolan in resignation. He turned and began trotting along the displacer beasts' path. Geth shrugged, smiled, and loped along after him.

The beasts' run slowed to a pace better suited for stealth—short bursts of speed interspersed with long moments of patient stillness. The mix of shallow toe-prints and deeper flat paw-prints told the story of their stalking. Woven among the beasts' trail were the sandal prints of their prey, light and staggering but—to Geth's surprise—still swift. "Whoever they are," he grunted, "they move fast."

Less than a dozen paces further on, Adolan grabbed his arm and pulled him quickly and silently behind a cluster of tall feathery grass by the stream's edge. He gestured ahead. Geth nodded and rose up just enough to peer past the grass.

Ahead, the stream turned to flow around a steep rise in the valley floor. One of the displacer beasts was climbing that slope. The other already crouched atop it, peering intently down the other side. In general shape, the beasts resembled mountain lions, but so thin that every muscle stood out on their spare, six-legged frames. The thin, flexible tentacles that sprouted from their shoulders reached out to twine around saplings and branches. The tentacles ended in flat pads covered in horrid barbs that stripped the bark away from the wood.

The beasts' blue-black fur carried a weird shimmer that made it hard to focus on them. One moment, they appeared to be in one spot—in the next, they seemed to have shifted by several feet. Geth had to squeeze his eyes closed and open them again to be sure there really were two of the creatures.

The beast still climbing the slope was easily the size of a horse. The one at the crest of the slope was bigger still, its tentacles as thick as fat serpents. A strange, throbbing growl was building in its lean, corded throat.

It took Geth a moment to realize that the huge beast was purring with bloodthirsty pleasure. A heartbeat later, it sank down low to the ground and slid forward out of sight. The second followed.

"They're closing in!" he snarled.

"Go!" urged Adolan. "I have your back!"

Geth tore through the tall grass. He surged up to the crest of the slope, bounding and leaping from side to side with an ease no human could have matched. At the top of the rise, he paused long enough to take in the scene below. Through the trees and a little off to one side was one of the rocky outcroppings that dotted the valley like enormous roots thrust up by the hills. The displacer beasts had joined together, the larger of the two taking the lead. Their prey stood cornered against the outcropping.

Geth's eyes narrowed. Adolan's assessment of the footprints by the stream had been right—the beast's prey was a woman and a human. His own judgment had been right as well, though. The woman must have come a long way because she certainly wasn't from the Eldeen. Her skin was an exotic bronze-brown color and her hair was long, straight, and black. Weariness showed clearly in her face, but Geth saw her push it aside and ready a short spear with a pale shaft and a strangely crystalline head, then look up to glare at the larger beast with single-minded determination.

She was brave, but bravery wasn't going to save her against two vicious displacer beasts. Geth swept his arms wide, drew in a deep breath, and . . . shifted.

Somewhere deep, deep in the past the gift of lycanthropy, the ability to take the form of wolves, bears, tigers, and other animals, had risen in humans. Those who possessed it, whether naturally or by way of a curse, found themselves shunned—as predators and worse—by those who did not. They began to keep to themselves, favoring secrecy or the company of other shapeshifters. Among those shapeshifters who bred only with their own kind, the lines of lycanthropy stayed true. Where they bred with normal humans, though, or where they fell in love and mated with those of another line, the blood of the lycanthropes mingled and combined. The children born of such unions weren't fully human, but neither were they lycanthropes. They were strong, they were fast, and they were marked by the blood of beasts. They might not have been able to take the animal form of their lycanthrope parent, but they could take on some of its qualities.

Generation to generation, the traits bred true. Over time a new race was born, neither human nor lycanthrope nor animal, but something of each. They became the weretouched. The shifters.

Geth's ancient heritage rose up from deep within him, spreading out from the core of his being. Some shifters manifested terrible claws, others massive fangs, still others astounding speed or heightened senses. Geth's gift from his lycanthrope ancestors was sheer toughness. Strength seeped into bones and flooded his flesh. His skin hardened and his hair became coarse like an animal's tough hide. A sense of invincibility swept through him. For the moment at least, he felt unstoppable!

He let out the breath he had drawn in a tremendous roar and bounded down the slope, heading straight for the smaller displacer beast. His sudden appearance had both the creatures and their intended prey off balance—the dark-haired woman stared in shock as the displacer beasts whirled around to face this new threat. They were slow, though. The smaller beast sent barbed tentacles questing toward them. He shouted out another roar and swung his axes in twin arcs.

The natural magic of displacer beasts made them difficult to fight and attacking one took a combination of both skill and luck. As the beast's tentacles lashed toward him, Geth spun aside and chopped blindly. His left-hand weapon bit into unseen flesh. More than a foot away, the beast's tentacle sheared apart and the horny barbed pad at its end fell to the ground.

The beast's screeches of pain as it scrambled away were almost loud enough to drown out the sound of Adolan's chanted prayer as he called upon the powers of the forest to lend them aid. A breeze seemed to blow through the trees, stirring vines, branches, prickly bushes and tall stalks of grass—except that Geth felt nothing in the air.

All around the retreating beast, however, the stirring intensified as the plants of forest answered the druid's call, whipping into sudden life and twining around the monster. The beast squealed and struggled to free itself from their entangling grasp. Geth bared his teeth. The weak plants wouldn't hold the creature for long, but they would slow it down. As Adolan came sliding down the slope, spear at the ready, Geth whirled to face the larger beast.

The creature was crouched low to the ground and growling, its eyes darting between Geth and the cornered woman as it tried to grasp the turn of events. Its wide green eyes shrank to slits and its tentacles swayed dangerously. "Get back!" it yowled. "Get back and live! My prey! Mine!"

Geth's teeth clenched. They do talk, he thought. Damn. He bent his knees, sinking into a defensive posture, and stretched out his arms, axes ready for an attack.

And an attack came—but not against him.

The determination that the dark-haired woman had worn like a shield seemed to condense abruptly into outrage. "Prey?" she cried. "Prey? I am no one's prey, you hideous *dahr!*"

She took a step forward . . . and her sandaled feet rose off the ground. As if lifted up by her anger, she floated a foot or more above the forest floor, her eyes and face shining with fury. Her hand stabbed at the beast. Abruptly, a sound like a chorus of voices seemed to fill Geth's ears and a stream of white flames lanced from the woman's hand toward the beast.

The monster screeched and twisted—and where Geth would have thought that the flames would lap against its flank, instead they hissed through empty air. The woman's aim had been fooled by the beast's glamer. It lunged at her, tentacles flailing. The move seemed to catch her by surprise. She managed to slip under one tentacle, her feet sliding across the air, but the other whirled around and caught her with a hard slap across the chest. Her spear flew out of her hand and she slammed backward into the rocks with an audible thud. Her still body slid back down to the ground.

The displacer beast whirled back toward Geth. "Die you now! Yes! Die!" A tentacle lashed at him. Geth raised an arm, blocking. The barbed pad at the tentacle's end ripped away the fabric of his sleeve and gouged at his flesh. Anyone else would have had their skin flayed by the attack. Geth's shifting-toughened hide was left with nothing worse than deep scratches.

"Die now?" he snarled in mocking imitation of the beast's screeching voice. "Yes!"

He leaped in close, hacking and chopping with his axes. The beast dodged back, countering with tentacles and—if Geth got too close—a vicious swipe from one of its six clawed feet. His shifting heritage protected him from the worst damage of its attacks, though, just as the beast's magic kept most of his blows away from it.

It still managed to hit him more often than he hit it, though. In moments, he was bleeding from a half a dozen deep gouges, and the displacer beast was grinning with mad blood lust. Geth stumbled back, breathing hard. A tentacle grabbed his leg, yanked, and he was on the ground, staring up at the beast.

"More prey!" the creature screamed. "More!" Its head darted down, jaws wide.

Geth dropped one axe and snapped the other up crossways against his body, clutching it with both hands. The stout wood of the shaft jammed across the beast's open jaws like a horse's bridle. The beast tried to shake it out, but Geth pushed back, pressing the axe up. The creature's tentacles wrapped around his arms and tried to pull them aside. Geth's arms were stronger—at least for the moment. "Ado!" he roared.

Out of the corner of his eye, he could see the druid. The smaller displacer beast had managed to rip its way free of the twining forest plants. Adolan held it at bay with his spear, shifting and thrusting to ward off the creature's lunging attacks. His eyes darted to Geth, though, then up to the sky. He feinted, then jumped away as the creature reacted to the false attack. In the clear for a moment, he drew a deep breath, folded his lower lip under his front teeth, and let out two clear, piercing whistles.

The sky seemed to fall on the displacer beast that had Geth pinned as Breek came plummeting down like a feathered lightning bolt. With an accuracy that no human eye could have matched, the eagle struck the displacer beast square in the back. Wicked talons tore at the creature's blue-black hide and the beast let out a deafening screech of pain and alarm. It twisted around on itself, desperately trying to strike at this new attacker. As it reared back and its tentacles released his arms, Geth threw himself away from it.

His hand closed on the shaft of the unconscious woman's fallen spear, and he rolled to his feet with the weapon in his grip. The weapon was lighter than he expected, its shaft carved from some light, almost-wood, and its head forged of a metal with a delicate, almost crystalline sparkle. It looked needle-sharp, though, and that was what mattered. "Ado, I'm clear!" he shouted.

The second beast had turned its attention back to the druid, its tentacles lashing like serpents. This time, though, it looked like it was trying to seize the spear and tear it away. Adolan let out another whistle.

With a harsh screech and a mighty flurry of wings, Breek launched himself from the back of the larger displacer beast straight toward the smaller. The creature wheeled to meet the bird's attack, but at the last moment, Breek's wings spread wide and he swooped up and out of reach. The beast twisted around again—only to be met with the point of Adolan's spear as the druid charged. Sharp metal buried itself deep in the creature's chest. Its tentacles lashed frantically at the air, then fell still as it slumped to the ground. The larger beast screamed in anger. "Chosen! Mate!" Its head snapped around to glare at Geth and it surged toward him.

Geth shifted his weight as the beast's tentacles swept at him again, swaying back, but not giving ground. The tentacles came close enough for him to hear the hiss as they lashed the air. Guided by sound rather than sight, Geth jabbed out sharply with the woman's spear—piercing the wide pad of the beast's tentacle and pinning it to the earth of the valley floor. The beast roared and tried to wrench the pinned tentacle free, simultaneously raking at Geth with the other. The shifter roared just as loudly with the scourging pain of the blows that hammered at his back, but he reached down and wrapped his hand around the tentacle. As the beast roared out again, he pulled hard on it, hauling himself forward. The displacer's beast's eyes went wide in sudden panic. Following the taut, struggling tentacle, Geth swung his axe in a powerful overhand blow.

The blade hacked straight into the beast's narrow skull.

A shudder passed through its body, then it collapsed to the ground and lay still.

Geth let go of the axe and staggered back. "They're both dead?" he wheezed as Adolan came trotting over.

Adolan glanced at Breek as the bird flapped down from above, settled onto a tentacle, and began to tear at the limp flesh with his hooked beak. "Breek says yes," he said.

"Good." Geth sagged to his knees and released his hold on his shifting-granted endurance. As it drained away, the wounds he had suffered seemed ten times as painful. He clenched his teeth as the shifting tugged on the worst of the injuries, but it was still too much. He gasped out loud and almost fell over.

"Easy," murmured Adolan. Geth felt the druid touch his bloodied back, then heard him murmur a prayer.

Nature's power swirled around them like a summer breeze. A sweet ache throbbed across Geth's back as his wounds closed. He groaned with relief and opened his eyes. "Twice tak," he said.

Adolan smiled briefly, then slapped Geth's newly healed shoulder. "A pair of displacer beasts between two men and a bird," said the druid. "We're lucky the beasts were still young!"

"Young?" Geth forced himself to his feet. "They would have gotten bigger?"

"Not necessarily. But they would have gotten smarter." Adolan knelt down beside the fallen woman and touched her face lightly with the tips of his fingers. She groaned quietly. Geth pulled her spear out of the ground and shook the beast's tentacle off of it, then moved over to stand above Adolan.

"How is she?" he asked.

"She'll be all right," Adolan replied. His fingers probed the back of the woman's head underneath her hair. Her face contorted and she stirred uneasily. Adolan's eyes drifted shut and he spoke a second prayer of healing. Once again, Geth felt nature itself stir to the druid's call. The dark-haired woman's face eased. Her breathing drifted and became regular. Adolan lifted his hand away. "I can feel her exhaustion. More than anything, she needs sleep," he said. "She'll stay this way until we can get back to Bull Hollow." He studied her face. "She's not like anyone I've ever seen. And the spell of fire that she cast was strange, too. That strange sound that came with it wasn't like any priest's prayer or wizard's invocation."

Geth tilted his head and looked closely at the woman. Her bronze-brown face was long and almost too elegant, her skin smooth and flawless, though darkened by long exposure to the sun. A twisted band of polished bronze circled her head and wide, decorative bracers of the same metal wrapped her forearms. A simple cord around her neck supported a woven spiral of thick bronze wires. Caught within the spiral was a cloudy green-yellow crystal the size of two of his fingers held side by side. Her clothes, as well as the sandals on her feet, showed the strain of long travel, though the woman was hardly dressed for it: she wore only a short, light shirt and tapered pants, with a fringe that wrapped around her waist. In spite of the wear on it, the fabric of her clothes was a rich, deep red embroidered with gold-colored thread in strange and exotic patterns. Geth glanced at the spear in his hand. The shaft below the crystalline metal of the head was worked in similar patterns.

"I don't think she's a wizard or a priest, Adolan," he said. "And that was no spell. I've seen her kind before."

Adolan looked up at him. "In the Eldeen?" he asked, his voice low and cautious.

Geth shook his head. "No. It was . . . before I came to Bull Hollow." Geth's jaw tightened. He gestured to the woman's distinctive clothes and spear, to her fine features. "She's a kalashtar."

Only the vaguest kind of recognition flickered in Adolan's eyes. "Kalashtar come from the east," Geth explained. "Far to the east—across the Dragonreach and the Sea of Rage, from Sarlona." He glanced down at the sleeping woman. "I saw some of her kind in Rekkenmark in Karrnath. A wizard told me that they have powers that aren't like any magic we know." He touched his forehead. "It's some kind of mind-magic."

Adolan's eyes narrowed and his nose crinkled. "Do they all float like that when they fight?" Geth shook his head. "What do you think she's doing in the Eldeen Reaches?

"I don't know," said Geth. He drew a deep breath. "But I don't think it's safe to take her back to Bull Hollow. We should leave her here."

"Geth!"

"Trouble followed every kalashtar I ever saw, Adolan." Geth gestured to the carnage around them.

"She stumbled across young displacer beasts looking for prey. We already knew they were dangerous." Adolan stood up. "And she's asleep. What trouble can she bring down on us?"

"She'll wake up sooner or later. There must be some reason she's stumbling through the hills in exhaustion."

Adolan crossed his arms and fixed him with a glare. "She's most likely lost. We can't just leave her, Geth. The displacer beasts were the most dangerous things in the forest, but they weren't the only danger. We need to take her with us." When Geth glowered, he raised his eyebrows. "Are your fleas bothering you again, furball?"

Geth bared his teeth. "I don't like it," he said.

"You don't like much of anything. Think on this: we dealt with the displacer beasts *and* saved a life today. Be happy with that."

Geth's lips pinched back together. "Ring of Siberys in a mud puddle, Ado."

"With you around, someone has to be the optimist." Adolan walked over to the area of brush that had been animated by his prayer. A few long vines still squirmed across the ground. The druid grabbed them and began gathering them like some kind of strange, wild rope. "Find me two long, sturdy branches. We need to make a litter."

CHAPTER

2

Twilight lay purple against the sky by the time the forest opened up and Singe looked down into the shallow valley that held—so a tavernkeeper had told them two days ago—the hamlet of Bull Hollow and the end of the long western road.

Given that the "road" was really more of a vague track, Singe didn't hold out any great hope for the "hamlet" either.

Toller d'Deneith urged his horse up alongside Singe's. The young man's face twisted as he looked down. "That's it?" he asked.

"I told you not to expect much." Singe studied the valley. The buildings of Bull Hole were shrouded by trees, but at least a dozen thin plumes of rising smoke were clustered together. A short distance away from the plumes, a broad clearing opened up around what seemed to be stone ruins. Here and there, other clearings broke through the trees where small farms had been cut from the forest. He grunted. Maybe the place had potential after all.

"Let's get down there," he said. "If we need to knock on doors looking for a place to sleep, it's best to do it while there's still some light."

"You don't think they'll have an inn?"

Singe's mouth curled into a grin. "We have a saying in Aundair: cow-paths don't lead to palaces. This is the very end of the loneliest cow-path in the Eldeen, Toller. Do *you* think Bull Hollow will have an inn?"

Toller sat up a straight, needled by the comment. "A little respect would be appropriate, Lieutenant Bayard!" His hand went, unconsciously, to the hem of the blue jacket that he wore in spite of the heat, pulling it taut so that the silver embroidered emblem of the Watchful Eye superimposed on an upright sword—symbol of the Blademarks mercenary guild of House Deneith—flashed in the fading light of the setting sun.

Singe brushed back a stray lock of blond hair, crossed his hands over the pommel of his saddle, and gave the young man a lazy stare. A similar jacket, though without Toller's insignia of rank, was folded up in his saddlebags in favor of a much lighter vest. Toller was sweating in spite of the cool of evening. He wasn't.

"Singe," he said calmly. "Call me Singe. Lieutenant Singe if you have to." He sat up straight. "Commander."

Toller flushed and glanced away. "Sorry, Singe."

Singe rolled his eyes. "Twelve moons! Stop apologizing!" he groaned. He twitched his horse's reins and the animal started to move again. "If you can't do at least that, your first command will be your last!"

"Right. Sorr—" Toller caught himself and closed his mouth. Singe nodded his approval and the young man allowed himself a half-smile. "Does this mean I can actually call you—?"

"No."

Bull Hollow, when they reached it, turned out to be a cluster of well-kept, mostly wooden buildings arranged around a central common like gamblers around a cock pit. The majority of the buildings were houses, a few were simple shops of various kinds, and at least one had the stout stone walls of a smithy. That the small community managed to support more than one commercial establishment at all was something of a surprise, but Singe supposed that Bull Hollow actually served as the trading hub for a region that spread far beyond its little valley.

Toller reached over and prodded him. "Look at that."

Singe looked. On the far side of the common was a large whitewashed building with a number of windows and what looked like a low-slung stable to one side. A goodly number of folk were gathered at the ground floor and, from what he could see through open windows, all of the visitors held mugs and tankards. He sat back. "Twelve moons," he said.

"It's an inn?" asked Toller.

"An inn or something enough like one that I'm willing to chance it." He nodded to Toller. "Maybe I was wrong about this place."

He turned his horse toward the large building, Toller wheeling his mount sharply in order to stay close. Their arrival was beginning to bring attention. More and more faces all around the hamlet's common were turning in their direction. Eyes were wide and he caught more than one over-loud whisper of excitement and curiosity. A good number were directed toward Toller and the insignia of House Deneith.

Toller was staring back. "Maybe now would be a good time to begin recruiting," he whispered. "We have their attention and they're clearly interested."

"We have plenty of time," Singe murmured back. He barely moved his lips as he nodded to a young lass in a homespun dress of a cut that looked like it had come out of another century. "Let them come to us. We'll have some dinner and give them a chance to get a few drinks inside themselves. When we've worked our way back toward civilization with a train of recruits for the Blademarks in tow, that's the time to talk fast and try to sell the benefits of becoming a mercenary. For now, relax and use your eyes. Reachers make good scouts and wilderness fighters—try and spot the best ones before they start posing for us."

"You're the veteran," said Toller. "Have you ever been out this far before?"

Singe pressed his lips together and fixed his gaze on the tavern. For a moment he was silent, then he said, "Almost. Once, years ago. During the war and much further north. My first recruiting trip—I was barely more than a recruit myself."

"And?" asked Toller.

Singe glanced at him. "And nothing," he said curtly. "It was during your uncle's command of the Frostbrand. He led the trip himself."

Toller's mouth clamped shut and his eyes dropped down to the ground under his horse's hooves.

Singe grimaced. Mention of Robrand d'Deneith was all it took to shut the mouth of half of House Deneith. None of them, not even Toller, liked to be reminded of how close he had been to the old man.

And Robrand, thought Singe, would be angrier than a hunting dragonhawk if he knew I was invoking his name just to change to a subject—though he might understand, given the consequences of that particular trip.

He forced himself to relax his grip on his horse's reins. "Drink lightly with dinner," he advised Toller, trying to ease the tension between them. "The real challenge will come after."

The young man took a deep breath and nodded, sitting up straight once more. Singe caught a glimpse of grateful relief in his eyes. He smiled at him. "You'll do fine, Toller. Have confidence and take charge."

A tall man with a shock of white hair was hustling out from the inn before they had even walked their horses up to it. His eyes darted from the crest on Toller's jacket to the swirling, ornate hilt of the rapier that hung at Singe's side. The Aundairian turned his smile on him. "You have rooms?" he asked. "And dinner?"

"Yes, good master! Of course!" The man practically fell over as he bowed. "Welcome, welcome! My name is Sandar." He spun around and bellowed. "Thul! Thul!"

A sleepy-looking boy poked his head out from the stables. Sandar gestured urgently for him to come forward. Singe swung his leg over his horse's rump and dismounted before the innkeeper could injure himself in his eagerness to serve. "We're not in any rush, Sandar," he said warmly. "Take your time!"

Sandar looked relieved. "Tak, master! That's kind of you. We don't see many of the dragonmarked in these parts, and to have two . . ."

"Only one, Sandar. I just work for House Deneith." Singe smiled and nodded to Toller.

Sandar's eyebrows rose so high they almost merged with his hairline and he spun around to face Toller. "Your pardon, good master!" he gasped. "I had thought your servant to be your equal!"

Singe's indulgent smile vanished into a glower while Toller's face lit up. "No apologies needed, Sandar," said the young man, "it's happened before." He stretched so that his dragon-mark—the shimmering, swirling colors of the magical pattern that marked a true heir of one of the great houses—peeked out from under the cuff of his right sleeve. Sandar's eyes opened even wider in awe.

"Good master!" he breathed. "The best of my inn is yours!" Sandar stepped back, licked his lips, glanced from Singe to Toller, and back again, then asked, "If it wouldn't offend you, masters, would you mind my asking what business brings you to Bull Hollow?"

"Not at all, Sandar," Toller said as dismounted. "We're here on a mission for House Deneith, looking for recruits for the Blademarks Guild."

A murmur of mingled excitement and concern rippled through the watching "Mercenaries?" asked Sandar. Singe thought he finally saw a hint of caution peek through the man's eagerness to serve. "But the war is over. Surely there's no more need for mercenaries."

Singe snorted. "There's always a need for mercenaries," he said. "Peace requires an iron fist. But I don't suppose you felt much of the war in Bull Hollow, did you?"

"No, master," Sandar admitted. "So far out from the center of the Five Nations, it barely touched us. We do have a veteran living in the Hollow—a great man, though not from here originally—but he doesn't like to talk much about the war."

"I understand."

Toller grinned. "We'll let the veterans swap war stories between themselves tonight, Sandar. Let's start with food." He threw a mischievous glance over his shoulder as Sandar led him inside. "Help the stable boy with the horses . . . Lieutenant Bayard."

Singe glared after him, but his mouth twitched with a certain pride. "We'll make a leader out of you yet, Toller," he muttered under his breath.

Dandra woke to the sound of voices and the distinctive sensation of having a roof over her head for the first time in weeks. Panic wrapped around her heart and squeezed. The reflexive discipline of a month of constant dread took precedent, however. She stayed still and silent, her eyes closed and her breathing regular, as she took stock of her situation.

She was lying on a bed, rough and slightly smelly, but a bed nonetheless. She was indoors—warmth, smell, and sound trapped around her. She could hear the crackle of a fire and the murmur of voices. Dandra concentrated on the voices, trying to sort them out. Two voices, one gruff, one softer and more pleasant. Both men.

A memory returned to her. Cold rock at her back, the strange six-legged creatures stalking toward her—and two men, a human and a fierce shifter, appearing from nowhere to come to her rescue. Her own outrage and the way it had drawn energies out of her she had thought drained by exhaustion.

The powerful slap of one of the creature's tentacles. Her impact with the rock she had chosen as her refuge. She focused her awareness on her body. To her surprise, she felt much better than she would have expected. The pains she had expected to find in her chest and in the back of her head were simply not there. The exhaustion that had all but crippled her—that was gone, too. She felt as if she had slept . . . for hours.

Panic's grip tightened around her heart. *Tetkashtai!* she called within the darkness of her mind. *Tetkashtai!*

Here! Like a lantern shone along a dark corridor, a yellow-green light blossomed in her mind's eye. The presence that was Tetkashtai swirled around her, wrapping her in a desperate embrace. *Il-Yannah, Dandra. I couldn't wake you. The human cast some kind of spell on you!*

Dandra returned the mental embrace. *It must have been a healing spell,* she said. *I feel better than I have any right to. How long have I been asleep?*

I don't know, Tetkashtai fretted. *Too long!* Images formed within her light. Views, seen from the perspective of someone being carried, of trees passing. The men who had come to her rescue, their faces distorted by Tetkashtai's fear. A climb up a long slope, then back down. A rough little cabin. The range of Tetkashtai's vision was too short to reveal anything meaningful, any landmarks in the distance, and her sense of time was disjointed. In spite of herself, Dandra swallowed.

We need to get out of here.

Yes! gasped Tetkashtai. *Oh, yes!* Another image formed: Dandra's hand rising, a cone of flame blasting out to envelope the men.

No! said Dandra, startled. *They rescued me. I can't do that!*

Tetkashtai's silent voice hissed, snake-like. *I can. Let me! They'll regret keeping us here. . . .*

I don't think they're keeping us. They're only trying to help. She forced the image of the men burning out of her mind and replaced it with another of them giving her directions, food, perhaps blankets. *They may be willing to help us more!*

Tetkashtai coiled in on herself. *All right,* she said. *But don't tell them anything! And if they can't help us, we run—immediately!*

Dandra bent her thoughts into a shape of obedience, the mental equivalent of a nod. *Yes, Tetkashtai.*

She opened her eyes and turned her head. "Hello?" she said.

It had been days at least since she had last spoken aloud. Her voice came out rough and cracking. It got the men's attention, though. They had been standing beside the fire. At the sound of her voice, they turned sharply. The shifter reacted as an animal would, arching his back and leaning onto the balls of his feet, ready either to fight or to run. The human, however, hurried directly to her. There was an earthenware pitcher on a small table beside the bed. He poured clear water into a cup and offered it to her.

"Here," he said kindly. "Drink." He settled on the bed and helped her as she sat up. The water was cool and good. She swallowed it with a gratitude that surprised her. The man poured her more. "Are you all right?"

She nodded and water splashed down her chin. She felt Tetkashtai draw back in slight disgust, but the man just smiled. He was ruggedly handsome under the beard and somewhat younger than she had expected—there was an air of responsibility to him that made him seem older. A simple collar of polished black stones etched with strange symbols and strung on a leather cord hung around his neck.

"My name is Adolan. This is Geth." He gestured to the shifter as Geth moved in closer, his wide eyes shining in the firelight. The shirt that the shifter wore was torn into rags and stained with blood. Through the gaping fabric she could see that his compact body was knotted with muscle and thick with dark hair. He carried no visible wounds—maybe Adolan had used healing magic on him as well—but old scars made a map of bald streaks on his hairy skin.

"Dandra," she answered, gulping past the water. She set the cup aside and looked at both Adolan and Geth. "You saved me from those—"

"Displacer beasts," grunted Geth.

"—displacer beasts." Dandra bent her head and pressed her hands together. "Thank you."

"You're welcome," said Adolan. He tried awkwardly to imitate her gesture, then gave up. "Geth says you're a kalashtar." She nodded and he smiled. "I've never met a member of your race before."

Enough pleasantries! snapped Tetkashtai. *Find out what we need to know—*

As the presence spoke, Dandra saw Adolan frown slightly. His eyes drifted down to the bronze-wrapped crystal that hung around her neck.

Tetkashtai! she hissed urgently, but the presence had seen the same thing. Her silent voice broke off sharply and her light shrank back in alarm. Her retreat left Dandra feeling slightly empty.

"That's an interesting crystal you wear," said Adolan. "I almost feel as if it's alive."

"In a way," Dandra answered as casually as she could manage, "it is. It's a psicrystal. For a psion, a psicrystal is an aid and a companion."

Adolan's frown deepened in confusion. "What's a psion?"

"A kalashtar wizard," growled Geth. "Which would make this psicrystal like a wizard's familiar." He gave Dandra a suspicious look. "I told you kalashtar had strange powers, Adolan."

"No stranger than magic," Dandra said defensively.

Adolan held out his hands. "Easy," he said. "I'm sorry, Dandra. I didn't mean to upset you." He glanced at Geth. "You should find the elders and let them know that the displacer beasts are dead."

The shifter darted a narrow glance at Dandra, but nodded. "They'll all likely be at Sandar's, and I could use a tankard."

He turned away and shrugged out of his shirt. He flung it into a corner and dug another out of a big chest that stood against the wall, pulling it on over broad shoulders. His big hand picked up one of a pair of fighting axes that stood by the chest and slipped it through a loop on his belt. For a moment, his eyes met Adolan's. The human gave a tiny nod, then looked to Dandra.

"I'll be back in a moment," he said, and followed Geth to the door of the cabin. When he opened it, Dandra's eyes went wide in alarm.

The little slice of the world outside was dark. *Tetkashtai, it's night!*

The presence let out the barest spark of yellow-green light. *Il-Yannah*, she whispered. *We need to go.*

Dandra glanced around the cabin. Her spear was leaning against the foot of the bed. Her sandals were on the floor at the bedside. A cupboard beside the fireplace stood open, revealing a loaf of bread and what looked like cheese. Her stomach growled. Food would be nice, but she had mastered the means of sustaining her body with mental energy alone. A blanket on the other hand—her fingers bunched into the rough, scratchy coverings on the bed . . .

Adolan stepped back into the cabin, closing the door behind him and smiling at her. Dandra forced her fingers to relax and smiled back at him.

In her mind's eye, Tetkashtai formed the image of a flame. Dandra answered with a reluctant mental nod.

"I don't trust her," Geth murmured as Adolan followed him out into the gathering night.

"I understand," Adolan whispered back. The druid glanced back through the door and into the cabin. His eyes narrowed.

"There's something about her—"

"Yes," Geth growled. "Something I don't trust!"

Adolan shook his head. "No. Something haunted. There's something she's keeping from us. I'll see if I can find out what it is. She may need our help."

Geth looked up to the skies overhead. The moons were rising, and the Ring of Siberys was visible in the southern sky, a shining, milky band. He pointed at it. "There's the Ring," he said. "You can stop searching mud puddles anytime."

"If she's trouble, I'll send Breek to fetch you," Adolan said with a smile. He turned for the door, then glanced over his shoulder. "Good hunting today, Geth."

Geth gave him back a smile that exposed just the tips of his teeth. "Good hunting, Ado."

Adolan stepped back into the cabin and closed the door behind him. The swath of light that had illuminated the patchy grass in front of the cabin vanished. For a moment, the night was dark, but as Geth's eyes adjusted, it seemed to grow steadily brighter—another legacy of his lycanthrope ancestors. From a high perch on the roof of the cabin, Breek gave a benevolent squawk as Geth crossed the little clearing and turned down the short path that led into Bull Hollow. A half-dozen paths converged at the cabin. The folk of the valley lived close to the land and the forest and carried great respect for Adolan. More than just the paths of Bull Hollow came together at the cabin. Even if Adolan hadn't been a druid, Geth suspected that he would have found himself at the heart of the community. He was pleasant and personable, naturally charismatic, trusting, patient—Geth's opposite in many ways.

Like the way he trusted Dandra. Maybe Adolan was right, Geth thought as he walked, maybe Dandra did need their help. Maybe . . .

Maybe seeing her was too much of a reminder of the last time he had seen kalashtar. In Rekkenmark.

Just before Narath.

The memory was like picking at a scabbed over wound—as soon as he thought about it, all of the pain came flooding back. All of the bloodshed. All of the fire. All of the screaming.

Geth stopped for a moment and clenched his jaw tight. The great war, the Last War that had consumed the kingdoms of Khorvaire and lured a young shifter away from the Eldeen Reaches with promises of glory and adventure, had ended officially two autumns past. The news had reached Bull Hollow with a wandering tinker the following spring. But for him, the war had come to an end nine years ago. In his mind, Geth saw the snows of northern Karrnath, their clean white stained red with blood and dusted black with ash . . .

He choked on his breath and forced the memories away, burying them behind other memories. A return to the Eldeen Reaches after two years of wandering Khorvaire like a ghost. His first glimpse of a certain valley, at the very end of the Eldeen itself, caught in the green of spring. His first encounter with Adolan.

Geth opened his eyes again and looked around at the scattered buildings, visible through the trees, of Bull Hollow. The lively noise of Sandar's tavern drifted on the air all the way from the common. Seven years in Bull Hollow, he thought, as long a time as I was away from the Eldeen before.

Not that all of those years had been easy. Virtually all of the other races that inhabited Khorvaire had an instinctive mistrust of shifters—a less than desirable part of the lycanthropic heritage. Even in the Eldeen, where shifters were more common than anywhere else on the continent, they tended to form their own tribes and communities. The humans of Bull Hollow weren't that much different than any other members of their race. With Adolan to speak for him, though, Geth had at least had a chance and Bull Hollow had come to accept, and even respect, him. He had more than enough good memories to blot out the bad ones.

Geth took another breath—a deep, confident one—and started walking again. When he stepped out of the trees and onto the common, his face was still grim, but his heart was lighter.

And at least the people of Bull Hollow were used to seeing him with a grim face. As he walked up to Sandar's inn, a cluster of men who had brought their drinking out into the open air hailed him. "Geth! How was your hunting?"

Geth forced his face to soften a little more and gave the men a restrained smile—one that didn't show all of his teeth. "Good hunting!" he called back with a lightness he didn't quite feel. "I have news for Sandar and the other elders. The beasts are dead!"

The men cheered and raised their tankards and mugs. "You'll find the elders inside," one man told him, "but if you want to talk to Sandar, you'll have to catch him on the run. He has guests!"

Geth's eyebrows rose. "Guests? Travelers?"

"Well, they're not from around here, are they? If they were, they'd know better!"

The cluster broke into laughter. Sandar's serving woman, a pretty young lady named Veta, raised her nose in the air as she came out of the inn's common room with another round of beer. "You ignore them, Geth!" she said loudly. "Our guests are proper gentlemen!"

"Veta," said Geth, "if they were proper gentlemen, they wouldn't be this deep in the Eldeen."

Veta gave him a disapproving look. "Well, they aren't like any of the men around Bull Hollow, I can tell you that. They're from a dragonmarked house—the younger one was wearing a crest and all! And the older one . . ." She sighed as she passed a tankard to Geth. "Oh, he was the finest looking man you've ever seen! Tall and lean, with beautiful blond hair and just a patch of a beard on his chin. And he carried himself so well!"

The shifter grunted. "Anyone can stand up straight, Veta, and there are more crests than the ones that great houses use."

"They're gentlemen for true, Geth!" Veta simpered. She turned to go back into the common room.

"Gentlemen or not," said Geth, "I hope they're peaceful. We don't need more trouble." He could hear a growing buzz from inside the common room. Word of the displacer beasts' deaths was beginning to circulate. People would be eager for the story. Taking a deep breath, he stepped through the door.

A cheer so loud it would have shaken leaves from a tree greeted him. The inn's patrons stood, roaring their approval. Sandar raised his arms high. "The hero of Bull Hollow!" he called. Geth turned, nodding with embarrassment as he acknowledged their praise.

At a table toward the back of the room, standing along with everyone else, were the two men who could only be Veta's gentlemen travelers. Geth had to admit that they did cut much more impressive figures than most visitors to Bull Hollow. The younger of the two was cheering along with the Hollowers, the pattern of a dragonmark flashing on his forearm.

The other man, blond and about the same age as Geth himself, was staring at him with stinging fury on his face. Geth met his gaze with a curious glance.

It took a moment for him to recognize the face behind the chin-patch beard and the burning rage. After seven years of peace in Bull Hollow, he had let his guard down. He'd forgotten what it was like to be pursued. He'd forgotten that he was being hunted.

"Geth!" the bearded man bellowed. His rapier cleared its scabbard in a single smooth motion. Sandar's patrons froze, their cheers silenced by surprise. "Geth, you bastard traitor!"

For a moment, Geth froze, too. The hair on his arms and the back of his neck rose sharply. His lips pulled back from his teeth.

Then the hero of Bull Hollow dropped his tankard and spun around, leaping for the inn door and the common beyond. There was a crash behind him and thundering footsteps. Shouts of alarm. Singe's shouts of anger. A voice he didn't know commanding Singe to stand down. Sandar's voice demanding that he put away his sword.

Geth ran as fast as he could, racing across the common. Singe's rapier was only as effective as his reach. But it wasn't the blond man's only weapon. Geth kept his eyes on the trees ahead.

Too late. Behind him, he heard Singe call out a simmering, sizzling word of power.

A dozen paces ahead, flame blossomed in the night, swirling into a sphere of seething orange fire that was almost as tall as the shifter. Geth skidded to a stop, his feet digging up strips of sod, then tried to dart around the sphere. The sphere rolled over on itself, moving to block him. He feinted left, then darted right. The fiery sphere moved with him, then rolled closer. Geth was forced to leap back or be burned.

"Geth!" Singe called.

The shifter whirled and dropped into a crouch, his sharp teeth bared and his pointed ears back like a cornered animal. His hand darted to his belt, groping for his axe. Singe was trotting across the common, his right hand holding his rapier, his left crooked in the arcane gesture that controlled the flaming sphere. He stopped a cautious distance away.

The two men faced each other in silence in the flickering, smoky light.

"Singe! Singe! *Lieutenant Bayard!*" The younger man who had been with Singe in the inn came dashing from the direction of the inn, his jacket hanging open, his sword already drawn. Behind him, the folk of Bull Hollow were gathering. Their voices were animated and alarmed. Some were jogging across the common, clubs and daggers in their hands. The young man's face was pale. "Have you lost your mind?" he gasped. "What are you doing?"

"Toller," Singe said tightly, "I spent four years trying to track this bastard down. I only came back to the Blademarks because I thought I'd never find him."

The wizard was cut off by the arrival of a number of the men of the Hollow, Sandar in their lead. The white-haired innkeeper carried a surprisingly large mace in one hand. "Good master," he said to Singe, "I'd ask you to lower your weapon and . . . uhhh . . ." He glanced at the fire burning behind Geth. "Dismiss whatever magic you command."

Singe didn't take his eyes off Geth. "They don't know, do they?" he asked.

If it was possible, Geth's lips peeled back even further. Singe took a step closer, his left hand gesturing. The sphere of fire began to roll forward . . .

The deep bellow that echoed across the common—across the entire valley—seemed to shake the very air itself. It sounded like the cry of some enormous wounded animal, caught in unimaginable pain. Around Singe, the people of Bull Hollow gasped. Toller yelped in fear. Geth's own gut clenched in sudden alarm.

Singe's hand trembled. He looked up into the night. "What was that—?"

In the second that the wizard's gaze was turned away, Geth's muscular frame uncoiled. His arm swung back and then snapped forward, sending his axe spinning through the air. Singe choked and flung himself down and backward.

It was a terrible throw, awkward and haphazardly aimed. Geth could see recognition of that flicker in Singe's eyes even as he dropped. The axe missed him by a good five feet, embedding its blade deep in the ground of the common. Geth didn't wait to see his reaction. He turned and darted around the resting ball of fire, putting it between him and Singe and hurling himself toward the woods once more.

"No!" howled Singe. There was another gasp from the folk of Bull Hollow. Geth glanced back over his shoulder in time to see the wizard charging after him, not around the fiery sphere, but *through* it.

He emerged from the flame without even a scorch mark on him. A ring on his finger shone with a sudden, hungry light.

But the trees of the forest were ahead. Geth flung himself into them as a second bellow rolled through the night.

"Adolan," asked Dandra, "where is Bull Hollow?"

We don't have time for this, Tetkashtai hissed.

We need directions, Dandra replied.

Once again, a frown flickered across Adolan's face, as if he was somehow aware of the silent communication. The druid crossed the cabin from the door to the open cupboard, reached in and took out the bread and cheese Dandra had glimpsed. "Just down the path," he answered. "It's very close."

"No, I mean where is it in relation to other places. Like Yrlag in the Shadow Marches, for instance."

"Yrlag?" Adolan turned and looked at her. His eyes narrowed. "Yrlag is a week and half's travel to the southwest. We're in the west of the Eldeen Reaches."

You came too far! I told you we had missed Yrlag!

Shut up, Tetkashtai! Dandra gave Adolan an embarrassed smile. "I'm lost," she said. "I was traveling from Yrlag to—" she searched her memory hastily for the name of a town or city in the Eldeen Reaches. "—Erlaskar."

Adolan's eyes didn't shift. "Through the Twilight Domain and the Gloaming?"

"Well, not *through* them, obviously," Dandra lied.

She had no idea what either place was, but the man's voice made them sound dangerous. Inside her mind Tetkashtai was tensed like over-wound clockwork, but she forced herself to remain calm as Adolan took a knife from the cupboard as well. He cut big pieces of bread and cheese, setting them on a grill by the fire to toast, then turned back to put plates out on a rough table. He worked without saying anything, though Dandra had the sense that he was only looking for the right moment.

Finally she broke the silence before he could. "Do you have a map of the Eldeen Reaches, Adolan?"

"A map?" He turned and looked at her.

Dandra swallowed hard. His eyes were sharp, but also compassionate.

When the druid spoke again, his voice was soft and cautious. "You're not going to Erlaskar, are you, Dandra?"

Tetkashtai gave another silent hiss, but to her own surprise, Dandra shook her head. "No," she murmured.

"I didn't think so." Adolan gestured to the table and said, "Sit down. Eat something."

"I can't," she told him. "I have to go."

Adolan's eyebrows rose. "Go? Go where? Dandra, it's dark."

"I know. I slept too long." She pushed herself up off the bed. "Show me the map," she said. "Please."

He nodded slowly. "All right," he said, crossing back to the cupboard. "Dandra, if you need help, all you have to do—"

Before he could say anything more, the air shivered under a deep bellow. It came from outside the cabin but not, Dandra thought, from somewhere close by. Adolan spun at the sound, his feet striking the grill and sending the bread and cheese sliding into the fire. He barely seemed to notice, instead leaping across the cabin and wrenching open the door. Dandra, eyes wide, turned to follow him as he leaned out into the darkness, twisted around to look up, and whistled through his clenched teeth.

"Breek!" he called. "Breek! Find Geth!"

There was a squawk from up on the cabin's roof and the sound of a bird launching itself into the night. Adolan pulled himself back inside and turned back to her. Any compassion in his eyes was gone, replaced by a harsh urgency. "There's trouble," he said, reaching for a spear, longer and heavier than her own, that stood by the door. "Something unnatural has entered the valley. You'll have to stay—"

They're here. Tetkashtai's voice was sharp—and frantic. *Dandra, they're here! We need to run!*

I know. Dandra looked at Adolan as another bellow rumbled in the darkness. "I'm sorry," she said.

She reached out to Tetkashtai through the connection that bound them together, drawing the presence close. As if she had turned a key in a lock, she felt power stir within her. With Tetkashtai's yellow-green light surrounding her, she drew on that power, shaping it with a disciplined will. The droning, disembodied chorus of whitefire swelled in her ears. Adolan's eyes went wide as the sound throbbed against his ears as well. With a flick of thought, Dandra gave the whitefire form.

Pale flames flared around Adolan. They lasted only an instant, but in that instant his mouth opened in a scream that never came out. He slumped to the cabin floor, stunned by the sudden, shocking heat, little flames licking at his clothes. Dandra focused her will and the whitefire chorus changed in pitch as another whisper of power snuffed the flickering flames.

Snatching up her spear, she fled into the night, running once again.

CHAPTER

3

'**N**o!" Singe howled. He shoved off from the ground and lunged back to his feet, sprinting after the fleeing shifter. The fiery sphere of his spell was in the way. Ignoring the startled cries of Toller and the folk of Bull Hollow alike, he dove through it without hesitation. The fire tickled his skin, but no more—the ring on his left hand shielded him, devouring any flame that touched his body. Momentarily light blind, he peered into the darkness ahead. Geth was a shadowy figure disappearing into a wall of trees.

The strange bellow sounded again, but Singe barely registered it, just as he barely registered the calls from the people left behind on the common. "You're not getting away again, Geth!" he hissed—and plunged into the trees.

The bare earth of a path glimmered briefly in the moonlight, then the silver illumination was cut off by the thick branches overhead. For long moments, Singe's only guide was the thrashing of Geth's progress through the bush. Jaw clenched, Singe followed as best as he could, rapier held low and one arm up in front of his face to ward off lashing branches.

Then he realized that the only thrashing in the woods was coming from him. He froze instantly, breath catching in his throat, as a thin silence spread out among the dark trees. He held up his rapier and murmured a cantrip over it. Clear, steady light spread out from the blade—but penetrated less than half a dozen paces in any direction around him. Leaves and trunks, branches and bushes, all cast shadows that made seeing any further impossible. Singe turned slowly, trying to spot the trail that he had made as he crashed through the undergrowth.

The shifting shadows made that impossible, too.

"Twelve bloody moons!" he breathed. He was alone and lost in a dark forest—with an angry shifter somewhere close by. Glowing rapier held high, he moved slowly forward.

With every few paces, the deep, mysterious bellow rolled through the night again and again. Singe gritted his teeth against it, then hesitated for a moment. Without a point of reference, he could end up walking in circles.

"Twelve bloody moons!" he cursed again. He turned and began moving in the direction of the bellow's source.

Geth emerged onto a trail while Singe was still crashing around among the trees. With any luck, the Aundairian would take precious moments—or even longer—to find his way clear. Nine years ago, Singe had been a skilled swordsman and he was still clearly every bit the wizard Geth remembered him to be, but unless a great deal had changed in nine years, he was no woodsman.

The shifter looked down at his thick, hairy hands. They were shaking. Geth clenched them into fists and darted along the trail. The roaring bellow continued to echo as he ran. He tried to put it out of his mind. He was lucky that it had distracted Singe and given him the chance he needed to break away, but of all the times . . .

Duty and fear tore at him. Geth bit his lip. "Grandmother Wolf, forgive what I do."

Three trails came together, part of the web of paths that laced the forest around Bull Hollow. His feet slid as he changed direction and charged down one of the other trails. Moments later, the trees opened up into the clearing around the cabin.

The door of the cabin stood open, spilling light into the yard.

Geth slid to a stop. Even if Adolan had left in a hurry, he

would have closed the door. Breek was nowhere to be seen. Geth approached the cabin cautiously. "Ado?" he called. "Ado?" He flattened himself against the outer wall and darted his head through the cabin's door.

The stink of scorched leather and singed hair stung his nostrils even before he caught the soft groan as Adolan stirred on the floor inside the door. Geth sucked in a sharp breath and bounded to his side. It took no more than a glance to see that the kalashtar woman was gone. He grabbed Adolan's hand and hauled him to his feet.

"What did she do to you?" he growled.

"A burst of fire," said Adolan. He rubbed a hand across his forehead and winced at his own touch. The skin of his face was reddened, but no worse. "The heat was so intense it took my breath away, but it doesn't seem like it did much real damage."

Another bellow rolled on the air. Adolan gasped and pulled away. "Ring of Siberys! The Bull Hole! How could I . . ." He darted around the cabin, snatching up a satchel stitched with strange symbols, his spear, and a jerkin of stiff, heavy hide.

Geth stood still, watching him with a heavy heart. After a moment, the druid realized that he wasn't moving and paused. "Geth, what's wrong?" His face tightened. "Where's Breek? I sent him to fetch you."

"Then he's still looking for me," Geth said. His gut twisted. "Ado, House Deneith has found me. One of the Frostbrand—one of Robrand's lieutenants. Singe. He was in Sandar's." Geth drew a shuddering breath. "I have to leave."

Silence fell heavily as Adolan stared. "Now?" asked the druid, his voice thin and disbelieving.

Yet another bellow punctuated the question. Geth spread his hands helplessly. "I told you Deneith might come looking for me."

"I know what you told me." Adolan ground his teeth together. He leaned his spear against the nearest wall and wrenched the hide jerkin over his head. When his face emerged, his eyes were angry. "But I can't believe that you'd leave now or ever. Are you just going to keep running? Bull Hollow needs you!"

"Bull Hollow isn't going to want me around when they find out the truth."

Adolan glared at him. "So you'll abandon your friends in the face of danger?" He paused for half a heartbeat and added, "Like you did at Narath."

The druid's word stung like salt rubbed into a wound. A growl tore itself out of Geth's throat. "It's not the same!" he snapped.

"Isn't it?" Adolan asked. He settled the satchel over his shoulders and picked up his spear again. He looked up and his eyes softened. "Geth, fight! Forget the Frostbrand. Forget Singe. He's in as much danger tonight as any of us. Tomorrow I'll either stand with you in front of the Hollow or we'll leave together."

He held out his hand.

Geth stared at it as the bellow rolled over Bull Hollow once more—then he bared his teeth and slapped his hand down to grasp the druid's forearm. Adolan's hand closed tight on his forearm in return.

"You have Grandmother Wolf's own honor," he said.

"I have Cousin Boar's own stupidity," Geth grunted.

He released Adolan's arm and turned to the chest against the wall. Digging down into its depths, he came up with a large, blanket-wrapped bundle that clanked as he set it on the cabin floor. Adolan stared at him in amazement. Geth responded with a glower, daring him to say anything.

Something lurked in the trees overhead, peering down out of the darkness. Singe prayed that it wasn't Geth. Half blind from the light that shone from his rapier, he could see little enough, but in the course of more than a decade of serving with the Blademarks, he had learned to recognize the feeling of being watched. He continued along the path that he had finally stumbled onto a short while earlier. The strange bellows still rolled out across the valley from somewhere ahead. If whatever was in the trees made any sound, the bellow drowned it out.

Singe kept his eyes on the ground or on the shadows ahead, anywhere but up. With every step, awareness of the thing in the trees prickled across the back of his neck. He forced himself to remain calm, to stay relaxed as he moved closer to the thing. It didn't seem to move, but he could feel it still watching him. Closer . . .

Directly underneath it, he stopped sharply, glanced up, and, flinging an arm over his eyes, snapped out a brittle word.

Up among the leaves, light burst in dazzling flash. There was a harsh croak and something crashed through the branches toward a clear patch of sky. Even with his eyes shaded against the flare, Singe only caught a glimpse of a big, ungainly bird flapping away. Scraggly legs trailed through the air behind it and a long neck curved back on itself. Singe's eyes widened slightly.

A heron, he thought. Twelve moons, what's a heron doing in the forest?

There was a soft rustle behind him.

Singe's heart leaped into his throat as he whirled around, sword outstretched, another spell smoldering on his lips and at his fingertips.

At the edge of the path, as if emerging from a hiding place, a woman crouched in a virtually identical pose. Her right hand held a short, pale spear at the ready. Her left was pointed at him in a gesture very much like a wizard prepared to unleash a spell. Her feet, he realized, didn't touch the ground. Instead, she hovered with no apparent effort.

For a long moment, neither of them moved. Singe studied the woman—he was certain she was doing the same to him—without moving his eyes. To judge by her sharp features and exotic clothing, she was a kalashtar.

And a kalashtar deep in the Eldeen was even stranger than a heron in the forest.

Very slowly, the woman uncoiled. Spear and hand both remained pointing at him as she drifted out onto the path and slid the length of a pace along it in the same direction Singe had been heading. He turned with her, keeping her boxed between the edge of his rapier and his own waiting spell. The woman slid another pace, spear and hand still rock steady—

The tension between them shattered as a lean figure leaped screaming out of the darkness. Singe didn't understand a word that it uttered, if they were words, and caught only a glimpse of the crude axe that it swung. He simply snapped around and spat the word of his spell.

The kalashtar woman's pointing fingers shifted at the same moment. A droning chorus of sound beat against Singe's ears, the sound of her race's weird power.

Twin blasts of churning energy caught the screaming figure and wrapped it in flame—red-orange from Singe's hand, white from the woman's. Its battle cry changed into a shriek of pain, then broke sharply as the figure spun around and fell to the ground. For a moment, the only sound in the forest was the soft crackle of fire.

Singe edged closer and peered through the burning brilliance. Their attacker had been a man dressed in rough, worn clothing, his hair strung with beads, his ears and his nose pierced through with lengths of wood and bone. The wizard turned to look at the kalashtar with respect.

"Singe," he said simply.

"Dandra," she replied. Her voice was rich like spices, but strained. "There will be more of them. We have to run."

The dull rhythm of feet pounding on dry earth pulled on Singe's ears. "Too late!" he hissed, and took two fast steps backward to stand at Dandra's side.

They appeared from the shadows at a run—three more men and a hard, thin woman whose head had been shaved and marked with tattoos. They didn't even glance at the flaming corpse of the first attacker, but at the sight of Singe and Dandra, they broke into the same weird war cry the dead man had uttered. If it was meant to frighten their victims, Singe thought, it was very effective. His hand clenched on the hilt of his rapier. "You strike left!" he gasped to Dandra.

He hoped that she understood, but didn't wait to see. He spoke a new word of magic and the fingers of his free hand flicked a trio of bright sparks at one of the men on the right. The man's war cry broke and he staggered—but kept coming. Singe saw Dandra point left and again he heard a choral drone. White fire lanced from Dandra's fingertips but this time the man she had chosen as her target ducked and rolled beneath the blast. Behind him, green leaves and twigs burst into flame like dry tinder.

Singe had the time to mutter a curse, then their attackers were on them.

He slid to the side as the man he had targeted with his magic swung with a thick club. His rapier darted out but the man flinched back, bringing the club around in a weak counter. Singe rocked back to avoid the blow—and almost lost a good portion of his head to a wild strike from an axe wielded by the tattooed woman. He staggered to the side, found his balance, and settled back into a fighting stance just in time to ward off the woman as she pressed her attack.

A glance showed that Dandra was having trouble as well. The two men facing her were armed with long knives, and while Dandra's spear gave her a greater reach, she was hard-pressed to keep both men back. As she thrust at one man, the other lunged at her. She moved with tremendous grace, spinning and shifting as if she only needed to think about moving. It still wasn't enough. She caught one with a crack of the spear shaft across his forehead—blood welled up and began to drip into his eyes—but the second slipped past her guard and got around on her other side.

And in the moment that Singe watched her, the man with the club got past his rapier long enough to swing a crushing blow at his sword arm. Singe twisted around and caught the blow on his left shoulder instead. His arm went numb and he staggered. The tattooed woman darted in again. Desperately, Singe turned his stagger into a low lunge.

The blade of his rapier sank into her thigh. She shrieked and fell back as he whipped the weapon free. Swaying to the side, he barely managed to avoid another punishing blow from the man's club. Dandra yelped and he shot a fast glance toward her. One of her attackers had managed to grab the butt of her spear. The kalashtar spun and kicked out with a sandaled foot but the move left her open. The second man dove in—

—and was tackled by a massive, growling form that seemed to explode out of the night. Singe caught only a glimpse of flashing teeth and thick muscles, but the man was swept off his feet and slammed back into the shadows. Over the noise of combat, he heard the wet crunch of a blade penetrating flesh and bone.

The sudden, ferocious attack gave him and Dandra the moment's chance that they needed. As the man with the club turned to meet this half-glimpsed new threat, Singe thrust his rapier under his momentarily upraised arm. Blood burst from his mouth in a sudden spray and the club tumbled to the ground as he fell. Dandra yielded to the pull of the man who grasped her spear; a hard push shoved him off balance. As he fought to regain his balance, she wrenched her weapon from his hand, reversed it, and, with a grim expression, jabbed the glittering head deep into his chest.

Her last ally dead, the tattooed woman flung herself away, limping for the safety of the forest.

A short, heavy sword—already slick with blood—whirled around and chopped deep into her torso. She slumped forward, her body seeming to fold over the blade.

Geth stepped back into the circle of Singe's light, sliding his weapon free and allowing the woman's corpse to collapse onto the ground. He raised his eyes and met the wizard's gaze with a simple, brutal directness.

Abruptly, Singe felt as though he had fallen through time nine years into the past. The backcountry hunter he had confronted on the common of Bull Hollow had barely seemed like the warrior he remembered. That warrior stood before him now. Geth still wore the clothes he had before, but in his left hand, he held his sword, a product of the smoke-belching war forges of Karrnath.

His right hand and arm were covered in an armor sleeve of blackened, magewrought steel. Flat spikes protruded from the knuckles of the great gauntlet and three low, hooked blades swept forward from the back. More spikes lined the ridge of his forearm. Interlocking strips of metal bulged around his upper arm, running all the way up to the plates of the wide, heavy shoulder guard.

Slowly, Singe lifted his rapier once more and braced himself for the shifter's attack.

"Stop."

From the direction that Geth had come, another man moved into the light. His only weapon was a spear with a cluster of dried leaves bound to its shaft and his only armor a jerkin of heavy, paint-daubed hide, but he carried himself with authority. A druid, guessed Singe—he had seen men and women with a similar look throughout the Eldeen Reaches. He had never, however, seen one with such a clear confidence and sense of purpose as this man. Under the weight of the nature-priest's gaze, he let his rapier drop. The druid gave him a measured look as he paced closer.

"You must be Singe," he said. "My name is Adolan." He turned and glanced at Dandra. To Singe's surprise, the kalashtar shrank back slightly and her feet settled to the ground. Adolan knelt to examine one of the fallen warriors. "Human," he muttered. He looked back up at Dandra. "I have the feeling you know who these people are."

Tension passed over Dandra's face, as if she was struggling with her response. Then she drew a breath and met Adolan's eyes. "They're the hunters of a clan called *Drumasaz*," she said. "In their language, it means 'the Bonetree.' They come from deep in the Shadow Marches."

"The Shadow Marches?" the druid said sharply. His eyes narrowed. "What gods do they follow?" he demanded. "Do you know?"

"No gods," Dandra whispered so quietly Singe could barely hear her. "They worship the dark powers of Khyber."

Singe couldn't hold back a nervous chuckle. "A cult of the Dragon Below? Are you serious?"

Adolan gave him unnerving stare. "The Shadow Marches breed many foul things—degenerate ideas and desperate beliefs among them." He prodded one of the bodies with the toe of his boot and rose slowly. "What would a Marcher clan be doing—"

Singe felt a prickling across the back of his neck. His eyes darted up into the darkness overhead. Geth must have felt something, too, because he hissed, "In the trees, Ado!"

The druid glanced up, then folded his lower lip under his teeth and gave an ear-splitting whistle.

A hunting bird's screech cut the night. Branches and leaves crashed above them as something struck from out of the sky—and something else sought to escape. Singe flinched instinctively. Wings cracked through the air, then the hunting bird screeched again.

A moment later, a big eagle with red-gold plumage settled onto the path. Clutched in its talons was a massive black heron. The eagle spread its wings and screeched once more, then waddled awkwardly back as Adolan approached and bent down. "Well done, Breek," he said. "Singe, your light?"

Stunned, the wizard stepped closer and raised his shining rapier high. Over Adolan's shoulder, he got a better look at the dead bird. Its long neck had been broken by the eagle's attack, but it looked almost as if the heron had been on the verge of death already: it was thin and its black feathers seemed strangely oily. The eyes that stared blankly into the night were an eerily bright acid green.

Singe swallowed. "I didn't know herons perched in trees," he said awkwardly, trying to fill the silence.

"The tops of trees," Geth said, "yes. The thick of a forest canopy? No. Ado?"

"It's tainted. But not enough to have triggered the Bull Hole. I've never seen anything quite like it." The druid stood. "We—"

"We need to go," said Dandra.

Singe, Adolan, and Geth swung around as one to stare at her. The woman's hands were clenched tight around her spear. There was a terror on her face, Singe saw, that hadn't been there when they were fighting the hunters.

"They'll be coming." She trembled. "They follow the birds."

Singe darted forward and steadied her. He glanced at Geth and Adolan. "There was a bird watching me before we were attacked."

"More hunters coming then?" asked Geth.

"Or worse," said Adolan softly. "Either way, we shouldn't stay here." He looked to Geth. The shifter nodded and spun around to lope away along the path, his gaze swinging right to left and back. Scouting the way. Singe felt another twinge of familiarity.

Nine years before, the shifter had done the same thing in service to the Frostbrand and House Deneith.

He turned back, however, to find Adolan staring at him. "Put your fight with Geth aside," the druid said. "You're in danger." He looked at Dandra. "Are you going to attack me again?"

She shook her head urgently. Adolan nodded. "Then come with us, both of you. Quickly." He made a clicking noise with his tongue and the eagle croaked in response, vaulting back into the air and flapping furiously to gain the sky. Adolan gestured with his spear, then turned and ran after Geth with long, confident strides. Dandra pulled out of Singe's arms and raced off in his wake. Her first few paces were on the ground, then she was floating again, moving as quickly as Adolan—faster even. Abruptly, Singe was all but alone, left to stare at the retreating figures of the druid and the kalashtar and at the bodies lying along the path.

"Twelve moons—" he breathed in confusion.

His voice froze as a weird fluting call pierced the forest. It was unlike anything he had ever heard: shrill, maddening, and haunting all at once. There was another sound underneath it as well, a vague muttering chant. Singe's teeth snapped together and he sprinted hard after Adolan, the light from his rapier bouncing and sweeping in the darkness.

The fluting call fell silent, but not the muttering chant. If anything, it seemed louder. Even another of the rolling bellows—louder than before and also closer—did nothing but drown it out for a moment. When the echoes of the bellow faded away, the chanting was closer still. Singe cursed under his breath. He glanced at Dandra, but the kalashtar's eyes were fixed on the path ahead. "Adolan," he gasped, "what's happening? Where are we going?"

"We're going to the Bull Hole," Adolan said. Even he sounded winded. "We'll be safe there."

"What's the Bull Hole? What's making that chanting?"

There was light ahead. Moonlight. Singe caught a glimpse of Geth's hulking form waiting for them. Abruptly, they shot out of the shadows of the forest and into a huge broad clearing. At its center was a jumble of stones.

He remembered seeing this clearing from the rim of the valley as he and Toller looked down on Bull Hollow. He remembered thinking the stones were the ruins of some building. He couldn't, he realized, have been more wrong.

The stones looked like they predated the hamlet, like they predated any human presence in the Eldeen Reaches. Weathered smooth, they shone and shimmered under the light of the moons and the Ring of Siberys. Many leaned sharply and a good number had fallen entirely, but it was easy to see that they had once stood in a carefully arranged, tightly clustered circle. Yet another bellow rolled through the night and this time Singe felt it rumble in his guts. He could have sworn that even the ground trembled with the sound.

Geth fell in with them, matching his pace to Adolan's. The shifter's face was grim and every few moments he glanced back over his shoulder. They were a little more than halfway to the stones when he let out a growl and spat, "Here they come!"

Singe risked a glance back himself. Bursting silently from the edge of the forest and into the moonlit clearing were a dozen or more tall, lean Bonetree hunters. More frightening than the human figures, though, were the hunched shapes that ran along with them, scuttling out of the trees on squat, misshapen legs.

The creatures stood less than half the height of a human. It looked as if their heads and necks had been crushed down into their shoulders. Each pumped four bandy arms as it ran. It seemed as if every arm carried a weapon: Singe glimpsed viciously spiked bucklers, light spears, ugly maces, and crossbows. All of the creatures wore a strange crest on their malformed chests as well. The moonlight caught a weird design shaped like a mouth full of teeth.

Then one of the crests shifted, opened wide, and let out a wild yell. Two mouths, Singe realized. The creatures had two mouths to go with their four arms! They were the source of the muttering chant, as if their two mouths had been talking to each other in a horrible chorus as they stalked the darkened forest.

"Faster!" grunted Adolan. "Get to the stones!"

None of them needed his encouragement. Geth ran with the

flowing stride of an animal, almost going down on four legs. Adolan opened up his pace. Dandra's floating form skimmed over the ground like a low-flying bird. Singe simply moved his legs as hard and fast as he could. A new roar rose up from their pursuers, humans and creatures calling out together.

Twenty paces to the stones. Fifteen. Dandra vanished among the stones.

Something whizzed past Singe and sank into the ground ahead. He caught a glimpse of a crossbow bolt, its head buried in the soil, as he raced past. Ten paces. Geth was under cover, then Adolan. He was alone in the open! Three more thuds came in rapid succession all around him. Three more bolts sprouted out of the ground. The archers were finding their range. Five paces.

Singe leaped and rolled into the shelter of the stones just as a cascade of bolts fell out of the air like deadly hail.

CHAPTER

4

Dandra felt Singe slam into her as he dove for cover behind the same fallen stone as her. She heard the rattle of crossbow bolts as they bounced off the stones. Adolan and Geth were somewhere close by, also under cover. She was aware of everything, but only peripherally, like a sound half-heard or a shadow half-glimpsed.

Tetkashtai's wailing filled her head. *They've caught us! Light of il-Yannah, we're captured. I won't go back there. I won't!*

The strength of her presence raged inside Dandra, clenching at her guts like the hands of a drowning swimmer. Tetkashtai's terror was contagious and so powerful that it was almost physical. She gasped for breath.

Tetkashtai! she shouted back in her mind. *Tetkashtai! Calm down! We have to—*

The presence lashed out at her, a vicious swipe of light that burned through Dandra's mind. *This is your fault! If you'd been faster, if you'd fled this place when I told you to, we'd be safe. This is your fault, you dahr!*

An image formed in Tetkashtai's light. Eyes. Wise, piercing eyes, full of secrets. Terrible, devouring secrets. In the presence's yellow-green light, the color of those eyes was distorted, but Dandra could picture them as well as Tetkashtai. They were bright, acid green. Like those of the black heron that Breek had brought down. When Adolan's eagle had first brought down the strange bird, the sight of those unnaturally bright eyes had stirred emotions in her. Fascination. Fear. Horror.

Tetkashtai's wails struck a fever pitch. She clawed at Dandra's mind as if she could rake the image and the memories away. *No! No! No!*

Dandra's head slammed back against the rock as her body stiffened. Bright sparks of pain popped in her vision. *Tetkashtai, be quiet!* she shouted, thrusting back against the terrified presence. Keening incoherently, Tetkashtai withdrew into the crystal, leaving Dandra gasping and clutching her temples.

"Twelve moons!" cursed Singe. He hauled himself up beside her, leaning his back against the stone and gulping air. He glanced at her, his face blotched red and white from their flight. "Dandra, are you all right?"

She nodded weakly. His hand scrambled for his rapier. The light that the blade shed seemed cold and feeble, as if the shadows of the stones were sucking it up.

"Rest," said Adolan. The druid was crouched behind a leaning stone to their left.

"Are you insane?" Singe's voice broke. "As soon as they're finished—"

The rain of crossbow bolts stopped. Singe tensed. "Here they come!"

"No," said Adolan.

Singe stared at the druid with astonished disbelief, but a moment later—when no attack had come—he stood up and peered over the top of the stone. Dandra heard breath hiss between his teeth. On their right, Geth moved as well. The metal of the strange armored sleeve that he wore scraped against rock as he moved, bending his neck to look out into the clearing. "They've stopped, Adolan," he reported.

"Twelve moons," Singe whispered. "What are those things?"

"Dolgrims," Adolan answered. There was a raw tension in the druid's voice. He was crouched behind a leaning stone to their left. "Aberrations, a blight on Eberron."

Dandra saw Singe's throat work as he swallowed hard. *"Those* are dolgrims?" he asked. "I've read about them. They're . . . not what I expected."

Dandra forced her limbs to move. Slowly and carefully, she leaned over and peered past the side of the stone. Perhaps halfway between the stones and the edge of the clearing, the dolgrims milled about in confusion. Moans and growls of frustration sputtered out of their double mouths. A few tried to move closer to the stones. They looked almost like they were attempting to walk into a strong wind. Behind them, the Bonetree hunters squatted down on the ground with an unsettling patience.

One of the dolgrims squealed and seemed to point directly at her. Half a dozen of the creatures swung around sharply, raising one or a pair of arms to fire off a new volley of crossbow bolts. Dandra, Singe, and Geth ducked back under cover. Even Tetkashtai seemed to take notice, gibbering out another wail of terror.

"What's holding them back?" asked Singe. "What is this place—?"

His question was drowned out by another of the rolling bellows, this one so loud that Dandra pressed her hands to her ears. She glimpsed movement as Adolan reached up and pressed his palm against the stone above him. His mouth moved in an invocation and the deafening roar ended. Out in the clearing, a frightened babble broke out among the dolgrims.

"We're safe here for the time being," said Adolan. "You can relax. They can't get any closer."

"Why not?" Singe asked.

Adolan settled back. "The Bull Hole is sacred to my sect. Our lore holds that our traditions began thousands of years ago as a defense against an invasion from a realm of madness. The leaders of that invasion were powerful creatures called daelkyr. They brought lesser creatures with them from their realm—and created others from the beings they found on Eberron. All of them are anathema to nature. The war that followed took place in the Shadow Marches, spilling over into the lands surrounding the Marches." He gestured around them. "Like the Eldeen Reaches. The Daelkyr War ended when the paths to the realm of madness were sealed. My sect, the Gatekeepers, is the oldest of the druid traditions and the one that sealed those paths and bound the greater aberrations left behind on Eberron into the depths of Khyber." He touched the stone again. "Ancient druids created the Bull Hole and places like it to warn and guard against such creatures as the dolgrims. Its power keeps them back."

Dandra watched as Singe stared at the druid, then squeezed his eyes shut, raked fingers through thick blond hair, and finally opened his eyes again. "That's ludicrous!" he sputtered. "There weren't even any humans in this part of the world that long ago. Historians have shown that the only cultures here were scattered orc barbarians and the hobgoblin empire of Dhakaan—and it fell almost six millennia ago!"

Adolan raised an eyebrow. "Historians?"

"Singe studied at Wynarn University," growled Geth. "He knows *everything*."

Dandra caught the dark glance that Singe shot toward the shifter. Adolan's eyes, however, never wavered from the wizard.

"What do your historians say," he asked, "caused the Dhakaani Empire to fall?"

Singe's jaw tensed. "There's evidence of a war."

"With who?" Adolan spread his hands. "Scattered orc barbarians?"

Singe opened his mouth, then closed it again. Geth turned his back on him and looked out into the clearing. "The Bonetree hunters are all just sitting back but the dolgrims are still milling around. It looks like a few have tried to go around the back of the circle."

"They won't get in there either," said Adolan. He glanced back at Singe. "Well?"

The wizard glowered at him. "You're telling me this circle was built by hobgoblins?"

"Of course not." Adolan rose to his feet, careful to stay in the shadow of his stone. "The first druids were orcs."

"*Orcs?*" Singe's eyes bulged in disbelief. "Orcs couldn't create something like this!"

"Not now, maybe," Adolan agreed. "But you believe that the

hobgoblins who spend most of their time fighting among themselves in Darguun today are the same race that once built an empire spanning half a continent, don't you?"

Singe's mouth closed with a snap. Adolan turned to look at Dandra. "At the cabin," he said, "you were desperate to escape."

Dandra bit her lip. "I'm sorry that I turned on you, but I had to—"

Adolan raised his hand, stopping her. "They're after you, aren't they? You're the reason they've come to Bull Hollow."

She felt blood rush to her face. With the eyes of all three men on her, she nodded.

"Why?" asked Adolan.

Her belly knotted at the question. *Tetkashtai*, she thought, *what should I tell them?* The cowering presence's only response, however, was a thin, mad gibbering. Dandra took a deep breath and looked back at Adolan.

"They were holding me captive," she said, trying to keep her story as simple as possible. "They kidnapped me from Zarash'ak and took me to their camp in the marshes. I managed to escape, but they've been pursuing me ever since." She paused, then added. "I've been running for almost a month, just trying to stay ahead of them. Until you found me, I didn't even really know where I was."

A harshness that crept into her voice surprised even her. Adolan's eyebrows twitched in surprise, but Geth actually cursed out loud. "Rat! Do you expect us to believe that?"

Dandra gave him an angry look. "Would you want to get caught by them?" She pointed over her shoulder, beyond the stones. "I can move fast and it's hard to track someone who doesn't leave footprints if she doesn't want to. They needed their herons to follow me."

"You were walking when we found you."

"I was exhausted!"

"Easy," said Adolan, raising a hand to both her and Geth. "Arguing isn't going to help us." The druid glanced at Dandra again. "Why did they take you?"

"Why me? I don't know," she answered. That much at least was the truth. She directed another mental prod toward Tetkashtai, but the presence whined like a child and batted her away. "I was in the wrong place at the wrong time, maybe."

"Maybe they wanted you for a sacrifice to Khyber," suggested Singe.

Dandra nodded. "Maybe," she lied. Her hand shifted to wrap tight around the yellow-green crystal that hung from her neck. She could almost feel Tetkashtai stirring under her fingers.

The sudden patter of another shower of crossbow bolts shattered the tension of the moment and sent all of four of them cringing back under cover. "Ado, we have to do something!" Geth snarled. "They'll soon get lucky and hit something other than rocks. We can't stay here."

Adolan nodded and said, "You're right. You and Singe keep watch. Dandra, come with me." He beckoned her to follow as he moved deeper into the circle.

Dandra drew a sharp breath and scuttled after him. Her movement roused Tetkashtai as nothing else had. *Yes!* she shrieked. *Yes, run! Il-Yannah's light, please run!*

The presence's fear rattled through her, so strong that Dandra almost stumbled as her legs started to respond to Tetkashtai's demands. She pushed back against her terror. *We can't run, Tetkashtai. We'd be abandoning Geth, Singe, and Adolan!*

So? Tetkashtai wailed. *Better them than us! They can distract the hunters while we escape.*

Dandra recoiled from the suggestion. *Tetkashtai! I can't do that!*

The presence wrenched at her, yellow-green light harsh and bright. *When did your opinion start to matter? Run!*

No! Dandra thrust the presence away, then sent an image to her, a vision of what had happened while she huddled in fear. *The hunters are waiting for us,* she said. *The dolgrims have crossbows ready—*

Tetkashtai stared at the vision—then whirled like an angry cat. *You told them!* she howled. *You told them what happened!*

Dandra stumbled again, her shoulder scraping against cold rock. *You wouldn't answer me!* she protested. *I only told them what I had to.*

It was too much! Tetkashtai raged. Dandra forced herself back to her feet, staggering through the presence's anger—and flinching as a hand gripped her arm. She looked up sharply.

Adolan held her upright, offering her support. His eyes met hers. They were blue, she noticed. Soft blue, clear and direct, a stark contrast to the green eyes that haunted her thoughts . . .

"You fight a silent battle, Dandra," he said.

Tetkashtai froze in the midst of her rant, her fury shrinking to a deadly, hate-filled point. *He knows!* she hissed. A sudden vision of flames washed through Dandra's mind. *Kill him. Kill him!*

The kalashtar's throat constricted and she shuddered, squeezing her eyes shut. *No,* she gasped. *No! I won't!* She gathered the flames and flung them back against Tetkashtai's venomous light. Startled by the force of her rejection, the presence backed down. Dandra groaned aloud in release and her body sagged. Adolan held her up.

When she opened her eyes, he was staring at the crystal around her neck. Dandra stiffened and pulled away reflexively. Adolan let her go. "How?" Dandra breathed. "How do you know?"

The druid shook his head. "Gatekeepers are attuned to the unnatural." He pointed at the psicrystal. "I don't understand your powers, Dandra, but I can tell that something is wrong. Is this why the Bonetree—"

Dandra clenched her teeth. "Don't say anything else," she told him harshly. "Just tell me why you needed me here."

Adolan's eyes widened, but he said nothing and motioned for her to turn around. Her body stiff, Dandra turned.

The stones of the Bull Hole clustered close together around the circle's center like old warriors closing rank. Symbols and drawings were etched into their cold surfaces, some trick of the pale moonlight making them seem fresh and new though they should have been weathered into illegibility by untold ages. The stones surrounded an open space less than ten paces across and carpeted in coarse grass. Lying on the ground at the very center of the circle was a thick, irregular slab as broad as Dandra's outstretched arms.

Breek perched on the slab. The bird's eyes were focused on the sky overhead. Dandra followed its gaze and saw the long, gangly shapes of two herons in the moonlit sky. Her breath caught.

"They're still watching us," said Adolan. The druid stepped around her and over to one side of the slab. "Breek would attack them, but he knows that he would be a target as soon as he rose above the Bull Hole. We need to know what we're facing. Lend me a hand." He gestured and Breek hopped off the slab onto the ground. Adolan bent down, working his fingers between the soil and the stone.

Dandra looked at the slab and allowed herself a thin smile. "I think I can do better," she said. She focused her concentration on the stone and imagined the feel of its cold, dense surface under her hands, then drew that sensation into herself, wrapping her mind around it. *Tetkashtai, help me,* she said as she reached out to pull the presence closer to her.

Except that Tetkashtai wrenched herself away with a chilly disdain. Dandra's concentration wavered in surprise, her mental connection to the stone fading sharply. She sent a swift, angry thought toward the presence's yellow-green light. *Tetkashtai, what are you doing? I need your help. We have to move this rock.*

Why? Tetkashtai drew herself up, her light gleaming harshly. *You know what I think needs to be done.*

More images of Adolan wreathed in flames, of herself fleeing the circle and leaving Singe and Geth to face the Bonetree hunters, flashed through Dandra's head. She clenched her teeth. *I'm not going to do that.*

Then you can move that stone with your hands like a dumb human. Tetkashtai pulled back. Dandra's jaw dropped open in shock.

"Dandra?" asked Adolan. He was staring at her in concern. "Are you all right?"

The kalashtar closed her mouth. "I'm fine," she said. In her mind, she snarled at Tetkashtai. *Help me!*

No. Move it yourself.

Dandra's hands curled into fists. *All right,* she spat. She stared at the slab, then stretched out her mind and wrapped her thoughts around it once more. "Step back," she told Adolan. A startled look crossed the druid's face. He snatched his fingers out from under the stone and scuttled backward away from it. Dandra turned her will against the slab, pushing against it in the same way that she pushed against the ground when she chose to glide above it.

There was a word for the invisible force involved in attempting to move something with willpower alone: *vayhatana*. It literally meant "ghost breath," a good word for something that was at the same time subtle, powerful—and often elusive.

The slab didn't move, but Dandra's feet slid back and she almost fell to her knees. In the darkness of her mind, Tetkashtai sneered. *Pathetic.*

Dandra didn't answer her. Climbing to her feet, she focused on the slab again. When she rose above the ground, the *vayhatana* that she used was soft and gentle, taking no real energy at all. This time, though, she hardened the *vayhatana*, throwing it against the slab while willing herself to remain where she was. Without Tetkashtai's aid, directing her powers was difficult, but the raw strength behind them—that was her own. Dandra wrenched at the core of her being, dredging up all of her reserves, and *heaved* at the stone.

Nothing happened. She strained harder, like any human hauling at a great weight. A shudder shook her body, flesh faltering beneath the strength of her will. Tetkashtai flinched, though she still managed to mock her. *Stop this!* she said imperiously. *You can't move that. Who do you think you are?*

Anger flickered in Dandra's heart. Her teeth grinding together with aching pressure, she seized it, weaving it into her effort, focusing the *vayhatana* until it was like a cocoon spun around the slab. She lifted her hand slowly and held her palm out toward the slab. She could feel the stone, feel the way it rested against the ground. It only needed something to slide on to make it move, the way that just a thin layer of water could make tiles slippery. Or the way that a gentle force could send her gliding over the ground . . .

It took less than a thought to draw the cocoon of *vayhatana* under the slab, slipping invisible energy between stone and soil. The fingers of her hand pressed forward slightly.

A faint ripple of force shimmered through the air. Dandra didn't even dare to breathe as, with the slightest of tremors, the slab slid smoothly away from her. A few inches . . . a foot . . . another foot.

Tetkashtai was silent in her head. On the other side of the slab, Adolan stared and moved his mouth in choked words of wonder. The moving stone revealed the edge of a hole in the ground. Adolan managed to find his voice again. "Open it all the way if you can."

Dandra gave a slight nod and pushed a little harder. Like a child's toy boat set down on smooth water, the slab floated aside. When the hole—no larger around than the ring of her own arms—was fully exposed, she took a breath and pulled her mind away from it. The slab settled back to the ground with a soft thud that brought a squawk from Breek. As Adolan hastened to kneel at the edge of the hole, Dandra lowered her hand. A hot pride spread through her—a pride that turned swiftly to shame. Tetkashtai's entire attention was turned toward her, the presence's light as cold as a winter dawn. Without a word, Tetkashtai retreated, shrinking into a yellow-green spark, no brighter than a star.

Dandra felt more empty and alone than she ever had before. She swallowed and stepped quickly to Adolan's side.

The druid was peering intently into the hole, his lips moving in quiet murmurs. Sounds were returning from the hole as well, though, soft, almost animal sounds like the lowing of a cow. Or a bull. Cautiously, Dandra peered over Adolan's shoulder, down into the hole. It might not have been very big around, but it was clearly deep. Far, far deeper than she would have expected. Frighteningly deep. She could feel a power in the hole, too, something very old and very primitive. Something that hated the abominations that had intruded upon the valley, something that remembered the ancient war that Adolan had described. The strength of that hatred seized her, pulled at her, tried to drag her down into the primal deeps. Dandra gasped and reeled back desperately, trying to escape it. Adolan's hand reached up to steady her.

"Easy," he said.

She swallowed, trying to recover her breath. "What is that?" she gasped. "If that's what the Bonetree worship . . ."

Adolan shook his head sharply. "The cults of the Dragon Below worship the powers of Khyber. The spirit of the Bull Hole was placed in the depths by the Gatekeepers to help make sure that they stay there." He rose to his feet, his face grim

"You were talking with it," Dandra said.

"The Bull Hole knows things," the druid replied. "It told me what we face."

"The dolgrims? The Bonetree clan?" Dandra asked.

Adolan shook his head. "The dolgrims, yes, but not the Bonetree—the Bull Hole only sees unnatural creatures. No, there's something else in the valley. Something worse than the dolgrims."

Acid-green eyes flashed in Dandra's memory and fear rose in her throat. "What?" she asked with dread.

"Ado!" Geth's voice rose from the outer ring of the circle before the druid could answer. "You'd better see this! Something is happening out there!"

"You and Singe keep watch. Dandra, come with me."

Geth's eyes narrowed as Adolan beckoned Dandra to follow him, then moved off among the stones toward the center of the Bull Hole. A growl rumbled into his throat. He twisted away from both druid and kalashtar before it could fight its way free.

He found himself face to face with Singe. The Aundairian had been watching Adolan and Dandra as well, but with Geth's sudden movement, his eyes flickered to him. Geth stiffened. Singe did the same. For a moment, both men were silent, then Singe turned back to scan the clearing beyond the circle. "Here's a funny thing," the wizard said. He nodded toward the dolgrims and the Bonetree hunters. "If it wasn't for them, I'd be trying my best to burn you alive. But here we are. Like old times."

The growl Geth had trapped before slipped loose.

Singe paid him no attention. "What Adolan said about druid history—is it all true?"

"His tradition says it is."

"Huh." Singe stretched his arms. "I didn't think there was anyone left who still cared that much for tradition. I thought the Last War killed all of them—one way or another."

"Adolan never left the Eldeen," said Geth. "He was lucky."

He turned to face out of the circle as well, leaning against the stone that had given them shelter. The great-gauntlet on his arm, a sword on his belt, one of the Frostbrand at his side . . .

Memories of a dozen battles, of hundreds of nights of guard duty, of cities and towns and fortresses, swarmed over him. The fingers of his right hand, encased in the black metal of his gauntlet, began tapping out a ringing rhythm on the stone.

Singe glanced down at the sound. Aware of what he had been doing, Geth forced his hand to be still. Old habits, he thought, came back too easily. Singe looked away again.

"That gauntlet doesn't look like it's had nine years of use," he said.

"It hasn't," Geth answered.

"I remember when you got it. A full year's Blademarks wages—with bonuses—to that artificer in Metrol. You didn't take it off for half a month. The smell was so bad Robrand was worried your arm was rotting inside."

The wizard's voice was brittle. Geth could guess what was going through his head: nine years of bitter anger channeled into resentment at being made to stand as allies.

He knew exactly how Singe felt. He closed his hand into a fist and looked out over the clearing. "The hunters have spread themselves out," he said. The words came out as tightly clenched as his fist. "They're not making themselves a target. They know we have a spellcaster."

"More likely they know we have Dandra and they want to avoid her psionics." He darted a glance down at Geth. "That's kalashtar mind-magic to you."

"Is it really? Maybe they *did* teach you everything at Wynarn," the shifter grunted back. He looked up at Singe. The wizard had stiffened. Nine years had changed the man—Geth could see it in Singe's eyes—but he still had the same sensitive points. Geth dug a little harder. "That big crystal she wears around her neck? It's called a psicrystal—it's like a familiar for psions."

"I know what a psicrystal is," snapped Singe. He stared out into what Geth knew could only be shadows to his human eyes. "How may of them are there?"

"Dolgrims?" Geth made a rough estimate of their opponents' numbers—with so many arms waving and mouths champing in the moonlight, it was difficult. Every so often, a little pack would split off to circle the clearing while others would tumble out of the woods, making an accurate count even more difficult. Still, he grimaced at the odds. "Thirty, maybe forty. Less than half that of Bonetree hunters, assuming all of them are out there and not in the trees—"

Even as he spoke, though, an eerie, fluting call floated through the night air and a ripple seemed to spread through humans and dolgrims alike. The humans rose silently, remaining where they stood, while the dolgrims shrieked and jostled themselves into a rough semblance of order. All of them turned to face the dark line of the trees. Both Geth and Singe stiffened.

"What's going on?" muttered Singe.

"I don't know." Geth raised his voice and called over his shoulder, "Ado! You'd better see this! Something is happening out there!"

Adolan and Dandra were beside them in only moments, striding swiftly from the inner circle. Dandra looked strangely fear-haunted and Adolan oddly calm. Geth wondered what had happened at the Bull Hole's heart—but only briefly.

Out in the clearing, three figures emerged from the trees. One was a lean man with tattoos that swarmed up his arms. Another was a tall woman, as big as any man in Bull Hollow, with beads the size of finger bones strung through dark blonde hair and two pale rings piercing her lower lip over her canines. Both were dressed like the other hunters and carried swords. Of the third figure, though, Geth could make out almost nothing: it was shrouded in a cloak and cowl. One of the hunters approached the trio, speaking with them. His words were soft, but Geth saw him point at the stones and glimpsed his face as it twisted into an ugly grimace. The tall woman glanced back toward the forest and nodded. The lean man's expression grew long and he bowed his head. They had found the bodies of the hunters he, Singe, and Dandra had killed, Geth guessed.

Only the cloaked figure made no expression of sorrow. Its

cowl turned not toward the trees, but toward the circle of stones. Adolan's breath hissed between his teeth.

"What is it?" asked Geth.

Adolan shook his head. His eyes were fixed on the cloaked figure.

It must have said something because the humans turned toward it. The hunter who had spoken first swept his hand through the air, palm up. The cloaked figure turned sharply and strode forward, the lean man and the tall woman in its wake. Hunters and dolgrims alike leaped aside to make way for them.

At the same point where the magic of the Bull Hole had blocked the dolgrims, the cloaked figure was stopped as well. It cursed, a horrible word that carried all the way to the stones and that Geth didn't recognize, though he understood the emotion behind it all too well. The figure turned away and spoke again in what sounded like the same language, this time addressing the dolgrims. The horrid creatures squealed with excitement and charged back toward the trees. Only the Bonetree hunters and the cloaked figure remained in the moonlight. The figure turned back to face the Bull Hole again.

"Gatekeeper!" it shouted. "Gatekeeper!" Its voice was harsh and oddly broken, as if it did not often speak. It reached up to draw back its cowl. Geth's guts tightened. Dandra gasped and Singe hissed. Adolan's hands, Geth saw, curled where they rested on the stone of the Bull Hole.

There were no eyes behind the cowl. Black pits stared out of an emaciated face. The creature's flesh was pale and hard, drawn close to its bones and muscles. Its ears flared broad from the sides of its head before narrowing to fine points. Strange, thick clumps of hair fell from its head to its shoulders and a light, shimmering fur seemed to cover its arms and a chest that was bare beneath the cloak. Long, thin tentacles that resembled nothing so much as unnatural tongues sprang from the flesh of its shoulders.

"Gatekeeper!" the creature roared again. "I know you hear me. There is only one thing we want here. Give us the kalashtar and we will leave your valley!"

Dandra shrank back in fear, but there was also relief on her face, as if she had almost been expecting something even worse to lie behind the cowl. Geth's eyes darted from her to Adolan. "What is that thing?" he asked in disgust.

"A dolgaunt," Adolan answered. "The Bull Hole felt its presence in the valley. It's leader of the dolgrims. As foul as they are, it's even worse."

"Hruucan," said Dandra softly. Adolan glanced at her. So did Geth and Singe. Dandra looked at them without meeting their gazes. "The dolgaunt—his name is Hruucan."

Adolan's expression was guarded. "This isn't the first time you've encountered him?"

Dandra shook her head. The look in her eyes was so haunted that even Geth flinched back. Adolan blew out his breath. "Ring of Siberys."

For a moment, conflict washed across Dandra's face, then she blurted out. "If you want to avoid a fight, let me go. They've just spent a month following me. If I get out of the valley, maybe they'll keep following me—"

Adolan turned a sharp glare on her. "No," he said. The druid clenched his spear and stepped out from behind the stone.

"If she's the one thing you want, dolgaunt," he shouted back, "then I swear by the Three Dragons and the Twelve Moons that she's the one thing you'll never have!"

The druid's defiance echoed across the valley. Behind Hruucan, the Bonetree hunters stirred angrily. The tall woman said something to the dolgaunt and raised the sword that she carried. Geth bared his teeth. Even with the protection of the Bull Hole, he flexed his hand instinctively inside the great-gauntlet. "Boar's tusk!" he muttered at Adolan as he ducked back in among the stones. "Couldn't think of a better way to get them angry, could you?"

But out in the clearing, Hruucan simply turned his back on the stone circle and lifted his hand, silencing the hunters. He leaned toward the tall woman and the lean man who had accompanied him out of the forest. Both nodded. Geth stared as the dolgaunt strode out of the clearing and vanished into the trees after the dolgrims.

The tall woman and the lean man began drifting among the hunters, whispering to them. Where they passed, the savage warriors stretched and readied their weapons, looking toward the Bull Hole with a violent glee in their eyes.

"Twelve bloody moons, what are they up to?" said Singe. He glanced at Dandra. She shook her head. The wizard looked to Geth and Adolan. "I thought you said the dolgaunt was the leader of the dolgrims, not the hunters!"

Adolan shook his head. "Dolgaunts are servants of the powers of Khyber. The cults of the Dragon Below revere all such aberrations as holy creatures."

"Can we make a break for it while their numbers are low?"

"No," Geth said. "We don't know where the dolgrims have gone." He studied the hunters, especially the man and woman. They seemed to be in charge now that Hruucan was gone. The woman kept glancing toward the Bull Hole, then back toward the hunters, as she paced back and forth across the clan's line. "They're waiting for something," he guessed. "Maybe they're expecting us to make a break."

"Maybe," agreed Dandra. The kalashtar was watching the hunters as well, her brow furrowed. Geth glanced at her.

"What's wrong?" he asked.

"Maybe nothing." She turned to Adolan. "You said the Bull Hole only saw unnatural things like the dolgrims. It couldn't see the Bonetree hunters. It was created to protect against aberrations."

The druid nodded.

Dandra gestured toward the tall woman. "The Bull Hole protected us from the dolgrims and Hruucan, but the hunters haven't even *tried* to approach yet, have they?"

Adolan's eyes narrowed, then went wide. "Ring of Siberys!"

Geth stared at him. "What?" he demanded. "What is it?"

"Humans and aberrations have never attacked the Bull Hole in concert before." Adolan leaned against the stone, peering into the night. "I don't know if the Bull Hole will protect us against humans or not!"

"This isn't a good time to find out!" growled Geth. He reached across his body and pulled his sword from his sheath.

"It's going to get worse!" Singe thrust an arm up toward the sky. "Look!" Geth, along with Adolan and Dandra, followed his gesture.

Up above the treetops in the direction of Bull Hollow, ruddy light lit the underside of a growing column of smoke.

"Grandfather Rat," Geth breathed. Bull Hollow was burning. He knew where the dolgaunt and the dolgrims had gone.

The hunters saw the fire, too. As if it was the signal she had been waiting for, the tall woman thrust her sword high into the air and shouted, *"Su Drumas!"*

Savage, screaming battle cries made the night tremble. The hunters sprang to the attack. The Bull Hole's defenses didn't even slow them down.

Geth's heart thundered in his chest. If they stood their ground, they would be trapped. "The Hollow, Ado!" he roared. "We have to get to the Hollow!"

"Just keep the hunters busy!" Adolan spun abruptly and raced back toward the center of the Bull Hole.

Geth bared his teeth and prayed the druid knew what he was doing. "Hold them back!" he shouted at Singe and Dandra. "Singe to the left, Dandra to the right!"

Roaring like Tiger, he hurled himself out from the circle of stones and directly at the massed heart of the Bonetree charge. A lithe little hunter with two long knives leaped out in front of the pack, faster than the other warriors. Geth's sword darted forward, then swept to the side in a lethal arc.

The savage warrior ducked and rolled under it neatly, coming up inside the shifter's guard with his knives slashing in a furious cascade of sharpened metal.

CHAPTER

5

Geth's right arm snapped in front of his body and the slashing knives grated harmlessly along the blackened plates of his great-gauntlet. High . . . low . . . outside . . . Geth caught every strike on his arm. A year's wages as Singe had said, but worth it. Enhanced by an artificer's magic, the armor sleeve was as effective as the heaviest shield. He took a fast step backward and cut in with his sword once more. The Bonetree warrior twisted to meet the blow—and Geth straightened his arm, bringing the gauntlet up and around in a brutal, heavy backhand. Driven by thick muscles, the ridge of his forearm came up under the warrior's chin. Bone shattered and flesh, snagged by a spike, tore. The little warrior flew back a good three paces to slam into the ground. Geth turned sharply, arm outstretched, and another warrior went down, knocked off his feet by the momentum of his own charge.

Snarling, Geth turned and plowed into the nearest knot of warriors, swinging with sword and gauntlet. He heard Breek screech and caught a glimpse of the eagle, finally freed from the threat of arrows and bolts, beating into the sky toward the strange herons that circled overhead. To one side of him, Dandra's spear flashed and sparkled in the moonlight as she traded blows with a hunter. The kalashtar's feet had left the ground once more; she floated as she fought, skimming and turning with a fluid grace.

To his other side, there was a flare of flame and a burst of heat as fire leaped from Singe's fingertips to engulf three of the charging hunters. Two screamed and stumbled back, beating charred clothing and skin. One went down and didn't rise again.

"Save your spells!" Geth howled at the wizard. "You'll need them in Bull Hollow!"

It was an empty warning—more hunters swarmed around Singe, pressing too close to allow him time to cast another spell. Singe drew his sword and plunged in among them. Geth found himself pressed as well. Wherever he turned, it seemed that a Bonetree hunter was waiting for him.

A wavering call broke the chaos of combat, and the warriors around Geth drew back. A lone hunter stepped out of their ranks a half dozen paces away. Geth recognized him—the lean man with tattoos swarming up his arms, the hunter who had stood with Hruucan. Up close, he could see more. The man was clearly the oldest among the hunters. The hair that fell to his shoulders and sprinkled across his chest was gray. His face was lined, his gaze vague and slightly unfocused. He carried a fine sword, though, and he pointed it straight at Geth.

"Weretouched! Beastling!" he called in a voice that was strangely accented, but clear. "You belong to Ner!" He flung himself forward with a mad howl.

The hunters around him took up the battle cry. Geth growled deep in his throat, tightened his grip on his own sword, and leaped to meet him. He swung the heavy Karrnathi blade in a high, sweeping arc that would draw Ner's defense up and leave him open for a fast punch from his gauntlet.

Instead of trying to block the falling sword, Ner spun lightly out of the way. Geth found himself open and off-balance as Ner's own sword slashed down. He flung himself down and rolled, barely getting his armored arm up in time to block the attack.

Magewrought steel rang with the force of Ner's blow and a jolt of pain shot through Geth's arm. Ner gave him no respite, but rained blows down on him, each one sending numbing waves vibrating through the gauntlet and Geth's bones. The shifter struggled to scoot back and away. Ner stayed right on top of him. Geth's lips drew back in alarm. If this was how the man fought when he was old, Geth wouldn't have wanted to face him in his prime!

He twisted and kicked out sharply, aiming for Ner's knee. The hunter jumped back to avoid the blow. In the slim instant of that opening, Geth scrambled back to his feet. He swallowed a gulp of air and reached deep into himself, letting a shifting spread through him. Invincibility burned in his veins and across his skin. He hurled himself back at Ner with a growl. This time he ripped his sword low. Ner stopped the blow with his own sword, the two blades clashing together as the Bonetree hunter deftly slid Geth's attack aside—then twisted his weapon free and brought it around to slice at Geth's hip.

The edge of the sword skated across his shifting-toughened hide, cutting cloth and creasing skin, but not drawing blood. Before Ner could pull back, Geth reached down and closed the fingers of his gauntleted hand around the shining blade. Ner tried to jerk the weapon away. Geth moved his body with the force of the hunter's jerk, letting Ner pull him close. Shoving himself up on the balls of his feet, his entire weight behind him, he bashed his heavy-browed forehead into Ner's face.

The old hunter grunted and staggered back. Geth staggered a little, too—he could feel blood from some small cut starting to trickle down his face—but he managed to stomp after him, swinging his sword and jabbing with his gauntlet. Now Ner was on the defensive, forced to give ground and parry as Geth hacked at him. The other Bonetree warriors shouted and crushed in. The tall woman with the pierced lips loomed close, pushing her way through the press of hunters. She towered over them—and over Geth, too.

"Get back!" he snarled, swinging his metal-sheathed arm wide. She rocked back in time to dodge it, but quickly moved forward again.

Rage flared in Ner's eyes. "Ashi!" he shouted at the big woman. *"An atit!"*

The woman—Ashi—fell back. Ner's sword rose high. Geth brought his gauntlet up to block it again, but the hunter dropped and spun around, lashing out with one leg to sweep Geth's feet out from under him. The shifter hit the ground heavily. His breath exploded out of his lungs. Ner came back to his feet, whirled his sword around, and, for a moment, held it poised to strike.

Before the fatal blow could fall, the ground under them shook hard, then rose and fell like a wave passing through water. Ner swayed. Many of the Bonetree hunters stumbled. In the shocked silence that followed, Geth could hear Adolan chanting.

The soil of the clearing behind Ner and the other hunters heaved, groaned, and rose, rumbling into a thick column. No, Geth realized in shock, not a column. A body, one that towered three times the height of a tall man. Thick legs tore clear of the earth, arms of grinding stone swung free, and a gaping mouth opened in a rough and primal face as it let loose a savage bellow. An earth elemental!

The thing's voice was like an earthquake. The hunters, even Ner and Ashi, jerked like puppets as they fought to keep their balance. For a moment, Geth was glad he was already down. But only for a moment—with the speed of a landslide, the elemental swung its arms down at the fragile beings around its feet.

A Bonetree hunter died on Geth's left. Another died on his right. Over the crash of tumbling rock, Geth couldn't even tell if they screamed. They were simply gone, buried abruptly under a cascade of stone that raised a choking cloud of dust and sent pebbles singing through the air. When the elemental's fists rose, they left behind bodies that had been broken like crushed insects.

The surviving hunters yelled and scattered. His challenge to Geth forgotten, Ner raised a hand to his mouth and gave a fluting call, then whirled and led the Bonetree savages in a stumbling, frantic retreat into the woods. Still on the ground, Geth stared at the flattened corpses of the elemental's victims and scrambled to his feet. Blood streaked his bare left arm where flying shards from the stone monster's attack had punctured even his tough skin. His hands curled tight—one around the hilt of his sword, the other inside a metal shell that felt all too delicate.

The elemental was staring down at him.

"Ado!" he croaked.

The druid was beside him. "Easy, Geth!" he rasped. His voice was raw, strained by whatever magic he had summoned. "It's the spirit of the Bull Hole!"

"Twelve moons," breathed Singe as he and Dandra joined them. The Aundairian's side was bloodied and his face was coated in a sheen of sweat.

In contrast, Dandra seemed almost fresh and relaxed. The only blood about her was what clung to her spear, staining the crystalline head and spattering the pale shaft. She tilted her head back and looked up at the elemental. "It's trembling," she said. "Why?"

"Because it's not here to fight the Bonetree hunters." Forcing his voice deep into his chest, Adolan spoke a command in some primal, ponderous tongue that Geth didn't recognize, but that tugged at his soul.

The elemental let out another roar and turned by simply flexing its entire body so that its rugged back became its front. One massive leg swung forward, then the other, as the creature stomped away in the direction of Bull Hollow. "Follow it!" shouted Adolan. He raised his spear and charged after it. Dandra and Singe followed without hesitation, the kalashtar still darting through the air as the wizard stumbled over ground broken by the elemental's passing.

Geth glanced up at the sky. The smoke of Bull Hollow's burning seemed to blot out half the night, the red of flames taking the place of moonlight. The shifter drew a ragged breath. Just like Narath . . .

No, he reminded himself. Not like Narath. Not yet. Bull Hollow still had a chance. Sword held low, he ran to the fight.

The effort of moving the stone, followed by the sudden, desperate fight against the Bonetree hunters, had taken more out of Dandra than she expected. It took an effort to will herself after Adolan and the elemental he had summoned from the Bull Hole—even so, she found the gentle force that held her feet above the ground faltering only halfway across the clearing. Abruptly, her feet were once more on the ground and she was stumbling. Singe was there, though, and caught her arm.

"Are you all right?" he asked.

"Just tired," she told him. She pressed a hand to her forehead. She had a horrible feeling she knew why she was feeling so drained. *Tetkashtai,* she called silently, reaching in her mind through her connection to the crystal around her neck. *Tetkashtai, I need you!*

The presence only held herself away, aloof and cold. Dandra shivered. *Tetkashtai!*

"Dandra?" Singe asked again.

She forced herself to stand straight, relying on the purely physical strength of her body. "I just need a moment to recover."

"I don't think we have a moment," Singe said. He was staring ahead of them. Dandra followed his gaze.

As it approached the dark line of the trees ahead, the great earth elemental was shrinking with each lumbering step. No, Dandra realized, it wasn't shrinking. It was sinking back into the ground as if walking down a flight of invisible stairs. In only moments, it was gone entirely. Geth caught up to them as they reached the edge of the forest. The knuckles of the hand that clutched his sword were white with tension. "Where did it go?" the shifter growled at Adolan.

"The trees would only slow it down. It will travel underground to Bull Hollow. We'll meet it there." Adolan glanced up into the sky and whistled sharply. A moment later, Breek settled to the ground. The eagle's beak and talons were stained dark with blood. He spread his wings and screeched as if in victory.

Adolan nodded. "We don't have to worry about the hunters' herons at least." He flicked his fingers at the fierce bird. "To Bull Hollow, Breek! On guard!"

The eagle screeched again and leaped heavily back into the dark sky. Adolan gestured sharply with his spear and spoke a ringing word. Light—similar to the light that shone from Singe's blade, but warm like fire where Singe's was cold—blossomed around the spear's head. His gaze swept across them all. "Follow me," he ordered. "Don't fall behind."

The druid strode into the trees—directly into what seemed

like the thickest of thorn bushes. There was no path where he had stepped. Dandra sucked in a sharp breath. Her eyes darted to Geth. He bared his teeth. "Go!" he snarled.

Dandra swallowed and plunged into the forest.

There *was* a path, or at least a barely clear track of some kind. Adolan's spear shone like a beacon. Dandra moved as quickly as she dared, staying close to his light. There was a rustling and Singe's cool steady light flashed briefly. She risked a glance over her shoulder. The wizard was right behind her and Geth, moving like a ghost, right behind him.

"Keep with me!" said Adolan. Dandra hastened to catch up and, in the shadows, stumbled again. Once more, Singe caught her.

"Stay close," he whispered. He lifted his rapier high to spread its light around.

At the very dimmest edge of the magical illumination, a face pierced with two hoops through its lower lips flashed pale, then vanished. In the yellow-green crystal, Tetkashtai flinched in fear. Dandra gasped and called out, "Adolan, the Bonetree!"

With the elemental's disappearance, the hunters had recovered their nerve—and with her warning, there was no need for them to remain hidden. The darkness exploded with the sound of bodies crashing through the brush to either side of them. Dandra raised her spear, Singe his rapier, and Geth his vicious gauntlet, instinctively putting their backs together to meet the attack. Adolan was faster than all three of them, though. Light and shadows whirled as he spun around and Dandra caught a glimpse of him throwing his head back to let out an undulating chant that was half words and half wild howl.

The sound of it made goose bumps on her skin and all around them, the forest seemed to stir in response to the druid's call. To their left, the night shifted, contracting for a moment, then opening wide.

A pack of wolves burst out of nature's rippling magic, leaping at the nearest hunters. The battle cries of the Bonetree turned to shouts of surprise and terror. Adolan howled again and magic brought forth more wolves on their right. Lean, savage bodies met snarling, bristling beasts. Dandra saw a flash of white as Geth bared his teeth in kinship with the animals. He almost started to pull away as if to join the fight, but Adolan was already moving forward, faster now. "Keep moving!" he said sharply. "The wolves will guard our backs!"

They plunged on. Every few moments, Dandra caught Geth glancing over his shoulder, watching for signs of pursuit. If there were any, she didn't see them, but she could hear increasing barks of wolfish pain mixed in with the shrieks of the hunters. Slowly, the shrieks became confident calls. The hunters were taking the upper hand.

Tetkashtai was stirring again, fear mingling with her cold rage. *Dandra, we need to get out of this place!*

It's too late for that now, Dandra snapped back.

But the brief contact with the presence also lent a fresh trickle of energy to her tired limbs. A second wind whispered across her mind. "How much farther?" she asked Geth.

"We're almost there."

Dandra looked ahead. Past Adolan, firelight was beginning to peek through the trees. She could smell smoke strong on the air. A little further on and she could hear screams as well.

Then they were out of the forest. Dandra froze on the edge of a scene of horror, her eyes wide and Tetkashtai's terrified moans echoing through her soul.

The sleepy hamlet that Singe had seen at twilight was gone.

More than half of the buildings that had clustered around Bull Hollow's open common were on fire. Two had already collapsed, one falling back into trees and setting them alight as well—luck seemed to be the only thing holding back a forest fire. Smoke drifted and whirled on the air, threatening to choke the wizard with every breath.

Figures raced back and forth across the common—dolgrims, bandy legs and arms twitching like demented toys, and the folk of Bull Hollow, some fleeing in terror, some trying to fight back. Screams tumbled from more than one burning building.

Mixed with the screams was the chuckling, gibbering chatter

of the dolgrims. If Singe could have blotted out that nightmare chorus, he would have. Through long years of war and service to House Deneith, he had seen more battlefields than he cared to remember. He could think of only one that might compare to the madness that had fallen on Bull Hollow.

Geth stood beside him. Singe glanced at the shifter. White showed around his eyes. His breath was coming short and shallow between his sharp teeth. Singe knew they were both seeing the same battle—if the massacre at Narath could really have been called a battle at all.

On his other side, Dandra stood stiff with shock. In front of her, Adolan was simply staring at the devastated hamlet with an expression of pure rage on his face. Stretching out his arms toward Bull Hollow, he let out a cry of anguished fury.

With an answering roar, the spirit of the Bull Hole exploded up out of the common, raining clods of soil and chunks of turf down everywhere. The dolgrims ran and screamed just as hard as the folk of Bull Hollow. Their chatter turned to shrieks and wails, and they scrambled like rats at the elemental lashed out with its rocky fists. Singe saw a dolgrim driven down into the ground, crushed so deep into the soil that it vanished from sight.

But for every dolgrim that died under the elemental's fist, three more slipped away. The elemental was so ponderous and so much larger than the twisted creatures that they had an advantage in dodging the earth-spirit's blows. And the hamlet was still burning.

"Move in!" Adolan yelled. His voice cracked with emotion. "Do whatever you can!"

Geth roared and charged like a mastiff released from its chain, sword and gauntlet catching the burning light. Adolan raced forward as well, the deep words that commanded the elemental rumbling out of his chest. Singe scanned the smoke and shadows of the common. When he had first glimpsed the hellish light of the burning hamlet rising about the trees, one guilty thought had shot through him.

He had left Toller alone while he pursued Geth. Now the young commander was somewhere in the middle of madness that would make even a veteran falter.

Dandra was still standing with him, the shock in her eyes seeming stronger than ever. She had her free hand wrapped around the psicrystal that lay against her chest. Her whole body was trembling. Her gaze was empty, as if her entire awareness had turned in on itself in reaction to the horror before her. Her mouth was moving, though. She was muttering to herself. "I won't run. I won't. They need us . . ."

"Dandra!" Singe shouted over the cacophony of screams and cracking flames. She didn't respond. He had seen too many recruits freeze with shock at their first battle to be gentle. He reached out and slapped her.

The kalashtar reeled back, then looked up at him sharply.

For a moment, Dandra's eyes burned with the feral, brittle fury of someone terrified beyond madness. Singe gasped and snapped up his rapier, but before he could do more than react, Dandra sucked in a deep, wracking breath. Her eyes squeezed shut and a shudder passed through her.

When she opened her eyes again, they were frightened, but clear and rational. "Singe . . ." She stared at his raised blade, touched her cheek, and swallowed. "Il-Yannah, what did I do?"

The truth of what he had seen—or thought he had seen—almost rolled off Singe's tongue. From somewhere behind him, though, a heartrending shriek tore through the screams of Bull Hollow's destruction. The wizard glanced over his shoulder at the fiery scene, then back to Dandra. He swallowed his answer.

"You froze," he told her. "That's all." He lowered his sword. "Have you recovered? Do you think you're ready to fight again?"

Dandra nodded grimly and shifted her grip on her spear. Singe took a breath. "Good. Stay with me. I left a friend in Bull Hollow. I need to find him."

He turned and plunged across the common, shouting for Toller. Through the smoke, he could see the towering form of the elemental as it slowly chased down dolgrims, swinging its immense fists at any that came within its reach. Adolan moved with the earth-spirit, his spear skewering any dolgrims lucky enough to escape the earth-spirit's fists. Geth was leaping and springing through the shifting shadows cast by the burning buildings, darting back and forth wherever dolgrims menaced the people of Bull Hollow. Singe whirled around, looking for some sign—any sign—of his young commander.

On the far side of the common, Sandar's proud inn was half ablaze, its northern end devoured by flame that was slowly working its way south. In the cover of the south end, sheltered between the inn and its stables, a makeshift barricade had been erected. A classic defense taught in House Deneith officer training. Behind the barricade, a blue jacket with the flashing silver insignia of the Blademarks flew like a rallying banner from a broken pole. Dark shapes crouched low around it. Hope leaped in Singe.

"Toller! *Toller!*" He grabbed at Dandra's arm and pulled the kalashtar around to point the barricade out to her. "My friend is there!"

He sprinted across the common without waiting to see if she followed. The barricade was intact and three dead dolgrims were scattered across the ground before it. "Toller!" he shouted again.

There was no response. The only sound beyond the barricade was the screaming of terrified horses in the stable.

Singe slowed to a stop with sudden dread. "Toller?" he called. "Anyone?" He approached the barricade, a spell ready on his lips.

The light from the burning inn danced across fallen bodies—the dark shapes he thought he had seen crouched around the banner of Toller's jacket. With his heart in his throat, Singe vaulted over the barrier. Toller sat slumped with his back against the banner's broken pole. The scion of House Deneith, a promising Blademarks commander, slumped to the side at the wizard's touch. Any sign of life Singe thought he had seen was, he realized stupidly, nothing more than the shifting of firelight.

Toller's shirt had been torn open. His exposed chest, his arms, and his throat were all strangely pockmarked, the skin shriveled and pale. His dead face was locked in an expression of agony.

Singe squatted down and touched the swirling colors of

Toller's dragonmark. The bright mark had faded slightly with its bearer's death, but it was hot to the touch. Toller had used its magic before he died.

There was a whimper from the deepest shadows alongside the stable wall. Singe lifted his glowing rapier sharply. Its light fell on a huddled woman—the serving woman from the inn. Her eyes were wide with terror, but she was alive and, except for minor bruises and burns, uninjured. Singe's jaw clenched. There was a slight shimmer about the woman. He recognized it. House Deneith carried the Mark of Sentinel, the ability of magical defense. Some heirs of Deneith could turn aside arrows or conjure phantom armor or block spells. Toller had been able to throw up a minor magical shield.

In his last moments, he had used it to protect a serving woman.

Singe rose and took a step toward her. "What happened here?"

The woman's response was to stiffen and press herself back against the wall, her wide-eyes staring at him.

Past him.

Singe whirled as the tall, emaciated figure of the dolgaunt emerged from the smoke and shadows. Hruucan, Dandra had named him. His shoulder tentacles twitched like an insect's antennae, probing the air. Up close, Singe had a better view of what he had thought at a distance to be thick hair and light fur on the dolgaunt's head and body. The truth was repulsive. Thick tendrils of flesh dangled from the creature's scalp and ran down his neck and onto his shoulders in a heavy pendulous mane. Hruucan was naked from the waist up and all over his exposed skin, tiny buds of flesh rose up in imitation of whiskers and body hair—except that those fleshy buds writhed and shivered in reaction to every speck of falling ash and every breath of hot, fire-born wind. The black pits of the thing's eyes turned toward Singe.

"Wizard," he said and the grating bluntness of the word made Singe shudder. There was no emotion in Hruucan's harsh voice, only cold acknowledgment of what he faced.

His tongue-like tentacles lashed forward.

The huddled serving woman finally found her voice and screamed, scrambling away over the barricade. Singe leaped away from the whipping tentacles. Hruucan, however, closed in behind them, moving with uncanny speed and fighting in silence. His tentacles swept the air again and this time the dolgaunt whirled with them, spinning up on one leg to reach and kick with the other. Singe jumped back again. He slashed his rapier at the tentacles, but the tough strands of muscle just twitched out of the way as if possessed of a mind of their own. He shifted and stepped back, trying to pick his target.

His foot came down on something hard and thick, yet yielding. An out-flung leg. Toller's leg. His arms flailed and he staggered, then lost his balance entirely. The ground—and Toller's sprawled body—rushed up at him. Singe tucked his shoulder in and rolled as he hit the ground, coming up in a crouch. One of the dolgaunt's tentacles hit Toller's corpse and seemed to dig into the flesh, almost sucking at it.

Singe gagged. Gathering his concentration, he stared at the dolgaunt and hissed the words of a spell. In his mind's eye, the creature's nightmare form seemed to come into sharper focus for a moment, the swirling of its tentacles, arms, and legs slowing into something comprehensible. A moment of certainty filled Singe and he snapped up out of his crouch to swing his rapier at empty air.

Except that when the blade reached its target, the air was no longer empty. As he swung around for another blow, Hruucan drove his arm straight onto Singe's waiting rapier. The weapon sank in deep, piercing the dolgaunt's arm above the elbow and sliding along the bone to emerge just below Hruucan's shoulder. The dolgaunt's whirling fury stopped. He froze.

So did Singe. There was a certain feel to the moment of a sword striking flesh. A solid connection, a tearing of muscle, a grating of bone. His strike on the dolgaunt carried none of those sensations. Instead, it felt as though he had driven his blade into spongy, rotten meat. There was no resistance as it penetrated muscle. When it struck bone, it glided silent and smooth along the hard surface. Singe choked and jumped back, tearing the weapon away. It came free as easily as if he was wiping it across fine velvet. It left no wound behind it and only the barest trickle of blackish blood. Hruucan flexed his arm and smiled.

And as Singe stared, the dolgaunt's tentacles swept around behind his back, crossed, and yanked him forward. His rapier tumbled from his grip as Hruucan swept his arms wide, pulling him into a horrid embrace.

The tiny writhing buds of the creature's skin crawled against him—and where his skin was bare, or his clothing thin, stung! Singe howled in agony. It felt like the buds were burrowing into him! He struggled, trying to push back against the dolgaunt, but silent as a ghost, Hruucan squeezed tight, his tentacles flexing to drag across Singe's back. Their touch stung as well, bringing a new scream out of the wizard. Even the thick flesh of Hruucan's scalp tentacles swung to brush at him! The Aundairian sagged, weak and dizzy as if the dolgaunt was draining his very life away.

"Singe, get away from him!" Dandra's voice.

Singe fought to wrench his head back enough to turn so he could see her. She stood on the other side of the barricade, one trembling arm extended toward Hruucan. When they had first met in the forest, she had hurled fire bolts with ease. Now it looked like she was fighting to draw on that power.

"Move!" she shouted. "I'll burn him!"

Singe wanted to shout at her to burn him anyway—he wasn't entirely sure his ring would protect him from her psionic flames, but he was willing to take the risk. There was no need, though. As Hruucan whirled toward the sound of Dandra's voice, Singe could feel his horrible body stiffen. He pushed Singe away, reaching instead toward Dandra. The wizard reeled back to stumble against the broken pole that flew Toller's jacket. He stared down at his arms. Where they had been pressed against the dolgaunt's squirming skin, his flesh was puckered like Toller's.

On the other side of the barrier, Dandra was backing away from Hruucan, her spear held ready, her hand pointing at the dolgrim. Hruucan vaulted lightly to the top of the barricade and just stood there, tentacles writhing in the darkness. He seemed to stare at Dandra for a moment, then raised his harsh voice. Gibbered words, the same language he had used outside the Bull Hole to command the dolgrims, rippled off his tongue. Singe couldn't understand any of them, but Hruucan's command was obvious. All around the common, dolgrims began streaming toward them in immediate response, their chattering rising into shrill cries. Adolan's elemental swung around ponderously, roaring in confusion as the sudden movement of its tiny enemy.

An instant later, the weird fluting call of the Bonetree hunters rolled through the air as well. Singe choked on a curse as savage figures leaped out of the trees and across the common, battered and bloodied after their fight with Adolan's wolves but still very much alive!

"Hand of the Revered!" called the old hunter Geth had fought. "Command us!"

A hard pleasure seemed to spread across Hruucan's horrid visage. Pointing at Dandra, he shouted to the hunters, "She's here! Take her!"

One of the hunters, a muscular brute streaked with blood and armed with a heavy, wide-bladed axe, raced ahead of the others. His face was weirdly pinched and too small for his body, but his eyes were even smaller, dark pinpricks gleaming mad with bloodlust in the firelight. *"Su Drumas!"* he screamed as he charged. *"Su Darasvhir!"*

With enemies on all sides, Dandra spun around in confusion, her spear and her hand wavering.

Then Adolan was there, darting through a wash of firelight to put himself between the Bonetree hunter and the kalashtar. The hunter shouted again and swept his axe around in a deadly arc, but Adolan jumped back out of reach and thrust with his spear, forcing the hunter to break his charge or be impaled. The blood-streaked warrior threw himself to the side. Adolan followed, stabbing his spear down. The hunter was faster though, rolling aside and leaping back to his feet. His next swing was even heavier than his first. Adolan barely managed to check it with the shaft of his spear. The blow still sent him staggering back and left a deep notch in the spear's shaft.

"Ado!"

Geth's roar rolled across the battlefield of the common.

Singe saw the shifter's sword and great-gauntlet flash as he tried to fight his way past a pack of dolgrims to the druid's side.

Atop the barricade, Hruucan's tentacles twitched in frustration. His eyeless face turned toward Dandra. He tensed, ready to leap at the kalashtar.

Singe's chest clenched. "Hey, wormface!" he bellowed. He jumped at Hruucan and grabbed the rough fabric of the loose pants the dolgaunt wore. Hruucan turned, kicking to try and shake him off, but Singe held on grimly. Spreading the fingers of his free hand, he pointed up at the dolgaunt's head and bony chest and let the words of a spell ripple from his lips.

Fire rushed from his fingers, washing over the foul creature. Some of the flame rebounded to pour down over Singe, but the magic of his ring protected him. Hruucan had no such protection. The dolgaunt let out a grating screech as his deformed flesh bubbled and charred. He tore himself from Singe's grasp and tumbled from the barricade, fleeing blind into the smoky darkness.

His flight struck confusion into the dolgrims. Their charge slowed, turning into a chaotic mass. Beyond Adolan and his big, black-eyed opponent, however, the rest of the Bonetree hunters were still closing rapidly. Singe scrambled up onto the barricade where Hruucan had stood only a moment before and spoke a word of magic. A tiny, intense tongue of flame sprang into the palm of his free hand.

Picking his target carefully, he drew back his arm and hurled it. The flame streaked through the air as far and fast as an arrow—though not quite fast enough. Singe caught a glimpse of the old hunter leaping back hastily with his eyes wide and heard him shout for others to do the same.

The tiny flame exploded with a roar, flashing in a sudden inferno so bright it forced the wizard to fling up an arm to protect his eyes. Even Dandra gasped at the blast.

So did Adolan.

The massive hunter—so caught up in his rage that he didn't seem to notice the fiery magic at all—swung his axe in a heavy, overhand blow that sheared through the druid's spear and into his chest.

Adolan fell to his knees. Dandra's gasp turned into a scream. Singe froze in shock. The hunter planted one foot on Adolan's chest and forced him backward as he wrenched at his weapon. The axe came free in a spray of blood. Adolan swayed but remained on his knees, his eyes watching the wide blade sweep up . . .

With a bellow of pure animal rage, Geth surged out of the night and leaped onto the hunter like a beast. His gauntleted hand seized the handle of the axe above the hunter's grip and wrenched it back so hard that Singe heard the man's thick wrists snap. In the same movement, he jammed his sword vertically into the hunter's belly and all the way up under his breast bone. Blood burst out of the warrior's mouth.

Geth's weight carried his body to the ground, but the shifter rolled free and groped for Adolan. "Ado! Ado!"

The druid was still on his knees, still staring up into the night. Blood trickled through his red-brown beard. At the shifter's desperate touch, though, his eyes seemed to clear. His mouth moved, shaping words that emerged as a froth of blood. His hand fumbled toward the collar of polished black stones around his neck—

—then fell away as his body shuddered. Somewhere in the sky above, Breek screamed. A moment later, Geth roared at the night.

CHAPTER

6

A sound like an avalanche brought Singe's head up. Out on the common, the elemental that Adolan had summoned from the Bull Hole was falling apart in midstride, the earth and stones that had formed its body tumbling to the ground. The dolgrims it had been pursuing stopped and stared—then advanced cautiously to prod the heaped stone with their weapons. Singe swung around to stare past the scorched circle of his spell. A few human bodies lay within the blackened ring, but not nearly enough to account for all the Bonetree hunters. In the shadows beyond, he could make out figures emerging from the trees and picking themselves up from the ground.

"Moons!" he cursed. He leaped down from the barricade and dashed to Dandra. The kalashtar seemed frozen, watching Geth as he held Adolan's body, his forehead touching the druid's. Singe caught her arm. "They're regrouping!"

She started and whirled around, picking out exactly what he had. Their enemies were gathering themselves for a new attack. "Il-Yannah," she breathed. There was an edge of terror to her voice. "Will they *never* stop?"

"We need to find somewhere defensible," Singe told her. "Somewhere we can put our backs to a wall—"

"No," said Geth.

Singe spun back to the shifter. He was standing, Adolan's

collar of stones around his neck. The druid lay at his feet. A line of dirt had been traced down his pain-twisted face. Geth's face was smudged with dirt as well. Beneath it, the shifter's features were hard with barely restrained emotion.

"We aren't staying here," he said. He bent and ripped his sword out of the Bonetree hunter's corpse. His eyes swept around the ruins of Bull Hollow. Singe followed his gaze and realized that there wasn't a living inhabitant of the hamlet left on the common. Dol Arrah, he prayed, let them be safe in the woods!

Geth strode toward him and Dandra. "You said before," the shifter asked Dandra, "that if you fled, the hunter and the dol-grims would follow you. Do you think they still will?"

Dandra nodded. "Yes. More than ever."

"Good. We're leading them away from here. All of us." He gestured with his armored hand toward still-closed doors of the stable. "Singe, get horses—battle measures."

The old words of the Frostbrand. Instinct pushed Singe to obey before he even fully understood what Geth was proposing. Understanding came as he fumbled at the stable doors.

Battle measures—act quickly, take the best, deal only with the necessary. They would use Dandra as bait to lead their vile enemies away from Bull Hollow, to give any survivors a better chance to hide.

He glanced at Toller's body behind the barricade, killed by the dolgaunt while defending a place and people he didn't know. His jaw tightened.

He pulled open the door of the stable. Inside, the building echoed with the cries of panicked horses. An everbright lantern hung beside the door. He took it and lowered the shade to expose the light within, then made his way down the center aisle of the stables.

His own horse, battle-trained, was waiting quietly. He saddled the animal with a speed born from long practice, then turned to Toller's horse, trained like his own, and a spirited-looking mare. Unused to strange hands, only the mare gave him trouble.

"Singe!" called Geth from outside. "We need those horses!"

"Almost ready!" he called back. He got a bit into the mare's mouth, then released his horse and Toller's before backing the mare out of her stall.

Outside, the hunters and the dolgrims were still sorting themselves out. A shout went up, though, as an alert hunter spotted the horses. Their enemies began to close, warily this time.

Geth took the mare's reins and nodded at the lantern in Singe's hand. "Keep it open," he said. "We want them to follow us." He swung into the mare's saddle. Singe climbed onto his horse, then held Toller's steady as Dandra scrambled awkwardly into the saddle. Geth watched her with an unpitying eye. "Hold tight and stay low," he advised her. "Now follow me!"

With a tight shout and a kick at his mount's sides, he galloped straight at the clustered Bonetree hunters. Singe darted a glance at Dandra. She nodded grimly—then raised her voice in a fierce, rippling cry. *"Adar! Adar! Bhintava adarani!"*

Toller's eager horse needed no other urging. It sprang after Geth instantly. *"Deneith!"* called Singe, pushing his horse into a gallop, too.

Geth's roar was less prosaic. *"Follow us, you murdering bastards!"* he screamed as he raced by the hunters, then pulled his horse around to flash past the dolgrims as well. *"Follow us!"* He plunged his horse into the forest along a path that Singe could barely see. Dandra, her voice shaking, vanished after him.

Singe turned in his saddle, waving the everbright lantern to be sure the hunters and the dolgrims had seen it. They had—they were charging across the battle-scarred common in a stream. Singe gave the fiery, bloody remains of Bull Hollow one last look, then turned back to bend low over his horse's neck.

Dawn's golden light found them riding across the bare slope of a hill. Dandra felt it wash over her back, warming her night-cooled skin. There were more hills around them, all blanketed in long grass and thorny-looking bushes. Further down the slope, thicker trees grew in abundance. If they'd ridden among them, they would have had cover from their pursuers. Dandra didn't need to ask why they weren't riding in the trees. She knew the answer.

Geth wanted to be sure they were seen.

Dandra clung to her horse in exhaustion. All of her reserves—physical and mental—were devoted to hanging on to the animal. Her arms ached and her legs burned. Her backside was so sore she was certain that she'd never walk upright again.

At least she would walk again. A vision of Bull Hollow flickered in front of her eyes. Burning houses, screaming people, silent bodies. Adolan, dead in Geth's arms. The same vision had haunted her all night. A community had been destroyed because of her brief presence.

She raised her head look at Geth's back. The shifter rode in front of her, guiding his horse with a light touch. He had held them to the same pace all night after their initial galloping flight from Bull Hollow—just fast enough to stay ahead of runners on foot, easy enough that the horses didn't tire too much. He sat stiffly upright, constantly alert. He hadn't looked at her or spoken a single word through all their long ride.

Singe was behind her. The wizard hadn't spoken either, but she could feel his gaze on her back. It made her want to wither up in shame.

Survival is nothing to be ashamed of, Tetkashtai said. *It's why you're here at all.* The long, dark hours of the night and the knowledge that they were once more fleeing the Bonetree hunters rather than standing against them had finally calmed the presence. She was rational again—if not entirely forgiving. Her yellow-green light pulsed righteously. *If you'd listened to me and left when I told you to, none of this would have happened.*

You don't know that, Dandra told her. *The Bonetree clan are savages. They could have overrun Bull Hollow just looking for us.*

You should have run when you had the chance. You could have made a clean escape.

Anger flared in Dandra's belly. *If you had worked with me instead of sulking, maybe I could have made a difference!* She thrust another memory at Tetkashtai: hunters and dolgrims she should have been able to stop with fiery blasts, flames raging out of control that she should have been able to control with a thought. Without Tetkashtai's cooperation, her powers had dwindled—

Your powers? Tetkashtai's voice filled with disdain. *You forget yourself! Without me, you're little more than a warm body with a few tricks in your head.*

Without me, Dandra snapped, *you're a rock!*

Coming from you, that's almost amusing, Tetkashtai struck back with seething hatred. *Give the crystal to Singe and we'll see what happens.*

A chill settled over Dandra. Tetkashtai sensed her apprehension. *Are you afraid of what might happen, Dandra?* she asked. *Are you afraid that I might find another—?*

Dandra wrenched her mind away. She couldn't shut the presence out entirely, though, and Tetkashtai pulled at the edge of her consciousness. The presence was laughing at her, an edge of madness to her silent voice. Dandra sagged down in her saddle.

They passed around the hill and onto another, winding their way through wild valleys of astounding beauty. Where the folds of the hills dropped away to her right, Dandra could see dark mountains in the distance. The forests of the Eldeen Reaches were spread out to her left, a green sea that filled valleys and turned hilltops into islands. She found herself staring in spite of her exhaustion. In her flight from the Bonetree, she had been too busy watching the ground to enjoy the sweeping vistas of the wilderness.

The sun had climbed twice its own width above the horizon when Singe groaned, "Enough, Geth! I need to stop, at least for a little while."

Dandra watched the shifter turn slowly in his saddle, surveying the land around them. The metal of his great gauntlet scraped as he flexed his arm. Dandra looked around as well, but could see nothing over the entire distance behind them. If the Bonetree hunters were back there, they were more stealthy than she would have believed possible. Finally, Geth nodded. Muttering a curse, Singe reined in his horse and dismounted to lurch a short distance away. He fumbled with his pants, then let out a tremendous sigh of relief. Dandra flushed and glanced away.

Her gaze met Geth's. He was staring at her as he dismounted. She jerked without meaning to and her horse shifted in alarmed reaction. Dandra clutched at the reins. The horse just swung its head around to fix one dark eye on her.

"Get down." Geth's voice was harsh, the sudden sound of it startling.

Dandra's eyes darted to him out of instinct. He wasn't looking at her this time though. Squatting by his horse's head, he stared out at the rugged horizon. There was a battered packet of what looked like dried meat in his hand. Thick fingers fished out a strip.

"Get down," he said again. "This rest is for your horse more than it is you." He stuffed the meat into his mouth.

Dandra felt blood rush to her face at the rebuke. She leaned forward and braced her hands on the front of the saddle, then swung her left leg back awkwardly. Her knees and hips were stiff. Moving was painful. Gritting her teeth, she got her leg around and slithered backward out of the saddle.

The instant she put her weight down on her aching legs, though, they started to fold under her. Dandra gasped and grabbed at the saddle, but her horse whinnied in alarm and danced sideways. She would have fallen if Singe hadn't stepped up and caught her. She nodded silent thanks to him and steadied herself on her feet, feeling very much like a child.

"Have you never ridden before?" Singe asked.

"Not so hard or so long," said Dandra. "I'm more used to walking."

"Or floating?"

His words were raw. She flushed again. "Or floating," she admitted.

She took a few tentative steps, rubbing her fingers into her muscles and stretching her legs. As she moved, she looked out at the landscape ahead. Hills, forest, and more hills—including one that bore a distinctive lopsided crest of white stone. Dandra glanced at Geth. The shifter was snapping at another piece of dried meat.

"I recognize that hill ahead," she said. "I passed it on the south side two days ago."

"And you'll be passing it again on the north side before sunset," Geth mumbled around the meat.

Dandra's breath caught in her throat. "What?"

"You came this way, didn't you? You came from the Shadow Marches? Well, you're going back."

What? screeched Tetkashtai. *Back? We can't go back there! Dandra, tell him—*

Dandra pushed the raving presence away and swallowed hard. A long moment of silence passed, the only sound the rustle of a cool breeze in the grass. Finally, Dandra took a slow breath. "Geth," she said softly, "I'm so sorry. Adolan was—"

Geth spun around so fast that Dandra barely even saw him rise to his feet. "Adolan was *what?*" the shifter roared, thrusting his face into hers. "What was Adolan to you? What was Bull Hollow to you? A place to stop? A place to hide?"

He bared his teeth and Dandra could feel the moist heat of his breath. His wide amber eyes stared into hers. His very presence was intimidating, as if he was some wild animal that had come leaping out of the trees to confront her. A primal fear seized her heart. Geth was an animal in every way: his teeth, his eyes, his flat nose, his dense hair, the thick muscles that corded his neck, shoulders, and arms.

"Geth . . ." she pleaded.

He lifted his right hand slowly, raising the hooked blades that stood out from the back of his gauntlet in front of her face. "By Tiger's blood, I wish we had left you to those displacer beasts."

His hand snapped down and he turned away. Dandra stood stiff in shock. Singe was standing nearby. She shot a frightened glance at him. He shook his head. "Don't ask me." The Aundairian's mouth twisted. "Geth wasn't the only one who lost someone at Bull Hollow."

Dandra's heart felt like it had been turned inside out. Geth asked the question that she wanted to. "Who?" he snapped from a distance. "Who did you lose?"

Singe gave the shifter a cold, flat look. "His name was Toller d'Deneith, Geth. We were recruiting. This was his first command." He stood up a little straighter. "He was Robrand's nephew. Do you know what House Deneith has done to the old man's name since Narath?"

Dandra didn't understand what Singe meant, but it was clear that Geth did. A look of haunted guilt flickered briefly in his eyes. Singe's anger wasn't spent though. The wizard turned to her.

"I thought I found Toller last night, but he was already dead," he said harshly. "Hruucan killed him." He held out an arm, tugging back a blood-stained sleeve so that Dandra could see the marks—fading a little now—where the dolgaunt's skin had pressed against his. "These *hurt*. Toller was covered in marks even deeper. He must have died in agony." Singe let his sleeve drop and looked up at her.

"You never told us how exactly you knew Hruucan's name," he said.

Geth growled and stood closer. "Or why a cult of the Dragon Below would want a random sacrifice back so badly they'd spend a month chasing her and be willing to destroy a hamlet in the process." He lifted his gauntlet.

Dandra's belly twisted along with her heart. In her mind, Tetkashtai's light rose like a yellow-green column. *Dandra, leave!* the presence urged. *They're turning on you. You're not going to get any more help from them.* A new image formed within her light, an image of Dandra sliding her body between the crevices of space to cover hundreds of yards in a single long step. The same power she had used to break her trail when the Bonetree had been hunting her. Without the hunters' black herons, Geth and Singe would be unable to track her. The long step could carry her over the hill and out of sight . . .

But through Tetkashtai's light, Dandra could still see Bull Hollow and all of the people who had died because of her. She clenched her teeth and turned, putting her back to the two men. Tetkashtai's voice rose in a shriek. *Dandra! What are you doing?*

What I have to do. Drawing a determined breath, Dandra twisted her arms over shoulders and pulled up her shirt to expose her back—and the deep puckered scars of the wounds that Hruucan's foul tentacles had left on her skin.

Both Geth and Singe were silent.

She lowered her shirt and turned back to face them. "Will you let me show you something?" she asked.

Dandra!

"Be quiet, Tetkashtai," Dandra hissed out loud. Before the presence could react, she pushed her thoughts outward. In her mind's eye, Singe and Geth were like dark, tangled clouds. Dandra thrust herself into both clouds, catching at the men's thoughts and binding them to her own.

The *kesh* was the simplest of powers, a gift that all kalashtar shared and that enabled them to touch the minds of others. Even with Tetkashtai struggling against her, trying to draw away as she had at the Bull Hole, Dandra felt the connection of the *kesh* surround her. She could sense both Geth and Singe resisting her, frightened by this sudden intrusion. She sent images of reassurance pulsing into their minds—then opened up her own mind to them.

Geth yelped and leaped away, swiping with his gauntlet at the glowing yellow-green presence that loomed around them. Singe stood still, perhaps as a wizard more used to telling the difference between what was and was not physically present. He couldn't conceal his astonishment, however, as Tetkashtai flailed at her sudden exposure. Dandra held the presence's angry screams of shame back from the thought-link.

"What is *that?*" Singe breathed in astonishment.

"That's Tetkashtai," said Dandra. She steeled herself and spread her arms. "I'm a part of her. This is her body." Through the *kesh,* she sent an image spinning out to the men, an image of the phantom presence condensed down to a solid form—the psicrystal that hung against her chest. She held that vision of the crystal before them. *This,* she said silently, *is me.*

Geth snarled and crouched like a frightened animal as Singe stared. "Tetkashtai is the kalashtar and you're her psicrystal?" the wizard asked finally.

Dandra nodded.

"Twelve moons. How?"

Dandra swallowed. "Dah'mir," she said. She sent an image speeding along the link between their minds: an image of a tall man, his skin pale and flawless, his hair jet black. He wore robes of fine leather as dark as his hair. In a fabulous display of wealth, three red dragonshards had been set into the leather of each sleeve and a blue shard in the center of his chest. His eyes, however, outshone the magical stones. They were green—bright, acid green.

Even in her memories, those eyes had power. They were like an ocean rising to engulf her. Tetkashtai shuddered, her light flickering. Dandra's heart skipped as she fell into those remarkable green eyes once more . . .

"Stop it!" howled Geth.

Dandra started, the sound of the shifter's anguish ripping through her. Singe started as well and blinked his eyes as if emerging from a daze.

Geth was down on his knees, clutching at his head and staring at her. "What are you trying to do?" he spat.

"I'm sorry," Dandra whispered. "That's Dah'mir. There's something irresistible about him. None of us could withstand him."

"Who is he?" Geth demanded. "Who is 'us?'"

Dandra grimaced in spite of herself. "'Us'? I should say 'them.'"

She pushed more memories into the minds of the shifter and the wizard. Of Tetkashtai, hovering above the small clear space in the middle of a sparsely-furnished bedchamber, the Adaran-forged crysteel head of her spear flashing as she glided through the forms of spear practice. Of another kalashtar watching Tetkashtai from the bed, a smile of pleasure on his face and a violet crystal laying against his bare chest. Of a third kalashtar, her middle-length, slightly curly hair shot through with streaks of premature gray, bending over a table littered with books and paper. A blue crystal glittered in the band she wore across her forehead.

"Virikhad," said Dandra, "and Medalashana." She focused her gaze on the white-crested hill in the distance as she spoke, trying to extract herself from the memories. "We . . ." She winced and corrected herself. "They lived together in Sharn, researching dragonshards and looking for new ways to blend psionics with the magic of the shards."

Singe's eyebrows rose. "Did they succeed?"

"No." Dandra showed him and Geth an image of the papers that had littered Medalashana's table, all drawings of dragonshards, meticulously sketched and colored by Virikhad, right down to the patterns that swirled at their hearts. The rosy red of

Eberron shards, broken from stones. The glowing gold of Siberys shards, fallen from the sky. The night-deep blue-black of Khyber shards, drawn up from the depths of the world. "They needed to experiment with raw shards that hadn't been claimed by wizards or attuned to the powers of the dragonmarked houses—and raw shards are rare."

She hesitated, then added. "When I told Adolan I was kidnapped from Zarash'ak in the Shadow Marches, it wasn't entirely true. Medalashana, Tetkashtai, and Virikhad were lured to Zarash'ak from Sharn. There are rich fields of Eberron shards in the Marches. Raw shards are more common there than anywhere else. Tetkashtai and the others received an invitation from a scholar who claimed to have himself moved to Zarash'ak so he could be closer to the source of the raw shards; he had heard of their research and invited them to visit him."

Another image flowed from her memory: that fateful letter, the three kalashtar all clustered around trying to read it at once. Dandra swung from Tetkashtai's neck. The signature at the bottom of the letter swayed underneath her, bold and clear. *Dah'mir.*

"Lies?" asked Geth.

Dandra's eyes hardened. She resisted the urge to glare at the shifter. "What do you think?" Her lips pressed together. In her mind, she could feel Tetkashtai tremble with dread at what followed. Dandra spoke the memories in words, afraid they might overwhelm her again.

"They went, of course. A servant met them at the docks, and escorted them to a grand house with blue doors. Dah'mir was waiting for them." The vision of acid green eyes swam in her head again. She forced them away and said instead, "He looked just the way I showed you and the moment he spoke, we drowned in the force of his personality. He fascinated us—kalashtar and psicrystals alike. It was like falling in love. We couldn't help ourselves." She drew a breath. "He led us into the marshes and we followed like children, carrying nothing but what we wore on our backs or held in our hands. After that . . ."

She struggled to find words, then abandoned the effort, letting the nightmare of her memories flow out.

The journey into the depth of the Shadow Marches was a blur of days, of half-remembered images. An escort of savage pierced and tattooed warriors—Bonetree hunters—meeting them. Tetkashtai and the other kalashtar, crouched impassively in the center of crude, flat-bottom boat as the hunters paddled up a shallow, reed-lined river in silence. Black herons flying overhead like gangly vultures, always circling. A new landscape of drier ground and long grasses, where strings of bones seemed to grow out of trees and clack in the shifting wind. An encampment of rough shelters where slack-jawed men and women and drooling children stared at them in awe. The river had been left behind and the kalashtar, surrounded by the hunters, stumbled after Dah'mir. As they passed the encampment, all the folk of the Bonetree fell in behind them, chanting the praises of Dah'mir and the Dragon Below.

A hill rose up out of the flat landscape, unnatural, a mound built by ancient hands. There was a tunnel in its side. Dah'mir led the kalashtar into it, leaving their Bonetree escort outside, still chanting. Inside, however, a new kind of escort took their place—an escort of which each member had four bandy arms and two gibbering mouths. They carried torches that gave off a blue-green flame, like burning copper. By the light of those torches, Dandra glimpsed other figures in the shadows, stalking the darkness with a lethal grace, their faces eyeless, long tentacles twitching from their shoulders.

Dolgrims. Dolgaunts. Terror sharpened and brought Dandra back to awareness, though Tetkashtai stumbled on, unheeding.

In a chamber deep within—or perhaps beneath—the mound, Dah'mir finally released the kalashtar. Medalashana, Virikhad, and Tetkashtai were free for only a moment, barely long enough to gasp at the horrors and the weird devices that surrounded them, before Dah'mir's warm embrace was replaced by a cold domination.

Among the devices of the chamber stood a half dozen nightmare figures with spindly bodies and limbs shrouded in dark, clinging robes. Their hands had only four spidery digits, their flesh was purple-green and rubbery, their heads . . .

Their heads were broad and round, with veins that pulsed beneath their skin of their hairless scalps. Dead white eyes peered from deep, bony cavities. And in place of a nose and a jaw—in place of any lower face at all—they had four thick, writhing tentacles.

Illithids, whispered Dandra to Geth and Singe. *Mind flayers.*

The creatures lived up to their name. Dandra's last moment of coherent contact with Tetkashtai dissolved in tearing mental anguish.

She could feel Singe's growing horror and Geth's growing rage. She held onto the memories though, wrenching them up into her mind and watching numbly as Tetkashtai—along with Medalashana and Virikhad—was subjected to the most gruesome of psychic tortures and probed by psionic powers to rival their own. Their bodies were bound to tables, their minds pinned back by bizarre devices of jointed metal and dark crystal clamped over their skulls. There was no way to know how much time passed. The light in the terrible underground laboratory never varied. The mind flayers came and went, but never in any pattern that made sense. Sometimes dolgaunts would come, torturing the kalashtar's bodies. Hruucan was the worst of them. He made certain the captives knew his name so they would fear him even more.

Always there were Dah'mir's eyes. Acid-green eyes. Watching.

Then spidery fingers closed on Dandra, ripping her away from Tetkashtai and placing her atop a tripod of long, crooked needles, suspended on their points. Virikhad's violet crystal and Medalashana's blue crystal were placed on similar tripods to either side of her. Dandra caught a glimpse of some strange device, an array of brass and crystal, wires and tubes—all of them writhing around a dragonshard, a huge blue-black Khyber shard as large as an anvil.

The mind flayers gathered around the device and their white eyes lifted to the shard. Their bodies grew still, but Dandra could sense the psionic energy building among them, growing increasingly more intense and more powerful—until it burst like a silent thunderclap.

Dandra's presence stretched horribly, her being expanding, then contracting. Her connection to Tetkashtai seemed to twist, to turn inside out. The kalashtar was wailing, screaming as she had never screamed before. When the power of the mind flayers' energy faded, though, Dandra realized that *she* was the one screaming. That she was breathing and physically struggling against her bonds. That Tetkashtai rested across the laboratory, her presence locked away in the yellow-green psicrystal.

The mind flayers retreated. The dolgaunts returned, and for the first time, Dandra felt pain directly.

On the hillside overlooking the Eldeen Reaches, she opened her eyes to sunlight. Singe and Geth were staring at her. Both men's faces were pale. Within her, Tetkashtai hung silent and still, a ghost. No one said anything for a long, long time, until finally Singe ran a tongue across his lips and croaked. "You escaped?"

The thought-link was growing tenuous, worn away by the horrors that had flowed across it and stretched thin as Dandra's powers flagged. She managed to send one last memory across it, a memory of waking in near-darkness, her spirit pared down to a lean core trapped in aching flesh. She shifted, writhing in agony—and realized that the dolgaunts hadn't bound her, perhaps thinking her too weak to escape. In Dandra's spirit, the core of her being steadied and grew strong. Although it sent new pain tearing through her, she sat up.

"When a psion creates a psicrystal," Dandra told Geth and Singe as she watched the memory play out, "she splits off some part of her own psyche to give personality to the intelligence that she creates. The psicrystal grows out of that simple personality."

In her mind's eye, she felt herself climb to her feet and, with single-minded focus, shuffle across the laboratory toward a seemingly distant yellow-green glow. At the time she had been conscious of nothing but reaching the source of that glow—her crystal—but as she focused on the memory, she became aware of other things. Of how slow and painful her progress had been. Of the two crystals that rested on either side of her own, one a violet ember, the other a dead blue shell. She could have taken them. She could have turned her head, sought out Virikhad's and Medalashana's bodies. She hadn't. She had one goal and no other.

"The core of my personality," she said, her voice thick, "was determination. That's what saved me."

The hand of her memory-self closed on the yellow-green crystal—and Tetkashtai exploded into her head. Maddened kalashtar and determined psicrystal combined with a single, wild instinct—*escape*. Their powers—once Tetkashtai's alone, now Dandra's as well—flared. A thought spun out a line of *vayhatana* and Tetkashtai's spear, carelessly thrown aside by Dah'mir's servants, soared through the air to Dandra's hand. Her feet floated free of the ground and she glided out of the laboratory. Dolgrims moved to confront her. She summoned whitefire out of the air and flung it against them. Her heart thundering, she raced on through half remembered tunnels as roars of outrage at her flight shook the mound behind her . . .

The thought-link finally collapsed, fading away and leaving her breathless at her own memories. She staggered, but caught herself. One hand, she realized was clutching her crystal so tight that the bronze wire that bound it pressed painfully into her skin. Dandra forced her fingers open and looked up at Singe and Geth.

"The rest," she said, "you know. I've told you the truth about that. The Bonetree hunters were after us before that first night was over. I was lucky that I could skim over obstacles that they had to wade through." She touched her belly. "And I can sustain myself with psionic energy, where they had to find food. But even with my powers, I could barely stay ahead of them. I just ran. I knew Yrlag was on the north edge of the Shadow Marches and I would have gone there, but clearly I went too far. If I'd gone a different way, I probably would have ended up in Droaam or lost in the mountains somewhere. When you and Adolan found me, Geth, I was exhausted. If I'd kept going, I probably would have killed myself—if those displacer beasts didn't kill me first."

She pressed her palms together and bent her body toward the shifter. "Thank you," she said sincerely.

Geth stared at her, his eyes wide, but Singe drew a deep breath. "Virikhad?" he asked. "Medalashana?"

"Dead if they're lucky."

"Why did Dah'mir do this to you? Why does he want you back so badly?"

Dandra's stomach clenched. "I've asked myself that a thousand times." She felt her cheeks burn. "I don't know!"

"Maybe," growled Geth, "we should go and ask him."

He said it so bluntly that for a moment all Dandra could do was blink and stare at him. "Revenge?" she asked finally. Geth nodded. Dandra felt numb—even Tetkashtai flinched at the idea. "Geth, you can't do that. Dah'mir is . . . powerful." She touched her chest. "He held three kalashtar in his grasp!"

"I'm not a kalashtar. I'll put my steel against whatever power he has. And I can't think of a better memorial to Adolan and the other Hollowers than snuffing out a cult of the Dragon Below!" The shifter closed his gauntleted fist with a clash of metal.

Dandra flung up her arm to point behind them. "But the hunters and the dolgrims are still after us!"

"I haven't seen a sign of them since dawn and even that was a long way back." Geth's lips curled back from his teeth. "We hurt them last night and they don't have horses. They'll need to rest and regroup. We'll ride through the day and be well ahead of them."

"I don't know where the Bonetree camp and the mound are!" she blurted. "Dah'mir had us all in a daze on the way there and I was lost on the way out."

"Then we'll start where you met Dah'mir—Zarash'ak." Singe stepped forward. "I'm with Geth."

Geth shot a dark look at him. "No," he growled.

"You're going to do this yourself?" the Aundairian asked. "You're not that good, Geth. I owe this to Toller." His eyes narrowed. "Not to mention that I've been looking for you since Narath. Do you think I'm going to let you out of my sight now?"

Dandra heard the growl that rose in Geth's throat, but she also caught the flash of white as his eyes opened—just for a moment—wide in fear. Singe leaned a little closer to him. "You need me for this, Geth. And I need you. Neither of us has any choice."

They're both mad, thought Tetkashtai. The presence was trembling, her emotions raw from the flood of memories. *Dandra, when they have you well away from the Bonetree hunters, leave these fools to get themselves killed.*

No, said Dandra. *They're not mad.* There was a new fire growing inside her. She had been running for so long that there hadn't seemed to be any other choice. But she had stood against the Bonetree at the circle of the Bull Hole and faced down Hruucan at Bull Hollow.

She looked up at both Singe and Geth. "I'm coming, too."

Tetkashtai's presence radiated shock. *Dandra, you can't do that! After what Dah'mir has done? How can I not?*

I'm not going back to that mound!

Dandra's jaw tightened. *Tetkashtai, running didn't get us away from the Bonetree hunters or the dolgrims. This isn't just revenge for us. Dah'mir isn't going to give up unless we make him. He'll keep hunting us. You know he will. I'm not running any more.*

Tetkashtai wavered, fear tearing at her.

What if, Dandra suggested, *there was something at the mound that could show us how to reverse what Dah'mir's mind flayers did to us?*

The question left the presence speechless. With a grim sense of triumph, Dandra looked back to Geth. "What are we waiting for?" she asked. "An escort from the Bonetree hunters?"

The shifter gave her a thin smile and turned to his horse, swinging up into the saddle. "We'll head to Yrlag," he said, nodding to the southwest. "It's a little more than week's ride and we should be able to find a ship there that will take us to Zarash'ak."

The grass of the hillside had been crushed down in a wide patch. The round dung balls of three horses were clustered in neat piles nearby and the summer grass cropped in patches. Ashi rose and walked back to where Ner, Breff, and Hruucan were waiting for her. Ner had squatting down and was tapping the hilt of his sword against his chin in thought. Breff was inspecting the bloody bandage that covered the wolf bite sunk deep into his right calf. Hruucan, once again shrouded in his cloak and cowl, simply stood still. The dolgaunt moved awkwardly and the stench of charred flesh clung to him. The wizard had burned him more badly than he would admit. Ashi looked away from him as she made her report. "They stopped for a time. They rested, but they're staying on the move." She pointed. "Their trail turns on the slope of the hill. I think they're heading toward Yrlag."

"When were they here?" asked Ner.

Ashi glanced at the sun. It stood just past its zenith, baking the hillside in warmth. "Midmorning," she estimated.

"A quarter of a day," Hruucan rasped at Ner. "And drawing further away all the time." He gestured toward the trees in the bottom of the valley where the other hunters waited with the dolgrims. "Less than a third of your surviving hunters would be able to keep pace, let alone catch them!"

Ashi drew breath and glared at the dolgaunt in spite of herself. "More than half of the children of Khyber under *your* command didn't walk off the battlefield at all." She bit her tongue as Hruucan's cowled head swung toward her.

"Ashi's anger leads her, Hand of the Revered," said Ner swiftly. The huntmaster looked up at her. "If we rest now, Ashi, how many hunters will still be fit for the pursuit?"

Behind Ner, Breff held up five fingers. Ashi looked back to the huntmaster. "Four," she said.

Breff scowled. "Five!"

Ner reached out with his sword and tapped the flat of the scabbard against Breff's injured calf. The hunter yelped and hopped awkwardly. "Four," Ner repeated. He looked back to Ashi. "Who?"

"Mukur, Sita, Pado, and me," she said. She flicked her tongue across the rings in her lip hesitantly, then added, "Even if we can catch her, though, Ner, we'd need surprise and luck to take them. They're good fighters. You faced the shifter yourself."

Ner scowled and tapped his sword against his chin once more. Hruucan's grating voice broke the silence. "Dah'mir needs to be told, Ner. You must contact Medala."

For a long moment, none of the hunters moved, then Ner shifted one arm, and reached into the pouch on his hip. His hand emerged with the glittering band of copper wire and crystals that Dah'mir had given to him. He held out his sword to Ashi. She took it and stepped back as the huntmaster rose, spread the band wide, and pulled it over the top of his head. The crystals caught the sunlight and scattered bright flashes across the hillside. Ner turned to face in the direction of the Shadow Marches and the distant ancestor mound.

"Medala!" he said loudly. "Ner calls you!" He waited a moment, then said again. "Medala! Ner calls—"

His voice fell silent as a blankness washed across his face. Ashi shifted uncomfortably. In the month of their pursuit, Ner had used Dah'mir's device only a few times. Each time it had been like this. Ner had told her that it was like dreaming, that he had no awareness of his body while he spoke with the outclanner woman. He simply heard her in his head and replied to her by thinking his response. Sometimes, he had said, her manner was rough, wrenching the thoughts from his head before they were fully formed.

The communication never seemed to last long—after only a few moments, awareness would return to Ner's expression and he would pull the crystal device from his head as quickly as he could. Ashi waited.

Except that instead of easing with awareness, Ner's face drew tight in pain. His body tensed. Breff gasped out her name in alarm. Ashi froze, uncertain of what to do.

Then Ner's mouth moved and he spoke. "Hruucan!"

The voice that came from Ner's mouth sounded like the old hunter's, but Ashi knew that it wasn't his. The tones were clipped and sharp and the huntmaster had never in a month called the dolgaunt by his name. The words that emerged from Ner's mouth, she recognized in her gut, belonged to Medala. The outclanner was speaking through Ner.

Hruucan reacted without surprise. "I'm here, Medala."

"Failure is written in this fool's mind. Dah'mir is disappointed."

Ashi's mouth went dry. Even Hruucan looked slightly distressed. "Medala—" the dolgaunt began.

Medala cut him off. "The Bonetree hunters will do no good hobbling in pursuit of an enemy. Dah'mir commands you to bring them back to the ancestor mound, Hruucan."

The dolgaunt relaxed visibly. Ashi, however, exchanged a look of shock with Breff. Gathering her courage, she looked into Ner's blank face. "But what about Ner, Medala? He's our huntmaster!"

"Is that Ashi?" snapped Medala without answering her protest. "Dah'mir has instructions for you as well. You are the best of the surviving hunters—he places the pursuit in your hands. Follow wherever your quarry goes. Be stealthy. If the opportunity presents itself, you may kill the shifter and the wizard. Your quarry is all that's important. Take the crystal band when I am finished. Use it more often than Ner has. When it is possible, help will be sent to you. Do you understand?"

"Yes," Ashi said automatically, then added quickly, "No. Why is Hruucan being placed over Ner, Medala?" There was no response. "Medala?" she asked, stepping closer to Ner.

The huntmaster's eyes rolled back. A thin gurgle broke out of his throat and before Ashi could even reach for him, he collapsed. Ashi stared down as a trickle of blood came dribbling out of his nose. His eyes stared directly up at the sun.

"Ner?" she whispered.

Hruucan tilted back his cowl to stare at her. She caught a glimpse of the burned, dead skin of his face. "Ner failed Dah'mir and the Dragon Below," the dolgaunt said harshly. "You have your instructions. Take the web."

Ashi bent woodenly and tugged the band from Ner's head. The light that flashed from the crystals seemed cold. Handling it as little as possible, she reached down and stuffed it into Ner's hip pouch, then tugged the pouch off of his body. She met Breff's gaze again as she stood. His eyes were wide. *"Su Darasvhir,"* he said in stunned voice.

For the Dragon Below.

"The trail grows cold," said Hruucan. "Do you need any supplies?"

"No," grunted Ashi. "I have everything I need." Her hand tightened on Ner's sword.

CHAPTER

7

Yrlag lay along the south bank of the Grithic River, a deep, cold waterway that marked the border between the Eldeen Reaches and the Shadow Marches. In actual truth, there was little to distinguish one region from the other—low, harsh scrubland rolled across either side of the Grithic, wild and ungoverned. The only reason that Yrlag existed at all was trade. The wilds of the Eldeen, the uplands of the Shadow Marches, and even the barrens of Droaam came together along the Grithic. The river was the gateway to Crescent Bay and the sea coast. With no other cities easily accessible, traders and outlaws of every race and morality passed through the town, exchanging the goods of the wilderness hinterlands for the luxuries of the wider world.

Geth had seen a lot of tough towns in the years he had served with the Blademarks of House Deneith. He had seen more in the years between Narath and his return to the Eldeen. Almost none were as tough and dangerous as Yrlag. Dandra, Singe, and he rode across the decrepit bridge that spanned the Grithic in the company of a mixed band of mangy gnolls and smelly humans. Bandits without a doubt. Dandra stared at them. Singe kept one eye on them. Geth rode in relaxed calm. The band looked like they were returning from whatever raid had taken them into the Eldeen. They were in a good mood and on their way into Yrlag to sell their stolen plunder. There was nothing to fear from them at the moment.

When Singe wasn't keeping watch on the bandits, he was staring at the bridge beneath them. About halfway across its span, with the din and stench of Yrlag growing in their ears and noses, he guided his horse close to the low rail at the edge of the bridge and peered over. When he straightened, he glanced at Geth.

"The footings on this bridge are massive," he said in wonder. "They look much older than the road surface, but they're in better condition."

"They are older," Geth said. "Adolan—" He grimaced. The druid's name lay across his tongue like the collar of black stones lay around his neck. "Adolan told me once that Yrlag is built on the ruins of a hobgoblin town from the time when the Dhakaani Empire spread across the whole south of Khorvaire. Yrlag was its westernmost outpost. New bridges have been built on top of the old hobgoblin footings ever since."

He turned away from the Aundairian and slouched down in his saddle. A week's travel had taught both Singe and Dandra when he wanted to be left alone. If the footings of the bridge still interested Singe, he kept his curiosity to himself. Geth forced his mind into the unthinking blankness that had become more of a companion to him in the last week than either the wizard or the kalashtar.

There had been too much time to think on the journey to Yrlag. None of the trio had felt much like talking. Geth almost wished that the Bonetree hunters had caught them—simple, mindless fighting would have been good—but there had been no sign of pursuit. Every night after Singe had cast the spell that created a simple, featureless black dome to give them shelter, Geth had backtracked along their trail, setting snares to catch the next day's food and watching the darkness. When he rose in the morning to collect his catch, he watched the empty landscape. By dark or by day, there was nothing to see. The Bonetree clan might almost have given up their hunt—but his gut told him they hadn't.

An old central street ran through Yrlag from the great bridge down to the deep pool cut into riverbank that served as a waterfront. Geth suspected that the pool, like the bridge, had been created by the ancient hobgoblins, an enhancement to the already deep riverbed. As they came off the bridge, he scanned the makeshift booths and stalls that lined the street, pulling the bundle that contained his great gauntlet from the back of his saddle and holding it protectively. Yrlag pickpockets would steal anything they could get their hands on.

In a niche between two booths, a tall figure draped in a badly fitting cloak caught his eye. From under the hood of the cloak, a woman's lean face stared back at him, framed by dark gold hair woven with beads and pierced through the lower lips with two small hoops.

Geth twisted around so sharply in his saddle that his horse whinnied and pranced in alarm. Singe cursed and reached out to grab the animal's bridle, bringing it back under control. "Geth! Watch what you're doing!"

"Singe, it's the Bonetree hunters! I saw one of them!"

Geth spun back to stare at the niche—and saw only a ragged old cloak hanging from a knotted post and shifting in the breeze. Geth blinked and rubbed his eyes. Singe followed his gaze and raised an eyebrow.

"I saw her!" Geth insisted. "The big woman." He dredged up the name the old hunter had called out during the fight at the Bull Hole. "Her name is Ashi."

Singe pressed his lips together. "The hunters couldn't have passed us, Geth. We would have seen some sign. We're well ahead of them. Come on. We need to find a ship and you need to rest."

The wizard released Geth's horse and urged his own through the crowd. Geth stole one last look at the hanging cloak, then glanced at Dandra. She shrugged and turned her mount after Singe. Even after a week's riding, it was clear that she wasn't comfortable on a horse.

After a moment, Geth followed as well. He kept his eyes open as they rode, though, scanning the shifting crowd. Maybe Singe had been right, he thought. How could the hunters have moved quickly enough to pass them? He probably had made a mistake. Still, he couldn't shake feeling that he *had* recognized Ashi.

Ahead, both Singe and Dandra reined in sharply. "Twelve moons!" Singe gasped. "I was hoping to find a fast ship, but this is Olladra's own luck!"

Geth looked up. Docked in the nearest berth was a sleek ship easily eighty paces in length. She sat low in the water with the weight of her cargo but still looked like she could outpace anything else on Yrlag's waterfront. Deep blue paint shot through with bright yellow trim ran around her hull in a wide band below her rails and the name painted proudly on her bow was *Lightning on Water*.

The ship had, however, no masts and no sails. Instead, massive wooden beams reached out from its stern to clutch a pale blue ring of enormous diameter that hung above and behind the ship's hull. Geth stared at it, then squinted. There was a strangely translucent quality to the ring. He couldn't tell if it was carved from wood or forged from metal—or maybe even cast from some heavy glass.

"What kind of ship is that?" he asked in amazement.

"It's a House Lyrandar elemental galleon," said Dandra. "I watched them docking in Sharn. Il-Yannah, I wouldn't have expected to find one here!"

"They'll go wherever there's a profit to be made," Singe said. He bit his lip. "There's nothing faster on the water, but—"

"But—?" asked a salt-hoarse voice. "But nothing! I'll bet you a silver ring there's not a ship west of Sharn that's faster than *Lightning!*"

Geth twisted in his saddle and glared at a slim, fair-haired man standing with a sheaf of papers in his hand beside a stack of barrels. The man gave him a sharp smile. "Nervous?" he asked. "I've noticed Yrlag tends to do that to be people."

The man wore a dove-gray coat with long tails and upturned cuffs. His voice carried, like Singe's, the accent of Aundair. His hair was long and drawn back, exposing the graceful tapering points of his ears and a bright, swirling pattern that spread up the back of his neck. The man was a half-elf—and carried a dragonmark. Geth took a second look at his coat. The man's smile grew a little wider. "Looking for these, my shifter friend?" He held up his cuff so that bright silver buttons flashed in the sunlight. Barely visible on each one was the kraken crest of House Lyrandar.

Singe slipped down from his horse and stepped up to offer the half-elf his hand. "A common sailor doesn't check manifests, the average clerk in my experience doesn't dress so well, and neither generally carries a dragonmark. I'll make a guess that you're the captain of this fine ship."

The half-elf took Singe's hand in hearty grip. "Captain Vennet d'Lyrandar, friend." Bright eyes flashed at each of them. "And in my experience, the average traveler doesn't stand on piers gawking at ships for the fun of it." He glanced back to Singe. "Looking for passage?"

"Yes," said Geth. He climbed down and joined Singe. The Aundairian shot him a dark look, but Geth ignored him. Crossing his arms over his chest, he told Vennet, "We need passage to Zarash'ak."

"My own destination! Five days to the City of Stilts." Vennet swept his hand grandly across the length of his ship. "As I say, fastest ship west of Sharn. And loaded to the rails—but you're lucky. My passenger cabins are full, but if you don't mind staking out a corner of the forward hold, there's room for the three of you." His eyes traveled over their horses. "No room for the beasts, unfortunately, but I can recommend an honest stable master who would be happy to buy them from you."

Geth grunted. He gave the smiling captain his hardest bartering look. "He'd better be honest. Those animals are the price of our passage."

Singe let out a quiet groan. Vennet's smile didn't even waver. "They must be very special horses, then," he said. "Passage to Zarash'ak is one thousand gold."

Blood rushed to Geth's face. "One *thousand*—!"

"It's a long way to Zarash'ak."

Geth took a step forward, but Singe grabbed him sharply, spinning him around and pulling him away from Vennet. "Close your mouth before you make this worse!" he hissed.

Dandra was off her horse as well now and at their side. "That's more than these horses are worth, isn't it?" she whispered. Geth gave an angry nod. "Light of il-Yannah." She looked down the length of the pier at the other ships they had passed. "None of these look like they'll be leaving soon. And the longer we wait, the better the chance the Bonetree hunters will catch up to us!"

Singe's lips twitched. "Leave this to me." He turned back to Vennet. "Captain, we're happy to pay appropriately for the speed and convenience of an elemental galleon," he said pleasantly, "but you *are* asking us to travel as freight. Perhaps a reduced rate?"

"Freight doesn't get up and move around the ship. It doesn't eat."

"Empty space is even less trouble than freight," Singe commented with a smile. "But it's a shame to see a ship sail without a full hold."

Vennet shrugged. "Room to pick something up along the way."

"Where?" asked Singe. "There isn't another port bigger than a fishing village between here and Zarash'ak." He ran a hand along the top of one of the piled barrels and said, "Five hundred." Vennet's eyebrows rose.

"You'd pay five hundred for deck space on any one of these tubs!" he snapped, jerking his head along the pier. "And you'd take two weeks to make the trip, eating salt pork the whole way."

"House Lyrandar eats better?"

"Take passage on *Lightning* and you'll eat at my table!" spat Vennet

"Six hundred."

"Eight hundred."

"Done." Singe stuck out his hand. Vennet clasped it heartily.

Geth flinched. "Singe, we can't pay that!"

"No, we couldn't pay a thousand. For passage from Yrlag to Zarash'ak on a Lyrandar elemental galleon, eight hundred is a bargain." He nodded to Vennet. "Especially with dinner at the captain's table thrown in."

The half-elf's eyes narrowed. "You're shrewd, friend."

"I did a turn as quartermaster for a Blademarks company." As Vennet's eyes widened again in surprise, Singe opened his vest and slid his fingers into an almost invisible pocket. They emerged with a flat case no larger than his hand. He flipped it open and extracted a folded paper. "We'll pay you the price that our horses fetch up front and any remainder from that when we reach Zarash'ak."

Vennet stared at the paper. Geth craned his neck to see what it was. He caught a glimpse of the crest of the Blademarks—overlapped with the crest of the dwarven bankers of House Kundarak. A complex mark of authentication shimmered in magical colors at the bottom of the paper. Geth's eyes went almost as wide as Vennet's. The paper was a Deneith letter of credit, allowing the bearer to draw on the resources of the great house. Generally such things were given to Blademarks recruiters to allow them to draw pay for new recruits. By using it to buy even a portion of the cost of transport on a Lyrandar galleon, Singe would be risking the ire of the lords of Deneith.

Then again, he realized, the wizard probably had enough to explain to the lords of Deneith already.

Singe gave Vennet a level look over top of the letter. "I presume there's a Kundarak bank in Zarash'ak."

The captain nodded, barely glancing up from the document. "Storm at dawn, a small one, but big enough for this. You should have said you were in the employ of another House!"

"You would have charged me more."

"True enough." Vennet looked up again. "Do you have identification proving you're authorized to use this?"

Singe flipped the flat case around and passed it to Vennet. There were stiff papers clipped to the inside of it. Geth watch the captain study the writing on them—and saw his eyes widen slightly once again. He handed the letter and the case back to Singe. "That's in order, then." He gave the wizard a glance of curiosity. "Etan Bayard. There's a family named Bayard with large vineyard estates near Fairhaven—"

"No relation," said Singe briskly as he returned letter to case and tucked both away securely. "Call me Singe."

He gestured to Geth and Dandra, introducing them as well. If Vennet was surprised by either the shifter or the exotic kalashtar, he gave no indication of it. "You'd best see to selling those horses," he told them. "We're almost loaded. The Grithic is a tidal river—we'll sail for the ocean as soon as the tide is full. There's a woman named Kirla who runs a stable on Madder Street. Mention my name and she won't cheat you too badly."

Singe kept aside a portion of coin from the sale of the horses and they made hasty visits to several shops for supplies, gear, and clean clothes to supplement what little they had ridden away with from Bull Hollow. They made it back to *Lightning on Water* with only a little time to spare. Vennet was pacing the deck and looking annoyed.

"Took your time, didn't you?" he said, looking at the small packs that each of them now carried.

Geth growled and tossed a heavy pouch filled with trade strips at him. Vennet's smile returned quickly enough as he weighed it in his hand, then gestured to a hatch near the bow of the ship. "Stow your gear. You can join the other passengers on deck or stay below when we take speed—it's your choice." His smile rose a little. "Welcome aboard."

He turned away, calling orders out to the ship's crew. The gangplank that Geth, Singe, and Dandra had just climbed was pulled up; massive ropes were loosened from the pier and drawn aboard. The ship lurched, caught by the river's current, as the three made their way forward. Geth stumbled and growled.

Singe raised an eyebrow. "Something wrong?"

"No," Geth spat, steadying himself.

"It's occurred to me," commented the wizard, "that I don't think I've ever seen a shifter on a ship before."

"I only need to get used to it." Geth staggered slightly, arms out and legs flexing to maintain his balance. Over the rail, Yrlag began to slip away as *Lightning* moved out into the river, escorted by smaller boats. "What did Vennet mean by 'taking speed?'"

"You've never been on an elemental galleon before?" asked Singe.

"I hadn't even seen one before today!"

Singe pressed his lips together as if he was trying to keep from smirking. "You'll enjoy this."

Geth snarled at him.

Stairs so steep they were almost a ladder led down into the forward hold. As Vennet had suggested, the ship was almost entirely full—there would be just enough open room, Geth guessed, to spread out the bedrolls they had purchased. He rolled his eyes, though, at the piles of slowly creaking crates and barrels that surrounded them. When Singe led the way back up onto the deck, Geth scrambled up hard on his heels.

It was easy enough to spot the other passengers: they were the only ones standing talking as the crew hustled around the deck. There were half a dozen of them, most merchants by their dress and manner. One man, however, stood out from the others—quite literally. An older half-orc, he was taller than Singe and easily as broad as Geth, with coarse features, stunted tusks, and a grayish cast to his skin. He was also the best dressed of any of the passengers, wearing a fine coat of red silk drawn over a charcoal-gray tunic, and he carried himself with strength and confidence in spite of his age. He was the first to notice their approach and broke off from talking with a thin, hunched man who reminded Geth of a quill pen to greet them.

"Friends!" he called in a booming voice. "Join us! This is Pandon—" He gestured to the hunched man, then spread his arms wide. "—and I'm Natrac."

"Singe, Geth, and Dandra," replied Singe smoothly. "A pleasure."

Natrac reached out to shake hands with all of them, his massive palm making even Geth's hand look small. A ring with a gaudy red stone too large to be real glittered on one finger. "The pleasure is mine. It's good to see new passengers come on deck for the start of *Lightning*'s run." He slapped Pandon on the back. "I had to drag Pandon here out of his cabin."

The watery smile on Pandon's face made it clear that he wished he was still there. Geth looked out at the banks of the Grithic. They were moving past them at a fast pace already, though he wasn't quite certain how. Yrlag was already a smudge of smoke against the sky upstream. "This seems like a good start," the shifter commented.

Natrac blinked in surprise, but Singe leaned forward and murmured to him. The half-orc's eyes went wide and he gaped, "He's never even *seen* an elemental galleon before?" He looked down at Geth in disbelief. "Balinor's stewpot, this isn't fast! Our captain isn't drawing on more than a whisper of his mark's power yet."

He nodded toward the stern of the ship. Standing on the aft deck before the massive bluish ring, framed by the great beams that supported it, Vennet gripped the handles of a big, ornate wheel and continued to shout out orders. The breeze caught at the twin tails of his hair and his jacket, tugging with playful familiarity at both.

There seemed to be mist streaming off the ring like the condensation of warm breath blown around an icicle in winter. As Geth stared, Singe slapped him on the back. "That ring's an air elemental—just like the earth elemental Adolan summoned out of the Bull Hole, but bound to the ship. Vennet is controlling it through his dragonmark. It will blow us all the way to Zarash'ak!"

Geth glanced back to the passing banks. "How fast will we go?" he asked.

Natrac's grin broadened. "Wait and see! It will be a while yet before the river opens up and Vennet can take speed. There aren't many rivers capable of running an elemental galleon at all. Even on the Grithic we need to be closer to the open ocean."

"It sounds like you've made this trip before," Dandra said.

"Twice a year at least," said Natrac. "From Zarash'ak to Yrlag and back."

The kalashtar looked alarmed. "That must cost you a lot."

"Hardly anything, really. It's the price of business."

"And what business is that?" asked Singe.

"Opportunity, my friend," Natrac answered. He swept his arms wide again, gesturing to the land around them. "There are always young—and not so young—men and women in these parts who want to leave the backcountry to seek their fortunes in the wider world, but don't have the means to do so. They agree to enter my service for a time and in return, I provide them with transportation and a livelihood in Zarash'ak."

"Young people from the wilds looking for adventure," Singe said. He leaned back against the ship's rail and gave Geth a blunt stare. "That sounds familiar. Do most of them adjust or do they just end up causing trouble?"

Geth fought back the growl that grew in his throat. Dandra was glancing between him and Singe. Even quiet Pandon noticed something was up. Natrac, however, carried on. "Some do cause trouble," he confessed. "Most adjust well enough, though—eventually." He rapped the ship's rail. "That's the value of taking passage on an elemental galleon. I used to book passage on ordinary ships, but you can imagine the effect of keeping ten or so strapping, half-wild savages on board a ship for two weeks or more. I saved on transportation, but the cost of damages was ruinous. On Vennet's ship, the trip takes less than half the time and I simply increase the period of my clients' service to cover the cost." He clapped his hands. "Happiness all around."

Singe nodded. "Aren't you worried about offending House Deneith?" he asked nonchalantly. "I've heard that the Blademarks Guild sometimes recruits in the Eldeen Reaches."

Natrac chuckled. "They never come this far and I'd be nothing to them even if they did. To be safe though, I never hire my people out as mercenaries. Porters in Zarash'ak, guides in the Marches, gladiators in Sharn if they have a knack for it—but mercenaries? No." He tapped a finger against the side of his nose and winked at Singe. "Not that I've ever turned anyone away if they're a tough fighter. There's always more that want to go than I can take in a trip. Just before we boarded, one of my clients broke another's jaw so she could take his place on the ship! If you need to hire a porter with a strong fist while you're in Zarash'ak, ask me."

"I'll do that," said Singe with a smile. His eyes scanned the deck. "Where are these fine porters anyway?"

"As much as I like to see other passengers come on deck to enjoy the view, my clients stay below deck in the aft hold except when necessary." He folded his hands across his stomach. "Part of my arrangement with Vennet. My clients can be a little . . . rough around the edges."

"That's often the way with backcountry types, isn't it?" agreed Singe. He turned around to look out over the river, deliberately putting his back to Geth. The shifter's hands curled into fists. Dandra frowned, however, and put a hand on his arm.

"Don't," she urged him.

Geth shrugged her off and stalked over to the far side of the deck.

Beyond the Grithic's northern bank—now a long bowshot away, even from *Lightning on Water*'s position in the center of the river—the land rose into the rolling, barren hills they had descended only that morning. Beyond the hills lay the great forests of the Eldeen. Fourteen years ago, he hadn't been able to put those forests behind him quickly enough.

Seven years later, he'd promised himself he'd never leave them again. How many of Natrac's clients below deck, Geth wondered, were wishing for some last glimpse of their own homeland? How many would eventually find their way back to Yrlag?

He stared at the hills as the river gradually widened and the smell of the land faded away, replaced by the growing salt-tang of the sea. The harsh croaking of gulls echoed across the water. It reminded Geth of Breek's familiar squawk—lost along with Adolan. He closed his eyes, shutting out the last sight of the distant Eldeen.

A sudden shout from Vennet drew his attention back to the ship. "All hands, prepare to take speed!"

Geth raised his head as, around the ship, the crew called back to the captain. A murmur of anticipation rose from the other passengers.

It was drowned out by another cry. "All clear, captain!"

"Taking speed!" Vennet cried out. "Taking speed!"

From where he stood, Geth saw the captain take a firm grip on the wheel. The half-elf's eyes narrowed in concentration.

A low, haunting whistle seemed to pass through the air. Geth's eyes darted up, following the sound to the great blue ring mounted behind the ship. Its translucent surface was quivering, like a pot of water coming to a boil. The wisps of mist it had given off before grew denser and became streams thick as smoke. The whistle screeched higher and louder, making Geth's ears twitch unbearably. The hair on his arms and on the back of his neck rose. The growl that he had suppressed before broke out of his throat and his lips pulled back from his teeth. The whistle faded away. The ship seemed to hold its breath.

In the next moment, the blue of the ring vanished like snow thrown on a fire, puffing away into a hoop of roiling mists as a howling gale blasted out behind the ship. *Lightning on Water* gave a tremendous leap and surged forward in a powerful burst of speed. Caught off-guard, Geth lurched and staggered. The wind of their passage took his breath away. He clenched his teeth and blinked against it as his fingers dug into the wood of the rail. The ship seemed to rise up underneath him. A few of the crew were snickering and pointing at him. He didn't care—he just held on.

"Geth!" called Dandra. "Geth!"

A hand tapped his shoulder. Geth glanced back at the kalashtar. Singe stood behind her.

"Relax!" she said. "It's not that bad."

"What is this?" Geth gasped. "What's going on?"

The ship shuddered and rose again. The roar of water rushing against the hull shifted in pitch. Geth's hands clamped around the rail even harder. Singe peered over the ship's side, then pointed down. Geth leaned over cautiously to follow his gesture.

Lightning on Water was moving so fast that her hull had lifted almost entirely clear of the water. Previously hidden below the waterline, a long wooden fin arced gracefully down from the ship's side to slice through the water like a paddle held sideways.

"There's another on the other side," said Singe. "As I understand it, because they're thinner than the hull, the ship can go even faster."

"That's good," gulped Geth. "Because we *need* to go faster." He looked at Dandra. "Now I know," he said, "how you feel on a horse." He forced his hands open and slid down to sit on the deck with his back against the rail and the racing water out of sight.

The first two days of the voyage were among the most physically miserable of Geth's life. Most of his time—day and night—was spent on deck. Even with the rushing wind of their passage, the fresh air was far more comforting than the disturbing creaks and eternal shifting below. It also alleviated the worst of his seasickness. Water and plain bread were the only things that could pass his lips without sending him rushing to hang over the ship's rail.

Some time on the third day, it seemed as if his body made a bargain with the sea. The shifter found that he was actually hungry and cautious sampling showed that a little food would stay settled in his stomach. The sea wind felt good on his face and in his hair and there was thrill to the rise and fall of the ship as it surged over the waves. The crew had grown used to his presence on deck; they seemed genuinely pleased when they discovered that he had started to enjoy the journey.

The only thing he couldn't get used to was the sensation of being below deck while the ship was moving. He'd never been afraid of tight spaces before, but onboard *Lightning on Water*, it was disquieting. Fortunately, the weather was warm in spite of the wind. If he'd survived two nights on deck while puking his guts over the side of the ship, he told himself, he could survive a couple more.

As the sun set over water and darkness fell, he found himself alone in the bow of the ship. The crew had gone to their hammocks and blankets. The other passengers, Singe and Dandra among them, had made a habit of remaining in the captain's cabin after dinner. It seemed that sharing Vennet's table wasn't exactly the exclusive invitation Singe might have thought it was. Geth stared out at the broad horizon—at the moons and stars above and the shining Ring of Siberys in the south—and finally allowed himself to mourn Adolan. The druid's loss was an empty ache inside him. Geth reached up and brushed his fingers over the collar of black stones, feeling the deep grooves of the ancient symbols that had been carved into them.

"Do you mind if I join you?"

Vennet's voice came from right behind him, so close that it made the shifter jump. He twisted around, his teeth bared out of instinct. Vennet raised a hand. "Easy," he said. "Sorry to startle you. If you'd prefer to be left alone . . ."

Geth hesitated, then relaxed. He'd been alone with his thoughts long enough, and he'd seen little of Vennet through the voyage. By day the captain manned the wheel, controlling both the ship and the elemental. A junior officer, also a bearer of the Mark of Storm that gave House Lyrandar its distinctive powers, took over by night. Geth patted the rail beside himself. "Stay," he said. "Plenty of room."

"I'd thank you for such a gracious invitation, but she *is* my ship." Vennet leaned against the rail, his back to the sea. In one hand he held a bottle. He offered it to Geth.

The shifter accepted it and took a cautious swig. The liquor inside was strong and harsh. He passed the bottle back to Vennet. "I would have expected something a little better of the captain," he wheezed.

"It's crew rations," the half-elf admitted. "But it's how you can tell a working windwright from a pampered drizzle-whistler in House Lyrandar." He raised the bottle to the starry sky. "We sailors develop a fondness for the rot." Vennet took a drink, then ran his gaze over Geth. "You're looking better than you have been."

Geth grunted. "It would be hard not to."

Vennet chuckled and put the bottle back in Geth's hand. "We missed you at the table tonight. I thought maybe you'd come now that you'd found your sea legs."

The shifter made a sour expression as he took another pull at the bottle. "I like it better on deck," he said. "Why? Have I missed anything?"

"Not much," confessed Vennet with a shrug. "The run from Yrlag to Zarash'ak is generally pretty much the same every time, although this voyage isn't going particularly well for Natrac. Some of his 'clients' have been getting out of hand, and he's finally realized that Singe works for House Deneith." He grinned. "He's been groveling like a goblin all night. Singe is drinking it up."

"I'm sure he is," Geth growled.

He drank again, then returned the bottle. Vennet looked at him over its end as he drank as well. When he lowered the bottle, he commented, "There's no love lost between you two, is there?"

"We served together," Geth said curtly.

"Ah." Vennet turned around to look out across the sea. "Where?"

The way he asked the question made Geth glance at him with new respect. When conversations turned to the Last War, he'd found over the years, people generally asked about his experiences in one of two ways. If they'd managed to stay out of the fighting, their questions tended to be curious and polite.

If they'd seen fighting themselves, on the other hand, their questions were blunt, tempered less by curiosity and more by a need to share their own experiences. While he'd avoided discussing the War through his years in Bull Hollow, Geth found himself opening up to Vennet. "All over," he said. "That's how it was with a Blademarks company."

"Was?" Vennet raised an eyebrow.

"Singe stayed in the Blademarks. I left."

Geth didn't offer anything more and Vennet didn't ask. "I can understand moving around," the captain said. He looked back at the water again. "I earned my commission doing transport work along the coast of the Bitter Sea, from Aundair across the Karrnathi coast to the Lhazaar Principalities. Sometimes a run down Scions Sound to Cyre or Thrane. That was a touchy trip."

The shifter gave him a smile. "I manned a ballista on the Cyran side of the Brey River for five months, shooting at any ship trying to make that run."

"Did you ever hit anything?"

"Did you ever get hit?"

Vennet laughed and they swapped the bottle again. "Where else?" he asked.

Geth dug into his memories, trying to remember the best of his time with the Frostbrand. "All over northern Cyre. Up into Karrnath. A little bit on the Talenta Plains. Wherever our commander drew a contract." He looked at Vennet. "Transport work sounds more peaceful."

The captain shook his head. "I saw trouble enough. It's hard to catch a Lyrandar ship if the captain doesn't want to be caught, but there are always pirates and hostile ships willing to give it a try. Lyrandar doesn't float warships, though. We leave the hard fighting to those on land—and they're welcome to it." Vennet rubbed his thumbs across the bottle. "There was one assignment. Transport accompanying an Aundairian raid on a Karrnathi logging town. After the Eldeen Reaches broke away, Aundair came up short on quality timber for shipbuilding, but Karrnath's forests were still thick." His voice dropped. "The town should have held out against the raid, but somehow the Aundairian soldiers broke through. I didn't get any further from my ship than the docks, but it was like they turned into monsters when they got into that town. What they did . . ."

Geth's mouth went dry. A queasy nausea returned to his stomach. "You're talking about Narath."

Vennet looked at him with haunted eyes. "You've heard of it." He gave a bitter chuckle. "Of course you have. Who hasn't?"

"Aye," said Geth. He drew a rough breath. "I wouldn't mention that story to Singe."

"Because it was Aundairians who did it?" Vennet grimaced. "I know how he feels. Believe me, I don't talk about it often either. For a long time, it was like a stain on my soul." He took another long drink from the bottle, then offered it to Geth again.

This time the shifter shook his head. Vennet nodded and shoved a cork back into the bottle's neck. "Enough for tonight," he agreed. He clapped a hand across Geth's shoulder. "Maybe when we reach Zarash'ak, though? There's a tavern I know—"

The sound of running feet on the deck saved Geth from having to decline the half-elf's offer. Both men turned at the same time as one of Vennet's crew slid to a stop in front of them. "Captain! Trouble in the aft hold!"

Vennet's eyes flashed angrily. "Natrac's gang again?" The crewman nodded and Vennet cursed, then looked to Geth. "I wouldn't normally ask a passenger to step into a fight, but some of Natrac's clients are brutes. A veteran of the Blademarks would be a good person to have at my back."

The prospect of a good fight stirred Geth's spirit. "I'm with you," he said.

"Good man." Vennet stuffed the bottle into a pocket and strode toward the stern of the ship, sparing a hard glare for the crewman. "Natrac's in my cabin. Tell him to get his backside aft!"

The crewman saluted and dashed off.

Lightning on Water's crew were gathered around the top of the ladder-like steps leading down to the aft hold—they leaped back at Vennet's approach. The sounds of a roaring brawl thundered up from below. One of the crew called out to Vennet. "They've been arguing for a while, captain, but the fighting only just broke out."

The sudden splintering of wood punctuated her report. "Kol Korran's wager, if they damage my ship, I'll take the price out of Natrac's gray hide!" spat Vennet. He pointed at two burly sailors who stood by with thick wooden pins. "You and you. After us."

He thundered down the steps into the hold with sure-footed ease. Geth sprang after him, ready for anything.

At least he thought he was ready for anything. At the bottom of the stairs, he froze and bared his teeth. A snarl tore itself out of his throat.

The dim, magical light that lit the hold shone on a dozen bodies, most struggling, a few stretched out senseless on the floor. In the center of the chaos—fighting in a whirlwind of fists, feet, knees, and elbows—was Ashi!

CHAPTER

8

Dandra bit her lip to hold back her laughter as Natrac spun out the punchline of a long and embarrassingly self-deprecating anecdote. He probably wouldn't have noticed if she had smiled, though. All of his attention was on Singe. The wizard sat near the head of the captain's table, to the right of Vennet's empty chair. His face was a stern mask of disapproval. He had to be working even harder than her, Dandra knew, to keep a straight face against Natrac's frantic attempts to ingratiate himself.

In truth, Singe had told her their first night on *Lighting on Water*, Natrac had been right all along. House Deneith had no interest in such a small, isolated operation as Natrac's. Still, he hadn't been able to resist winding up the blustering half-orc. The ship's other passengers had picked up on the joke as well. Even thin, hunched Pandon kept his face buried in a goblet to hide his grin as Natrac's anecdote lurched to an end. The cabin was silent. Dandra was certain she saw a drop of sweat run down the half-orc's face as he waited for a reaction from Singe.

In the back of her mind, Tetkashtai gave a silent sniff of disapproval. *Childish.* Dandra ignored her. Singe straightened and she could see a grave and measured response growing in his eyes.

It never reached his lips. The door of the cabin swung open and a panting crewman burst through to point at Natrac. "Captain says get yourself aft!"

Natrac's gray skin grew even paler and for a moment he seemed frozen between responding to the captain and toadying to Singe. The urgency in the crewman's face was obvious, though.

"Go!" Singe shouted at Natrac. "Go!"

The half-orc leaped from his seat and raced out of the cabin. Vennet's crewman went with him. The silence around the captain's table was real.

Dandra stood up. "We should see what it is."

Singe nodded and rose as well.

They reached the hatch of the aft hold hard on Natrac's heels. Dandra could hear the sounds of fighting below. A brawl had broken out. The crew of *Lightning on Water* were clustered around the hatch. Vennet, Geth, and two big crewmen were disappearing down into the hold.

Only a heartbeat later, a terrible snarl ripped up from below.

"Geth!" Dandra exclaimed.

"Twelve moons," cursed Singe. "That can't be good!"

He pushed through the clustered crew, shoved past Natrac, and darted down the steps into the hold. Dandra followed close behind him. Down below, the two big crewmen were laying into Natrac's brawling clients. Vennet had waded into the fight as well, pulling the combatants apart with a ferocious ease that belied his slight frame, cursing blasphemously the whole time.

Geth, however, was bounding straight to the heart of the free-for-all. The tall woman who fought there whirled at his approach. Anger washed over a face flushed from combat and Ashi gave the screaming battle cry of the Bonetree hunters.

Light of il-Yannah! wailed Tetkashtai. *Where did she come from?*

Dandra watched Geth shift as he charged—his hair bristling and growing thicker, his body becoming subtly tougher, even the features of his face turning coarser and more beastlike. As he closed with Ashi, the hunter snapped a leg around in a fast kick that smashed into his side. Geth shrugged it off.

He responded with hammering punches of his own. Ashi stumbled backward under the flurry, barely able to block the shifter's fists. When she managed to react with punches and kicks herself, Geth swung his right arm to defend himself with blocks that just as often turned into heavy blows. Dandra could see why Geth's weapon of choice was the massive great-gauntlet—it was a extension of his own natural fighting style. Spinning and darting around Ashi, he took all of the punishment that she served out and returned it in equal measure.

But the Bonetree hunter had the advantage of height and the beams in the ceiling of the hold ran only a couple of feet above her head. Ashi caught Geth with a solid, double-fisted blow that seemed to rattle even the tough shifter, then as he shook off the strike, jumped up and wrapped her hands around the top of one beam. Hanging from it, she snapped her body forward, putting her entire weight behind a stomping kick with both feet square to Geth's chest. The shifter made a wheezing noise and flailed back away from her.

Ashi dropped to the ground in a crouch. Across the hold, her eyes met Dandra's. The kalashtar froze. Geth was down. The burly sailors had their hands full keeping back Natrac's struggling brawlers. Singe stood in front of her protectively, but he was unarmed—and his fiery spells were as useless on a wooden ship as most of her own powers. Most, though not all. She reached desperately for the *vayhatana* she had used to move the stone in the Bull Hole. If she was fast, she could use it hold Ashi back. *Tetkashtai, I need your help!*

The only response from the presence was another wail of despair.

To one side of the hold, though, Vennet turned from bashing a man's head against a barrel. Dandra saw his eyes narrow as he took in the hunter's menacing stance. He shoved the man he had been struggling with away and turned to face Ashi. Even as her crouch turned into an outstretched leap for Dandra, concentration flickered across the half-elf's features. The dragonmark that patterned the back of his neck shimmered.

The roaring of a gale filled the hold. Dandra felt it only as a strong breeze, but in a path in front of Vennet, loose objects and abandoned clothing flapped and tumbled, blown up into the air. The worst of the windstorm, however, was focused directly on Ashi. Its unseen force snatched the leaping hunter out of the air and slammed her back into a stack of crates. Her impact scattered them and left her sprawled on the floor, struggling to climb back to her feet in the face of the howling wind. She grabbed at a big, heavy barrel and clung to it.

Now, Tetkashtai, urged Dandra. She reached into herself and forced an image of what they needed to do onto Tetkashtai. The frightened presence finally responded, entwining her skill with Dandra's raw power.

A ripple of force passed through the air as invisible *vayhatana* wrapped around Ashi's taut body—and around the barrel she clung to. With all of her will, Dandra held the two together. Trapped even as Vennet's wind died away, Ashi spat and struggled, but the best she could do was rock the barrel from side to side.

Out of the corner of her eye, Dandra could see Vennet staring at her. All of Natrac's other "clients" were staring, too—at her, Vennet, and a slowly rising Geth. The brawlers were silent, shifting uncomfortably.

Natrac peered down from above. "Is it over?" he asked.

Vennet's angry gaze shifted to the half-orc and rage fell over his face. Natrac flinched and slowly slipped back through the hatch.

The mood around the captain's table a short time later was far grimmer than it had been earlier in the evening. Vennet sat at the table's head, Natrac and Geth to one side, Dandra and Singe to the other. In the aft hold, Ashi had been placed in shackles and chained to bolts driven into the wood of the ship. *Lightning on Water* had no brig. Chains had been the best solution Vennet could come up with. For the remainder of their voyage, the rest of the men and women who had taken Natrac's offer of passage would sleep on the ship's deck, their good behavior guaranteed by a promise from the captain that if they stepped out of line they would have to deal with him and Geth directly.

A few swift questions had already uncovered the instigator of the brawl: an ugly man who was still unconscious after Ashi had slammed the back of his head against the floor of the hold three or four times in quick succession. It was generally acknowledged that she had been defending herself against the man and two of his cronies—at least initially. Once the fighting had started, everyone had joined in, most siding with the ugly man. Ashi, it seemed, had not made herself popular among Natrac's clients.

Natrac also held the key to how the Bonetree hunter had come to be aboard the ship in the first place. "It happened at the last moment," the half-orc said, shrinking back from the combined gazes of the others at the table. "I was loading my clients on the pier at Yrlag when she came running up and demanded a place onboard. When I explained that there was no more room, she turned to the biggest man in line and hit him so hard that she broke his jaw with a single blow." He spread his hands. "How was I supposed to pass over someone who fights like that?"

"Grandfather Rat," cursed Geth. Dandra watched as he glowered at Singe. "I *knew* I saw her in Yrlag. She must have run ahead of the other hunters and guessed where we were heading—on her own, she could have slipped past us. The Yrlag Bridge is the only way across the Grithic from the north. All she had to do was wait for us there, then follow us through the town."

"And when she found out we were taking passage on *Lightning on Water,* decided to get on, too," Dandra added. She shivered. "She could have crept out and killed us at any time. We should be lucky that she was the only one."

Vennet glared at all of them. "So she's on my ship because of you three," he said angrily. "Whatever's going on here, I'd like to know about it now!"

Dandra hesitated, unsure of what to tell the dragonmarked half-elf. Singe came to her rescue. "Her name is Ashi, Vennet. She's part of a Shadow March clan called the Bonetree. They're a cult of the Dragon Below."

"Sovereign Host protect us," said Natrac.

Vennet's face settled into a mask of intensity. "Tell me what this is about," he said tightly. His eyes grew hard and bright as Singe recounted Dandra's flight from the Bonetree, the attack on Bull Hollow, the trio's escape to Yrlag, and their determination to see an end to Dah'mir's power. The wizard made no mention of Tetkashtai, Medalashana, Virikhad or the cult leader's terrible experiments, instead implying only that Dandra had been abducted as a potential sacrifice to the dark powers that the cult worshipped.

When he was finished, Vennet sat back, his expression blank. Natrac, on the other hand, was pale. The half-orc stood slowly. "Vennet," he said, "if there's nothing else you need from me, I'd like the return to my cabin and barricade myself inside until we reach Zarash'ak." He made a sign of protection against evil. "If you do the sensible thing and drop that cultist over the side, let me know."

"I'm not going to drop *anyone* over the side, Natrac," Vennet growled. "House Lyrandar has rules against that. She's chained up well enough. If you want to shut yourself in your cabin for two days, you're welcome to. Keep what you know to yourself. I don't want a panic onboard."

Natrac nodded tightly. "I'll be in my cabin as long as she's alive." He turned to go, but laid one heavy hand on Dandra's shoulder on the way out. "You're lucky to have escaped," he said. "I had a cousin who was taken by a cult in Zarash'ak itself. We kept finding pieces of him in the canals for a week. And they say the cults in the marshes are even worse."

He walked out, shutting the door softly behind himself. Vennet looked after him for a moment, then glanced at Dandra. "Is it true?" he asked. "Are they worse?"

Her belly tightened. The horrific memories she had shared with Singe and Geth surged back at her, forcing a whimper from Tetkashtai. "I don't know," she answered truthfully. "I don't have anything to compare them to."

"If Dah'mir commands dolgrims and a dolgaunt, he must be very powerful," Vennet said.

"You know what dolgrims are?" asked Singe.

"I've seen a lot of things I've tried to forget." said Vennet. Dandra thought she saw his eyes dart briefly toward Geth.

The shifter only grunted. "What are we going to do with Ashi? Dropping her over the side sounds like a good idea."

"Dropping people over the side is bad for business," the half-elf said firmly. "The crew sees it, they start talking, word gets around . . ." He sat back in his chair. "When we reach Zarash'ak, we turn her over to the authorities there."

"I've been to Zarash'ak," Dandra reminded him. "The authorities there seemed as likely to turn her loose as imprison her—if she didn't just escape from them. Either way, she's going to start tracking us again!"

Vennet frowned. "What am I supposed to do then? Carry her all the way to my next stop at Sharn?"

Dandra glanced at Singe and Geth. The wizard raised his eyebrows. "Why not?" he asked. "Even if she escapes or is turned loose there, she's going to be hundreds of miles away from us."

"You're asking me to carry a dangerous cargo," Vennet said darkly. He steepled his fingers in front of his face for a moment, then looked up. "An extra five hundred gold from your letter of credit when we reach Zarash'ak and I'll do it."

Singe's eyebrows climbed even higher. "Twelve moons, you're mercenary!"

"No," said Vennet, "that would be the province of House Deneith." He gave the wizard a biting smile. "And unlike Natrac, I wouldn't dream of cutting into Deneith's business." There was a knock at the door. "Come in!" Vennet called.

One of the big crewmen who had gone into the hold along with Geth and Vennet opened the door. "Beg you pardon, captain, but we may have found out why the fighting started. It sounds like the woman had valuables with her—the first men into the fight were trying to intimidate her into handing them over."

"Not a very successful attempt," commented Vennet. "Have you looked for these valuables, Karth?"

The crewman shook his head and flushed. "They'd be in the hold, captain, and none of us want to go down with . . ."

His voice trailed off, but Dandra could guess what he meant. None of the crew wanted to be around Ashi. The hunter had done a lot of damage and even chained up she was intimidating.

Vennet rolled his eyes. "Is there any word what kind of valuables we're talking about?" he asked crossly.

"Some kind of jewelry," said the crewman. "Some of Natrac's gang say it was like a headband set with diamonds."

"I find it hard to believe that a Marcher savage is going to be carrying a diamond bloody headband, Karth. Or that one of Natrac's thugs would recognize diamonds if he saw them."

Tetkashtai stirred uneasily within Dandra's mind. *Dandra, a headpiece set with crystals* . . . An image of the spidery, crystal-studded devices Dah'mir's mind flayers had used on them flickered within her light.

I know, said Dandra. "Vennet," she said aloud, "I'd like to look for this headband."

Geth and Singe stared at her, but Vennet tilted his head, then nodded slowly. "If you want to," he said. "You can't go down alone, though—"

"I'll go with her," Singe said. He shot a glance at Geth. The shifter growled agreement as well.

"We'll all go," said Vennet. "Karth, fetch a couple of lanterns. We'll need more light down there."

As they left the captain's cabin and paced back along the ship's length, Vennet leaned close to Dandra. "You think there's something special about this headband?"

Dandra clenched her teeth. "I think it might be connected to the cult of the Dragon Below." The half-truth seemed to satisfy Vennet.

Karth was waiting by the hatch down to the aft hold, two ever-bright lanterns in his hands. Vennet took them, passing one to Singe, then nodded at Karth to raise the hatch.

The hold was silent. Geth crouched down and peered into the dimness, then nodded and went in all the way. Vennet followed. Singe gestured for Dandra to go ahead of him, but she swallowed and stepped aside. Ashi might have been shackled, but facing the hunter was still going to be difficult. "After you," she said. Singe nodded and descended the steps. Dandra swallowed. Tetkashtai had already drawn herself into a tight, tense spark. Cautiously, Dandra stepped down into the hold.

From where she sat chained to the floor, bound hand and foot, Ashi glared at her. The Bonetree hunter's face was bruised and swelling from the brawl and her ferocious fight with Geth, and there was fierce hatred in her eyes.

Vennet and Singe kept their distance from the bound hunter, but Geth strode right up to her. His lips peeled back from his teeth and he growled in Ashi's face. The hunter's gaze shifted slowly from Dandra to Geth. Her lips twitched as well, but they didn't part. She kept her silence. Her arms, however, tensed against her shackles.

"Get away from her," said Vennet. He grabbed Geth and pulled him away, then faced Ashi himself. "Where's this headband trinket that started the fight?" he demanded.

Ashi didn't answer. Her eyes didn't waver from Geth. The shifter growled again. "Beat it out of her," he said, his voice thick and almost irrational.

Ashi's jaw tightened, but her expression of angry resolve didn't change.

"Geth!" Dandra hissed. A part of Dandra understood what Geth wanted: a measure of revenge against their enemy. The temptation to hurt Ashi as she had been hurt herself was strong. Dandra pushed the urge away. She stepped up to Geth and grabbed his shoulders. The shifter's chest was heaving. "We're better than that," she said. "Beat her while she's bound or kill her in cold blood and we bring ourselves down to her level."

To her surprise, the statement provoked more of a reaction from Ashi than any of Geth's threats—the hunter drew a sharp breath and spat out a harsh, deeply accented rebuke. "Blood in your mouth, outclanner! I'm not a torturer. Or a murderer either!"

Geth turned on her. "One of your clan murdered Adolan!"

Ashi's eyes narrowed. "The Gatekeeper? He died fighting, like the hunters you killed, shifter. If that's murder, then there's more of my clan's blood on your blade than yours on mine!"

Dandra felt Geth's body stiffen under her hands, his massive muscles flexing. She shoved him back several more steps from the bound hunter. Singe grabbed him from the other side, helping to restrain him, though Dandra was reasonably certain that he could have wrenched himself away from both of them easily. After a moment, he slowly relaxed. Dandra let him go, then looked at Ashi.

"The headband," she said. "Where is it?"

The hunter lapsed back into sullen silence. Dandra looked around the hold. Searching the stacks of crates, barrels, and sacks—not to mention the blankets and packs Natrac's clients had left behind—would take hours. There was another possibility though. If the "diamond headband" was, as both she and Tetkashtai suspected, some kind of psionic-empowered creation, it would more than just a physical presence. She cleared her thoughts and opened her mind's eye.

A swirling mist took shape in her vision, similar to Tetkashtai's presence but shadowy instead of glowing with light. The feel of it filled her dread, but she focused her mind and pointed where the aura seemed strongest. A heavy sack rested in front of a pile of crates. "Behind there," she said.

The slight tightening of Ashi's face told her she was right. Singe stepped forward and dragged the sack aside to reveal a gap between the crates. He held his lantern close, peering inside, then got down on the floor and stretched one arm deep into the gap. His hand emerged with a well-worn pouch of soft leather. He passed it to Geth. Dandra watched Ashi for any further reaction, but the hunter's expression had taken on the harsh coldness of stone. Geth drew the string on the pouch open and spilled its contents into his palm.

A band, perhaps three fingers wide, of loosely woven copper wire studded with large, roughly cut crystals slid out. The crystals caught the lantern light and flashed brightly, but Vennet said, "Those aren't diamonds."

"No," agreed Dandra, "they aren't."

There was something strangely familiar about the aura of the band, like a face half-recognized. She reached out to touch the band.

The aura that surrounded it flickered and reacted like a living thing, rearing back then snapping toward her hungrily. Dandra snatched her hand back with a gasp. The band sought a living host—it clearly had little power on its own—but there was still a mind behind it, a mind reaching out for a connection. And the mind behind the band . . .

Tetkashtai recognized that mind only a moment before Dandra did. A name echoed in Dandra's mind. A haze of horror settled on her as she turned and stared at Ashi.

"Medalashana," she said, her voice trembling. "Medalashana is alive. This band lets you communicate with her."

The hunter's face went pale with a mix of anger and surprise. She looked away—enough of an answer to tell Dandra that she was right.

"Who's Medalashana?" asked Vennet.

Dandra hesitated, then answered. "A friend. Dah'mir took her at the same time he took me. I thought she was dead."

"You don't look happy to know she's alive."

"I . . ." Dandra looked back to the crystal band. Geth was still holding it, though he looked a little unsettled. He'd be even more unsettled if he could see what she saw: the aura of the device, coiled and writhing like a snake. "I don't think I am. The band has a sense of her mind about it, but it's dark. Mad. If Medalashana's alive, if she has her powers . . ." She swallowed. "It's only because she's given herself to Dah'mir and become one of his followers."

Geth's hands trembled. Dandra gestured for him to put the band away and he slid it back into the pouch, then quickly handed it to her. Dandra could still feel the device's aura, seething inside the leather.

"Twelve moons," said Singe from the floor. "Natrac's thugs saw Ashi with the headband, didn't they? That means she used it while she's been on the ship. Dah'mir knows we're coming!"

"If he doesn't," Dandra said grimly, "he at least knows we're on our way to Zarash'ak." She looked at Vennet. "We can go now."

"Wait, Dandra," said Singe. He leaned back down to the gap between the crates and wriggled his arm inside again. "I felt something else in—"

Ashi howled at his words and lunged forward as far as her shackles would allow. Dandra gasped, the disembodied chorus of whitefire snapping into her mind out of instinct. Geth growled and brought up his fists. Vennet's hand went to a cutlass he had strapped on in his cabin. Ashi paid no attention to any of them, however. Her eyes were fixed on Singe.

"Outclanner! Touch that and I promise I will hunt you down and kill you!"

The hunter's threat washed over Singe. He looked at her as he sat up. "I thought you were trying to do that anyway, Ashi," he said calmly. He held out the long bundle, wrapped in a length of torn blanket, that his fingers had found jammed into the gap. A flick of his wrist and the cloth fell away to reveal a sheathed sword.

Vennet spat at the sight of it as Ashi let loose another howl of outrage. "Storm at dawn! I told Natrac to make his thugs didn't bring any weapons onboard!"

"If Natrac was as eager to get Ashi onboard as he says, I don't imagine she had any trouble slipping it past him."

Singe stood up to examine the sword in lantern light. The scabbard that it rested in was crude, but the sword was much more sophisticated work, fifty years old or more to judge by its shape and the design of its hilt. The pommel had been worn almost smooth, but hints of gilt clung to the metal and there was still a trace of some kind of symbol on it. He turned it to the light.

The faded remains of a lion, a ram, and a dragon stared back at him—the heads of a chimera. Singe gasped in surprise and whipped the sword free of the scabbard. Light flashed on a fine magewrought blade, patiently honed to razor sharpness. The years had not, however, obscured the inscription on the bright metal: *Words teach and spirit guides*.

"Grandmother Wolf!" said Geth. "That's the sword Ner used when I fought him."

"It's the sword of the huntmaster of the Bonetree!" Ashi raged. "Sheathe it, outclanner, or I'll tear out your innards with my bare hands!"

"What it is," said Singe, "is an honor blade of the Sentinel Marshals of House Deneith. These aren't given out to just anyone." He looked at Ashi. "Where did a Marcher clan get this?"

The hunter closed her mouth and snarled at him.

Singe shrugged. "It should be returned to House Deneith. They'll know who it was presented to." He slid the sword back into its scabbard and looked at Ashi again. "If it was Ner's weapon, why isn't he carrying it now?"

"Ner is dead," Ashi said. She glared at Dandra. "Medala killed him when we failed to capture you."

Dandra's hands tightened on the pouch containing the crystal band. Vennet glanced at Ashi, then leaned in close to Singe and the kalashtar. "I'd keep those safe if I were you," he murmured. "I have a strongbox in my cabin . . ."

Singe glanced at Dandra, then shook his head as he sheathed the honor blade. "I think we'll keep both of these close."

"What about her?" asked Geth, jerking his head toward Ashi. The hunter glared back at them, hunched over in her bonds.

"Two days to Zarash'ak," Vennet promised. "I'll put a watch on her and check in myself. You don't have to worry about her anymore."

The next two days passed with a strange tension onboard the ship. Vennet's crew trod warily around Natrac's clients, who themselves seemed intimidated by the powers and strength that Geth, Dandra, and Vennet had displayed in taking down Ashi. Natrac remained locked away in his cabin, his absence causing great confusion among the other passengers. All of them knew about the brawl and somehow word got around that Vennet had confined Natrac to his cabin as punishment for bringing Ashi onboard. There were no more meals at the captain's table—the passengers took their meals with the crew or in their own cabins. Singe didn't see Natrac emerge from his frightened seclusion even for food.

True to his word, Vennet made sure two big sailors kept watch on the aft hold at all times. Ashi herself remained disturbingly silent. For his own part, Singe spent time with his spellshard, studying magic that he could use against the hunter—should she escape—without risk of setting *Lightning on Water* on fire. As she had on previous occasions when he had studied the arcane text captured in the fist-sized dragonshard, Dandra watched him with quiet fascination.

"Why fire?" she asked as he finished his studies in the ship's bow late in the morning of the second day.

Singe smiled at her, then looked out beyond the rail. Some time during the night they had entered Zarash Bay, the gateway to the Shadow Marches. The low marshy southern coast of the Marches lay across the horizon like a haze, drawing closer as the day passed. "Fire challenges me," he said. "You have to be careful with it. Spells of fire only have one purpose: to destroy. And if you're not careful, you can destroy a lot more than you intend to." His grin twitched to one side as he looked back to her. "Most people, even a lot of other wizards, are afraid of fire for that reason."

"But you're not?"

"Probably less than I should be." He tucked his spellshard away in the belt pouch that kept it close to him at all times—the only reason it had stayed with him at Bull Hollow and through all kinds of battles over the years—and held out his left hand to show Dandra the ring he wore. "This was an inheritance from my great-grandfather. I was given it on my sixteenth birthday. It protects me from fire. Probably not the best gift to give a rebellious adolescent, but I don't think my parents knew what it really was."

Dandra examined the ring. "I know a power that does the same thing," she said. She reached out and took his hand, her fingers parting his to look at the ring from all sides. Her touch tickled.

"What about your powers?" he asked and immediately regretted it as Dandra stiffened. He felt blood rush to his face. "I mean, what about Tetkashtai's . . ." he began again awkwardly but Dandra shook her head.

"It's all right," she said. "I know what you mean." She released his hand and sat back. "A psion's powers are a reflection of her psyche. Tetkashtai is . . . forceful. She's a fighter and she chose to follow a path suited to swift victory: the powers that she honed, her combat skills—" Dandra pressed fingers to her chest "—even her creation of me to augment her own resolve. Fire suits Tetkashtai."

Singe hesitated for a moment, then asked a question that had lingered in his mind since Dandra had opened her memories to him and Geth. "Is that why Virikhad loved her?"

"Loved? I—" Dandra winced, then shook her head. "Tetkashtai would prefer we didn't talk about that."

"Oh." Singe glanced at the yellow-green crystal around Dandra's neck and shifted uncomfortably. "Sorry, Tetkashtai." He looked back at Dandra. "She can hear me, right?"

"In a way, yes."

"Is it very different being . . ." He gestured to the crystal.

Dandra nodded. "To Tetkashtai, it's torture, able to see and hear but unable to do anything more," she said. "The only influence she has on the world is through me and even that's limited. We share our powers—we both have the knowledge, but I have most of the raw energy and she has most of the skill. Do you remember after the Bull Hole, when I was so drained? It was because Tetkashtai was trying to punish me by drawing away. Without her, I exhausted myself moving the stone that capped the Hole. But without me to work through, Tetkashtai can't use her powers at all."

Singe cocked his head. "How is Medalashana able to use her powers to communicate through the crystal band?"

Dandra's lips pressed together and she hesitated before answering. "Singe, when I told you that Medalashana could only be alive if she yielded to Dah'mir, there was . . . something else. I couldn't say it because Vennet was with us and later, I wasn't sure how to tell you." She looked him in the eyes. "If Medalashana has her powers back, it's because she has been returned to her body, either by Dah'mir or by her own twisted will. Either way, it means it's possible to reverse what Dah'mir did."

"That's good!" Singe said—then the underlying meaning of what Dandra was saying hit him. He struggled to keep a smile on his face. "So you and Tetkashtai would switch back if you could?"

"It's her body."

"I guess it is." He stood up. "What about Virikhad?"

"What about him?" Dandra asked, rising as well. Singe felt blood rush to his face again.

"I mean, do you think he's alive?" he said quickly. "Like Medalashana?"

Dandra paused, then said. "Tetkashtai hopes he is."

"And you?"

She shook her head.

A shout interrupted them. "Shallows ahead!" called a lookout. "Approaching land."

Up ahead, the long bay narrowed to the mouth of a meandering river, by no means large enough to allow *Lightning on Water* to progress at her full speed. As they came up on the river, the elemental gale that had howled in Singe's ears for five days faded away. The misty ring that bound the elemental to the ship shimmered and solidified once more and their speed dropped. Without the elemental's speed, the hull of the ship slid back down into the water, hiding the great running-fins once more. It seemed like they were crawling through the water, though Singe knew they were still making as good time as any conventional ship could hope for.

Glancing back, he saw Vennet surrender the helm to a junior officer, then make his way forward, collecting Geth as he went. Shifter and half-elf joined them in the bow of the ship. Vennet gathered them all close together in a conspiratorial huddle. "Listen," he said quietly, "we'll reach Zarash'ak at about dusk. You can disembark with the other passengers then if you want to, but I've got a problem I'd appreciate if you help me with." He jerked a thumb over his shoulder toward the stern of the ship. "I have cargo in that aft hold that needs to be taken ashore here."

"And you can't unload it with Ashi tied down in the middle of the hold," guessed Dandra.

Vennet nodded. "Aye. I have a plan, though." He glanced at each of them. "I know a man who lives close to the docks and he has a strongroom in his house. Between the four of us and Karth, I think we can walk Ashi that far. Because we're docking so close to dark, it won't seem odd if I give the crew the night on shore and leave unloading for the morning. Once they're all off the ship, we can get Ashi away without anyone getting alarmed. Then when the unloading is finished . . ."

" . . . we bring her back onboard, shackle her down again, and you carry her off for Sharn." Singe scratched at his chin under his beard. The plan struck him as risky. "Can't you unload the forward hold, move her up there, then unload the aft?"

Vennet looked at him like he was an idiot. "The ship needs to be balanced, Singe."

"Really?" He felt half like the captain was pulling his leg, but Vennet's expression was serious.

"Leave questions of sailing to House Lyrandar and I'll leave questions of defense to House Deneith." Vennet glanced at them all, then looked back to Singe. "Help me with this and I'll waive the fee for taking her to Sharn."

That was five hundred gold. "Done," Singe said quickly. Vennet clapped him on the shoulder.

"Good man. Thank you." The half-elf stepped back. "It won't take long for the crew to clear off once we're tied up. Be ready." He grinned at them all. "In the meantime, you might want to keep yourselves out of the way. If you thought leaving port was busy onboard a ship, you don't want to see how busy the crew is coming *into* port."

Vennet hadn't been joking about how busy the crew would be. As *Lightning on Water* slid up the river, the ship's crew scrambled all over her, above deck and below. Vennet was as busy as his men, maybe even busier. Singe and Dandra tried to find a moment to get into the forward hold to collect their meager gear—including the honor blade Singe had taken from Ashi and the crystal band, cunningly hidden by Dandra to avoid the necessity of carrying it constantly—but so many sailors moved through the hatch that it was easier to avoid it.

"It will only take a few moments to gather," Dandra pointed out. "It can wait."

Singe grimaced. "I'd feel better about having everything to hand." Geth grinned at him and patted his own gear, brought up on deck days earlier. Singe gave him a cool glare.

At least he and Dandra were unencumbered as they gathered with the other passengers to watch as the ship came into port at Zarash'ak. The City of Stilts was, Singe thought critically, far from the most impressive port he had ever seen. True to its name, the city's wooden buildings and plank streets sprawled above river and marsh on a forest of stilts, props, and piles. Singe couldn't help but think of a child's makeshift fort carried to extremes. Still, there was something curious to the way Zarash'ak almost hovered above the water, long rickety bridges leaping from platform to platform. Small boats skimmed the shadowed water around and between the piles. Smoke rose above the city, mingling with evening mist and merging with the twilight sky. Croaking frogs and calling marsh birds made a soft chorus, broken only by the rhythmic shouts between dockworkers and sailors as *Lightning* was guided into her berth. The entire scene was surprisingly beautiful.

As the ship bumped against the dock and the other passengers waited patiently for the gangplank to be lowered, Singe looked around. There was a figure missing from the small crowd. The wizard reached out and tapped Pandon. "Where's Natrac?" he asked. He would have assumed the half-orc would be among the most eager to disembark.

Pandon, however, gave him an awkward look. "I suppose you wouldn't have heard," he said.

"Heard what?"

The thin man shifted and sighed. "He's not coming ashore at Zarash'ak. He's staying in his cabin and going on to Sharn. He's afraid that you've ruined his business and House Deneith will be investigating him."

"What?" said Singe. "Pandon, you know that was just a joke!"

"Apparently Natrac thought otherwise," Pandon said. "Captain Vennet told me himself. Natrac has even released his clients from their contracts. They're free to do as they please."

He pointed. Singe followed his gesture and his eyes widened as he took in the sight of the Natrac's thugs, held back by the crew, waiting eagerly in the stern of the ship for their turn at the gangplank. Singe smacked a hand against his forehead and groaned.

"Twelve moons! What is he thinking? Dandra!" The kalashtar looked around. "I have to go to find Natrac and talk to him," he told her. "Can you gather my gear when you fetch yours? You know where all of it is."

Dandra nodded and Singe strode back toward the hatch that led to the tiny passenger cabins. The thud of the gangplank hitting the dock followed him. Shortly afterward, he heard the murmur of Vennet's disembarking passengers, then the excited calls of Natrac's former clients as they rushed to embrace a new life.

The crew would follow next; they had certainly already abandoned the rest of the ship. Singe stopped at the door of Natrac's cabin and banged loudly on the thin wood. "Natrac!" he called. "We need to talk. You're making a mistake. There's no House Deneith investigation. I was just having you on!"

There was no response. "Natrac!" Singe called again. Was the half-orc even inside? He paused and listened closely at the door.

A soft moaning met his ear—and a vile smell his nose. A wretched stink like an overflowing chamber pot wafted through the door. "Natrac?"

He tested the door. It was latched, but nothing more. It opened easily.

Natrac lay on the narrow bed, struggling fitfully. His clothes were soiled with his own excrement and only an open porthole vented the reek out of the ship. His face was flushed. His wrists and ankles had been lashed securely to the bed's frame and a gag forced into his mouth. Singe bit back a curse.

A heavy bottle nestled in a little boxshelf attached to the wall inside. Singe eased carefully into the cabin and fished it out. When he opened the bottle, a sickly sweet smell wafted out. There was a bluish stain around the cork. Singe hissed and glanced at Natrac's flushed face. A matching blue stain colored his lips and trickled down his face. Singe hesitated for a moment, then stepped out of the cabin and hurried back up to the deck.

Dandra met him at the hatch. She had her spear, but not their gear. Her face was pale. "The crystal band and the honor blade are gone!"

Singe clenched his teeth and touched the rapier at his side. "Something's wrong. Where's Geth?"

"He wandered down onto the dock with the other passengers. He said he wanted to feel something solid under his feet again." Dandra's nose crinkled. "What's that smell?"

"Natrac," said Singe grimly. "He's been drugged." The ship

was entirely silent around them. Everyone had gone. "We should join Geth." He started across the deck toward the gangplank.

A curved sailor's cutlass swept out of the shadow of the captain's cabin, barring his way. He leaped back as Vennet followed the weapon into the light. The crystal band was clutched in his free hand. Behind him, Ashi glided out the shadows as well, the unsheathed honor blade held low before her.

"I have a better idea," said Vennet. "Let's wait for Geth to come back and join us."

CHAPTER

9

Singe stared at the crystal band in the half-elf's grasp, then studied his face. His eyes narrowed. "Have you worn it already, Vennet?"

He heard Dandra draw a sharp breath and stretched out a hand to her. Vennet's cutlass twitched sharply. "Don't move," the captain said. "Not a muscle."

Singe let his hand fall slowly back to his side.

Vennet nodded as Ashi came up beside him. "That's good," he murmured, "that's very good."

"Vennet, what are you doing?" Dandra said.

"He's turning on us," Singe answered for Vennet. Everything was clear in his mind. "He planned this. Convincing us to stay behind on the ship, arranging for the crew to be busy in the hold so we couldn't check on our gear until the last minute." He glanced at Ashi then asked Vennet, "Was the crew really too scared to go into the hold or did you order them to stay out so you could talk to her alone?"

"A little of both," Vennet said tightly.

"And House Lyrandar's prohibition against throwing people overboard?"

"Ironically," said the captain, "that's the truth."

"Singe," Dandra said, "what's going on?"

The wizard risked turning slightly to give her a dark smile.

"The cults of the Dragon Below aren't something you find just in the Shadow Marches."

Dandra turned pale.

Singe looked back to Vennet. "I think our good captain has decided to make a move for power. If he hasn't done it already, he's going to contact Medala and offer his services to Dah'mir."

Vennet's face tightened. "You're too smart for your own good, Singe."

"I've been told that before," Singe said casually. At least he hoped he sounded casual. His stomach felt like it had squeezed down into a rock. "Why did you drug Natrac? No, let me guess." He followed a line of reasoning through his head. "Natrac was the only other one in your cabin when we told our story. He was the only other person on the ship besides us who knew that Ashi was a follower of the Dragon Below. You had to be sure that he didn't let that information slip out, so you made sure he couldn't talk to anyone on the ship and you spread the word that he was giving up his business and traveling on to Sharn. That way no one would suspect his disappearance afterward." He smiled. "And there's Captain Vennet d'Lyrandar, with no one left to give away his secret."

"Storm at dawn!" Vennet snapped. "Would you shut up?" He slid closer cautiously, cutlass at the ready. "If either of you moves or makes as much as a sound to cast a spell or—" the cutlass wavered slightly toward Dandra "—do whatever kalashtar do, you'll regret it. Ashi, hide by the rail. When Geth comes back aboard, make sure he dies."

The hunter nodded and darted across the deck, hunching down to stay out of sight. When she reached the rail, she peered over cautiously. She grimaced and snapped the fingers of her free hand softly to attract Vennet's attention. He turned slightly, enough to see her and still keep an eye on his captives. Ashi mimed someone wandering back and forth on the dock below. Vennet's teeth clenched and he cursed softly.

In the instant that the captain's attention wandered, Singe felt the brush of Dandra's mind on his, just as he had when she'd shared her memories on the morning after Bull Hollow. Trying his best to keep his face neutral, he relaxed and accepted the touch of her thoughts. The voice that rang in his head was taut. *Singe, what are we going to do?*

It took a conscious effort not to turn his head and look at the kalashtar as he answered her. *Can you warn Geth the same way we're talking?*

He's too far away. He'd need to be almost at the top of the gangplank for me to reach him and if he's that close, it will be too late!

Vennet was turning his full attention back to them again. *Be ready to tell Geth to get back fast,* Singe told Dandra. A plan was taking shape in his mind. He formed an image and sent it flickering at her—then swiftly focused back on Vennet as his cutlass flicked close.

"Call Geth!" the half-elf ordered. "Get him up here."

Singe looked him straight in the eye. "How long have you followed the Dragon Below, Vennet?" he said, buying time. If he called, Geth would come bounding up the gangplank. The shifter needed to come up slowly if Dandra was going to have any chance at warning him.

Vennet tensed. "Just call him!"

"Not too long, I think," Singe continued. "You don't seem obviously insane yet."

"You're baiting me," Vennet said. He pushed the cutlass forward until its tip pricked Singe's chest through his shirt. The wizard held back a wince. Vennet looked at him coldly. "You think I'm going to get angry and you're going to distract me? It's not going to work. You want to know how long I've followed the Dragon? Nine years—and that faith is the only thing that *saved* my sanity. I know you'll understand why." His eyes were hard. "You're a veteran of the Last War. You saw the things that men and women who claim to be good and righteous are capable of doing. *That* almost drove me mad. The powers of Khyber don't make those claims. The cult of the Dragon Below draws power from darkness. Two years after the darkest day of my life, I came to the cult and it made sense."

He leaned close, pressing down on his cutlass. A bright spot of red sprang up on Singe's shirt. Over Vennet's shoulder, he could see Ashi, still watching the dock—and, presumably, Geth down on it. The wizard swallowed and looked back at Vennet. "I saw dark things during the War, too. I got through it."

Vennet gave a thin smile. "Are you trying to convert me, Singe? Bring me back to the light?" His hand, the one holding the crystal band, trembled. "Geth told me there are things about the War you don't like to talk about. Like Narath. Narath bothers you." His lips twisted as Singe stiffened. "Well, I was on one of the ships that sailed against Narath. I had to stand on the docks and watch while our fine Aundairian soldiers ripped Narath apart."

Blood roared in Singe's veins, pounding in his head and burning hot across the skin of his face. Ashi, Dandra, and even Geth vanished from his mind as he met Vennet's gaze. "You weak, pathetic coward," he breathed. "That's your darkest day? *Watching* Narath die?" He seized Vennet's sword hand and shoved the cutlass away from his chest, heedless of the line of pain that the blade's tip traced across his skin. "I was *in* Narath."

It was only Dandra's piercing shout inside his thoughts that broke through the rage that gripped him. *Singe! Geth's coming!*

Singe's head shot up. The gangplank was shaking as someone climbed it. Ashi crouched like an animal ready to pounce.

Clenching his teeth, Singe flung Vennet back hard. The half-elf growled and charged back, the sharp blade of his cutlass raised.

Out of the corner of his eye, Singe saw Geth's face appear above the gangplank—only to stiffen with Dandra's silent warning and vanish again, even as Ashi leaped out of her hiding place. In the same instant, the wizard flung himself down and back before Vennet's blade, dropping onto his hands and kicking out blindly with his feet. The kick was wild and soft, but it was enough to make Vennet stumble back a pace. Singe rolled over and came up onto his knees, shouting the words of a spell.

It felt strange, given the time he had spent studying magic that wouldn't harm *Lightning on Water*, that it was still a fire spell he invoked. Bolts of flame leaped from his hands to sear across the ship's deck, setting wood ablaze in a fiery streak that pointed straight toward the gangplank. Ashi shouted and jumped aside as the fire reached for her, but the hunter had never been Singe's target. Thrusting himself to his feet, he grabbed Dandra's hand and charged directly along burning path he had created, protected by his ring as Dandra's powers protected her.

But for all that the fiery path roared and crackled, it wasn't very wide—only an arm span or so. Vennet or Ashi could have reached through the flames and skewered him or Dandra easily. If he had judged the captain correctly, though, violence would not be his instinctive reaction to fire on his ship.

He heard the half-elf bellow with rage.

"Get ready!" Singe gasped at Dandra.

The powerful wind generated by Vennet's dragonmark struck them from behind so hard that it sucked Singe's breath away. The flames around them stretched out flat, guttered once, and vanished, utterly extinguished.

Just as it had battered Ashi when Vennet had trained it on her in the ship's hold, though, the wind also caught both the wizard and the kalashtar in its grip, forcing them along before it. Where Ashi had tried to struggle against the wind, however, Singe and Dandra ran with it. Singe caught a brief glimpse of Ashi, clutching the ship's rail helplessly, as they swept by her.

Then the top of the gangplank was in front of him. Still propelled by the wind, he seemed to leap out into empty air, only to come crashing down about halfway along the gangplank's angled length. He fell, rolled heavily, and spilled out onto the dock as limp as a rag doll.

Dandra twisted in the air, landing like a cat in a graceful crouch.

Before Singe could even catch his breath, Geth was kicking him out of the way. The shifter planted his feet on the surface of the dock, grabbed the rails on the sides of the gangplank, and *heaved*. With a groan almost as loud as Geth's own, the gangplank lifted away from the brackets that held it steady at the edge of the deck above. Geth staggered back a step, grunted, and released his grip. The gangplank grated against the ship's side, then slid down to splash into the water. At the same time, the eerie droning chorus of Dandra's own fiery powers hummed in the air. Singe twisted around in time to see her release a cascade of carefully aimed flames at three of the thick mooring ropes. Intense white-fire burned into the twisted hemp and the ropes, already under tension, snapped like whips. *Lightning on Water* shifted and swayed out from the dock sharply.

In the half-dark of early evening, the docks of Zarash'ak were far from abandoned, however. People turned to stare at them—and up on the deck of the ship, Vennet and Ashi leaned out over the rail. Singe scrambled to his feet, grabbed Geth with one hand and Dandra with the other, and pushed them across the dock into the nearest and deepest shadows.

"Keep going!" he spat. "Dandra, keep your feet on the ground—we don't need any more attention!"

The shadows were the mouth of a narrow alley and Singe found himself squeezing between tight walls toward ruddy light at its far end. Geth, with a broader chest, had to force himself through. His great-gauntlet, wrapped up and stuffed in a bag that hung across his back, scraped the walls harshly.

"What happened back there?" the shifter asked. "I start back up onto the ship and all of the sudden Dandra's screaming in my head, Ashi's jumping out at me, there's fire and wind . . ."

"Vennet has loyalties to more than just House Lyrandar," said Singe.

"He follows the Dragon Below! He was going to sell us out to Dah'mir!" Dandra's voice was hot with outrage, but Singe shook his head as he squeezed another pace closer to the alley's exit.

"You, Dandra. I'm pretty certain he was only selling out you. I don't think Geth and I figured as anything more that obstacles. Like Natrac."

"Natrac?" grunted Geth. Singe told him what he had discovered in the half-orc's cabin. "Tiger's blood!" cursed the shifter.

They popped out of the alley onto the edge of a market, still bustling in spite of the gathering night. Singe breathed a prayer of thanks for undeserved blessings and led the way into the crowd, slowly and casually. "Follow me," he ordered. "Geth, keep an eye out behind us."

The crowd in the market was mixed, mostly humans mingling with brawny half-orcs, but a few full-blooded orcs, delicate-looking elves, and lithe little halflings moved through it as well. Geth's shifter features and Dandra's exotic beauty barely stirred a second look. Singe himself felt practically invisible. Still, it seemed like forever before the press of bodies opened up ahead of them and they were on their own again, heading deeper into Zarash'ak with the crowded market between them and the docks. Singe let a little of the tension to ease out him. "Geth?" he asked cautiously.

The shifter shook his head. "No sign of Ashi or Vennet," he reported.

Singe gave a slow sigh of relief. "Twelve moons. We're away."

"We are," said Dandra thinly. Singe glanced at her. Her face was pale. "Light of il-Yannah, Singe—Vennet still has Natrac!"

It took an effort of will to hold back the memories of the horrors Dah'mir had inflicted on her. The thought that Natrac might suffer similar tortures was almost too much to bear and sent Tetkashtai retreating to the furthest recesses of her mind. When Dandra looked at Singe and Geth, though, she saw only harsh determination on both men's faces. They shared a glance—and pressed on along the street, putting more distance between them and the docks. Dandra stopped dead. "We can't leave Natrac as Vennet's prisoner!" she protested.

Singe paused long enough to hook his arm around hers and pull her forward. "Dandra, I know." He glanced into her eyes. His gaze was dark. "We shared your memories, didn't we? But we can't go back to *Lightning on Water,* not tonight. They'll be waiting for us."

"Vennet and Ashi? There are three of us and two of them!"

"You have a go with Ashi then, Dandra," said Geth. The shifter's voice was a quiet rasp. "She was tough with her fists and now she's got her sword back. Have you watched the way she moves? She'll be waiting if we go back. If she gets a chance to ambush us in the dark, the odds won't be in our favor for very long."

Singe's arm tightened on hers. "And remember, it's you they want. If we go back, we're delivering you right to them."

Dandra tensed. "But Natrac . . ."

"Vennet went to the trouble of drugging him," Geth pointed out with cool practicality. "He's not going to kill him now. He'll be all right until the morning." His hands tightened on the bag containing his great-gauntlet. "We'll go back then."

Singe still had a little money left from the sale of their horses in Yrlag. They found a small inn well away from the docks and took a room for the night. The innkeeper looked at Geth, but a smile and a word from Singe eased his worry. Once they were in their room, Geth flung himself down on one side of the bed and seemed to be asleep almost instantly. Dandra stared at him.

"How does he do that?" she asked. "How *can* he do that?"

"He's been able to sleep whenever he wants for as long as I've known him. No matter what's been happening, give Geth a moment of quiet and he can go to sleep." Singe shook his head in awe. "It's a valuable gift when you're a mercenary."

The wizard turned away, moving to the room's window and throwing back the shutters. The window faced away from the street and out over the low rooftops of Zarash'ak's ramshackle sprawl. A cool breeze drifted in from the distant sea, pushing back some of the pungent marsh smell that clung to the city. After a moment, Dandra slipped across the room to join him.

"You haven't said much about the time that you and Geth served together in the Blademarks," she said.

Singe looked down at her, then away. "No, I haven't," he said.

"Being an inanimate crystal gives you a lot of time to watch what's going on around you. The only time I've seen people with the depth of anger you two have is when they were friends before they became enemies."

Singe's face twisted. For a moment, Dandra wondered if maybe she'd pressed too hard, but then his eyes closed and he let out a long sigh.

"Not too long after I joined the Frostbrand—our Blademarks company—the commander of the company, Robrand d'Deneith, took a few of us on a recruiting mission," he said in a low voice.

"Folk from the Eldeen Reaches generally make good scouts and the Frostbrand had developed a specialty in taking winter assignments, so we headed into the northern Eldeen. Not quite so isolated as Bull Hollow, but still more wild than civilized. In a little place that was hardly more than a crossroads, Robrand started his recruiting speech." Singe's expression grew nostalgic. "Twelve moons, the old man could talk! Recruiting was a hard sell in that region—the Eldeen Reaches had seceded from Aundair only a generation or so before and most Reachers didn't want to have anything to do with the world outside their forests. But there was one eager young shifter who came forward with a hunger for adventure in his eye and signed up on the spot."

"Geth," said Dandra and Singe nodded.

"There's a tendency in every Blademarks company for new recruits to band together. Eight of us joined the Frostbrand within a couple of months of each other. I was the first, Geth was the last. The bunch of us were practically inseparable for the next five years." He reached up and ran a finger along his cheek-bone, high under his left eye. Dandra looked closely and saw a thin scar. "Geth gave me that during a tavern brawl in Metrol. He was aiming for the Cyran soldier who was holding me from behind and missed."

"That can't be what broke you up though."

"*That* was nothing. We laughed about it."

"Then what happened?" Dandra hesitated, then said, "Tonight when Vennet mentioned 'Narath' . . . you've said that name to Geth before and he doesn't like to hear it either."

The wizard gave no response.

"Singe," Dandra said, "what happened at Narath?"

"Go to sleep, Dandra," said Singe. His voice was cold and empty. "Take the bed next to Geth if you want. I'll sleep on the floor."

Dandra glanced at the bed. There was plenty of room for three people to lie side by side. She looked back to Singe. He was still staring out of the window, his face a harsh mask. Dandra held her tongue and turned away, leaving him to whatever dark memories were running through his head.

The sound of the room's door closing woke her. Dandra sat upright, her mind snapping alert and the drone of whitefire throbbing on the air. On the floor under the window, Singe came to his feet with his rapier in his hand.

Geth stood inside the door, a big bundle of rags and three broad conical straw hats in his arms. He looked at both of them critically. "I walk out of here and you don't stir, but I come in and you're both ready to strike me down?" He walked over to the bed and dropped the bundle. "Here. I've been to market."

The rags were clothes, simple and well worn—by fisherfolk previously if the smell that rolled off them was anything to judge by. Dandra wrinkled her nose. Singe stared. "Did you actually *pay* for those?" he demanded.

"More or less." Geth tossed a muddy brown shirt to the wizard. "We can't just walk up to *Lightning on Water*. We need something to disguise ourselves."

"No one will recognize us by smell at least," Dandra pointed out with a grin. Singe gave her a dim glower.

It was the middle of the morning by the time they left the inn and stepped back onto the street. Zarash'ak was alive around them. The air was humid and close, but the people of the City of Stilts moved around in a hurry, as if eager to get their errands finished before day grew any hotter. Dandra found herself staring around as she, Geth, and Singe wandered back toward the docks, unexpectedly aware of what she had missed of Zarash'ak when she had passed through as a crystal around Tetkashtai's neck. The city had sounds, sights, and smells she hadn't really appreciated before. Musicians on a street corner made strange music that mixed a chirping stringed instrument with a deep, thrumming pipe. On streetside grills, vendors cooked long strips of meat brushed with a thin sauce that smelled both spicy and sour. Other vendors made thick rounds of dark gold bread, flapping a pale yellow dough back and forth between their palms before slapping it onto hot iron griddles. People seemed to buy the yellow bread at one stall, then wander on to another to buy meat or blackened roast vegetables to stuff inside.

"What is that?" she asked as they passed one grill stall.

"Snake," said Geth. He pointed at the bread. "That's made out of a flour pounded from a kind of marsh reed called *ashi*."

"When it's cooked, it's the same color as Ashi's hair."

Geth grunted at the observation. "Let's buy some and ask her about it, shall we?"

They followed a different route to the docks than the one that they had taken the night before and approached *Lightning on Water* from a distance. Singe had suggested they would find Vennet's crew busy unloading the ship—the half-elf might be a treacherous serpent, but he was also a Lyrandar captain and clearly took his business seriously. To Dandra's surprise though, they could see as they approached that activity on the ship was subdued. Most of the crew seemed to be hanging over the side, watching as crowds surged around on the dock below. Geth held both her and Singe back while he scanned the dock and the ship thoroughly for any sign of Vennet or Ashi. Finally, he shook his head.

"I don't see either of them," he reported.

"What do you think's happening on the dock?" asked Dandra.

"Let's find out."

Dandra tilted her hat slightly toward the ship as they passed, trying to conceal her distinctively dark skin from the sailors above. Although it didn't seem likely that any of the crew shared their captain's vile faith, even a casual greeting could give them away. Once they were among the crowd, it was a little easier to hide and she relaxed a bit—at least until she realized that the attention of the shifting, gawking crowd was focused on the narrow alley down which she, Geth, and Singe had made their escape. The three of them pushed their way carefully to the front of the crowd.

A long, thick stain of dried blood painted the wall to one side of the alley mouth. At the top of the stain was a deep ragged hole, as if a spike had driven into the wood. The hole was also bloodstained.

Beside the stain, two words had been scratched into the wood: *blue doors*.

"Rat!" breathed Geth. He nudged the man who stood next to him. "Do you know what happened here?"

"*Dagga*. Word is that the ship over there"—the man gestured to *Lightning on Water*—"was transporting a mad woman. I hear she got loose, kidnapped someone from his cabin, and even tried to set fire to the ship. When that didn't work, she came down here, hacked off her prisoner's hand, pinned it up to the wall, and ran off with the rest of him!"

"It was more than his hand!" chimed in a half-orc woman on his other side. "It was a whole *arm*. My boy saw it hanging there before the watch and took it away!" She held up one hand and made a circle over it with the finger and thumb of her other hand. "Big ruby ring on it too! The woman would *have* to be mad to leave that behind."

Natrac's ring, Dandra realized. Her hand sought out Singe's and squeezed it tight. If they'd come back last night, they could have stopped this.

The wizard must have realized the same thing. He looked slightly pale. "The watch," he said, "will they investigate? Will they look for the man whose hand or arm it was?"

The half-orc woman laughed. "Not unless someone wants to come forward and pay the fee!"

"Or unless this mad woman starts cutting off more parts," said the man darkly with a glance at the woman. "Only the cult does that and not even the watch will stand for their type in the city!"

"Any idea what 'blue doors' means?" asked Geth.

The man and woman shook their heads, but Dandra seized Geth's hand as well as Singe's and pulled both men out of the crowd and down the dock. When they were out of sight of *Lightning on Water,* she stopped and looked at them. "I know what 'blue doors' means." She took a deep breath. "When Tetkashtai, Virikhad, and Medalashana came to Zarash'ak, they met Dah'mir in a house with blue doors."

"Are you sure?" asked Singe.

She nodded. "It's all a message for us," she said. "Do you remember what Natrac said after the fight with Ashi? The cult of the Dragon Below kidnapped his cousin and left parts of him in the canals. Vennet and Ashi left Natrac's hand and ring as a message to say that they had him. They left the words to show where they've taken him, knowing I'd understand but not anyone else."

Singe's eyes narrowed. "But how could Vennet know about this house?"

"The crystal band," Dandra told him grimly. "Vennet has used it to contact Dah'mir and Medalashana. One of them must have told him what to do."

"Twelve bloody moons," cursed Singe. He looked at Dandra. "Suppose Dah'mir wants to come to Zarash'ak. How long do you think it will take?"

"More than a week," Dandra answered. "Even if he left the Bonetree mound as soon as Ashi told Medalashana we were coming to Zarash'ak, he'd still be days away from here."

"And you can find this house with blue doors again?"

She nodded.

A growl rumbled up out of Geth. "It's going to be a trap—and after all that last night about not going back because we'd deliver you right to them . . ."

"I know," Dandra answered.

Tetkashtai's presence shook inside her. *Dandra, this is too much! We don't even know that Natrac's still alive. Light of il-Yannah, he's had a hand cut off!*

Then we have to go to make sure he's dead, Dandra said. *I won't leave him to the cult of the Dragon Below.*

Dah'mir and Medalashana will know we're in Zarash'ak for certain now.

The suggestion sent a tremor through Dandra's belly, but she forced it away. *All the more reason to confront Vennet and Ashi and get the crystal band back.* She glanced up at Singe and Geth. "When should we go?"

"I don't think we have anything to gain by waiting." Geth tapped a fist against his right arm. Hidden under a loose sleeve, the metal of his great gauntlet rang solidly. "Let's go now."

Dandra looked to Singe. The wizard nodded. Dandra steeled herself. "All right then," she said. "This way."

The ship that Tetkashtai and the other kalashtar had taken from Sharn had made port at another part of Zarash'ak's dock.

Dandra led Geth and Singe along the waterfront until she found the point where the ship had berthed. Dredging her memory, she began pacing through the city, following landmarks and tracing the route that the kalashtar had taken those months ago. At one intersection, though, she had to stop. To the right, the plank street broadened into a wide and busy thoroughfare lined with fine, large homes.

To the left, it became narrow and crooked, leading away into an older, more rundown part of the city.

It would have made more sense for the house with blue doors to be to the right—it was big and very pleasant and would have fit that neighborhood. Memory, however, suggested that the kalashtar had turned *left* at this spot.

Tetkashtai, she asked, *which way?*

The frightened presence confirmed her memory. Left. Dandra moved on, turning where memory prompted her. The district, however, was nothing like she remembered. Empty windows gaped like black eyes form the faces of dilapidated houses. Occasionally, feet scampered on the wood ahead as figures scrambled back into the shadows.

"Squatters," said Singe.

Not all of the figures ducked away. A lanky orc—full-blooded, with coarse features, lean muscles under his gray-green skin, and heavy tusks that made Natrac's look small—stared at them from the shadows of one house, red eyes gleaming. His clothes were rough and swamp-stained; he looked like some kind of marsh nomad, looking for easier prey in the lawless places of Zarash'ak. Dandra's grip tightened on her spear and Geth made sure that the orc saw the heavy sword at his side.

"Dandra," he asked, "are you sure about this?"

"Yes," she said. She turned a corner.

In her memory, the house with blue doors was a grand and luxurious building, three stories high with dormers along the pitched roof. It stood alone on its own platform, surely a luxury in a city where walkways and platforms had grown haphazardly together over time. The doors that had stuck in her memory and in the minds of the kalashtar were tall and striking, their bright polished surface painted a deep blue that was exactly the color of an autumn night's sky.

The building that she faced now might once have been much like what she remembered. It had the shape of something grand, but it had been a long time since it could have been considered luxurious. Much of the roof had fallen in and the dormers with it, leaving the house looking like a crushed skull. The wood of the house had gone gray with age. If it stood alone on its own platform, it was because its neighbors seemed to lean away, as if shunning the decaying structure.

The blue doors were still there, as tall and striking as in her memory, but the color on them was faded and old, a stain on the wood. One door hung askew. Dandra could say nothing, struck dumb by her memory's betrayal. "This isn't what we saw," she managed finally.

"Dandra, is it possible that Dah'mir's domination of you and the kalashtar began *before* he met them?" asked Singe after a moment. "Some kind of illusion spun into your minds . . ."

Dandra nodded slowly. "It's possible, I suppose. This is the house, though. I'm sure of it."

"If this isn't the right place, we don't have anything to worry about," said Geth. "If it is the right place, they'll be expecting us. Be ready." The shifter studied the broken house carefully, then loosened his sword in its scabbard. "We should make getting Natrac back and out of here our goal, but I don't think dealing with Ashi and Vennet would be a bad thing either."

"I agree." Dandra shifted her grip on her spear and took a step into the air, skimming the ground and ready for combat.

They moved forward, stepping cautiously over the gap that had opened between the building's platform and the planks of the street. The murky water that lapped the shadows beneath Zarash'ak was visible far down below. Dandra glided up to the faded doors. She was about to put a hand to them when Geth pointed at the step beneath her feet. "No dust," he said. "It's been swept clean."

"Wind or rain?" suggested Singe.

The shifter shook his head. "Probably not."

Dandra pushed open the door. She recalled a beautiful foyer

with stairs rising up to the second floor and the distant sound of trickling water. What actually lay beyond the door was a rickety, broken room with huge gaps in the walls. Stairs—every second step seemingly broken—rose to a second floor that sagged so badly she wasn't sure she would have risked crossing it. The sound of water was the splashing of the river, echoing up from somewhere below.

A trail of blood led deeper into the house. Dandra gestured silently to the trail and started across the floor.

"No, Dandra!" snapped Geth. "There was no blood outside—"

His warning was too slow. A chunk of hurled wood cracked against the side of Dandra's head and sent her stumbling to the ground. Gasping in pain and with Tetkashtai screeching in alarm, she twisted around. She caught a glimpse of movement as Singe shouted and darted to her side—only to be met by Ashi's screaming battle cry as she leaped down through a broad hole in the ceiling. A kick caught Singe's shoulder, spinning him around and driving him to the floor—

—which cracked and broke under the impact of Ashi's landing. The tall woman's battle cry turned into a yelp of alarm as the crumbling floorboards gave way beneath her and Singe. Stunned by Ashi's blow, Dandra froze as both the hunter and the wizard plunged down into the darkness below.

CHAPTER

10

'**R**at!" Geth sprang to the splintered edge of the hole as two solid impacts below shook through the frame of the old house. Debris rained down around him. He held his gauntlet over his head and peered down. Singe and Ashi lay, tangled together and stunned, on the floor of a lower level about fifteen feet down and apparently much more solid than the one above.

There were shouts of alarm coming up from below as well. Ashi and Vennet weren't alone! Geth glanced up at Dandra.

"Looks like this is the right house!" he spat. He spun around and slithered backward past the edge of the hole, lowering himself swiftly down. When his fingers clenched wood and he hung from outstretched arms, he grunted and kicked out.

Old wood screeched in protest but held firm as he swung and released, arcing through the air to hit the ground in a roll. He came up in a crouch and spun around as Ashi wrenched herself away from Singe. Geth leaped forward to stand over the wizard, his gauntlet up, his sword clearing its scabbard in one fluid movement. He had only a moment to take in the great chamber around him. Once it might have been a private water landing of some kind: there was a huge square opening in the center of the buckled floor with broad stairs running down and the sound of lapping water drifting up. Another long flight of stairs rose to the upper levels of the ruined house. Holes broken in the high ceiling let day's light stab into the shadows.

Ashi drew her own sword and took a fast pace back—and then took another as Dandra fell through the hole above to land with an unnatural grace and lightness. Her spear glittered in her hand. Alarmed shouts turned to frightened cries, but one voice rode above them all.

"Hold your ground!" roared Vennet in a voice used to calling across the deck of a ship at sea. "Follow the plan, Fause! Temmen, be careful not to hurt the woman!"

The Lyrandar captain, his cutlass drawn, charged around the hole in the floor. A lean man wielding a thick quarterstaff followed close behind. From the hole's far side rose the unified chanting of half a dozen men and women dressed in dark, shapeless robes, a wild-haired man with a look of madness on his face leading them. "Powers of Khyber, great Dragon Below, hear our prayer and lay low our enemies!"

"Grandfather Rat's naked tail!" cursed Geth. Had he really thought an easy rescue might be possible?

Natrac slumped against the wall behind the chanting cultists. His already-fouled clothes were drenched with blood; his right hand had been brutally amputated at the wrist, the wound fire-seared to seal it. The half-orc's skin looked waxy, but he was still breathing. He needed a healer. Geth had an unpleasant certainty that if they got out of the chamber alive, they would *all* need a visit to a healer.

He shifted and leaped at Ashi. He could feel the magic called down by the cultists fall over him like a shadow, trying to drag at his arms and fill him with self-doubt. The sensation of invincibility that flooded his veins flung the dark prayers back, though, and as Ashi's sword flashed in the dim light, he caught her blow on his gauntlet and replied with a thrust of his own heavy Karrnathi sword. Ashi twisted aside, then arched her back to avoid a punch from the gauntlet as well. Her teeth clenched and she smiled, eyes shining as bright as her blade.

"You fight well, shifter!" she said. Her sword flicked high, then dove low. Geth anticipated the feint and caught the sword on his own, turning it aside. He and Ashi sprang apart, and she added, "I can see why Ner claimed you at the Gatekeeper circle!"

Geth settled into a defensive posture, sword and gauntlet both up. From the corner of his eye, he could see Dandra skimming toward Vennet and Temmen. Her spear darted out like a shining crystalline serpent, a fast and lethal strike.

Temmen knocked the blow away with one end of his staff, then struck back with the other end, forcing Dandra to parry wildly with the butt of her spear. Vennet slipped easily around both combatants, a wicked grin on his face. "Not a spearman as such," he called out, "but on short notice, I think an expert in the quarterstaff will do!"

Geth managed to block a flurry of hard blows from Ashi that left his arm stinging. "Singe!" Geth yelled. The wizard was on his feet, but fumbling as he drew his rapier. The fall had knocked the wind out of him. "Singe, we could use a spell!"

"Then stop leading us into places made of wood!" wheezed the wizard. He hauled himself upright and jumped clear of both Ashi and Vennet. He moved his hand in an arcane gesture and spoke a word of magic. Three of the cultists pitched over, their eyes closed in unnatural sleep. The chant of the others faltered and Geth felt the baleful shadow of their prayer fade.

"Storm at dawn!" cursed Vennet in frustration. The half-elf wasn't, however, looking at the fallen cultist, Geth realized. As he whirled in combat with Ashi, he saw Vennet dodge back and forth for a moment, then heard him curse again. "One will do!" he spat. "Ashi, move!"

"No!" the hunter snarled. The same battle lust that Geth had glimpsed in Ner's eyes at the Bull Hole flared in Ashi's. "I claim his death!"

"Neither of you can have it!" gasped Geth. He spun around Ashi and slammed his gauntleted elbow back in a hard blow that sent her reeling away.

And left a clear path between him and Vennet. The Lyrandar captain's eyes narrowed.

There was no parrying or blocking the gust of wind that blasted out from him. It hit Geth like a moving wall and shoved him back. He caught half a glimpse of mold-slick stairs running down to dark and murky water before the wind battered him right over the edge of the hole in the chamber's center.

He slammed into the stairs hard and started rolling and sliding on the slimy surface. Instinct opened his hand, releasing his sword before some random jarring bounce could send it plunging into his own body. The bone-jarring, teeth-rattling impacts of his body and limbs on the stairs came too fast to count, but as abruptly as the wild ride had started, it was over—with a tremendous splash, he hit water.

It was brown-green, cloudy, and warm. Geth felt unnamable lumps and ropy strands touch him as he sank and it was all that he could do to overcome the instinct to inhale. He spread his limbs and kicked hard back toward the surface. As soon he broke the surface, he gasped for air—then gagged and choked as something slimy rippled off his face and slithered into his mouth. He spat convulsively. The water *stank,* foul with all the detritus of the marshes and Zarash'ak combined.

The enormous pillars and piles that supported the platforms of the City of Stilts spread out around him like a drowned forest at twilight. The bottom of the stairs were in front of him, though, a long broken smear on them marking his tumbling fall.

He kicked for them, threw an arm over a sludge-coated step, and hauled himself out of the water as a new wave of chanting rolled down from the cultists above.

The sound of it sent a chill through Geth.

"Grandmother Wolf!" he breathed, staggering to his feet. A sudden bubbling noise snapped his attention back to the water. Its foul surface was boiling as something rose from deep below.

The head that emerged from the water as big across as a large shield and armored, too—the vile slickness of the water shimmered on a mottled carapace like that of some enormous crayfish. Four powerful legs and a thick tale propelled the creature to the surface, while massive arms clacked jagged pincers as long as Geth's own legs. Tentacles hanging below the enormous creature's head writhed, questing toward him.

Geth scrambled up the stairs, scooting backward to avoid turning his back on the monstrous beast. His feet and hands slipped on the muck that coated the wood, but he kept going as the creature reared back and hauled its bulk out of the water onto the lowest step. Geth grabbed the step nearest him and held on desperately as the stairs pitched under its weight. A high snarl of fear ripped free of his throat.

Dandra whirled around in time to see Geth plunge down the stairs and out of sight. A moment later, she heard a splash as he hit the water below. Temmen tried to take advantage of her distraction and pressed her hard. She beat back his staff, desperately trying to get away. Over the crack of wood against wood, she heard Singe speak the words of a spell—words that became an abrupt gasp of pain. She slid to Temmen's side and twisted to look over her shoulder.

Singe was on his knees, clutching at the knife that sprouted from his arm. Ashi lowered the hand that had thrown the knife and took a step toward him. Vennet turned to Dandra, a look of triumph on his face. Temmen moved back in, his staff already falling.

We're doomed! wailed Tetkashtai. *Dah'mir will take us back—*

"We're not doomed!" hissed Dandra through clenched teeth. She swept her spear up to block Temmen's blow, then spun the weapon, slid her right hand down on the shaft and wrenched back hard with her left, snapping the butt of the spear up and into the man's groin. He skipped back before it could hit him, but it gave her the opening she needed. "And Vennet," she spat as she pulled Tetkashtai close and reached into herself, "is *not* Dah'mir."

The air rippled around her as she slid her body through the crevices of space. When she had used the power to escape the Bonetree hunters, she had stepped across hundreds of yards at once, pushing herself as far as she possibly could. The long step moved her much shorter distances as well, though.

She was beside Singe before Ashi had moved more than a pace. The wizard cried out in surprise, but Dandra dropped a hand on his shoulder. Her spear snapped up, swinging between the hunter, Vennet, and Temmen, all of them startled.

"Stay back!" she ordered. She glanced down as Singe pulled the knife free and clamped a hand around the wound. "Singe—"

"I've taken worse," he hissed, then flinched as the cultists' chant rose to a pitch.

Dandra's breath caught in her throat as something big thrashed down in the water, bubbling and splashing and making a hard clacking noise that sent shudders up Dandra's spine. The stairs leading through the hole in the floor flexed and moaned under some massive weight and a high-pitched snarl rose on the air.

"Geth!" Dandra moved toward the hole.

Singe grabbed her hand. "That was a summoning spell, Dandra! Get out of here!"

"Not a chance!" she said.

Ashi slid forward slightly. Dandra's spear darted toward the hunter, but the instant she moved, Vennet and Temmen slid closer as well—and a figure dropped down through the gaping hole in the ceiling that Ashi and Singe had created. It fell right onto Temmen's back, slamming him to the floor.

As everyone—Dandra, Singe, Ashi, Vennet, and the cultists—stared, an orc rolled away from the dazed man, darted to the head of the stairs and began chanting as well.

"Storm at dawn!" choked Vennet. Ashi spun around and leaped for the orc.

Dandra reacted without thinking. Power throbbed on the air as she drew whitefire up from within herself and gave it a tightly focused form. Pale flame flashed around Ashi and the hunter seemed to crumple in mid-stride, stunned by the intense heat.

The orc's eyes widened, but he didn't stop his chanting.

"No!" Vennet howled. He swung between Dandra and the orc as if trying to decide who to attack—then lunged toward Dandra. "Dah'mir *will* have you!"

Geth scrambled to one side and shoved himself a little higher up the bouncing, slippery stairs as one of the creature's enormous pincers closed on the step where he had been perched—and snipped right through the wood.

"Tiger, Wolf, and Rat!" the shifter yelped. He kicked ineffectually at the pincer. The creature's head turned to him, its tentacles making a horrid slithering whisper as they writhed together. It drew its pincer back and opened it, ready for another strike. Geth tried to haul himself higher, but his bare hand slipped in the slime on the stairs and he had to fight just to stay where he was. "Singe!" he shouted. "Dandra! *Anybody!*"

The chanting that rolled down from above was a gruff counterpoint to the cultists' chorus. It tugged on Geth, both foreign and strangely familiar. In the water below, ripples seemed to contract, then burst open wide.

The scaly snout of a large crocodile broke the surface. The reptile snapped at the broad, crayfish-like tail of the creature on the stairs, hauling it back toward the water. The creature's head reared back and it let out a screech like steel on slate.

"Quickly, shifter!"

Geth twisted around. An orc stood at the head of the steps, stretching a long staff with a tight crook in the end down to him.

"Climb up!" he urged. "One crocodile can't hold a chuul!"

The stairs gave another ominous groan and bounced as the creature below twisted to flail at the crocodile while still clinging to its precarious perch. Geth glanced over his shoulder in time to see a pincer close around the crocodile and bite deep into its scaly hide. Geth grabbed for the staff and climbed up the slick steps. The orc hauled back, lending his strength to the effort, the muscles of his hairy arms straining under the short sleeves of a pale, swamp-stained shirt.

Recognition stirred in Geth's memory. "You!" he gasped at the orc as he staggered to the top of the steps. "We saw you outside on the street!"

"I was only supposed to watch this place, but I couldn't just watch anymore!" the orc said tightly. His voice had the defensiveness of someone who wasn't completely certain he was doing the right thing. Geth realized with a start that in spite of his size and bold actions, the orc's gray-green face was still smooth with youth.

The stairs shook again, the chuul screeched once more, and there was a frantic hissing from the crocodile that ended with the muffled snap of the chuul's pincer closing. The creature let the crocodile's body fall and turned back toward him, scrambling up the stairs with gore-smeared pincers extended and the tentacles under its head lashing in a frenzy. Geth yelped in shock.

"Geth!" shouted Singe. Geth spun around to see the wizard staggering to his feet. One of his arms was a bloody mess, but he was gritting his teeth against the pain and extending his hands in a gesture of magic. Geth gasped and grabbed the orc, yanking him aside.

As the chuul's head lurched up above the level of the floor, Singe called out a rushing word of magic and a bolt of intense flame roared from his fingers to wash over it. The chuul let out another horrible screech and crashed backward down the stairs, enormous pincers flailing, shell burning and melting. The monster hit the water with a splash and the hiss of extinguished flames.

The orc shouted triumphantly and spun away to lunge for the clustered cultists, his staff swinging. They broke at the orc's charge, their chanting vanishing into a chorus of yelps as they ran for the stairs leading up to the rest of the ruined house. Only Fause, their wild-haired leader, held his ground, pulling a cudgel from his robes and meeting the orc with a frenzied counterattack.

Geth whirled the other way. Ashi lay stretched out, scorched and stunned, and Singe was sinking back, but Vennet was still on his feet, swinging his cutlass as Dandra dodged and parried desperately. Geth snarled and leaped for him.

The half-elf's eyes widened at the sight of him. He threw one final slash at Dandra, then tried to scramble back away from Geth. "You don't know how badly Dah'mir wants her,

Geth," he gasped. "He's not going to let you rest. He's already on his way!"

"Not here yet though, is he?" Geth said. He twitched to the side in a feint.

Vennet took it. He thrust out with his cutlass, but the shifter sprang to the outside of the blow and caught the blade with his gauntleted hand, forcing Vennet's arm up high—and punching hard at the Lyrandar captain's exposed side with his free hand. Vennet gasped and let go of his cutlass to twist around and punch back. Geth flicked the cutlass away and swept his gauntlet down to knock the blow aside. His left fist smashed into the side of Vennet's face, jerking his head around.

"For what you did to Natrac," Geth growled, then grabbed the half-elf's shoulders as he stumbled, bent him over, and slammed a knee up into his gut. "For betraying us." He dragged Vennet upright and drew back his arm. "And for dumping me," he roared, "in that damned water!"

His arm and shoulder snapped forward, catching Vennet full in the face, and sending him reeling back, blood pouring from a shattered nose. The half-elf swayed briefly, then crashed to the floor.

The entire structure of the old, ruined house around them groaned and shuddered. Dust and boards fell from above. Ashi stirred. Across the room, Fause went pale and dodged away from their mysterious orc ally to run for the stairs. Geth stared at Vennet's fallen form in shock. "I didn't hit him *that* hard!" he gasped.

Singe had a scrap of torn cloth out and was trying to bind it around his wounded arm. He spun around and stared up at the ceiling, with one end of the cloth clenched in his teeth. "That came from up above! What's going on up there?"

The orc had gone as pale as Fause had. "Vvaraak's wisdom," he breathed, staring up as well. "The Servant of Madness."

Geth looked at him. "Who?" he demanded. "Who's the Servant of Madness?"

Dandra was the one who answered him. The kalashtar's feet were sinking back to the floor. Her eyes were wide and terrified, her body stiff. "It's Dah'mir," she said. "I can feel him. Dah'mir is here!"

"What?" Singe exclaimed. He yanked the makeshift bandage tight and spat the cloth out of his mouth. "How? He should still be days' travel away!"

Overhead, the fleeing cultists let out cries of surprise—and awe. There was a cascade of thumps as knees hit the old floor and then Fause's voice rose in a wild, ecstatic chant of praise. Even over the chant, Geth could hear the measured pace of steady footsteps. "Grandfather Rat's naked tail," he hissed. He crouched down, ready for a new battle.

"No!" said the orc. "You can't fight him! Into the water—I have a boat nearby." Gripping his staff tightly, he ran for the stairs and darted down them.

Geth hesitated and exchanged a fast glance with Singe. He could guess what the wizard was thinking: could they trust the stranger? It didn't seem to him that they had much choice. The orc had helped them. If the footsteps overheard really did belong to Dah'mir . . .

"See to Dandra!" Geth grunted. He darted to Natrac and heaved the half-orc's body over his left shoulder with a groan and a curse. He staggered back to his feet and turned around.

Singe stood at Dandra's side, murmuring to her, easing down her spear, and trying to get her over to the top of the stairs. Beyond them, Ashi was rising to her feet.

"Singe!" shouted Geth.

The wizard whirled and Geth could hear him try to gasp out the words of a spell, but the hunter was faster. She leaped, lashing out with a fist. Her blow spun him around and sent him sprawling. A snap of her leg sent a hard kick into the softness of his belly.

Like someone waking from a bad dream, Dandra blinked and started to turn away, but Ashi grabbed for her. For a moment the hunter's hand raked the air and it seemed that Dandra might dodge away from her, but the cord that hung the yellow-green psicrystal around the kalashtar's neck snapped tight. She jerked back with a strangled cry.

"No!" Geth yelled. He managed a stumbling step forward even as Ashi wrenched on the cord and hauled Dandra into her grasp. Dandra tried to strain away—

—and the cord around her neck snapped. The psicrystal flew free.

Geth stretched out his right hand and snatched the crystal out of the air, clenching the steel-cased fingers of his gauntlet tight to keep it from slipping through. He spun back to Ashi and Dandra. The Bonetree hunter had her arms wrapped around Dandra, lifting her off her feet and squeezing her in a crushing grip.

"Let her go!" Geth roared. He stuffed the psicrystal hastily into his pouch without looking and started to let Natrac slide to the ground.

"No," called a deep, oil-smooth voice, "hold her. Give up your struggle, shifter—there's nothing more for you to fight for."

Geth spun around.

He had seen and heard Dah'mir in Dandra's memories, but even memory paled in comparison to the majesty of the man himself. Robed in black leather set with priceless dragonshards, just as Dandra had first seen him, the tall, pale-skinned man stood at the bottom of the steps. The gloom of the chamber made his acid-green eyes seem to shimmer. His presence was almost overwhelming—Geth gasped as it washed over him. His gut clenched. Dah'mir was right. There was nothing more to fight for! His grasp on Natrac tightened . . .

Then he gasped again as the stones of Adolan's collar grew shockingly cold. A new clarity burst inside his mind, driving back Dah'mir's power. Geth shook his head, blinked, and looked at Dah'mir again.

The green-eyed man's presence was strong, but not so overwhelming as it had seemed a moment ago. There were cultists crowded onto the stairs behind him, peering down like a gang of children. A woman in dirty green robes stood at Dah'mir's side. Her face was sharp and almost feral, though it had the look of having once been plump and joyful. Her tall body was hunched and crooked. Beneath smudges of dirt, her skin was dusky; her hair, clumped and matted, was shot through with gray.

It took a moment for him to recognize Medalashana—the kalashtar bore only a distant resemblance to Dandra's memories. Geth drew a sharp breath.

Dah'mir's eyes narrowed. Geth's heart skipped. He glanced quickly at Dandra and Singe. The wizard was still down. Dandra was still folded in Ashi's arms—but she was no longer struggling. She had frozen, staring at Dah'mir as if he was the center of her world.

"Shifter—" said Dah'mir.

Geth whirled, bared his teeth, and snarled.

Medalashana howled in outrage. "Dah'mir! Let me take him! I'll shred his mind and lay his thoughts out before you!"

Geth flinched at the venom in the kalashtar's voice, but Dah'mir held up a hand to her. "Hush, Medala. We have the one we came for. He's nothing. If he wants to defy me, let him."

His raised hand made a pass in the air. A flash of light seemed to grow out of that gesture and arc across the chamber. It took on a shape as it moved: a spectral claw, gnarled and inhuman.

Geth froze, then dodged to one side. The claw drifted after him. Geth growled and swatted at it with his gauntlet, but his fist passed right through it, leaving a chill on the metal.

On the ground by Ashi's feet, Singe raised his head. His lip was swelling where Ashi had hit him. "Get out, Geth!" he slurred. "Run—"

Ashi kicked him hard and he collapsed once again. Geth swallowed. His eyes darted from Dah'mir to the open square in the floor and the water beneath. If their mysterious orc ally was down there . . .

Dah'mir's other hand made another gesture and a soft, ugly word passed between his lips. The claw swooped around abruptly and slid through Geth's chest.

The shifter gasped and staggered as a terrible ache seized his joints and nausea worse than he'd felt even on Vennet's ship wracked his guts. His skin burned with a sudden fever heat. His vision blurred—he could only just make out the spectral claw as it drifted away from him, then faded into nothingness. He blinked, straining against a growing brightness in the air.

Medalashana was watching him with naked glee, Dah'mir with distant interest. Ashi seemed to wear an expression of anger and disgust.

The room spun around him. Geth stumbled under Natrac's weight, then reeled sideways, blinded by the light and disoriented by fever. He tried to focus his thoughts. The hole in the floor. Escape. The water under Zarash'ak was horrible, but the idea of dropping dead from whatever plague-curse Dah'mir had placed on him was worse. He staggered forward, one step after the next.

The ache in his joints seemed to penetrate all the way into his bones. A mewling whine crawled out of his throat as he stumbled again and a horrible thought wrapped around him. *He wasn't going to make it . . .*

He pitched forward and fell—fell until he splashed into darkness and water's cool embrace.

Ashi looked away as the shifter plunged into the foul waters below Zarash'ak. She heard a splash and then silence. Both the shifter and the half-orc would sink and drown. Her gut clenched and she fought to keep anger and disgust from her face. It was wrong for such a strong and powerful warrior to be struck down without a chance to defend himself. To die as Ner had died . . .

The raw strength of her hidden emotions drew the attention of Medala. The woman stiffened and wheeled toward her. "Dah'mir!" she seethed. "Your savage disapproves!"

Dah'mir lifted his handsome face and raised an eyebrow. "Do you, Ashi?"

The hunter ground her teeth together, trying to guess what best to say, then simply spoke what was in her mind. "He was a good enemy, Revered," she said. "For an outclanner, he showed bravery and commitment to his friends, too. He deserved to die fighting."

Medala's face twisted in a vile grin and she barked out a coarse laugh. Dah'mir's lips pulled into a shallow smile as well. "He was fighting *me,* Ashi," he said. "Is that less of a challenge than facing you over steel?"

Ashi's fist tightened. She said nothing for a moment, then bowed her head. "No, Revered," she admitted.

Dah'mir's smile grew deeper.

"Ashi, haven't I always said you are as bright as you are strong?" He folded his hands and paced across the room to her, Medala stalking along at his heels. Ashi felt her captive stiffen in her grasp as he approached. By her feet, the blond wizard stirred again. The hunter quickly put a foot down hard on the small of his back.

Dah'mir ignored him to examine the woman, taking her chin in one hand and forcing her head up. Her breath quickened as she met Dah'mir's green gaze. "Ah," the pale man murmured softly, "you just can't help yourself, can you?" Dah'mir's hand fell away. "You can let her go, Ashi. She won't go anywhere."

Dandra released her hold cautiously, but the woman did nothing more than turn to stare at Dah'mir with doe-eyed fascination.

Beneath Ashi's foot, the wizard shifted and struggled to climb to his feet. He twisted around to glare at Dah'mir. "Twelve bloody moons!" he cursed, outrage on his face. "What have you done to her, fiend?"

Dah'mir stepped back sharply, gesturing for Ashi to let him rise. She reached down and dragged the squirming man to his feet, but kept a tight grip on him. Dah'mir moved back in front of him. Unlike the woman, the wizard didn't succumb to Dah'mir's mere presence—but Dah'mir didn't seem surprised or bothered by that. He simply gave the wizard a level look. "This is how it will be," he said. "You will come with us. If you attempt to use magic, I will know and I will give you to Medala."

He lifted one finger and Medala's eyes blazed. The sound of a chime seemed to ring in Ashi's mind. In her hands, the wizard's body tensed as tight as a bowstring and he screamed. Dah'mir's finger fell, but the chime and the wizard's screams both continued to ring in Ashi's ears. Medala stared at the man like a dolgrim stared at a wounded rabbit. "Medala!" Dah'mir spat.

The sound of the chime broke off abruptly as the woman cringed. The wizard collapsed in Ashi's arms, gasping for breath. In the wake of his screams, the chamber seemed deadly silent. Dah'mir folded his hands and bent his head to the shuddering man. "Apologies," he said. "Medala sometimes tries too hard to please me. If you've ever tried to train an animal—" he shrugged "—you know how it can be."

There was a groan as Vennet sat up from the floor and touched his bloodied face—and then a gasp as he realized who stood before him. He struggled to his knees and bent his head. Blood pattered from his nose to the floor. Ashi found a bitter pleasure in the injuries that the shifter hand inflicted on him. Vennet might have freed her on his ship and arranged the trap that had finally brought down her quarry, but she was glad the shifter had bested him. Vennet was a good fighter, but he was a bad enemy.

The half-elf snuffled awkwardly around his broken nose. "Dah'mir! Medala! We weren't expecting you for another two days! How did you get here so quickly?"

"When you contacted Medalashana last night and told her about your plans, I decided to leave my escort behind and travel ahead," said Dah'mir. He offered, Ashi noticed, no further explanation. She was found herself disappointed. The terrible sound that had announced his arrival had been like nothing she'd heard before. If she wanted to know more, though, she wasn't going to learn it from Dah'mir.

Vennet's mouth opened as if to ask another question but then closed again. He fumbled at a pocket, then seem to scrape together the courage to look up at Dah'mir. "Lord," he said respectfully, "this is yours." He held out the crystal band—and cringed back as Medala darted forward and snatched it away with a cry.

"Captain d'Lyrandar," said Dah'mir as if nothing had happened, "you've been of tremendous service." His eyes narrowed. "I've found that men of such faith as yours, however, do not give their services away. Name your price."

Ashi saw Vennet's throat work as he swallowed. "Power, Dah'mir," he blurted. "Power and your blessing!"

Dah'mir's full smile was a radiant thing that made even her heart lift with joy. "Greed is honest. I anticipated your request, Captain d'Lyrandar." He reached into his robe, then extended his closed hand to Vennet. "Make what power you can of these," he told him. He opened his hand to reveal two dragonshards—one midnight blue, the other dawn gold, each of them as thick as Ashi's thumbs and twice as long.

Color drained from Vennet's face as he took the crystals. "Dah'mir," he said in awe, "this is more than—"

Dah'mir waved his hand dismissively. "Consider it a down payment on future services, then. Cunning and strength of the Dragon Below be yours."

The green-eyed man touched him on the shoulder, then gestured for him to rise. Vennet climbed to his feet and bowed his head humbly.

"Whenever you need me, lord, just send word," he said, then turned and walked out of the chamber, a vaguely stunned look on his face. The cultists who had crept down the stairs after Dah'mir reached out to touch the half-elf as he passed, as if something of the Dragon Below's blessing might rub off on them.

As Vennet climbed the stairs, Fause thrust past him and threw himself at Dah'mir's feet. He groveled, smearing his face against the floor. "Dark master!" he babbled. "A blessing! Please! A blessing!"

Dah'mir looked down at the wild-haired man, then stretched out a foot and pushed at him. Fause toppled over, squirming in ecstasy. Dah'mir raised an eyebrow. "Find me boats, Fause," he said. "We'll be returning to the marshes. And prepare your followers to accompany us. I'll need a new escort."

"Yes, dark master! At once!" babbled the man. Ashi stared at him in loathing.

"They play at power," murmured Dah'mir to her. The green-eyed man stood close—possibly closer than he had ever stood to her before, close enough that Ashi could smell a slight metallic, acrid odor clinging to him. "They do not live with the Dragon Below. They are not the pure servants that the Bonetree hunters are." He bent down and retrieved the huntmaster's sword from where she had dropped it in her final charge and returned it to her. "I am pleased with your service. When we return to Bonetree territory, you will be the new master of my hunters."

"Thank you, Revered," Ashi replied tightly. "And until then?"

Dah'mir touched the groaning wizard, then the woman who had been Ashi's quarry for so long. "They are in your charge," he said. "Guard them and see that they survive the trip into marshes. The children of Khyber await their return to the mound."

His touch lingered on the woman. "Especially your return," he told her blank, staring face. "I'm very curious to learn how you slipped free of my control, Tetkashtai."

Ashi blinked, but touched her lips and forehead as Dah'mir glanced at her. "I will watch over them, Revered," she said obediently.

CHAPTER

II

'Come on," Singe said with frustrated patience. "Come on, eat."

He held a little chunk of meat to Dandra's lips. He wasn't exactly sure what kind of meat it was—fowl, snake, or something else—but it was cold and weirdly greasy. At least it was soft and shredded easily under his fingernails. "Eat," he urged Dandra again.

She paid no attention to him. Her eyes were on Dah'mir, watching the green-eyed man in rapt fascination as he laughed and spoke with Fause and the other cultists around the fire of the night's campsite. Virtually all she had done for the last two days was stare at him. Singe pushed the food against her unresisting lips. Her mouth finally opened and she took the meat, chewing it absently.

"Good," Singe told her. "Now swallow." She did, and that was a minor triumph, too. The first time Singe had tried to feed her, Dandra had just kept chewing, the food still in her mouth. Singe had never had to feed a child himself, but he was certain it would be something like this. He plucked another morsel from the small heap that he cupped in his palm and held it to Dandra's lips. The slow process of coaxing her to take another bit of food began again.

At least it gave him something to focus on besides their situation. Two days spent in the broad boats that Fause had scrounged at Dah'mir's command, two days spent rowing slowly upstream along the sluggish river that lay beyond Zarash'ak. Only Dah'mir, Medalashana, and Dandra had been spared the labor of rowing; Singe had been forced to take an oar alongside Ashi and the cultists. His shoulders and back burned and he had big welts wherever marsh flies had landed to nip at the salt on his sweaty skin. On the first day, the wound that Ashi's thrown knife had inflicted on his arm had open up and bled profusely. Singe had faltered like a lame horse, with so many flies buzzing around the wound that he'd begun to imagine the wriggling of maggots and the stench of infection.

Ashi took the charge of looking after Dah'mir's captives seriously, though. When the boats had been drawn up on a patch of dry land along the marshy riverside for the first night's camp, she had dragged Singe before Fause and forced the cult's leader to use his prayers to heal the wound.

The touch of the Dragon Below's power had made Singe long for his imagined maggots. Fause's prayers brought no gentle healing—Singe's flesh had flowed and knit together in a horrible, unclean rippling. All through that night, he had found himself touching his arm, half-expecting to find some vile cyst left behind where the wound had been. He'd stared up at the cold stars and shivered, feeling more alone than he ever had before.

The image of Geth plunging into the foul water under Zarash'ak—defiant to the last, Natrac and Dandra's psicrystal lost with him—played itself out in his memory again and again. The anger he had carried for nine years seemed as empty as the revenge against Dah'mir that they had planned on the hillside above the Eldeen Reaches.

But they hadn't seen Geth's body, Singe told himself, or Natrac's. And the orc who had come to their aid had leaped into the water like a child into a swimming hole. There was a chance, wasn't there?

Wasn't there?

Singe forced desperate hope out of his head. He couldn't afford to dream. He had to keep his eyes and his mind clear. His chance would come. He bent his thoughts back to Dandra. "Come on," he murmured. Dandra ignored him. He clenched his teeth. "Twelve moons, how did you eat the first time you made this journey?"

"We didn't," said a harsh voice over him.

Singe jerked and flinched back from Medalashana—Medala as Dah'mir insisted on calling her. The abbreviation suited her. Compared to the woman he had seen in Dandra's memories, she was like someone cut short, half of her substance and half of her soul stripped away. The kalashtar crouched down, staring at Dandra as if Singe wasn't even present.

"We starved. The Bonetree clan tolerates weakness in no one. Dah'mir forced them to give us water, but they didn't feed us and we were too enraptured by Dah'mir's presence to feed ourselves."

Singe said nothing. He couldn't bring himself to it. When Medala had forced herself on his mind, the experience had been nothing like Dandra's gentle touch. Just having her close made his breath catch as little else ever had.

Medala's lip curled. "Don't try to hide your fear, Singe," she said without looking at him, "I can feel it pouring off of you without even trying." The kalashtar reached out to brush Dandra's hair. Dandra gave no reaction and Medala hissed. "But I can't read you, can I, Tetkashtai? Dah'mir's hold presses your mind down into places even I can't reach. We'll be back at the mound soon enough, though, and when he releases you—"

Shadows stirred in the gathering twilight. "Medala!" snapped Ashi as she strode up to them. "What are you doing? Get away from her!"

The gray-haired woman stood slowly, her eyes flashing. "Are you challenging me, Ashi?"

The camp went quiet, even Dah'mir's smooth voice fading away. Ashi leaned in close, face to face with Medala. "In this," she said gruffly, "yes! Singe and Tetkashtai are in my charge. Dah'mir said so."

"Dah'mir has placed me above the hunters," Medala hissed back, "and thus above you. I'll do as I please!"

A chime rang in Singe's mind and pain lanced through him, just as it had in Zarash'ak. He fell back onto the ground, scattering

Dandra's food as he curled up into a ball and gasped for breath. He heard Ashi yelling angrily—and then Dah'mir's voice rose sharply. *"Ashi! Medala!"*

The green-eyed man's shout was like a slap in the face. The chime in Singe's mind vanished—and with it the scourging pain of Medala's power. He rolled over onto his side, panting and shaking. Medala was on the ground, prostrate before Dah'mir's approach. Ashi kneeled as well, but through watering eyes, Singe could see that her back was rigid with fury. Dah'mir stopped in front of both women, his black robes whispering softly, the dragonshards set into them shimmering softly in the gloom. His presence was like a tangible force in the air and there was the trace of an edge in his voice when he spoke. "Medala, control yourself. I have plans for the wizard and I don't want him damaged beyond use."

The words sent a shiver down Singe's back, but not quite so much as the sight of the powerful kalashtar groveling in the dirt before Dah'mir. "Forgive me!" she begged. "I wouldn't have harmed him! I only wanted to make Ashi understand her proper place."

The pale man frowned slightly and turned his gaze on the kneeling hunter. "Ashi, your obedience to my instructions is a credit to you, but you must show respect to Medala. She has my favor—and the favor of the powers of the Dragon Below as the first of a new line of servants."

"Yes, Dah'mir," said Ashi. Singe saw her big frame cringe. "I mean, yes, Revered!" Her fingers darted to her lips and her forehead in some sort of ritual sign. Dah'mir's eyes flashed.

"Have a care, Ashi! Your service has been outstanding, but there are limits to my patience." He reached down a hand and helped Medala to her feet. The green robes that the kalashtar wore were filthy. Dah'mir spoke a word of simple magic and passed his hand in front of her. The dirt fell away. He took Medala's arm and led her back to the campfire. Medala's face shone with adoration.

Through all of it, Dandra hadn't moved except to follow Dah'mir's movements.

Groaning, Singe forced himself off the ground and back to

her side. There were a few fragments of meat still crushed in his palm. Woodenly, he held another up to Dandra's lips.

I have plans for the wizard and I don't want him damaged beyond use. Singe's belly twisted with more than his hunger—and, he realized, with more than fear for just himself. If Medala was the first of a new line of servants to the Dragon Below, what were Dah'mir's plans for Dandra?

"Leave off, outclanner," Ashi growled. Singe flinched around to stare at the hunter. The big woman was rising, anger on her face—but anger that was, thankfully, not directed at him. She held out a flask. "Her body needs water more than it needs food. Leave off trying to feed her and see that she drinks."

Singe hesitated, then took the flask. Dandra took the water more easily than she took the food. As she drank, Singe glanced back at Ashi. The hunter was glaring at Medala and Dah'mir as they sat by the fire. An idea slid into his mind. He let it brew for a few minutes, turning it back and forth in his mind. After a moment, he said, "Ashi?"

She looked back at him and her mouth curled, the pale rings in her lip catching the light of the fire. "You have nothing to thank me for, outclanner. Dah'mir placed me in charge of you and I do my duty to the Bonetree."

"I wasn't going to thank you," he told her. "You're holding us prisoner, you've kicked me in the stomach, and I think there was a promise to tear out my guts with your hands."

Her teeth clenched. "Dah'mir has forbidden that."

"I'm glad to hear it." Singe drew a deep breath and said, "In Zarash'ak, the things you said about Geth . . ."

"I meant them. He was a good enemy—*rond e reis*, fierce and tough. He didn't deserve to die as he did. Take comfort that he probably drowned quickly."

Singe closed his eyes for a moment, then opened them again. "You're a woman of strange honor, Ashi."

"You don't understand the Bonetree, outclanner," Ashi said harshly. "Our ways are simple. If an enemy deserves my respect, I will give it to him. Death in combat is honest. Murder, torture—those are the weapons of the weak."

"You cut off Natrac's hand."

Her eyes flashed and she lunged forward, slapping him sharply. "Don't make me forget my duty," she seethed, then sat back. "Vennet cut off the half-orc's hand. It was a shame to me."

"You didn't like Vennet," said Singe. Ashi shook her head. Singe paused, then added carefully, "And you don't like Medala either."

She stiffened for a moment before grunting, "The falling man finds the ground. What of it? My duty to the Bonetree comes before anything you can say, outclanner."

"But not a duty to the powers of Khyber? You're hiding something from both Dah'mir and Medala, Ashi."

The hunter froze.

"For all that you insist on calling me 'outclanner,' you know my name," Singe murmured. "You know Geth's and Natrac's. I think you know her name, too." He pointed at Dandra. "But I've noticed that you do the same thing Dah'mir and Medala do—you call her Tetkashtai."

"Medala gave us Tetkashtai's name before we began the hunt," Ashi said stiffly.

"Still, you haven't told Dah'mir or Medala that you also know her by another name. And you didn't exactly jump to tell Dah'mir about that orc."

It had been Fause who'd let mention of their mysterious ally slip to the green-eyed man. Singe had glimpsed anger in Dah'mir's face at mention of the orc's interference, though he'd acted as if it was nothing. The wizard looked up at Ashi. "Why are you holding back?"

Ashi glared at him. "Perhaps it makes me happy to know something that they do not," she said. "We are taught that Dah'mir is all-knowing and infallible, one of the favored servants of the great powers of the Dragon Below—even speaking his name out loud is forbidden among the clan. But when he set Medala, an outclanner, above his people, I doubted. As I doubted when he set Hruucan to lead the hunters after I was sent to follow you."

"So you know that Dah'mir isn't infallible," said Singe. He leaned forward. "And if he wrong about one thing, it might be that he was wrong about something else."

Ashi's eyes narrowed. "I may not like Medala, outclanner," she said, "but if you're trying to turn me against my clan, you will fail. And Dah'mir is the heart of the Bonetree clan. I may doubt, but from the day we're born, we're taught to revere him!"

"From the day you're born?" Singe blinked and twisted to look at Dah'mir. The man had a strangely ageless quality about him, but he was no more than decade older than Singe was himself. "Ashi," he said in mocking disbelief, "maybe you were taught that way, but think—your parents wouldn't have known Dah'mir as anything but a young man!"

Ashi snorted. "Now you're the one who's wrong about something. Did you think Dah'mir was some trickster-priest taking advantage of our beliefs?" She rose. "He *created* the Bonetree. He has shaped and guided the clan for more than ten generations."

For a moment, Singe gaped at her. "What—? How?"

"He's favored by the Dragon Below," said Ashi. "Do you need to know more?"

She turned away as Singe sat back, stunned, his nascent plan of exploiting her dislike for Medala shaken. Ten generations, he thought in wonder. Elves lived that long, and dwarves sometimes too, but even they carried their years in their face and eyes. Dah'mir was neither elf nor dwarf, and his acid-green eyes were as bright as a youth's. One of the undead might exist unchanging for so long, but the undead didn't bask in the light of day as Dah'mir did.

"Twelve bloody moons," he breathed. In all that Dandra had described, he had never thought that they might be facing someone so ancient! Was that the secret of his unnatural presence and his power over the kalashtar? What other secrets, he wondered, lay behind those acid-green eyes? He looked around Ashi.

She was standing less than a pace away, her eyes raised to the sky and the rising moons. Singe followed her gaze—and drew a sharp breath.

Silhouetted against the silver glow of the night sky, circling down to land near the campsite, was a heron, its legs dangling and its long neck folded back on itself. The bird landed beyond the firelight, but he could see that its feathers were black and greasy, When it cocked its head, its eyes flashed green. Singe saw Dah'mir glance toward the bird and give an almost imperceptible nod.

Ashi took a fast step back to Singe and Dandra. "Don't move, outclanner. As you value your life, *don't move!*"

Bonetree hunters burst out of the night all around the campsite, screaming and howling their battle cries. Knives, spears, and clubs flashed. The cultists who had come from Zarash'ak leaped to their feet instantly, stumbling over each other in frightened surprise. They weren't unarmed, though, and they snatched up weapons quickly. Confusion surged across the campsite as they met the hunters' unexpected attack.

Singe looked up at Ashi, standing in front of them, her arms spread wide to let the attackers know that he and Dandra were her prisoners. His rapier and Dandra's spear were strapped across her back. For two days the weapons had been tantalizingly close, but Ashi had never been so distracted as this before! For a moment, Singe gauged his chances of seizing his rapier and making a break for the boats the cultists had drawn up at the river's marshy edge beyond the camp.

Then he looked at the attacking hunters again and let the idea fall away. Five of the eight cultists were already down, skulls smashed in, throats slit, or chests run through. Seeing Dah'mir and Medala still seated calmly by the fireside, one of the cultists attempted to surrender, dropping her weapon and throwing up her hands.

A long knife opened a gash from her chest to her belly. Another cultist went down to the combined attack of two hunters, their clubs rising and falling in horrible rhythm. Fause and the final cultist spun around, back to back, facing the closing ring of hunters.

"Dah'mir!" Fause called desperately as recognition seemed to finally sink into him. "These are your followers! Call them off!"

The green-eyed man shrugged. "I only need one escort, Fause—and unfortunately, the Bonetree tend to be jealous folk."

The cult-leader cursed and raised his hands, trying to cast a prayer to the foul powers he followed. A club spun out of the ring and hit his head with a hard, hollow sound. He staggered—then straightened as another hunter thrust a spear into his body. The last cultist screamed, but the hunters closed in and dragged him to the ground. His screams ended in an ugly, bloody bubbling noise.

Dah'mir rose at last, holding out his hands in blessing. The hunters broke away from their victims to kneel before him. Singe stared.

They were all children, gangling and awkward adolescents—though there was nothing awkward in the way they had wielded their weapons. All displayed tattoos and piercings, just as the adult hunters had. All looked lean and tough. Ashi glanced down at Singe and gave him a thin grin. "The elder hunters were sent in pursuit of Tetkashtai," she said. "The next generation takes their place while they are gone."

Some of the young hunters turned toward him and Singe shivered at the intensity in their blood-spattered faces. Ashi drew her sword and raised it before them. "*Su Drumas!*" she called.

"*Su Darasvhir!*" the hunters shouted back. They spun away from Ashi to raise their weapons to Dah'mir—and to Medala. "*Su Darasvhir!*"

Singe saw Ashi stiffen. He leaned closer toward her. "What is it?" he asked her.

"They've changed since I've been gone," Ashi said. She stared at the hunters as Dah'mir dismissed them. The young men and women moved swiftly, hauling up the bodies of the cultists and dragging them away from the campsite.

"You said Dah'mir has shaped the Bonetree clan," Singe pointed out. "What do you think he's shaping it into?"

"Close your mouth!" the big hunter snapped. She squatted down, her face troubled. Singe hesitated, then shifted a little closer.

"Maybe they're not the ones who've changed," he murmured. Ashi tensed and Singe flinched back in anticipation of a blow, but Ashi didn't move. He slid back again. "While you tracked us to Yrlag and while we were on Vennet's ship—was that the first time you'd been away from the clan?"

"I said close your mouth." Ashi stood. She glared down at

him. "You should start to learn the ways of the Bonetree," she said. "You'll need to."

"What are you talking about?" Singe demanded—but a vile suspicion was already growing in him. "Twelve moons," he cursed in disbelief. "Dah'mir's plans for me . . . he wants to bring me *into* the clan?"

"How did you think he shapes the Bonetree?" growled Ashi. She stalked away, leaving Singe to turn and stare at the savage youths of the clan.

Geth's eyes twitched open to a hot white light that stabbed all the way through into his brain. He whined and squeezed them shut again, but the light pierced his eyelids. He tried to fling up an arm to cover his face, but he couldn't move. Something held his arms at his side. Every muscle and joint in his body ached; every inch of his skin burned. Under the metal of his gauntlet, his right arm felt like it was itching and crawling. His whine rose into an uncontrollable howl. He twisted desperately—and the twisting seemed to shake his entire world.

A gruff voice cursed in words he didn't understand. His world shook a little more, but a shadow cut off the excruciating torment of the light. Geth forced his eyes open.

An orc stood over him, a shroud in one hand and a club in the other.

Geth shouted and tried to writhe away from him, but the orc cursed again, dropped the shroud and the club, and reached for him. "Rest, shifter! Rest or you'll tip the boat!"

Awareness forced itself on Geth. The house in Zarash'ak, Vennet, the cult, the monstrous chuul, the orc . . . Dah'mir's spell. A vague memory of a plunge into foul water. An even more vague memory of something or someone nudging him to the surface. He focused on the orc.

"You saved me," he gasped. Another thought tugged at him. "Natrac!"

He twisted again, looking around. Natrac lay close beside him, pale but breathing slowly in sleep. Both of them lay in the bottom of a flat-bottomed boat. Over the boat's sides, Geth could see the tops of trees and the nodding heads of reeds. The hot light that beat down on him was the sun, sailing across a blinding blue sky. The club the orc had been holding, he realized, was actually an oar of some kind. The shroud was a blanket.

"Where are we?" he croaked. "Where are Singe and Dandra?"

The orc's face tightened. "Your friends were taken upriver by the cult." Geth cried out and tired to sit up. The orc held him back. "Be still!" he commanded.

"My arms," Get moaned. "I can't move my arms!" He struggled to raise his head and look down his body.

"I've bound them," said the orc. "You've already come close to tipping us once before with your thrashing." He eased Geth back down. "Dah'mir's spell infected you with disease, and swallowing the waters of Zarash'ak didn't help you. You're too sick for my skill and knowledge to cure you. I'm taking you to someone who can."

He picked up the blanket and draped it across a kind of frame to make a rough sunshade. The scorching light of the sun vanished. Geth's vision seemed to swim with the plunge back into fevered darkness. "Who are you?" he asked thickly.

"My name is Orshok." The orc's rough hand reached out of sight for a moment, then reappeared cupping a number of knuckle-sized red-purple berries. He held the fingers of his other hand over them and murmured a prayer. Geth felt magic like a sweet breeze swirl around them. Nature's magic.

"A druid," he said. "You're a druid!"

"Rest," said Orshok. He picked a berry out of his hand and placed it in Geth's mouth. The tiny fruit burst on his tongue, filling his mouth with tart-sweet juice. A feeling of ease spread though him, pushing back his fever and aches a little bit. His eyelids drooped . . .

He was tearing the wet meat off a half-cooked chicken carcass when he felt the presence of someone watching him. The hair on his neck and forearms bristling, he whirled around, one hand still clutching the chicken, the other snatching up his sword from the grass beside him.

Both ended up pointed at a man of about his own age, a human with red-brown hair and a beard that was just filling in. The man leaned casually on a heavy spear decorated with a spray of fresh green oak leaves and contemplated the blade and the bird. "I hope you don't get those mixed up while you're eating," he said in a pleasant voice.

Geth didn't move. The other man shrugged. "Don't mind me," he added. "I didn't mean to interrupt."

"You're not," growled Geth. When the man still made no move, he settled back down to the ground, though he made sure to keep one hand free and his sword close. The sack that held his great-gauntlet was nearby as well—he wouldn't have time to don the armored sleeve, but its weight made a decent weapon on its own.

The bearded man moved slowly out from among the trees, deliberately giving the shifter plenty of time to react. Geth's eyes darted around the small clearing, trying to see if he had brought anyone else with him. The forest was thick with the new growth of spring and the shadows were growing deep as evening settled over the valley, but neither growth nor darkness were so dense that he couldn't see through them. The man was alone.

As the stranger settled down on the other side of the small fire, Geth became conscious of how he must look. Chicken juices shone on his face and hands, mingling with the grime of long travel. His thick hair was matted. His clothes were stiff with dirt and a foul stink rose from both them and his body. How long had it been since he washed? He choked off the thought and bit back into the chicken, sharp teeth ripping off a big chunk of flesh. He kept his eyes on the bearded man as he chewed.

"My name's Adolan," the man said after a time.

"Geth," the shifter answered around a mouthful of meat. He looked over the other man's well-worn leather clothing and the rough collar of polished, rune-etched stones that hung around his neck. He swallowed and, in between bites, grunted, "You're a druid?"

Adolan nodded. "I watch over this valley." He twitched his spear toward the forest. "There's a hamlet back that way. Bull Hollow. You might have noticed it?" Geth grunted and Adolan continued. "Some of the farmers on the edge of the Hollow have noticed someone suspicious skulking around the forest. One of them asked me to look into the theft of a couple of chickens."

"Might have been a fox," said Geth, licking his lips.

"Might have been," agreed Adolan. The druid looked at him. "Are you just passing through?"

The question sent a flash of heat through Geth. "Maybe," he rasped angrily, returning his gaze. "Maybe not."

Adolan's eyes seemed to sharpen with such intensity that, even in anger, Geth hesitated. "Yes," he said after a moment. "Just passing through."

"Mind if I ask where you're headed?"

Geth seized a bone in his teeth and pulled it loose from the chicken, then spat it away into the night. "West," he answered. "As deep into the Eldeen as I can."

The druid actually chuckled. "You can't get much deeper into the Eldeen than Bull Hollow—unless you want to turn south and live with the fey in the Twilight Demesne." He fell silent for a moment, then said, "I know you're not from around here. Your voice has the sound of the northern Eldeen in it, though. Is that where you're from?"

Geth's lips twisted. "A long time ago," he said.

To his surprise, Adolan let the matter drop entirely. Geth waited for the inevitable questions—where have you been? what did you do?—but they didn't come. The druid said nothing. After a long silence, Geth looked back at him, then nodded at the fire and the other chicken that was roasting unevenly above it. "Want some?"

Adolan glanced at the plump carcass and Geth could tell he was appraising the way its skin, tufts of singed feathers still clinging to it, was turning black on one side while remaining pale and raw on the other. "Was that the red one or the white one?" he asked.

"Red," said Geth. Adolan nodded.

"That was a fine-looking bird." With nimble fingers, he flipped the chicken on its spit, then produced a knife and sliced a leg free. He settled back and bit into the steaming meat. "Would be better with salt," he said after chewing thoughtfully.

"My chef took it all when he ran off with the chambermaid," Geth said.

Adolan laughed and stripped another mouthful of meat from the leg. Geth found himself laughing as well—and he hadn't laughed since well before the last time he'd bathed. A feeling of peace settled over him and the faint warmth of tentative friendship stirred in his belly as he looked into the fire—

—that rose all around him. He spun and blocked the blow of an Aundairian soldier's sword with his gauntlet, then punched the man in the gut. The blood-smeared mail shirt that the soldier wore soaked up the worst of the blow, though, and he laughed.

He stopped laughing when Geth's sword sliced through his neck. Geth didn't wait for his body to fall, but leaped away, sprinting through the madness that Narath had become, searching for the next Aundairian. He didn't look at the carnage around him. The atrocities. The massacre. Rage gripped him, crushing his heart and snuffing the light in his spirit.

Rage—and shame. He howled as he ran, screaming out names. "Nilda! Coron! Singe! Dew! Treykin! *Frostbrand, answer!*"

More Aundairians fell to his blade and his black gauntlet. He took three at once, stabbing one from behind, gutting another, and crushing the throat of the last with a single punch. Their victim was already beyond his help. Geth left her and ran on.

His head throbbed from the blow that had laid him low, his chest and face were still cold and wet from having lain unconscious in the winter snows of Karrnath. Blood and water had frozen his hair into thick clumps that slowly melted in the heat of the burning town. The flames around him scorched his skin, making him feel like he was burning as well. He was sweating heavily and he ached right down to his bones. He kept going, though, shouting for his friends, for any member of the Frostbrand. Narath seemed to have turned into a maze. Every corner he turned opened onto the same scene of fire and blood. Geth sobbed as he raced through horrors that in only a few short weeks would become infamous throughout the Five Nations . . .

Some part of him knew that the tale of Narath couldn't possibly have reached so far when it was still unfolding around him; another part wondered why he was back in Narath when he had just been in Bull Hollow with Adolan. The rest of him didn't care. He shouted again. *"Frostbrand, answer!"*

He was running through corpses. Faceless. Broken. Bloody. The mass of them dragged at him, pulling him back. He had to force his way forward, as if he was walking against a powerful wind. The dead of Narath just kept piling higher. He started to recognize faces among the corpses, too. Treykin. Dew. Coron. Other mercenaries of the Frostbrand whose names had vanished from his head. Sweating and aching and burning from the inside out, Geth climbed a hill of death. His voice had fallen away to a constant moan.

The faster he tried to climb, the slower his progress. All around him, the corpses began to slide, slipping and running like a slope of loose earth. Geth struggled to stay on his feet, to stay on top of them, but more bodies came at him. Singe slid by to one side. Dandra to the other. Sandar. Natrac.

Red-brown hair flashed. "Adolan!" Geth screamed. He lunged, trying to get to the druid, but Adolan's body just sank down among all the others. Geth dug down through death, desperate to reach him.

Living figures rose above him. Geth looked up as Medalashana, her face drawn tight with madness, swooped close. "Let me take him, Dah'mir!" she shrieked. "I'll shred his mind and lay his thoughts out before you!"

But Dah'mir stood aloof, untouched by the death and fire all around. "Hush, Medala," he said. "We have the one we came for. He's nothing."

The green-eyed man reached out toward Geth. His hand was a scaly claw. As it plunged into Geth's chest, all of the fires of Narath seemed to come together in the shifter's body. Geth howled in agony and toppled into darkness.

CHAPTER

12

He woke up shouting names he hadn't spoken in years. Strong hands grabbed his shoulders, pushing him back down onto rough blankets, and a gruff voice muttered words he didn't understand. Geth thrashed, trying to sit up, to climb out of whatever bed he lay in. The gruff voice rose sharply, grunting more gibberish. Geth picked out one word though: Natrac.

A hand grabbed one of his arms while the weight of a body pinned his other. "Geth! Easy!" called Natrac's voice. "We're safe. Relax!"

Geth squeezed his eyes shut, then opened them again. The weight across him was the half-orc, though it took Geth another heartbeat to be certain. Natrac's face was drawn. The fine red coat and gray tunic he had worn on Vennet's ship were gone, probably too fouled to be salvaged. He wore rough leather clothes like those Orshok had: patched pants and a pale shirt with sleeves that ended just below his shoulders.

His right arm ended at the wrist. The burned and angry flesh had been replaced by skin that was still soft and smooth from magical healing.

The sight of Natrac's stump shocked him into relaxation. The pressure on his shoulders eased and the gruff voice grunted again—this time in approval. Geth twisted his head around to look up at the speaker. It was an old orc woman, her gray-green face deeply wrinkled and speckled with coarse white hairs, her tusks dull and yellow. In spite of her age, though, her limbs were thick with muscle. She patted his shoulders and said something else in what Geth guessed was Orc. Natrac answered her in the same language. The old woman patted Geth's shoulders again, then stood and stepped away from him.

Geth looked around. He lay on a low blanket-covered platform in a hut built from rushes and hides. The old woman picked up a shallow bowl from a packed dirt floor strewn with more rushes and waddled to a doorway that had been hung with a hide. When she brushed it aside, the red light of sunset flashed through.

"She'll fetch Orshok," said Natrac. He rolled off Geth. "How do you feel?"

The shifter lay back, taking stock of his body. "Good," he answered after a moment. He was slightly weak and ravenously hungry. There was an ache in his chest, but the pain was spiritual rather than physical, the aftermath of the fevered dreams that had ravaged him. He drew a long, shuddering breath against the images—some half-remembered delusions, some all too real—and sat up.

He was naked under the blankets except for Adolan's collar of stones. Natrac reached out and grabbed his clothes from on top of a chest. They looked and smelled like they had been washed. There was the sour odor of illness in the air, though. Geth's skin felt damp and he realized abruptly that the old orc had been washing him. He looked up Natrac.

"Where are we? How long have I been sick?"

"We're in an orc village called Fat Tusk," the half-orc told him. He sat back, his amputated arm cradled in his lap. "From what Orshok tells me, it's been five nights since you tried to rescue me from Vennet and the cult—and he ended up rescuing both of us from someone he'll only describe as the 'Servant of Madness.' "

"Dah'mir," Geth growled. "Five nights? Rat, Natrac! Do you remember what we told you about Dah'mir and the Bonetree clan?"

Natrac grimaced and thrust the stump of his arm forward. "*Dagga*, I remember," he said.

Geth flushed and words stumbled on his tongue. "Natrac, you shouldn't have gotten caught up in this. Vennet was using you as bait. He drugged you on the ship to keep you quiet, then when we discovered he followed the Dragon Below and escaped—" His fists knotted in his clothes. "I can't make it up to you."

The half-orc waved away his apology—or tried to. There was no hand for him gesture with. His face twisted in frustration and anger. "You came for me, Geth. What more could I have asked for?" His remaining hand curled tight. "But by Dol Dorn's mighty fist, I swear that Vennet is going to wish he killed me outright! That bastard should have known better than to leave me alive!"

There was a hardness to Natrac that he hadn't shown onboard *Lightning on Water*. The façade of the blustering merchant had been stripped away to reveal a raw fire underneath. It would have taken a lot more than just bluster, Geth realized, to deal with the thugs Natrac had brought onboard Vennet's ship. He wondered what the half-orc had done in his younger days.

"I'll stand with you, Natrac," he promised. "There's a lot that Vennet needs to answer for."

He held out a fist. Natrac bashed his fist against it, knuckle to knuckle. *"Kuv dagga!"* he said in harsh agreement. He looked at Geth. "Singe only told us part of your story on the ship. I've told Orshok what I know, but there's more to it. What did Singe leave out?"

The hide covering the door flipped back and Orshok stepped into the hut. "Wait, and tell us all," the young druid said in his thick accent. He nodded at Geth's clothes. "If you feel well enough to walk, get dressed and come with me."

There was apprehension on Orshok's face. Geth scrambled to his feet and pulled on his clothes quickly. "I feel fine, tak to you," he said. "What happened? I remember Dah'mir casting a spell on me—and then waking up in your boat."

"You stumbled into the water," Orshok told him. "The Servant of Madness must have thought you were already dead. I was close enough to go back and pull you both to safety."

"Then twice tak—that's two times you saved me," said Geth as he pulled his vest on over his shirt. "What were you doing in

Zarash'ak anyway? When you saved me from the chuul, you said you were only supposed to be watching the house."

"My teacher had a vision that the Servant would go to Zarash'ak and sent me to watch what he did there." Orshok's gray-green skin flushed dark. "When I saw that you were in danger, my hatred for the cults of the Dragon Below moved me more than my teacher's instructions. I couldn't stand by any longer."

"I'm glad you didn't." Geth nodded to the door of the hut. "Tak to your teacher as well. You said curing me was beyond your skill. Was she the one who broke the disease?"

The young druid looked confused. Natrac said something briefly in Orc and Orshok's eyes widened—then narrowed. "Meega was only tending to you, Geth," he said. "She isn't my teacher—and it wasn't my teacher who cured you."

Geth paused in the act of buckling on his belt. The scabbard was empty, his Karrnathi sword lost in the water below Zarash'ak, but the pouch on the belt's other side was still intact. His great-gauntlet was sitting on the chest where the rest of his clothes had been. It would need some time to check the straps and plates—he had already decided to leave it for now.

"Who cured me then?" he asked Orshok.

A loud voice shouted from outside in Orc. Geth caught Orshok's name, but didn't understand the rest. The voice's owner didn't sound pleased, though. Orshok shouted back and glanced at both Geth and Natrac. He threw back the hide covering on the hut's door.

The village of Fat Tusk stood on a low rise that pushed up from the reeds of the marsh, a flat hill that was large enough to hold a half dozen small huts and one large longhouse. In the twilight of the day, orcs were stirring—drawing water, preparing food, washing, even praying. In front of the longhouse, a handful of squat-bodied orc children tussled and screamed at each other. Closer to hand, however, three big adult orcs stood around a blazing firepit, all of them watching the hut. Orshok called to them as he ducked through the doorway. Their eyes narrowed slightly as Geth emerged.

But they grew even narrower a moment later, and the face of

the biggest of the three screwed up into a glower. Geth glanced over his shoulder to see Natrac stepping out of the hut. Orshok's voice took on a frustrated tone, but the biggest orc spat a few harsh words over top of him. Natrac flushed. Geth leaned close to him as they approached the fire. "What did he say?"

"Keep the half-breed back, I'm through speaking with it," translated Natrac. His eyes flashed in the firelight. "Full-blooded orcs don't always take kindly to half-orcs."

The apprehension that had been in Orshok's face was quickly turning into anger. "Geth," he said, "meet Krepis. The druid who cured you."

Geth stepped into the circle of firelight and studied Krepis— just as the orc was studying him. Krepis stood at least the width of a hand above everyone else around the fire. His shoulders were broader and his features heavier as well. The teeth of a crocodile were strung around his neck, six white points gleaming on either side of a larger disc of red-stained wood. He looked like he was about Geth's own age, older than Orshok, but definitely younger than Natrac. Geth bit back anger at his dismissal of the half-orc and glanced at Orshok.

"How do I say tak to him in Orc?" he asked.

"I talk you language," Krepis grunted before Orshok could answer. His accent was even thicker than the younger orc's. His voice was arrogant. He slapped his chest. "You talk to me!"

Geth looked him straight in the eye. "Then tak, Krepis," he said with all the respect he could muster. He bent his head. "Tak for curing me."

Krepis stood tall, puffing out his chest with pride—at least until Geth's shirt collar fell open as the shifter straightened. Krepis's eyes seemed to bulge and the orcs who stood with him stiffened. Krepis snapped at Orshok in Orc once again. The younger druid's face turned dark. Geth glanced at Natrac.

"He wants to know why you're still wearing the stones," the half-orc said.

Geth reached up to his open collar. His hand encountered the stones of Adolan's collar.

"Rat!" he hissed. He tugged his shirt closed again and stepped closer to Orshok. "What about the stones?" he asked. "How does Krepis know about them?"

"He saw them when he was breaking your fever," said Orshok. He had to try and squeeze his answer around Krepis's continued tirade. "They're sacred, a holy sign of our tradition. He wanted to take them away, but I wouldn't let him."

On all sides of them, the village had gone quiet as orcs watched and listened to the big druid. The more Krepis ranted, the darker Orshok flushed.

"Ignore him," he said, his voice strained. "Just tell us all what's going on."

Geth's eyes had narrowed, however. "Wait," he said. "Your tradition?" He reached up and put his fingers under the stones, holding the collar out boldly. "You're Gatekeepers?"

As Orshok nodded and Krepis sneered, it seemed to Geth that he could almost hear Adolan proudly recounting the history of his sect—telling how the Gatekeepers were first druids and how the first Gatekeepers had been orcs. Geth's hand fell away.

"The collar was given to me by a Gatekeeper," he said, "after a hunter of the Bonetree clan struck him down. His name was Adolan. He was the guardian of the Bull Hole in the Eldeen Reaches."

"Bull Hole?" Krepis spat. He jerked his head at Natrac. "Old half-breed told this story. I not hear of Bull Hole. Druids of Eldeen Reach fallen from old ways. Not Gatekeepers anymore."

Geth drew a harsh breath. "Adolan *died* because he was Gatekeeper!"

"Stones belong to true Gatekeepers!" Krepis grabbed for the wooden disk strung around his neck together with the crocodile teeth and held it up so Geth could see it. There was a symbol on this disk, a symbol identical to one of the symbols on Adolan's collar. "Belong to orcs. If druid of Eldeen had stones, must be stealing. Must be thief!"

Blood burned in Geth's cheeks. With a roar that echoed across marshes, he dove over the fire, hands grabbing for Krepis. His ancient heritage flooded him as he leaped—a feeling of invincibility surged in him. He slammed into Krepis, knocking the big orc flat to the ground.

"By Tiger's blood, you take that back!" he howled. Crouched on top of the orc, he twisted and drove a knee into Krepis's belly. "Adolan was as true to his faith as—"

Krepis got an arm free and hammered a punch straight up into Geth's jaw. The shifter shrugged it off, bared his teeth, and grabbed Krepis's thick arm with both hands, wrenching it hard. Krepis bellowed in pain.

Then the druid's cronies darted in and hauled Geth off him. Shifting might have made Geth tougher, but it didn't make him any stronger. He thrashed and fought as they tried to get a grip on him, lashing out with fist and foot against their grabbing hands. There was a rip as his shirt tore and for a moment Geth spun free—until Krepis rose up behind him and grabbed for him with both hands. Geth tried to twist away but Krepis's meaty fingers closed on the pouch at his side, yanking the shifter off balance. Geth fell heavily. The pouch tore open.

Dandra's psicrystal tumbled out and skittered across the ground, glittering yellow-green in the firelight. The eyes of one of the other orcs lit up with greed. He snatched at the shining crystal.

The instant that his hand clenched around it, his red eyes opened wide and his body stiffened. Geth gasped as a droning sound like a hundred, disembodied voices speaking at once pulsed on the air and the firepit exploded upward into a seething white pillar of flame. Krepis—all of the orcs in Fat Tusk—froze in terrified awe.

"Il-Yannah's light!" sobbed the orc clutching the psicrystal. His voice soared up into a crazed shriek. "A body! I have a body again!"

"Grandmother Wolf," breathed Geth. *"Tetkashtai?"*

The orc spun around. "You!" Tetkashtai raged through his tusked mouth. "Where's Dandra? What's happened to Dandra?" The disembodied chorus of her power throbbed. A shower of sparks burst out of the towering fire.

One of the memories that Dandra had shared with him and Singe flashed in Geth's mind: a vision of her hand closing on the yellow-green crystal in the darkness of Dah'mir's terrible laboratory, a rush of power as Tetkashtai exploded in her mind and the connection between kalashtar and crystal was restored.

He'd caught the crystal with his gauntlet and stuffed it straight into his pouch. He'd never touched the crystal, but Dandra had grasped it just as the orc had—with naked flesh. Tetkashtai didn't need Dandra. She could forge a connection with whoever held the crystal.

But even with Dandra's determined will to control her, Tetkashtai had been half-mad. Without that strength of mind . . .

Not even pausing to think, Geth lunged at the orc and grabbed his arm, twisting it hard enough to hear bones grind. The orc's voice rose in a high-pitched scream—that dropped into a deep shout as his fingers opened and the crystal fell to the dirt.

The fire sank down to glowing coals.

Geth thrust the orc away quickly and whipped off his belt, hastily sliding the pouch free. With trembling fingers, he turned it inside out like a clumsy mitten around his hand, then grabbed the crystal and tugged the pouch back up around it.

He could almost imagine that he heard a thin wail of despair from Tetkashtai as he pulled the drawstrings of the pouch closed. The orc village was utterly silent around him. Orshok and Natrac were staring at him in astonishment, Krepis in rage. For a long moment, no one moved, not even the orc children.

Then an orc rose from in front of one of the huts. He was old—the oldest person, Geth was certain, he'd ever seen in his life. He moved painfully and leaned heavily on a staff with a crooked end, much like the staff Orshok had carried in Zarash'ak. His hair and beard were pure white; his gray-green skin looked as fine and brittle as parchment. Everyone in the village turned to him as he hobbled forward.

He paused beside the orc—now whimpering and clutching his wrist—who had picked up the crystal. The old man batted his hand away and examined his wrist, then stretched out his fingers and murmured a word of nature's magic. The younger orc's breath caught in his throat and he gasped with relief. The old orc turned to look at Geth.

His left eye was as white as his beard, but his right eye was bright and alert. "You have a strong grip, shifter!" he said without any trace of an accent.

As if his words had opened a floodgate, sound rushed back into Fat Tusk. The orcs of the village clustered together to babble in amazement while both Orshok and Krepis converged on the old orc, each trying to talk over the other. The old orc's good eye, however, was fixed on Geth.

Natrac stepped up beside Geth. "What was that?" he gasped.

"That was what Singe didn't tell you about on Vennet's ship," the shifter said grimly. He stood still as the old orc approached and planted his staff in front of him. Krepis and Orshok fell silent, taking up positions behind him, while he considered Geth. His gaze lingered on the collar of stones and Geth stood up a little straighter.

The old orc nodded. "My name is Batul," he said finally. "I'm the teacher of these two arguing idiots." His staff flicked back twice, faster than Geth would have expected, to crack against Krepis's shins and Orshok's toes. The younger druid hopped painfully, though Krepis only grimaced. Batul nodded at the pouch in Geth's hand. "Open that," he said. "Let me have a look at that crystal."

Geth opened the pouch again and held it out so that Batul could peer inside. The elderly druid's eye narrowed. He moved a hand through the air and spoke another prayer. For a moment, it seemed that the night around the pouch grew sharper. Geth could feel a tingling around his hand. Batul, however, drew his eyebrows together and shook his head. The tingling in Geth's hand vanished.

"It's not an aberration," Batul said, half to himself, "though by the Ring of Siberys I'd swear it's nothing natural either." He looked up at Geth. "I've heard parts of your story," he said. "I'd like to hear it all."

Geth closed the pouch once more, knotted the drawstrings tight, and told him. Batul didn't move at all through the long tale, but listened intently. Orshok, Natrac, and Krepis didn't move either, though Krepis's face ran through a range of angry glowers. When Geth had finished, the big druid reached out and smacked Orshok in the back of the head with a curse. "Stupid!" he snarled. "Bring Bonetree hunting for us now!"

Batul closed his eyes and sighed, then opened them again, his good eye fixing itself on Geth. "Has Orshok told you why he was in Zarash'ak?"

Geth nodded. Batul grunted and hobbled to a nearby log set as a seat around the firepit. He settled himself on it and looked up at Geth.

"Visions and dreams have haunted me since I lost this," he said, tapping his cheek under his milky right eye. "For more than a month, they've hinted at danger to Fat Tusk—danger that would come from Zarash'ak when the green-eyed Servant of Madness appeared at a certain place there. I tried to protect my tribe by sending Orshok to watch, hoping to learn what was coming and avert it. Instead, I've drawn us into your struggle."

"I don't understand," said Geth. "Why would Dah'mir send the Bonetree here? He has Dandra!"

"It seems to me that maybe Dandra isn't what the Servant of Madness wants." Batul pointed his staff at the pouch in Geth's hands. "If Dandra and Tetkashtai are incomplete without each other, Dah'mir has only one half of the whole."

"Grandmother Wolf." Geth stiffened, his grasp on the pouch tightening. "I'll leave."

"If Dandra had fled after visiting Bull Hollow, the Bonetree hunters would still have come on her trail," Batul said flatly. "Even if you leave now, you've still been to Fat Tusk. We could abandon Fat Tusk and the hunters would still try to track down each member of the tribe to find you." His face tightened. "There are many orc tribes and human clans living across the Shadow Marches, Geth. At least half of them follow the Dragon Below. Even among so many, the Bonetree clan is one of the worst. What you describe of Bull Hollow is not the worst they can do—or have done."

"Why not stand up to the Bonetree then, teacher?" asked Orshok. Batul glanced at the young druid. Orshok stood tall and said fiercely, "We should join Geth. He's come this far. He's faced the Servant of Madness. He's fought the Bonetree clan and dolgaunts. If we put our support behind him, we'll be freeing

Dandra and Singe, saving Fat Tusk, and striking a hard blow against both the Bonetree and the Dragon Below."

The suggestion brought a sudden, daring hope to Geth's heart. Krepis, however, groaned loudly and spat out a rant in Orc.

It ended in a taut silence between all three druids, with Krepis and Orshok glaring at each other, their tusks thrust out in challenge, as Batul stroked his beard thoughtfully. Geth turned to Natrac. The half-orc's face was pale. "What did Krepis say?" Geth asked him.

"He asked if Orshok was deliberately trying to make sure Batul's visions came true," Natrac said softly. "First Orshok brought us to Fat Tusk, now he's proposing to stage a raid that will certainly bring danger to the tribe. Attacking the Bonetree clan is suicide." Natrac swallowed. "Krepis's suggestion is that they appease Dah'mir by handing us over to him."

Geth ground his teeth together and looked back to Batul. "If you're thinking of taking Krepis's suggestion, remember that Natrac was only bait. Whatever happens to me, I'd appreciate it if you saw him to safety."

Natrac's mouth dropped open, but Batul's eyebrows rose. "That's brave," he said.

"I'm not brave," growled Geth. "I like Orshok's idea a whole lot better. It would be good if you picked that one." He glared at Krepis. "Tak again," he spat at him.

Krepis stepped forward, a snarl curling his lips.

Batul's staff rose in-between the orc and the shifter. "No," the old druid said. "No fighting between us. We'll either help Geth or send him on to the Bonetree."

"Which then, teacher?" asked Orshok.

Batul lowered his staff. "A test," he said slowly. "Let Geth's own actions decide."

Geth crossed his arms. "That sounds good to me."

"And to me," said Natrac. He moved to stand behind Geth. The shifter twisted around to glare at him. Natrac glared back at him and shook his head. "You came for me, Geth. I'm going to stand by you."

He held out his fist. Geth stared at it—then bashed his own

fist against it, and turned back to Batul. "We'll try your test together," he said.

Batul nodded in approval. "Fetch boats," he said to Orshok. "They'll cross Jhegesh Dol."

The color drained out of the young druid's face and he gasped something in Orc that sounded like a curse. Batul cut him off sharply, dismissing him with a gesture. Krepis gave both Geth and Natrac a look of deep satisfaction before Batul dismissed him as well. The old orc turned to them with a stern face. "Prepare yourselves," he said somberly, then hobbled away, leaving them alone by the dying fire.

Geth looked at Natrac. "What's Jhegesh Dol?" he asked quickly. There was a sudden hollow in the pit of his stomach.

"I don't know," said Natrac. "But the words sound like Orc. A *dol* is just a place, a structure or even a stretch of marsh. *Jhegesh...*" He shook his head. "There's a word like it, though: *jegez.*"

"What does that mean?"

"Cut."

Singe was trying to feed Dandra again when she drew a sharp breath and froze, turning her head to fix her gaze in the distance. "Tetkashtai!" she croaked. Her hand rose to clutch at her chest, at the place where her crystal had hung.

The wizard's heart skipped as he stared at her. He glanced around, checking to see that neither Dah'mir nor Medala was anywhere nearby, then leaned closed. "Dandra?" he whispered. His voice almost stuck in his throat. "Twelve moons, Dandra, can you hear me? Dah'mir has some sort of hold on you again. You've got to fight him!"

She didn't react at all. Before Singe could even speak again, she relaxed and started breathing normally. Her head swung back around and once again she was staring with placid fascination at Dah'mir. Her hand fell back to her lap. Singe's fingers curled tight and he held back a curse of frustration.

Was she trying to fight off Dah'mir's control? He was certain that if she was capable of it, she was trying! Why had she called

Tetkashtai's name then, he wondered, and reached for her lost crystal? A reflex, maybe, an attempt to draw on the presence's power—but she had peered off into the distance as if there had been something out there. Singe looked out into the night. There was nothing that he could see. That didn't mean, though, that there wasn't something that Dandra, even through Dah'mir's hold on her, might be able to sense. Like the psicrystal.

The journey through the marshes had disoriented him, but there was one thing he knew: Zarash'ak lay to the south, under the shining haze of the Ring of Siberys. If Geth was dead, the crystal would be in or under the City of Stilts, either resting with his body or looted and sold off as nothing more than a pretty bauble.

Dandra had stared off to the west—and Singe couldn't imagine that the crystal would find its way inland unless Geth was alive and carrying it.

"Twelve moons," he breathed, hope flickering in his chest. "Twelve bloody moons!"

His elation was shattered by the screaming battle cry of the Bonetree hunters, and a sudden, brief clash of blades. Singe whirled around, but the fight was already over. Ashi was crouched over the quivering, wounded body of one of the young hunters. Her sword was drawn. So was his. There was blood only on Ashi's blade, however. She reached down and wiped her sword on the young hunter's shirt, then turned her back on him as the other hunters moved forward and surrounded their wounded comrade. To Singe's surprise, Dah'mir and Medala, seated by the fire, did nothing more than glance up before returning to their conversation.

The young hunters' glares and mutters followed Ashi as she stalked across the camp to fling herself down beside Singe and Dandra. She pulled a whetstone out of a pouch and began stroking it along the blade of her sword as if utterly unconcerned by what had taken place. Singe could see her hands trembling though.

"What was that?" he asked softly. He had discovered that unlike Ashi the young hunters spoke only their own language, though they seemed to understand Dah'mir's commands well enough, reacting as much to the green-eyed man's dominating presence as to his actual words. He had no fear that they would overhear him but Medala's hearing sometimes seemed uncanny and he had no desire to attract her attention.

"Any hunter can make a challenge for the huntmaster's blade," said Ashi. "If they're successful, they become the new huntmaster. That pup has been working himself up to challenging me for the last two days. He won't be the last." She growled as she worked at the sword's edge. "Stupid children. I don't know if they honestly think they can lead the hunters or if they just want the sword!"

"Why would they just want the sword?"

"Because they're greedy. By tradition, the huntmaster carries the best weapon in the clan. No one else is allowed to even touch it."

"I remember that," said Singe. "You threatened to disembowel me when I unsheathed it."

"Don't let anyone hear that you did," Ashi said, "or I don't think even Dah'mir would be able to save you. You've touched the blade and that puts you above everyone else in the Bonetree except me." She held up the sword, turning it so that firelight flashed on the polished metal. After a moment, she lowered it and looked at Singe. "On Vennet's ship, you called this a sentinel's honor blade."

"An honor blade of the Sentinel Marshals of House Deneith," Singe corrected her. "The patriarch of House Deneith would have given it to a Sentinel Marshal in recognition of some great deed. They're rare, maybe one or two are awarded in a generation. This was the weapon of a hero." He glanced up and saw a blank look in her eyes. "What is it?"

"I don't know what a Sentinel Marshal is," Ashi muttered.

Singe blinked in surprise. "I guess maybe they don't get into the depths of the Shadow Marches too often," he said. "The Sentinel Marshals enforce justice across the borders of kingdoms. When a criminal tries to flee from a kingdom to escape the king's troops, a Sentinel Marshal will pursue him." He pointed at the motto on the honor blade. *"Words teach and spirit guides* is a Sentinel Marshal saying. The words of the law teach and direct them, but the spirit of the law guides them in their duties. Because they're members of House Deneith, ancient treaties put them outside of the laws of any one kingdom." He gave Ashi a level look. "You know what House Deneith is, don't you?"

"A clan from beyond the Marches," said Ashi. "A clan with magic in its blood."

"That's one way of putting it," Singe agreed with a nod. "House Deneith carries the Mark of Sentinel—magic of protection—the way that Vennet's house, Lyrandar, carries the Mark of Storm."

"Do all children of Deneith have this Mark?" Ashi asked curiously.

"Children never bear a Mark," Singe told her. "If someone carries a dragonmark, it appears as they enter adulthood. Sometimes they grow larger and become more powerful—the rarest and most powerful appear fully formed—but usually they're small. Most members of a dragonmarked house don't carry a mark at all."

Ashi actually looked disappointed. Singe cocked his head and looked at her sideways. "Ashi?"

The big hunter shrugged, then extended the honor blade. "Two generations ago, an outclanner was taken captive in the marshes. I've heard that he was so badly wounded that the hunters wanted to kill him, but Dah'mir insisted that he be kept alive and brought into the Bonetree—as you will be. The outclanner's name was Kagan. If he had another name, it isn't remembered. Kagan couldn't fight anymore, but there was still enough man in him to bring many children into the clan." She twisted the sword. "His weapon was so fine that the huntmaster claimed it."

Singe stared at the sword, then at her. "You're saying that there's House Deneith blood in the Bonetree clan?"

Ashi grimaced and shook her head. "If Kagan was a member of your House Deneith, his blood in the Bonetree is thin," she said. "The elders say that after a few years, Kagan went mad and managed to kill all of the children he had sired—except one." She smiled softly. "The elders claim it was the will of the Dragon Below that he grew up to become the longest-lived huntmaster to ever lead the Bonetree hunters."

"Ner?" asked Singe.

She nodded.

"Did he have any children?"

Ashi looked up at him.

"Twelve moons!" Singe spat. "You?"

Ashi nodded again.

Singe sat back, stunned. After a moment, he asked, "Do you carry the Mark of Sentinel?"

"It would be the only way to know for certain if I had the blood of House Deneith, wouldn't it?"

"Yes," admitted Singe.

"Then I have no clan but the Bonetree," Ashi said. She slid the honor blade back into its sheath.

The orc-crafted boats skimmed through black water so still that it mirrored the night sky. Thick strands of reeds and grass made clouds; the trees that grew up through the water were like gnarled pillars pressed down by the weight of the sky above.

The boats carried no lights. Like shifters, orcs could see well in the dark. Geth sat in the bow of Orshok's flat-bottomed craft, Natrac in Krepis's. Batul squatted between the half-orc and the big druid to keep the peace. No one spoke. Batul had forbidden it.

The clouds of reed and grass grew broader, the stretches of open water narrower. Finally Batul spoke a word in Orc, and Krepis and Orshok guided the boats toward a grassy crest. Geth felt the wood underneath him crunch over solid ground.

"Out," said Batul. "We're here."

Geth glanced at the sky. It was, he guessed, roughly the middle of the night: the thin crescents of three of the twelve moons had already dipped below the horizon and the full, pale orange disk of the moon Olarune was rising to its zenith. He picked up the long staff with the angled crook at the end, the same as Orshok's and Batul's own, which was all the old druid would permit him as a weapon. Natrac had one, too. "It's a traditional orc marsh tool," the half-orc had muttered before they'd climbed into the boats. "A hunda stick. It's a probe, a support, a weapon . . ."

"What the hook on the end for?" Geth had grunted.

"Catching snakes," Natrac had answered.

Geth missed his gauntlet and sword. He even missed the paired axes he had wielded in Bull Hollow after he had put the gauntlet away in rejection of his past, but the little hamlet seemed more distant than Narath now.

He leaped lightly onto land, then held the boat so Orshok could clamber out. Natrac tried to do the same, but ended up slipping halfway into the water, thrown off balance because he had only one hand to pull with. It earned him a sneer from Krepis. "City-born half-breed."

Natrac's remaining hand tightened on his hunda. Batul grunted at them both.

When they were all on solid ground, Batul led them forward. Geth looked around as they walked. Under the light of the moons and the Ring of Siberys, the marsh was still. It also stretched almost completely empty for nearly as far as he could see. The only feature that stood out was a lone tree, twisted and dead.

Batul stopped under the shadow of the tree and stared ahead across the desolate marsh. After a moment, he spoke. "The Gatekeepers were created to defend the Shadow Marches against magical invasion from Xoriat, the realm of madness. For thousands of years, we waited and we trained. When the invasion finally came, though, even we weren't ready. Our tribes were devastated. The hobgoblin empire of Dhakaan was beaten back. The daelkyr, the foul leaders of the hordes of Xoriat, held the Marches in their fingers until orc and hobgoblin, Gatekeeper and Dhakaan, came together to drive them back and close the pathways to Xoriat." He stretched out a hand, sweeping it across the landscape before them. "Nine thousand years ago, before it was torn apart and its master put to the sword, this place was a daelkyr stronghold. Jhegesh Dol."

Geth studied the marsh. The only sign that a stronghold of any kind might once have stood here were a few large, scattered dark rocks. The grass and reeds of the marsh looked the same as anywhere else. The wind that blew over them smelled no different. The shifter glanced at Batul. "All we have to do is cross this?" he asked.

"Dagga." The old druid pointed. Geth followed his gesture; in the distance, he could make out the shape of another dead tree. "We will wait for you there. Cross Jhegesh Dol by dawn and Fat Tusk will fight with you."

Geth noticed that the orc didn't bother to mention the alternative. He glanced at Natrac. "Ready?"

The half-orc nodded. Geth took a breath and stepped out past the dead tree.

Nothing happened. He walked a few paces more. There was still nothing. He twisted around. Natrac was right behind him, looking as puzzled as he felt. Batul, Orshok, and Krepis had turned away from the dead tree and were pacing back toward the boats. "Batul!" he shouted. "Is this a trick? Nothing—"

Natrac sucked in a sudden, sharp breath and terror settled over his face as he stared beyond Geth. The shifter whirled back around.

The marsh was empty no longer. A misshapen fortress, cold and black, rose above them.

CHAPTER

13

'W'here did *that* come from?" Geth growled in disbelief.

Natrac shook his head. "I don't know! One moment there was nothing and the next . . ." He swallowed and said thinly, "It happened when you turned around. When you took your eyes of the marsh. There are legends about what orc tribes and dragon-shard prospectors have found deep in the Shadow Marches. Old ghosts from the dark times of the Daelkyr War."

"There are legends about the deep forests in the Eldeen Reaches, too," Geth told him, a chill on his skin. He craned his neck back, looking up at the fortress. It was a hideous thing. The black stones that it had been built from were rough and irregular yet shone slick in the moonlight, as if grease or fat had been rubbed into them. High up on the fortress walls were tall windows that were no wider than his palm. Higher still, narrow platforms and towers jutted out, like vile growths. The battlements at the very top of the walls were jagged with blades set into the stone.

The fortress sprawled out to either side of him and Natrac, but directly in front of them was a gate, tall and narrow like the windows, set with blades like the high battlements. "We can't go around it," said Geth. He jerked his head at the gates. "I think we're supposed to go through."

Natrac nodded in reluctant agreement.

The blades that covered the gates looked dull and weathered, but Geth didn't feel like taking the chance of touching them. He and Natrac set the butts of their hundas against a flat space on one gate and leaned hard on the stout wood, pressing until the great gate swung open enough for them to slip through.

A rank stench of blood engulfed them. Natrac doubled over, retching at the smell. Geth clenched his teeth, biting down on his tongue, and fought the urge to do the same. Instead, he forced his head up and looked around them. The moonlight that bled through the open door made a tenuous silver path through a great, shadowy hall. Even away from the sliver of moonlight, though, there was enough light for him to see clearly. He almost wished that he couldn't.

Every part of the walls was decorated with blades and spikes. Empty torch sconces were formed from jagged swords of strange design. Knives made fantastic pinwheels on the walls. Halberds and other pole arms were bound in ranks around columns, their heads jutting out like sharp-edged frills. Doorjambs and archways wore crowns of iron spikes. High above, the ceiling was shingled in the overlapping blades of battleaxes.

The brown and black of long dried blood stained every surface.

Geth turned around, staring. "Grandmother Wolf," he murmured. The grating sound of Natrac's retching filled the air, echoing off the cold, hard metal. His whisper and even the soft scuff of his feet rose to join the cacophony. There was something else as well, though. He froze and gestured for Natrac to do the same. The half-orc wiped his mouth and staggered upright. They stood still and listened.

The echoes of their intrusion died out. For a moment there was silence—then a faint heart-wrenching scream of pain burst out from some unseen distance. Geth spun again, trying to locate the origin of the ghostly sound, but it seemed to come from everywhere at once. It rose and broke, falling away into a series of wordless, anguished sobs.

"Mercy of Dol Arrah, what was that?" gasped Natrac.

"It was the sound of someone with their tongue cut out," said Geth grimly.

The great hall narrowed ahead, shrinking down slightly to become a tall corridor that seemed to lead in the direction they wanted to go. Geth pointed his hunda silently. They crossed the hall and entered the corridor, both of them moving with swift stealth. Doors that bristled with clusters of long, tooth-like arrowheads lined the corridor, but neither Geth nor Natrac glanced at them, instead driving forward in unspoken agreement to get out of the fortress as quickly as possible. Geth's gut tightened with every step, though. It couldn't be that easy, he thought.

It wasn't. The corridor ended in another great chamber. At its far end stood a pair of metal-clad doors. To either side of them, stairs swept up, meeting at a broad landing and a dark archway. Natrac leaped forward to grab eagerly for the handle of one of the doors. Geth threw himself at the half-orc, holding him back. "Wait!" he ordered, and bent to examine the handles.

Long, knife-edge blades lined the inside of them. Anyone grasping the handles to open the doors would likely lose several fingers. Natrac hissed and clenched his hand quickly. Geth reached out with the crooked end of his hunda, hooking it around the handle and giving an experimental pull.

Nothing happened. The doors were locked or barred from the other side. Geth released his hunda—the wood now deeply scored from the blades in the door handle—and glanced at the stairs. "Looks like we're going up."

The room at the top of the stairs was darker than the hall and corridor below and it lacked the bizarre bladed ornamentation of the fortress's lower level. Geth wasn't certain he found that comforting. The upper room was cold and stark. If it had been an alley, he wouldn't have walked down it without a sword in his hand.

"Can you feel it?" Natrac whispered. "There's been murder here."

"More than murder, I think," muttered Geth. There was another corridor. They moved down it cautiously.

Natrac heard the whispers first. Geth felt him stiffen and turned to glance at him. The half-orc touched his hunda stick to an ear. Geth cocked his head and listened. After a moment, he heard the whispers, too. They were like a gentle wind blowing through the forest, each rustling leaf creating its own quiet sound. Leaves didn't sound so frightened or desperate, though.

Most of the whispers were the grunting, snuffling sounds of Orc. Mixed in among them were hints of another, harsher language—Goblin, Geth guessed. He looked Natrac. "Can you make out what they're saying?"

"They're begging for release," the half-orc said, his voice shaking. "They're in pain. They want to die." He pressed his lips together. "I don't hear any human voices."

"There wouldn't be," Geth pointed out. "There were no humans around to witness the Daelkyr War."

Out of the corner of his eye, he saw something shift in the shadows. He held back the urge to leap toward it and grabbed Natrac's arm. "Keep moving," he said tightly. The half-orc obeyed without question, though Geth could see his eyes darting around as they hastened on.

The whispers stayed with them. So did the shapes in the shadows, except that soon they weren't just in the shadows anymore. Geth staggered to a sudden stop as a pale orc, all color leached out of it, seemed to flow out of the very stones of the wall—he could see the corridor ahead through the filmy substance of its body. The orc's mouth moved in a pleading whisper and it reached out to Geth. Or tried to. Its hazy arms ended in ragged stumps, hacked off at the elbow.

"Tiger's blood!" choked Geth. He grabbed for Natrac, but the half-orc seemed frozen. Geth twisted around.

There were more phantoms emerging from the walls and shadows, rising from the floor and gliding down through the ceiling. There were bulky orcs and lean hobgoblins, scrawny goblins, and even hulking bugbears. Some looked almost as old as Batul. Others were little more than children. All of them were whispering. All of them had looks of horror and desperation on their faces.

All of them held out the stumps of arms and the stubs of legs. Some were missing fingers, some feet, others whole limbs. Many had been disfigured in other ways as well, their ears or noses or lips or eyes torn away, their bodies flayed and gouged. Natrac was staring at all of them in stunned numbness.

"Jegez," he croaked, his eyes wide. He stretched out his right arm, holding up his own blunt wrist. The phantoms' whispers rose and they pressed forward as if welcoming their kin.

Geth snarled at them, trying to push back. It was like grabbing a broken egg—he could feel the phantoms' insubstantial flesh, but not hold it. He seized a sharp-toothed hobgoblin by the neck and thrust it away from him for an instant. Even as he thrust, though, his fingers sank into the phantom, then through it. The hobgoblin clutched at him with pleading in its eyes. Geth jerked backward, plunging through several other phantoms and slamming into the floor.

"Geth!" called Natrac from the middle of a growing mass of colorless, tormented figures. The half-orc was beginning to look frightened. "Geth! Help me!"

Baring his teeth, Geth rolled back to his feet and lunged into the crowd, sweeping his hands through ghostly flesh until he grabbed something solid. Natrac's arm. He hauled the half-orc toward him, batting and growling at the phantoms as they tried to follow. Natrac was pale and stumbling, but Geth dragged him on down the corridor. "Move!" he urged. "We can't hurt them, but they can't hurt us either. We can get through this!"

"I don't know if we can," gasped Natrac as a new noise, a scraping noise, began to rise against the desperate whispers. "Look!" He flung out an arm. Geth turned from the phantoms behind them to look ahead—and froze.

Creeping along the floor and across the walls of the corridor was a swarm of amputated limbs: feet and hands, legs and arms. They scuttled on fingers and writhed like snakes.

The scraping noise was the sound of the bloody razors and blades that many of the creeping limbs clutched between gnarled fingers and overlong toes, dragging the metal against the stone of the corridor as they crawled.

A growl rumbled in Geth's throat. "Tiger, Wolf, and Rat!" His fingers closed tight around his hunda. The weapon was no use against the phantoms, but if the creeping limbs were solid enough to carry blades, he prayed that they were solid enough to take a blow.

Whether it would kill them, that was something else.

"Dol Dorn's mighty fist," spat Natrac. "What I wouldn't give to have a wizard or one of those druids here right now!" He scrambled to his feet and put his back against Geth's. "Singe's or Dandra's fire would be very good, but I'd even take Vennet's wind if he could blow those things away!"

Desperation sparked an idea in Geth's head. "Grandmother Wolf guide me," he gasped—and dropped the hunda stick to tear at the pouch at his side. Natrac glanced down as he ripped frantically at the knotted drawstrings.

"Sovereign Host!" the half-orc choked, understanding flashing instantly in his eyes. "You're not going to—"

Geth looked at him as the knots parted and the pouch gaped open. "You know what to do if you have to," he said.

He glanced up and down the corridor as the phantoms and their severed limbs closed on them, then he squeezed his eyes shut, plunged his right hand into the pouch, and seized Dandra's psicrystal.

Dandra's scream brought Singe flailing out of sleep—and, all around them, the young hunters of the Bonetree clan leaping to their feet with their weapons drawn. Singe flung himself at Dandra. The kalashtar was once again stiff, her eyes open and staring to the west, but this time her body was trembling.

"Relax!" he gasped at her, "Relax!"

A shadow fell over him. He glanced up. It was Ashi, her sword drawn, but Medala was leaping forward as well, Dah'mir pacing after her.

"What is this?" Medala said. "What's wrong with her?"

"Maybe she had a bad dream," Ashi said tightly.

"Kalashtar don't dream!" spat Medala. A chime rang in

Singe's head and pain lanced through him. Ashi was staggering as well, clutching at her head. The wizard clung to Dandra desperately.

Twelve moons, he thought through the dazing agony, what was Geth doing with that psicrystal?

Tetkashtai swept into Geth like a wildfire. She burned within him, her presence huge and powerful. When Dandra had first shown Tetkashtai to him and Singe, it had been like standing in a yellow-green mist. Having Tetkashtai actually within him was more akin to standing inside a raging, wailing inferno.

If this was what the orc in Fat Tusk had experienced, Geth realized, it was small wonder he had succumbed so quickly to Tetkashtai's possession! At least he knew what he was dealing with. Straining to focus all of his concentration on the presence, he threw out a single, silent shout. *Tetkashtai!*

You! Tetkashtai screamed back. Her voice was like thunder. A deluge of images blasted through him, eerie memories of him as seen through someone else's eyes. Geth staggered under the weight of Tetkashtai's attention. How did Dandra cope with this?

Tetkashtai ripped the thought out of him. *Even if she's nothing more than a rogue psicrystal,* the presence howled, *Dandra's mind is more advanced than yours and she occupies a kalashtar's body—one that I will reclaim!*

You can claim it later, Geth shouted at her, *you have something else to worry about first!* His words came out like a child's whine, overwhelmed by Tetkashtai's forceful presence. He abandoned words and flung a memory at her, his last glimpse of the phantoms and the creeping limbs that menaced him and Natrac.

The presence caught the image and swallowed it. The whirlwind of yellow-green light tensed slightly. *Stupid shifter!* Tetkashtai seethed. *What have you done?*

You'll help us?

What choice do I have? Tetkashtai spat. *Open yourself to me, Geth! You're no kalashtar. I will need everything you can give just to access the simplest of my powers!*

Geth hesitated, then gave up any attempt at holding Tet-kashtai back.

She seized him, and he felt like a stranger in his own body. His eyes snapped open and his head turned. Natrac whirled past him as Tetkashtai glanced at the phantoms, then at the creeping limbs. *The limbs are more dangerous*, Geth tried to tell her. *The phantoms can't actually—*

Be silent. Tetkashtai ordered him. She stretched out, reaching down into some place within him that was not quite his spirit and not quite his body. Whatever it was, pain ripped through him as Tetkashtai pulled something of him into herself. He sagged down. She heaved his body upright.

"A trickle," she said with his voice. "Pathetic, but it will have to do."

"Geth?" asked Natrac.

"No," said Tetkashtai.

Geth felt her concentrate, felt the storm of her presence draw together into a shining, focused spark. A little bit of the energy she had stolen from him spun out from that spark. Something seemed to open up within him, a pulse, a beat. It rose from his chest. He could feel it in his throat, and then in his ears: the droning chorus that had always accompanied Dandra's fiery powers. *Whitefire.* The word whispered itself into his mind through the connection with Tetkashtai.

"The spirits!" shouted Natrac.

In the corner of Geth's vision, he saw the half-orc whirl as the colorless shapes of the phantoms surged around them once more. Natrac's hunda stick lashed out, sweeping through the disfigured shapes again and again, trying to keep them back. It didn't work. They swarmed over him—and over Geth. Tetkashtai paid no attention to either the spirits that tried to tug at her or Natrac's calls for help All of her attention was fixed on the creeping limbs as they crawled closer. And closer.

Tetkashtai, what are you doing? Geth asked. His voice seemed weaker than ever, a pitiful mewling. *Hurry!*

Patience. The focused spark of her presence flashed. She curled his left hand into a fist and raised it, pointing at the approaching swarm. As the chorus of whitefire rose like a triumphant song, Tetkashtai opened Geth's hand.

Pale flames poured out in a roaring cone that seemed to fill the corridor. Hands, feet, legs, and arms shriveled like spiders flung into a candle, reduced in an instant to nothing more than hunks of burning, charred flesh. The knives and razors that they had dragged with them fell to the floor with a clatter. Only a few skittering hands escaped the inferno, scattering back into the shadows. Whispers rising into wails, the phantoms fled as well, their ghostly forms vanishing through walls and back down the corridor. Shivering, Natrac forced himself upright.

"Dol Arrah's mercy," he panted, leaning heavily on his hunda.

The tight spark of Tetkashtai's concentration unraveled, whirling back out into a yellow-green storm. Geth let out a silent gasp as the presence wrenched at him. *Still there, Geth?* she asked.

Speaking was an effort. *Let go of the crystal, Tetkashtai. Give me back my body!*

Tetkashtai laughed, both in his mind and out loud. *Give it back?* she said silently. *Why would I do that? I know what you're planning, Geth. A return to Dah'mir? No. A return to the crystal? Never.* Tetkashtai's voice rose into a shriek. *Do you have any idea what it's like to be trapped in that crystal? I'm not going back there!*

Tetkashtai turned Geth's body to face Natrac and the throbbing chorus of whitefire rose again. A look of new fear flickered across Natrac's face. The half-orc's hand tightened on his hunda and he lashed out, staff aiming for Geth's wrist, trying to make Tetkashtai drop the crystal as Geth had in Fat Tusk.

But Tetkashtai was faster. She slid Geth's toe under the shaft of his own hunda and flipped it up into the air. His left hand caught the staff in mid-air, twisting it and knocking Natrac's clumsy blow away.

"What was it Vennet said to Dandra in Zarash'ak?" Tetkashtai asked with Geth's voice. "Not a spear as such, but on short notice, I think a staff will do?"

A thought set the hunda stick ablaze in her grasp, though Geth felt nothing of the flames. Tetkashtai flicked the hunda again and the burning wood cracked across Natrac's good arm. The half-orc yelped and dropped his staff. Geth felt Tetkashtai's surprise at the ferocity of her strike. "Harder than I intended," she said. She flexed his muscles. "Strong. Fast. You might not be a kalashtar, shifter, but I think I like your body."

If you like that, growled Geth, *you're going to love this.* Gathering all of his remaining strength, he struck deep into himself, into a place the presence hadn't even tried to approach—and shifted.

Tetkashtai gasped at the wild power that surged through his veins, swooning as his lycanthrope heritage rushed over her. The yellow-green storm of her being flared and guttered like a torch in the wind. In that moment, Geth pushed out against her control, spinning his body around fast and slamming the back of his right hand against the cold stones of the wall. Pain shot up his entire arm and his clenched fist twitched in pure reflex to the impact.

Before Tetkashtai could do more than wail in frustration, the psicrystal slipped between his fingers and bounced across the floor with a soft ringing sound. The pain in the shifter's right hand was matched by a searing burn in his left. Geth hurled the flaming hunda away from him and collapsed back against the wall, his chest heaving.

As suddenly as she had stiffened, Dandra relaxed, her eyes gliding closed. Singe held onto her, clutching her tight until the chime of Medala's power faded and the kalashtar wrenched him away. She examined Dandra, then spun to the wizard. "What happened?" she demanded.

"I don't know," Singe choked. His head spun and throbbed. It was a good thing that his ignorance was the truth, because whatever Medala had done to him had left him without the will or energy to spin out a lie.

Maybe she knew that too, because she didn't press him any further. She turned to Dah'mir as the green-eyed man stood watching. "Something's wrong," she said. "Tetkashtai is fighting your power."

"Amazing," murmured Dah'mir. "She's doing what you failed to, Medala."

A chill ran through Singe's body. Someone else might have been intimidated by the possibility but Dah'mir seemed intrigued. Maybe even proud.

Medala's face twisted with jealousy but Dah'mir took no notice. He glanced at the young Bonetree hunters as he turned to sweep away. "Keep a watch on her and the wizard both," he told them.

In spite of her rage, Medala trotted after him like an obedient dog. Singe shrank back as the hunters turned to him with the smiles of foxes set to watch a chicken coop—smiles that faded as Ashi stepped over Singe and took up a position facing her own clan. Her eyes were dark from whatever attack Medala had inflicted on her, but her jaw was set and her sword was drawn. Muttering in frustration, the hunters slid back into the shadows.

Ashi didn't speak. Neither did Singe. His head pounding, he crawled back to Dandra and lay down close beside her.

"Lords of the Host," hissed Natrac. The crook end of his hunda poked Geth's chest. The shifter slapped it away and looked up at him.

"She's gone," he growled. He leaned his head back against the stone wall for a moment more, and released his shifting. It faded away, taking the worst of the pain in his hands with it. Some of whatever energy Tetkashtai had drawn from him trickled back as well. He heaved himself to his feet. There was a stink of burning flesh that he hadn't been aware of while Tetkashtai controlled his body. He clenched his teeth and tried to breathe shallowly.

The whitefire had scoured the corridor, scorching the stone. Dandra's crystal lay shining against the black remains of a goblin foot. Geth slid the pouch from his belt and approached the crystal with caution. His head told him that Tetkashtai couldn't take hold of him again unless he actually touched the crystal, but his heart was still afraid; he could feel the presence's touch ripping at his essence, bending his body to her will. Taking up a fallen razor—still warm from the blast of flame—he flicked the crystal gingerly back into the pouch.

"You're going to keep it?" Natrac spat in amazement.

"Dandra can control Tetkashtai," said Geth stiffly, knotting the pouch's drawstrings again. "She'll need the crystal when we rescue her and Singe."

"If we can rescue them."

"*When.*" Geth stood up and replaced the pouch on his belt. "We're going to get out of here. How's your arm?"

"It hurts," Natrac said, "but at least it's still attached to me." He looked down at the remains of the creeping limbs and grimaced. "Do you think there's more of them?"

The shifter glanced at the shadows that the few remaining hands had fled into—he thought he could still see them, hiding like bugs in the crevices. The final wails of the vanished phantoms continued to hang in the air, too. They changed slowly as he listened, becoming less frightened and more anguished, as if the defeated spirits were somehow reliving their ancient torture. The hair on Geth's arms rose. A darkness seemed to settle over the corridor.

"Geth . . ." said Natrac softly.

"Aye," Geth grunted. "We need to keep moving."

His hunda stick was burning bright, more than half its length afire from Tetkashtai's touch. The blades that the severed limbs had carried were scattered across the corridor, but Geth's skin crawled at the thought of wielding one of them. He needed a weapon of some kind, though. He snatched up the burning hunda carefully. Thrusting it ahead of him like a long torch, he set off along the corridor at a brisk trot. Natrac followed close, his eyes on the shadows behind them. Though both he and the half-orc could see well enough even without the added light, the fire gave Geth back a feeling of control and strength.

Especially when the phantoms' wails rose into wrenching screams. Especially as the smell of blood grew stronger. Especially as the corridor narrowed and passageways opened off of it, plunging away into the darkness of Jhegesh Dol.

Geth stopped short, pulling up so quickly that Natrac bumped into him and yelped before clamping his tusked jaw shut. "What is it?" the half-orc whispered.

"The corridor. Look." Geth held out the burning staff. The corridor they had been following split into three passageways, all identical.

"Just keep going," urged Natrac.

"I don't know which passage to take!" Flame hissed and popped as Geth switched his makeshift torch from one side to the other. "What if we're not supposed to keep going straight? What if we're supposed to turn?"

"What if we're not?" Natrac asked desperately. "How much time is there before sunrise? How long have we been in here?"

A terrible roar, as close as if something very large and very frightened was being tortured nearby, rolled over them—then was broken by the heavy, wet chop of a falling blade. The roar rose sharply, then subsided into deep, horrified weeping. Geth clenched his teeth and stepped into the corridor straight ahead.

The stones of Adolan's collar grew so cold that they burned his skin. Gasping in pain, Geth leaped back, almost trampling over Natrac. "Not that way!" he snarled, his teeth bared. He touched the stones with his free hand and scraped a fingernail against them. It came away with white specks of frost melting on it. He showed it to Natrac. The half-orc grimaced.

Geth turned to the passage on his right. Fingers held against the stones, he stepped forward carefully. The collar grew icy again—not quite so cold as before, but distinctly frigid. He swallowed. "I don't think this is the way either," he said. He moved back to the left-hand passage and walked into it.

The eerie chill fell away from the collar and Geth let out his breath. "Here," he said with relief. "This way—"

His relief melted like the frost on his fingertip at the thin noise that came hissing along the passage. It was the coarse, sliding whisper of metal on stone, the sound of a knife blade pressed against a grindstone.

"Host," choked Natrac. He looked back to the right-hand passage.

Geth tightened his hand on the end of his flaming hunda. "No," he said. "This is the way." He could hear the fear in his own voice, but he pushed forward. After a moment, Natrac cursed and followed him.

The sound of the grindstone grew louder, though there were other sounds around it. More falling blades. The grating of bone saws. Sobbing. Screams. Always screams. The fire of the staff began to falter. Wordlessly, Natrac held out his hunda, offering it to him. Geth pressed it back.

The passage ended ahead, opening into some wide, dark space. Burning hunda held low, Geth crept up to the mouth of the passage and peered out.

He stood at the edge of a small balcony like a private box in some fancy Sharn playhouse, except that this box overlooked a wide, shadowed stone chamber. On the far side of the chamber, atop a short series of shallow steps, a long block of black stone stood like an altar.

In the center of the chamber, a figure hunched over a grindstone. Orange sparks flashed from the long steel blade that it held to the spinning stone. The figure was nothing more than a silhouette against the fiery spray, but there was something about it that made Geth's skin crawl. He bared his teeth and the whisper of a growl rose in his throat.

The dark figure straightened. The rasp of metal on stone and the shower of sparks ended as it lifted the blade. The grindstone spun on in silence and the figure looked up at Geth and Natrac. The strange light of Jhegesh Dol fell on a man's face so pale and beautiful that it might have been the model for Dah'mir's own, except that where Dah'mir's eyes were at least human, the eyes of the man below were pale, solid lavender without any iris or pupil. He paused and then stepped forward so that the light slid across shoulders and arms that rippled with muscle and flashed on a chunky amulet that hung against a broad, hairless chest. Shadows seemed to cling to him, obscuring his torso and legs like insubstantial black robes. Another spirit, Geth thought, another phantom.

Then the lavender-eyed man stretched his arms and spread his hands with a clash of metal. His fingers were blades, long as swords, heavy as axes, and so sharp they seemed to cut the light itself. The blades weren't stiff though. They bent and flexed with life, merging with the man's flesh, a part of him. He hadn't been sharpening a sword. He had been sharpening his own hand.

Nine thousand years ago, Batul had said, Jhegesh Dol had been a daelkyr stronghold.

The man was no mere phantom. He might have been put to the sword seven millennia before, but the master of Jhegesh Dol stood below them—at least in spirit. A shadow of a nightmare from a realm of madness.

Geth's growl rumbled louder; his fingers clenched the burning hunda.

"That other passage," Natrac urged, his breathing harsh. "The second one. We can still go back." He started to turn.

The daelkyr's shadow brought its fingers together in a slow metallic scrape. The screams of the victims of the dark fortress echoed down the passage behind them. Natrac's face turned pale.

Around Geth's neck, though, Adolan's collar had gone cold again. Not painfully cold the way it had before, but sharp and bracing, like armor donned in winter. The sacred stones of the Gatekeepers' tradition were offering him protection, just as they had protected him from Dah'mir's influence in Zarash'ak and given him guidance at the intersection of passageways.

Guidance that had led him and Natrac to the daelkyr's shadow, not away from it. Geth's belly tensed and he knew that they weren't meant to run from this fight.

His growl rose into a roar. He jumped up onto the rail of the balcony, caught his balance—and leaped to the floor of stone floor below. To the sound of Natrac's frightened astonishment, he darted forward and thrust his flaming hunda at the daelkyr's muscular chest.

The spirit slid aside with an eerie grace and its hand came up to swipe at the hunda. The wood bucked in Geth's grip, then fell into burning chunks where the daelkyr's bladed fingers had cut it. Geth stared at the truncated section of staff still in his grasp.

Ten flailing swords stabbed at him. Geth yelped and threw himself back. The daelkyr's hands swept the air in front of his chest, so close he could hear the metal sing. He tumbled to the side, trying to stay out of the way of the shadow's lethal reach. His shifting-granted toughness wouldn't protect him from those steel claws; Geth wasn't sure that even his gauntlet would have stopped them!

And he wasn't at all certain he wanted to put the protection of the Gatekeeper's stones to the test.

Geth spun again. He ducked and blades hissed above him. The daelkyr's shadow moved in absolute silence except for the clash of its long fingers. Geth lunged in under its reach, extending himself to jab what was left of his hunda stick right into the shadow's belly.

It was like attacking mist. The flames that still clung to the stick flickered and dimmed. The daelkyr barely seemed to notice. Geth rolled quickly as its fingers darted at him again. "Tiger's blood!" he spat. The spirit could hurt him, but he couldn't hurt it?

"Catch!" Natrac called. He had his hunda stretched out, offering it to him. Geth cursed and shook his head.

"It's not going to do me any good!" The shifter dodged back again as the daelkyr's shadow pressed forward. "I need something else!"

He tried to duck around the thing, to get to its back at least, but it wouldn't let him pass. It surged ahead in a storm of bright metal, forcing Geth back by three fast paces. Abruptly, his heels hit the low stone steps of the dais he had glimpsed across the room and he stumbled. The daelkyr's claws flashed. Geth wrenched his body around, one palm planted on the steps, and tumbled out of the way as the blades met the stone in a skittering impact that sent sparks flashing in the shadows. He scrambled to his feet and leaped to the top of the steps, seeking the frail advantage of higher ground.

The black stone altar atop the dais was like a block taken from the walls of Jhegesh Dol, rough but greasy slick. Blood had gushed over in the stone in centuries past, drying thick in its pitted crevices. The altar's top was scarred, gashed and slashed by ancient blades like a butcher's wooden board.

In the middle of the altar lay a sword, its blade wide and heavy, flaring into a spreading fork like a serpent's tongue at its end, deeply notched along one edge. The metal had a weird sheen to it, dark and purple as twilight—but the sword was clean, as if none of the horror and corruption of the place had clung to it.

Geth vaulted onto the top of the stone and snatched up the sword. As the shadow of the daelkyr came charging up the steps, he whirled and swept the sword up to block its outstretched hands.

The twilight blade clashed against the spirit's steel claws—and cut through them. Falling metal clattered against the altar. The shadow staggered, mouth open in a soundless scream that revealed a dagger tongue. Its severed fingers trembled and black blood pumped out of the living steel.

Geth slammed the sword up in a chopping blow that cut under the daelkyr's arm and deep into its chest. The notched edge of the weapon bit deep in shadowy flesh. The spirit shuddered. For a moment it seemed that it might pulled itself backward off the blade. Geth grabbed the amulet around its neck, holding the foul ghost close as he jerked the sword higher.

The shadow of the daelkyr made no noise, but suddenly it seemed as if all of the tortured spirits of Jhegesh Dol gave one last wail.

The black fortress and the daelkyr faded into pearl-gray mist on an empty marsh. Geth froze. Natrac, standing on a low hillock of grass gasped and pointed with his hunda stick. The shifter spun around.

Less than ten paces away, Batul, Krepis, and Orshok stood under the branches of the tree that marked the edge of Jhegesh Dol. Behind them, the eastern sky showed the pale pink of dawn. Geth leaped down from the broken chunk of rock that he stood on and sloshed across the wet ground to face them.

"We're here," he spat, still breathing hard from his phantom battle. "Satisfied?"

But all three druids were simply staring at him. Even Batul's eyes were wide. Geth looked down at his hands. In his left he held the notched sword. In his right, the big amulet that had hung from the daelkyr's neck. There was something inside the amulet he saw now, a coarse, dull black object nearly as large as his palm.

"Gatekeeper legends," said Batul in an awestruck voice, "tell that when the daelkyr lord of Jhegesh Dol was brought down, two treasures vanished from Eberron. One was the sword, forged by Dhakaani smiths, of the hobgoblin hero who struck the killing blow. The other was a sacred relic, a scale from Vvaraak, the dragon who taught the first druids." He swallowed, his eyes fixed on the amulet.

Geth held it out to him. "Keep your word and stand with us against Dah'mir," he growled, "and you can have one of those treasures back."

CHAPTER

14

They arrived at the Bonetree camp with the sun high in the sky. The young hunters leaped out of the boats and splashed through the shallows to draw the vessels up on shore. On the riverbank above, there were excited shouts that rose into one of the fluting trills that Singe had learned to identify as Bonetree hunting calls.

"What are they saying?" he asked Ashi.

"That Dah'mir has returned," the hunter whispered. "That the hunt was successful."

There was no emotion in her voice. She'd said almost nothing to him since the night Dandra had woken screaming, but neither had she strayed far from his side. The young hunters were always watching Singe now, at least as much as they watched Ashi. True to Ashi's prediction, there had been two more challenges for her sword. The second challenger she wounded as she had the first. The third she killed, her face hard.

That hardness hadn't lifted.

As they climbed out of the boats, one of the young hunters began shouting at the others, forming them up into a pack, ready to lead Dah'mir and Medala up the riverbank. A ragtag honor guard, Singe realized. Out of the corner of his eye, he saw anger flicker in Ashi's eyes. She started to move toward the hunters but Dah'mir glanced at her. "Stay with the prisoners, Ashi," he told her.

"My place is leading the hunters, Revered," she said, but the green-eyed man shook his head.

"You have a greater honor," he said and once again Singe could feel the persuasive touch of his presence. "Bring the prisoners behind me so that the clan can see them."

Even Ashi's anger softened before his charm. She nodded and moved forward obediently. Dandra needed no encouragement to follow Dah'mir, of course. She stumbled after him like a zombie. Even after days of travel, it still hurt Singe to see the proud, bright woman reduced to a dim automaton.

Singe, though, froze on the river's edge. This was the end of their journey—and Geth hadn't come for them. The hope of rescue that he might have nurtured over the past several days wavered like a candle flame.

Ashi reached back and took his arm. "Come," she said.

At the top of the riverbank, the Bonetree encampment spread out around them, a scattering of rough shelters that seemed to be half hut and half tent. Men, women, and children—the first of the Bonetree clan he had seen, Singe realized, who were not hunters—hurried forward, calling out to the hunters and kneeling down to Dah'mir. The young hunters marched with all the self-conscious stiffness of fresh recruits to the Blademarks, but Dah'mir smiled and held out his hand, offering blessings freely. At his side, Medala's eyes darted across the gathered clan as if seeking out any hint of a threat to her lord.

Calls and praise turned to stony silence when Singe and Dandra passed.

As they passed a cluster of better shelters, a handful of older hunters stood watching. Singe's gut sank a little lower. He thought he recognized some of the hunters. They were the ones who had attacked Bull Hollow.

Ashi's face lit up. "Breff!" she called out to one tattooed man. Singe saw her eyes dart among the older hunters, then narrow. She said something to Breff in the language of the Bonetree clan. *"Ches azams esheios?"*

Breff shook his head.

For the last several days, Singe had been listening to the

hunters as they traveled upriver, trying to unravel a little of their language. He strained to make some sense of Ashi's words. *Azams* were other members of the clan. *Shei* was to hunt. *Sheios*—they hunt . . . *Are the others hunting?*

"Ashi," he murmured, "should there be more hunters?"

"Yes." She called to Breff again, waving him closer. *"Gri'i ans kriri?"*

"We're the only ones," Breff said. Singe felt a shock at hearing him speak another language. The hunter's words were low and his voice was brittle, as if he was discussing some terrible, haunting secret he wanted no one else to hear. "Hruucan set a hard pace on the journey back. Anyone who was too badly wounded . . ."

He stopped, glancing up.

Dah'mir stood beside them.

Ashi's face fell and Singe's belly trembled, but Dah'mir ignored them both and instead looked at Breff. The tattooed man's gaze slid to the ground.

Dah'mir took a step back. "Hunters," he said gently, "come to me." He gestured to the younger hunters as well as the older. "All of you."

They clustered around him, pierced and tattooed savages kneeling before a dark, immaculate priest. Only Ashi stood back, staying in her place between Singe and Dandra. Dah'mir stretched out his hands, laying one on Breff's shoulder. "First among the Bonetree," he said, "my loyal servants, be glad! To fall at the command of a child of Khyber is an honor! The clan will tell tales of the fallen for generations. Yours was a hunt to be remembered." He gestured with his free hand, indicating Dandra and Singe. "What you sought has been found and new blood for the Bonetree along with it." He smiled and his green eyes flashed. "Be blessed, hunters of the Bonetree! May the Dragon Below restore your ferocity!"

Singe felt the breath of magic as foul as Fause's healing of his arm and shivered. He couldn't imagine that more than few of the kneeling hunters understood Dah'mir's words, but when they looked up, there was a new light in their eyes. Their fingers rose, darting to their lips and their foreheads. Breff's eyes seemed brightest of all. *"Harana!"* he moaned, and leaned forward to kiss the hem of Dah'mir's leather robes. The green-eyed man raised his hand and all of the hunters leaped to their feet, joining in his honor guard.

None of them looked at Ashi a second time, so caught up were they in reverent adoration of Dah'mir. Singe glanced at her, but her expression was once again hard. He turned away and looked ahead.

The Bonetree mound rose above them. Singe bit his tongue. It was as large as a hill, but after the flatness of the Shadow Marches and with no other hills around, it looked enormous. "That can't be natural!" he said.

"It isn't," Ashi grunted. She didn't look at him, but she said, "There are stories told by the elders that describe how the earliest members of the clan built it in honor of the Dragon Below. It's said that once a Gatekeeper circle stood here, but that Dah'mir shattered it and raised the ancestor mound in its place. Now he lives beneath the mound with the children of Khyber. No member of the clan sets foot inside it, but there are other stories of passages that lead deep into Khyber and of Dah'mir's treasure."

Singe knew that it could only be a sign of growing desperation that his mind fixed on the least appropriate fragment of Ashi's words. "Treasure?" he repeated.

"Dragonshards," said Ashi. "For all the generations that he's guided the Bonetree, he's gathered dragonshards, like those he wears the and the ones he gave Vennet. The elders say that he's building a great shrine to the Dragon Below and when it's complete, the clan will be allowed to worship there."

She didn't sound like she believed it, but Singe had a vision of a shrine as large as one of the great halls of Wynarn lined with ten generations' accumulation of dragonshards.

"Twelve moons," he choked, feeling like a greed-maddened dwarf.

It was a feeling that lasted only until Dah'mir's procession reached the tunnel that gaped in the side of the mound. Standing inside the shadows of the stone-lined tunnel was a dolgaunt. His face and chest were terribly scarred, patches of the writhing buds that covered his skin replaced by tissue that was smooth, shiny, and raw. Clumps of his thick hair-tendrils were limp and dead, and the tentacle that sprouted from his left shoulder moved sluggishly compared to the right. Singe's belly felt hollow and cold.

It was Hruucan.

The dolgaunt stood stiff as the crowd of hunters split apart. When Dah'mir and Medala stepped forward, he bent to them—stiffly—in respect. Dah'mir's eyebrows rose. "Hruucan, when Medala said you had been injured . . ."

"I recover," Hruucan answered in the same harsh, grating voice that Singe remembered from Bull Hollow. "The scars are . . . inconvenient." His shoulder tentacles lashed the air with an agitation that betrayed his words. "Dah'mir, you have the one who did this to me with you!"

Dah'mir looked over his shoulder and his eye fixed on Singe. "I have plans for Singe, Hruucan," he said. "He will be brought into the Bonetree. His blood will make the clan stronger."

"Scars don't pass through the blood," Hruucan rasped. "If you command, any woman of the Bonetree will mate with him no matter how ugly he is. I'll leave him a man. That will be enough." The dolgaunt's empty eye sockets turned to Singe. "A rematch, wizard," he said. "A duel to finish what we started."

The smile that spread across Dah'mir's face was at once both horrible and entrancing. "He'll do it," he said.

Singe's hollow belly shrank even further. He felt Ashi's hand, still on his arm tighten sharply.

Dah'mir swept his arms wide, his voice full of a terrible joy. "A spectacle!" he declared. "Here before the mound. To celebrate my return!"

"Varda!" shouted Breff, translating for the Bonetree. *"Varda su teith e harano!"*

Those were words Singe knew. The younger hunters had used them as easily as they drew weapons. *A fight! A fight for blood and honor!* He watched matching smiles break across the faces of the Bonetree hunters. Their arms punched the air and their voices rose enthusiastically.

Dah'mir looked back to Hruucan. "Will tonight be soon enough for you, Hruucan?" he asked,

The dolgaunt bent again. "I welcome the sunset!" His tentacles quivered as if in anticipation.

"Excellent!" Dah'mir looked to Ashi. "You've taken care of these two admirably, Ashi," he said, "but you can relax now. They aren't going anywhere." His charming smile broadened but it didn't seem to Singe that Ashi relaxed at all. He turned to look at her, but she wouldn't return his gaze. When she did force her hand to drop, it almost felt like she had to wrench it away. The instant she let go, though, she stepped back and looked away from him.

Dah'mir's voice seemed like it was coming from a distance. "Breff, put Singe in an empty hut and see that he rests and has food. I'm sure Hruucan wants a challenge tonight. Guard him carefully—he is a wizard, after all."

"Yes, Dah'mir." A new hand replaced Ashi's on Singe's arm and pulled him back toward the camp.

Singe pulled away and spun to Dah'mir, a desperate plan trying to put itself together in his head. Maybe there was something he and Dandra could do together . . . "Please," he pleaded to Dah'mir. "Wake Tetkashtai. Let me say good-bye to her, at least!"

The green-eyed man's smile didn't falter at all. "I don't think so!" he said. "Breff?"

The hunter wrenched at him hard. Ashi, Singe realized, had been gentle with him. Breff dragged him off his feet. Singe twisted his head around as he stumbled after the hunter and managed to catch one last look at Dandra.

Dah'mir and Medala were leading her away into the mound with Hruucan walking behind them.

The journey, like the one before, had passed in a blur, as if Dandra stood still while everyone and everything sped by around her. There had been only two constants in that crazy rush. She was one. The other was Dah'mir, the bridge between her and the madness around her, the center of her world.

Was the blur worse, some small part of her had thought, because she was on her own this time? She didn't have Tetkashtai to guide her—one of her last lucid memories was the struggle with Ashi, the shock as Tetkashtai was torn from her, a glimpse of Geth catching the crystal. Her powers had vanished with Tetkashtai.

Then Dah'mir's presence had washed over her. Dandra was dimly aware that Geth was no longer part of the rush around her, though she couldn't recall why. Singe was there, however. Medalashana, too, though the gray-haired kalashtar called herself something else now. She was simply Medala, as if she had rejected her kalashtar heritage.

There were two moments on the journey that Dandra remembered, two moments when the world around her slowed down and she rose like a swimmer to the surface of Dah'mir's encompassing presence. The first came like a shock, abrupt and unexpected. There had been a spark on the horizon of her mind, familiar yet distant. "Tetkashtai!" she'd gasped. There had been a sense of confusion and a shook, the feel of an unfamiliar mind, a glimpse of savage orcs around a blazing fire, of Geth seizing her . . . but the moment had ended before she knew anything more.

If the first moment came as a shock, the second moment came like a knife in the back. Without warning, it felt as if a piece of her was being ripped out and the spark of Tetkashtai's presence seemed, if not closer, than at least stronger and more intense.

This time she knew what has happening: Tetkashtai was trying to take a new host. They'd guessed from the very beginning that it was possible, but Tetkashtai had never made good on her threats before—and it was the one thing that Dandra had never confessed to Singe or Geth.

But surely neither she nor Tetkashtai had guessed how painful it would be. Dandra hadn't been able to hold back a scream. She'd felt Singe holding her, trying to soothe her. Strangely, she had felt Geth, too, though in a different way. Then Tetkashtai's host had rejected her and Dandra had tumbled back down into the embrace of Dah'mir's strange power, grateful for peace . . .

She woke again with words echoing in her ears. "Wake up, Tetkashtai."

The world rushed back into sudden focus.

Dah'mir stood in front of her with Medalashana—no, Medala—at his side. Over them towered the device that had torn her from Tetkashtai, wires and tubes, brass and crystal, the big blue-black Khyber dragonshard still pulsing at its heart. There was one psicrystal remaining in the device, flickering like a violet ember.

She was back in the Bonetree mound, back in Dah'mir's horrible laboratory. Her mind reeled, disoriented. "Singe . . ." she gasped, then blinked and saw what lay behind Dah'mir and Medala. Three horribly familiar tables, two empty. On the third lay a corpse that had once been a kalashtar man. Now it was shriveled, slowly mummifying in the atmosphere of the mound. Its head had been ripped apart. Virikhad.

Dah'mir turned his head, following her gaze, and clicked his tongue in disapproval. "Confronted with your old love and the first name you call is the wizard's?" he said. "Fickle!"

"What happened to him?" choked Dandra.

"Isn't it obvious?" asked Dah'mir. "He couldn't—or wouldn't—return to his body the way you and Medala did. At least it wasn't a complete waste." He glanced into the shadows. "Although you did say his brain was . . . how did you put it?"

Tall, thin figures with dead white eyes and writhing tentacles in place of a lower face moved forward. Dandra felt a brush against her mind, then a sudden rush of alien sensations. Dry. Hollow. Weak.

It took a moment for her to realize the illithids were describing the taste of Virikhad's brain.

The horror was too much. Dandra screamed and flung herself backward. She hit stone. There was no running. As the mind flayers closed around her, she dredged for her powers. Without Tetkashtai, there was so little she could do, but she wasn't going to let the mind flayers take her without a fight. She stretched her thoughts, trying to reach for whitefire, for the invisible web of *vayhatana*, for the long step to carry her away from this place.

They all fell through her grasp like water. The cold minds of the illithids touched hers. She tried to empty her thoughts, to dive deep into herself for protection, but the mind flayers only grabbed her and dragged her back. They skated through her, grappling with her psyche—then froze, their collective will drawing away as if in alarm.

Dandra looked up to see their tentacles twitching in time to the gestures of their long fingers. One of their number turned to Dah'mir and Medala, and an icy voice spoke in Dandra's mind. *This is not Tetkashtai.*

"What?" roared Dah'mir.

Another presence pierced Dandra's mind, a savage attack that scattered the illithids' powers, tore at her thoughts, and left her gasping and swaying. She knew this presence—or at least had known it. Medalashana's touch had been gentle, organized, and disciplined. Medala's was raw and violent. As Dandra fell forward, sprawling onto the floor of the laboratory, she saw the gray-haired kalashtar's eyes go wide.

"How—?" Medala cursed in disbelief. She looked at Dah'mir. "It's her psicrystal! Tetkashtai's psicrystal walked off in her body!"

Dah'mir's eyes narrowed. "Find out everything you can, Medala," he said. "I want to know how this is possible."

Medala crouched down in front of Dandra. "Look at me," she snarled. Dandra forced her gaze down, trying to build some kind of mental defense against what she knew had to be coming. Medala's hand shot out, though, closing on Dandra's jaw with cruel strength and wrenching her head up.

A chime rang in Dandra's ears, a pure sound that drove all the way through her. Medala's eyes seemed to shimmer with silver light. Dandra tried to force her back and out of her thoughts, but it was no good. As the chime rang on and on, Medala slid deep into her mind. Dandra watched helplessly as the other kalashtar raked through her memories. The moment she had first struggled to her feet in Dah'mir's laboratory. Her flight from the Bonetree hunters. The desperate fight in Bull Hollow. Yrlag. *Lightning on Water.* Zarash'ak.

Dandra strained and thrust, trying to find some way to fight back. Medala held her with an easy contempt. *Stop that,* the gray-haired woman said with disgust as she flickered through the memories of Dandra's struggle with Ashi and Vennet beneath the house of blue doors.

You know I won't, Dandra spat back at her.

Medala swatted her like she was a fly. *You're a psicrystal, Dandra. That you walk in a kalashtar's body doesn't make you a kalashtar. How Tetkashtai bore the shame of having you carry her—*

How do you bear the shame of what you've become? demanded Dandra. She forced a vision on Medala, an image of her pinched and feral face held against a memory of how she had looked only months before in Sharn. *What happened to you?*

What happened? Medala shredded the vision with a thought. *What happened? I refused to die!* For a brief moment, the flow of memories from Dandra's mind to Medala's reversed.

Dandra saw Dah'mir's laboratory again, but this time from another point of view and washed with blue instead of yellow-green. She saw the tortured bodies of the three kalashtar laid out on the tables, inhabited by the feeble minds of their psicrystals. She felt Medalashana's fear and distress at her sudden imprisonment, felt powerlessness stretch her mind toward near-madness just as it had Tetkashtai's.

But Medalashana did something that Tetkashtai hadn't. At the moment when madness and eternal imprisonment had seemed closest, Medalashana had found the strength to reach back through the connection that bound her to her psicrystal.

Her crystal had been called Pok, a gentle spirit formed out of Medalashana's thirst for knowledge. It had taken no effort at all for Medala to murder him, snuffing out his light and reclaiming her body.

Dah'mir had come to her then, had taken a soul broken and mad, and made her his own.

Dandra cried out and wrenched herself away from Medala's memories. *Il-Yannah!* she gasped. She recalled her own memory of the moment she had taken up Tetkashtai's crystal: Medalashana's blue crystal had been dark. *You sacrificed your psicrystal to free yourself!*

It's the only way, Medala seethed. *Take back your body or be locked in the crystal. Virikhad couldn't do it.* She gave Dandra another memory, of standing at Dah'mir's side and watching Virikhad's body starving and growing weaker as the spirit of his psicrystal faded—until there was nothing left and Dah'mir allowed the mind flayers their feast. *And Tetkashtai . . .* She laughed madly. *We thought it was some hidden strength in her, but she was as weak as Virikhad!*

Dandra shuddered with loathing. Medala gave a final thrust into her mind—and found Dandra's fragile memories of the second journey from Zarash'ak to the Bonetree camp, the fragments of her distant sense of Tetkashtai's efforts to take a new host. Dandra felt her excitement. "Dah'mir!" Medala said out loud—and slipped away from Dandra's mind.

The chime faded from Dandra's ears. Somewhere Medala was telling Dah'mir everything she had discovered, babbling about Dandra's nature, about Tetkashtai's ability to force herself on anyone who held the crystal, about Geth and orcs. Dandra didn't listen. She just dragged herself up into a crouch and huddled back against the wall, trembling with rage at the violation of her mind.

Someone asked her a question, She didn't answer. A foot prodded her. She didn't move. The foot prodded harder. "Dandra," said Dah'mir, "if you don't want to talk to me, I can let Medala pry the answers I want from you again."

Dandra turned her head and looked up. Acid-green eyes looked down at her. She glanced away sharply before she could lose herself in them. "What is it about you that we can't resist?" she snarled angrily. "I've never felt anything like it. Neither had Tetkashtai. It's not psionic. It's not magic. What is it?"

"Why should I give away my secrets?" asked Dah'mir jovially. "Would you give away yours?"

"I don't have any left!" Dandra hissed at him.

Dah'mir's pale face stretched out as his eyebrows rose. "True enough." He squatted down. Dandra felt as if he was staring right through her, as though there was something that his eerie eyes alone could see. "I didn't expect something like you," he said after a long moment.

"Really? What did you expect?" Dandra asked. "Something like Medala, sacrificing a part of herself in her desperation to survive? Or something like Virikhad, clinging to his principles until he died?"

"Oh, Virikhad's not dead. Only his body has died so far—well, and the spirit of his psicrystal, of course." Dah'mir nodded at the violet ember of Virikhad's crystal. "He's still there. I think he'll let go soon. They—" He gestured toward the mind flayers, hovering on the fringes of the conversation like vultures around carrion. "—say it's not possible for him to let go, that he really is trapped in the crystal forever. None of us have touched the crystal, so we don't know if he's still capable of forming a new connection as you've shown us that Tetkashtai can."

His attention came back to her. "What I didn't anticipate was that a psicrystal might actually take control and attempt to rescue the psion." Dah'mir reached out and rested his fingers on her forehead. His touch was cool. "I should thank you."

Dandra twitched her head away angrily. "Is the only reason you lured Tetkashtai, Virikhad, and Medalashana to Zarash'ak because they were psions with psicrystals?" she snapped. She could feel a formless rage building inside her, an anger at whatever chance fate had attracted Dah'mir's attention to them—and her.

The green-eyed man smiled. "Only partly. They were convenient. Believe it or not, what I told them in my letter was partly true. I shared their interest in the interactions between magic, dragonshards, and psionics. I lured them to Zarash'ak because I *hate* having rivals." He stood and walked toward his towering device, staring up at the big blue-black stone at its heart. "In magical practice, Khyber shards have binding properties. I found a way to apply that to psionic practice as well. You've seen the results of my work for yourself. It needs refining, of course . . ."

Dandra stared at his grinning, handsome face, then choked out the only word she could manage. *"Why?"*

"Why?" Dah'mir turned and darted back to her, leaning in so close Dandra could feel the cool on her ear as he drew breath to whisper his answer—

—then stepped back, winking at her and waving his finger. "Not yet, Dandra. Maybe when Tetkashtai is here with you."

Dandra drew a sharp breath in spite of herself. "What are you talking about?"

Dah'mir laughed. Behind him, Medala gave a sharp grin.

"Ah, Dandra," Dah'mir said, "you've found yourself some very loyal friends. Maybe too loyal." He stood up. "I made a mistake in Zarash'ak when I killed Geth."

A sharp pain thrust through Dandra at the news and she gasped. Dah'mir waved her alarm away. "Hush. He survived, didn't he? Apparently, I didn't do as good a job as I thought. Given that he has Tetkashtai, that's a good thing." His lips tightened. "But his survival and the glimpses you've given Medala of his presence in an orc village go a long way toward explaining why there's a large raiding party of orcs trying to sneak through Bonetree territory right now."

Dandra stared at him. "The Dragon Below has many eyes," said Dah'mir with a shrug. He looked over his shoulder at the illithids. "Restrain her," he said. "I don't want them to have any warning."

He stepped back as one of the mind flayers moved forward. In its spindly fingers it bore a strange device with long, delicately jointed arms of bone and copper. Dandra tensed and started to rise but two more mind flayers narrowed their white eyes and the air seemed to ripple. A force like *vayhatana* seized her, holding her immobile. The first illithid reached out and slid the device onto her head.

A numbness seemed to fall over her. She saw and she heard, but it was if she couldn't actually *think* at all. Horror built within her but it had nowhere to go.

The mind flayers turned to the table that had held her captive once before and began preparing straps of thick leather. Dandra watched as Dah'mir took Medala's arm and paced out of the laboratory.

"It's a shame that Vennet isn't here," Dandra heard him tell the gray-haired kalashtar. "I think he'd have liked to see how a real trap is laid."

CHAPTER

15

Geth stared up at the black heron that soared overhead—the fourth that afternoon, the second since the sun had begun to settle below the clouds that choked the horizon and were spreading across the sky. He glanced at Orshok. "You're certain they can't see us?" he asked.

"Batul's prayers hide us from the senses of all animals," the young druid said confidently. "You could walk up to a rabbit right now and it would just sit there. The Bonetree's herons can't see us."

"Adolan examined one of the herons in Bull Hollow. He said it was tainted by the Dragon Below. Are you sure they're still just animals?"

"*Dagga,*" growled Krepis from his other side. "Many things tainted here. Trust Gatekeepers and walk."

He prodded Geth with the butt of the spear that he carried. The shifter bared his teeth at him but trotted on. Krepis still grated on his nerves, but the big orc's attitude toward him—and toward Natrac—had improved significantly since they'd emerged from Jhegesh Dol. The three druids weren't the only ones who'd been astounded by their retrieval of the dragon scale amulet from the ghostly fortress.

He looked ahead across the dry grassy folds of the Bonetree clan's territory. A dozen orcs prowled through the twilight. Twice that number strode behind him. Not all of them were Fat Tusk orcs, either. Word of the raid on the Bonetree had spread. Orcs had emerged from the marshes to join them as they traveled, all of them eager to strike against the clan.

In the center of the raiding party, Batul—the dragon scale amulet around his neck—moved with the speed and grace of an orc half or maybe even a third his age. Krepis and Orshok had both tried to persuade him to stay at Fat Tusk, but Batul had insisted. "The return of the amulet is a sign," he'd told them. "Great things will happen on this raid. You'll need me with you."

Geth had already been glad of the old druid's presence. His prayers had done more than hide them all from the Bonetree's herons: speaking with crocodiles from the riverbanks and birds from the air, he'd located Dah'mir's party with an ease that left even the other orcs amazed. The animals remembered Dah'mir. His passage disturbed them like something unnatural. Small animals remembered him with fear. Larger animals—crocodiles and marsh eagles—remembered him as a threat, like a stronger predator intruding on their territory.

None of the animals had good news for them, though. No matter how swiftly they traveled toward Bonetree territory, it seemed that Dah'mir was always just ahead of them. Geth had hoped they would catch the green-eyed man before he was able to return Dandra and Singe to the Bonetree mound.

Batul had calmed him and suggested a different course of action. They'd abandoned the river that morning at the edge of Bonetree territory for an overland approach to the mound. Again Batul's prayers had aided them. None of the orc raiders had knowledge of the land ahead but Batul had stretched out on the land at dawn and risen with an eerie insight into the lay of the region. Throughout the day, he'd directed the raiders to streambeds, gullies, and folds in the land that had hidden them from view.

Some among them had benefited from the druid's wisdom in a less magical fashion. Geth glanced sideways to where Natrac marched on the other side of Orshok. Out of the entire raiding party, the half-orc was the least used to the wilderness. Hampered as well by the loss of his hand, he'd been feeling out of place. His confidence had ebbed—at least until Batul took him aside and told the half-orc some of what he'd discovered after becoming blinded in one eye. "Learn your strengths," he'd advised. He'd tapped Natrac's scarred wrist. "You're probably not going to start having visions with this, but you shouldn't feel helpless."

The next evening Natrac had approached Orshok with a long knife begged from one of the raiders and asked for the young druid's help. A prayer from Orshok had tapped into nature's power, shaping and smoothing a piece of wood into a long shape like an oversized drinking cup with the knife blade sticking out of the closed end. Geth had guessed what they were doing and offered suggestions learned from his gauntlet. By the morning, Natrac had a wicked, if crude, weapon to lock over his severed wrist and take the place of his missing hand. "Dol Dorn's mighty fist," he'd rumbled with delight, "that's more like it!"

The way that he strode along, lopping off the nodding heads of grass stalks and thistles, filled Geth with a confidence he hadn't felt since . . . since he'd tracked two displacer beasts through the valley beyond Bull Hollow with Adolan. He bared his teeth and let a soft growl loose into the gathering night.

Up ahead, though, the scouting orcs were hunkered down, refusing to move forward. Geth moved forward. "What is it?" he asked. One of the scouts grunted out an answer.

"He says there's a ghost in the copse ahead," translated Natrac. "They've all heard it. They can't go on until Batul's examined it."

Geth looked at the small cluster of trees maybe a hundred paces ahead that had inspired such fear in the orcs. It didn't look like there was anything unusual about it, but it stood just below the crest of a low rise from which, Batul said, they would be able to get a good look on the Bonetree encampment. Geth could already smell the smoke of fires. He glanced back—Batul was still a distance behind them—then at Orshok and Krepis. "We need to get to that rise. Do we have to wait for Batul?"

Both looked taken aback at the question. Geth grimaced. Ever since Jhegesh Dol, he'd discovered while orcs could be great warriors and powerful druids, they also tended to be superstitious and skittish about ghosts and spirits. "Wait here then," the shifter grumbled. "I'll look myself."

He jogged past the squatting orcs and toward the copse. Halfway there, he could hear the eerie noise that had frightened the scouts, a soft and almost musical clacking. Geth clenched his fist inside his great-gauntlet and touched Adolan's collar with his free hand. The stones were as warm as the evening air. He walked on, a little more cautiously. There was no one in the copse and no visible source for the haunting sound—at least not until he was practically under the trees themselves.

Hung up among the branches and hidden by the leaves were dozens of dry bones, most of them human and orc, a few clearly more monstrous. As they stirred in the rising wind, they struck each other like macabre wind chimes.

"The enemies of the Bonetree—"

Geth stifled a yelp of surprise at the sound of a soft voice behind him and whirled around, his gauntlet leaping up protectively. Batul leaned calmly on his hunda stick, looking at him. "And the source of their name," he finished. He nodded at Geth's left hand, still in the act of reaching for his waist. "You have two weapons there," the old orc commented. "Which were you going to draw?"

The shifter glanced down. The ancient Dhakaani blade he'd seized in Jhegesh Dol hung from his belt in a makeshift sheath; the heavy, jagged sword felt good in his grasp and he'd elected to keep it. Batul had approved the choice.

But hanging next to the ancient weapon was the pouch that contained Dandra's psicrystal and Tetkashtai. The pouch was tightly knotted—there was no way that he could have touched the crystal—but a chill still passed through Geth as he realized that it had been the pouch and not the sword that he had been reaching for. He pulled his hand away, his teeth bared.

"I feel Tetkashtai in there, Batul," he said. "Ever since I held the crystal in Jhegesh Dol, I've been aware of her, slowly going mad from her imprisonment. It's like a thread of the connection between us is still there."

"Until you can give the crystal to Dandra," Batul replied,

"you'd do better to remember your other weapons." He stretched out his hunda and tapped the black metal of the great gauntlet, then the purplish metal of the Dhakaani sword. "That sword is forged from a metal called byeshk. It was made for killing aberrations like the daelkyr and their creations. Use it well tonight and you may live until morning." The druid turned from the clacking bone trees. "Let's have a look at what we're facing."

They crawled up the rise, stretching themselves out on the ground to avoid making a silhouette against the sky. When they reached the crest, Geth raised his head and looked over. The mound was close, so close he could see the grass on it bend in waves before the wind. To the right was the river and the ugly, rough shelters of the Bonetree clan's encampment.

All the members of the clan, however, were crowded into the stretch of ground that separated the camp from the mound. A number of tall torches stood in the center of the crowd. The rise was high enough that Geth could tell that they lit a broad, flat open space with the crowd gathered like spectators.

The humans of the Bonetree weren't the only ones in the crowd, though. He could see the squat, four-armed shapes of dolgrims. clustered with them, especially toward the mound. Like the humans, they were shifting and unsteady with excitement.

"What is this?" Geth growled at Batul. The old orc shook his head.

"They're waiting for something. A ritual fight maybe."

Geth almost choked. "Singe or Dandra?"

"Not likely Dandra." Batul's eyes narrowed. "Singe maybe. Or maybe not." He gave Geth a hard look. "Don't let it distract you."

The shifter drew a harsh breath and nodded. He turned back to the mound and picked out the dark mouth in its side that he recalled from Dandra's memories. It faced toward the crowd, but wasn't so close that the crowd was likely to interfere if they were fast and stealthy. In fact, whatever event the humans and dolgrims had assembled for could even serve as a distraction from their approach. He stretched out his arm and pointed. "The mound isn't all that high. We'll come in from the west. Orshok, Krepis,

Natrac, and the raiders you've picked out will come with me around the side of the mound. You and the rest climb the back of the mound. My group will take any guards at the mouth of the mound. Once we're inside, you attack from the high ground and keep everyone busy."

Batul nodded. *"Dagga.* That sounds good. Are you sure you don't want me to come with you? You may need my help."

Geth reached down and rapped his gauntlet against the hilt of the Dhakaani sword. "Tak, but I've got all the help I need." He glanced up as another black heron flew low overhead and circled down toward the river's edge.

The door—or rather the collection of crudely lashed together timbers that had been placed over the doorway—shuddered and was pulled aside. Voices outside spoke the language of the Bonetree and then Ashi ducked through the low opening—and froze.

"Come in," said Singe from the other side of the darkened shelter. "I'd offer you something to eat, but the larder's empty." He held up his hands, trembling fingers poised and ready to throw a spell. "If you're cold, though, I could warm things up."

Ashi didn't move. Neither did he.

After a long moment, Ashi swallowed. "Dah'mir will know if you use magic," she said softly. "Medala will come. You can't escape."

"I can try," Singe told her. "If I die, at least it would be better than living like this." He nodded around the hut. The walls had gaps, the tent-like ceiling had rips. The floor was dirt. The whole place smelled of mice and human sweat. "Especially if Hruucan has his way with me."

Ashi's face tightened. "At least you're not just killing yourself."

"I considered it. Then I thought, no, what would Ashi think?" His voice cracked.

The hunter took a step forward. "Singe . . ." she said. His hands tensed. A spell rose on his tongue. She froze again. Singe could feel his chest heaving.

He lowered his hands and swallowed the magic. "Twelve

moons," he croaked. "Why did you have to come? If it had been Breff, I could have blasted him and half of this damn camp at the same time!"

Ashi said nothing. Singe sighed. "I'm sorry. They're your clan."

"We're Dah'mir's clan," Ashi whispered bitterly. She reached behind her back. "It's time, Singe. Hruucan is waiting." She held out his rapier. The edge had been honed bright. Singe gave her a crooked smile as he took the weapon.

"Thank you. Not that it will do much good. I drove this through Hruucan's arm in Bull Hollow and he barely even bled."

"Use magic," Ashi advised him. "Use magic or strike for a killing blow. A dolgaunt will shrug off anything less." She hesitated for a moment, then looked down at the dirt floor. "Singe, I'm sorry I didn't help you escape when I had the chance."

The Aundairian started. "Ashi?"

She looked up at him. "I think you were right. I think I changed while I was away from the Bonetree." She drew a deep breath. "It won't be an honest death, but if Hruucan lets you live, I'll kill you."

Singe winced. "I know you mean that in the best possible way, but it really doesn't sound reassuring. But thank you. I hope it won't come to that." He sighed and slid the rapier into his scabbard, then looked down at himself.

Two weeks' travel from Zarash'ak had left him and his clothes filthy. If he was going to end up dead or crippled shortly anyway, he thought, he might as well risk a little magic. He spoke a simple spell, straightened his clothes and ran his fingers through his hair. Dirt sifted down onto the ground and a pleasant smell of spices surrounded him. "Better?" he asked Ashi.

The big hunter nodded. Singe stood straight and steeled himself. "Let's go meet Hruucan." He marched to the doorway and ducked through.

The Bonetree encampment was abandoned. From somewhere up ahead, he could hear the murmur of an excited crowd. With Ashi following him close, he strode toward it. They were almost out of the camp when a roar rose on the air, a weird muttering echo forming part of it. His bold step faltered. Ashi caught him and urged him on.

"That will be Hruucan entering the ring," she said grimly.

"And the echo?"

"Dolgrims. Dah'mir has brought the children of Khyber out of the mound to watch the duel."

Singe blinked. "The mound is empty?"

"Maybe," answered Ashi. "There's no way to know for certain."

The wizard looked at her. "Were you serious about rescuing me if you had the chance?"

She nodded.

Singe's guts twisted. "Then if you get the chance while I'm fighting, go into the mound and rescue Dandra," he said. "Get her out of here. Kill her if you have to. Just make sure that she's beyond Dah'mir's reach!"

Ashi's pierced lips hung open. "Into the ancestor mound?" she asked. "No one goes into the ancestor mound."

"Dandra's done it," Singe hissed. "Twice. Forget about me, but help Dandra." He searched her eyes. They were wide and frightened. "Please, Ashi!" he begged her. "Dah'mir has nothing in store for Dandra but torture. She needs your help."

Ashi swallowed. "I—"

But suddenly they were on the edge of the crowd and approaching a broad aisle that opened through the mass of the Bonetree clan. Breff and another hunter were waiting. They grabbed Singe and shoved him forward. Singe looked back for Ashi.

The crowd was already closing in eager anticipation. The tall hunter vanished behind him. Singe's teeth clenched. Was she going to help or wasn't she?

Either way he was on his own. "All right then," he growled to himself. "Let's put on a show." He shrugged his arms, pulled himself away from Breff and the other hunter, and fixed them with a cold glare.

"Touch me again and I'll remember it." The two hunters pulled up short. Singe turned and marched down the remainder of the rapidly closing aisle.

The "ring" was more like an oval, perhaps twenty paces at its widest point and twice as long. Dolgrims and the Bonetree clan stood all around it, a simple rope holding them back. Big torches burned atop six tall poles spaced around the ring, casting their flickering, ruddy glow down onto the dusty ground below and making the night beyond seem even darker.

The crowd fell silent as Singe stepped into the light. At the far end of the ring, the end closest to the mound, stood Hruucan, tentacles twitching hungrily. Behind him, Dah'mir and Medala sat like monarchs in great chairs raised up on a low platform. Dah'mir stood up. "Begin!" he shouted.

The roar that burst from the crowd was deafening, a buffeting wave of sound. Hruucan launched himself down the length of the ring, sprinting with a speed the wizard wouldn't have thought possible. Singe thrust out his arms and spoke the first of the spells he had carefully studied over the course of the afternoon. The words of the magic vanished in the roar of the crowd, but that didn't matter.

Light shimmered blue around him, then faded away. Singe could feel the protection of the magic clinging to him, though, an invisible skin of force that would help keep the buds and tendrils of Hruucan's skin from digging into his flesh quite so easily.

Then Hruucan was on him. From a dozen feet away, the dolgaunt leaped at him, curled fists leading, tentacles whipping around. Singe ripped his rapier free and threw himself to the side. Hruucan landed in a crouch and twisted back to his feet, turning smoothly to face Singe. His horrid, eyeless face was expressionless, but there was emotion in his every movement—he glided into a ready stance with a contemptuous grace.

Singe took a slow step back, putting a little distance between them, keeping his rapier up. Hruucan didn't move. Even his tentacles were still, poised like serpents. Singe risked another step.

Hruucan darted forward. His hands, open flat, thrust out in a flurry of short, sharp strikes that seemed to twine together with the attacks of his tentacles. Singe flung up his rapier, trying to put the blade in the way of that rain of blows. He stumbled backward as he parried, his feet raising little clouds of dust from the ground.

Then the dolgaunt pulled back, leaving him staggering—and wondering if he'd actually stopped Hruucan's attack or if the foul creature had only been toying with him.

The noise of the crowd was slowly dying back, overwhelming roars giving way to rippling shouts. Singe drew a hissing breath and moved to the side, circling around Hruucan. The dolgaunt moved to match him, always staying low and ready to strike. His tentacles swayed and stirred to either side of him as if each was trying independently to lure Singe into an attack. He didn't fall for it.

His free hand darted forward and he snapped a seething word of magic. Flames flared from his spread fingertips, splashing across the ring—but abruptly it was as if Hruucan was simply no longer there. To the soaring cheers of the crowd, the dolgaunt whirled aside, flowing away from the fiery magic in a tight spin of arms and tentacles. Singe turned to follow him but Hruucan was faster. His spinning form almost seemed to unravel, tentacles stretching out to slap at Singe. The wizard dodged away from one, but the other caught him with a hard slap across his face.

As he stumbled and reeled from the force of blow, the other tentacle snaked back and lashed around his legs, ripping his feet out from under him. Singe slammed down hard onto his back. He sucked in breath desperately and scrambled to regain his feet.

Hruucan met him with a pair of punches so fast and hard they lifted him up and threw him back. Singe hit the ground a second time, his chest aching, his lungs sucking hard for air.

The night shook with the roars of the Bonetree clan and Dah'mir's dolgrims. Singe rolled over onto his side and looked up to see Hruucan sinking back into his ready stance. The wizard cleared his throat, spat blood onto the dry ground, and climbed back to his feet. Forcing himself to stand straight, he lifted his rapier and offered the dolgaunt a taunting salute.

Hruucan's tentacles lashed the air angrily and he threw himself forward.

Ashi clenched her teeth and hissed as Hruucan unleashed another flurry of blows against Singe. Unlike his first furious attack, though, it was clear that the dolgaunt was no longer playing with his opponent. His strikes were real and hard. A hand, fingers curled like claws, slipped past Singe's guard to tear at him.

Whatever magic the wizard had cast on himself seemed to offer him some scant protection though: Hruucan's blow skittered across Singe's torso without even tearing his shirt. Singe slapped away his arm and thrust hard with his rapier into the dolgaunt's side.

But not hard enough. Hruucan lurched away and stood upright easily without a mark on him. A tentacle darted at Singe, slamming at his side in return. Singe lurched as well, but he didn't stand upright so easily.

He was going to lose, Ashi knew. It was inevitable. Hruucan was too fast for the wizard's magic and too powerful for his blade.

Ashi glanced beyond the crowd toward the dark mouth of the ancestor mound. No one was watching it. Nothing moved within. The fire of the Bonetree hunter who should have been standing honor guard guttered low, abandoned.

She hadn't told Singe all the tales about the mound that were spoken around the fires of the Bonetree. Stories of passages into the sacred depths and shrines built from dragonshards, yes—but also whispers of halls home to ghosts, of dark vaults where Dah'mir "prayed" with the outclanners who were sometimes led into the mound, of the lairs of Khyber's children and monsters too horrible to bear the light of day.

The crowd let out another roar. Ashi twisted back to the ring. Singe knelt on the ground, clutching at his belly. His rapier lay on the ground several paces away. Hruucan walked over to it—and kicked the weapon back to him disdainfully. Singe grabbed it, but Ashi could see the pain on his face as he rose.

Her eyes darted to Dah'mir, watching the fight with the benevolent expression of a doting father. At his side, Medala wore the staring hunger of a hunting panther.

All around the ring, she could see a similar bloodlust on the faces of people she knew as friends and comrades in arms. Breff leaped and shouted, cheering for a monster who roused only disgust in Ashi, a monster who had—by Breff's own account—driven the returning hunters almost to death. This is my clan, she told herself.

Would any of them have stood by her as Singe had stood by Dandra? Dah'mir hadn't stood by her, that was certain. By her or by the Bonetree.

Her hand fell to the huntmaster's sword. In spite of Singe's explanations, she wasn't sure she fully grasped the idea of Sentinel Marshals. "Honor blade," though—that was something she could understand. Maybe she carried the blood of Deneith, maybe she didn't. Either way, she knew that she carried the sword of a hero.

As Singe stumbled under another blow, Ashi slipped back from the crowd and darted for the mound. Scooping up a flaming brand from the absent guard's fire, she drew the honor blade and walked cautiously into the darkness of the tunnel.

"Someone's getting beaten bad out there," said Natrac.

"How do you know?" Geth asked. He checked the byeshk sword on his hip again, making certain the weapon would slide easily from the makeshift scabbard. Behind them, Krepis and the half dozen orcs that Batul had judged to be the best fighters among the raiding party were doing much the same thing and giving their weapons one last check. Orshok was offering up a last prayer for guidance and protection. Somewhere above them, Batul and the other raiders would be reaching the top of the mound.

"Listen to the crowd," said Natrac. "You can tell by the way they cheer. It's always the same voices—they're only cheering for one person. That means one person is giving all the good hits so the other must be taking them."

"Maybe they're all on one side."

"No, when that happens they boo a lot more and groan when the favorite takes a hit," Natrac explained—just as a collective gasp rose from the front of the mound.

"Like that?" Geth asked.

Natrac shook his head. "Crotch hit. A crowd will groan for that no matter who takes it."

Geth glanced at the half-orc. "You know a lot about crowds," he commented and Natrac gritted his teeth.

"*Dagga,*" he said. "You pick that up in an arena."

The shifter's eyebrows rose. "You were a gladiator?"

"I didn't say that, did I?"

Orshok moved up beside them. The young druid looked nervous. "Are you all right?" asked Geth.

Orshok nodded.

Geth snorted. "Grandfather Rat's naked tail. You're terrified."

The orc flushed. "This is a bigger fight than I've ever faced before," he admitted.

Geth reached out and punched him in the shoulder. "You did good when you came to our rescue in Zarash'ak. You fought like a veteran."

"I fought without thinking about it," Orshok said. "I just acted. I wasn't standing and waiting for a signal!"

"Then when Batul's signal comes, just do that again. Waiting may be hard, but it's the fighting that kills you."

The unseen crowd exploded with another roar. Geth bared his teeth and growled—then twitched at the feeling of something climbing up his leg. He looked down to see a tiny blue lizard blinking at him. Batul's signal. The old druid and the raiders had reached the top of the mound. Geth brushed the lizard away gently.

"We're ready," he rasped.

Natrac, Orshok, Krepis, and the rest of his band clustered close. Drawing a deep breath, Geth led the way around the mound.

The crowd came into view, a thick press of humans and dolgrims. Geth resisted the urge to try and see who was in the ring. The mouth of the mound was close and the way was clear. No one was watching them. A sentinel's fire beside the mouth had burned low. He turned for the shadowed tunnel.

Krepis's breath hissed at same moment that Orshok froze. "What is it?" snarled Geth sharply, glancing back. Even as the words left his mouth though, the stones of his collar turned cold. He choked on a gasp and spun around.

In front of the mouth of the mound, the shadows rippled and two figures seemed to step out of the air. One was a mind flayer, its probing mouth-tentacles glistening in the torchlight, a nightmare out of Dandra's memories.

The other was his own nightmare: the hulking, clacking, chitin-armored horror of a chuul!

CHAPTER

16

Geth's hand darted to his belt and snatched out his sword. The ancient weapon seemed even heavier than it had before, and the twilight sheen of the metal had taken on a dull glow, as if the sword somehow recognized that the creatures it had been made to destroy were near.

He heard shouts and screams from Batul's party on top of the mound. It was a trap. Dah'mir had been ready for them.

"Ambush!" he yelled. He raised his sword high and lunged—

The mind flayer's foul, tentacled head turned sharply. Its white eyes flashed and a wave of pure mental power blasted through Geth. He staggered under the assault, struggling to resist the illithid's power. The orcs in his band cried in fear and pain, caught in the same unseen attack. Some of those cries ended abruptly.

Around Geth's neck, though, Adolan's collar was icy, like a shocking slap of winter. Geth clung to that clean cold and forced himself to stay on his feet. A fast glance over his shoulder showed him that most of his band hadn't been so fortunate. Batul's hand-picked orc raiders were down and twitching on the ground. Krepis was supporting Natrac. Orshok stumbled like a drunkard.

"They knew!" the young druid gasped. "How did they know?"

"Those herons!" Geth roared. "Those damn herons!"

He whirled back to the mind flayer. Its tentacles thrashing, it slapped a spindly hand against the chuul's armored shell and the monstrous creature scuttled forward, pincers snapping.

Geth howled and shifted as he leaped forward to meet it. Invincibility flowing through him, he swung the byeshk sword hard at one of those grasping claws. The blade hit the chitin with a crunch, shattering it, and bit deep into the flesh beneath. The chuul screeched in pain and thrust out with its pincer, trying to slap him aside, but Geth soaked up the blow and stood his ground. He wrenched his sword free and dodged back, then swept the blade down the center of the pincer.

The heavy blade found the joint of the claw and cleaved through it in a spray of strange, thin blood. Half of the chuul's pincer sagged and fell, crippled. Once again, the creature screeched and thrashed, but Geth rolled under the sweeping, useless claw and threw himself at the mind flayer. The chuul was big and dangerous, but if the illithid had the chance to unleash another one of those mental blasts . . .

But the illithid was rising into the air, floating up as Dandra did—except higher. Safely out of his reach, it peered down at him with its dead white eyes.

The chuul's broad, armored back turned on Geth as Orshok, Natrac, and Krepis closed with it. Without even hesitating, the shifter jumped onto the creature, planted one foot at the curve above the thing's tail, vaulted up onto its shoulders, then—as the startled chuul reared back—leaped off and hurled himself at the hovering mind flayer.

He had a brief glimpse of the illithid's tentacles stiffening in sudden shock an instant before he slammed into it.

They tumbled through the air, his metal-clad right arm wrapped tight around its narrow, bony hips. Geth could feel thin fists pounding at his shoulders and tentacles groping and scraping at his head. He thrust upward with his sword.

The ancient Dhakaani smiths who had forged the weapon had ground sharp edges onto the spreading curves of its forked tip. The purple blade might not have pierced like a normal sword—but it cut very well. A palm's width of metal chopped deep into the mind flayer's back. Metal grated through bone. The mind flayer went limp.

They fell. Geth twisted and flung himself free from the creature, rolling as he hit the ground. He came up in crouch. The mind flayer's tentacles were still writhing, straining toward him. A whirling slice with the byeshk sword made certain the illithid was dead before he spun around.

Their tumble through the air had carried them away from the chuul and from the mouth of the mound. He was closer to the crowd now—and the people in the mob had finally realized that there was a larger battle going on than just the one they were watching. Roars and shouts rose into shrieks and battle cries. At the head of crowd, Dah'mir stood on a platform, arms thrust out.

"Attack!" he bellowed above the tumult. His green eyes flashed and a hand stabbed toward Geth. "The shifter! Bring the shifter to me!"

Geth's stomach knotted. "Tiger's blood!" he choked as Bonetree hunters and dolgrims alike split away from the swarm of the crowd.

Then Natrac and Orshok stood on either side of him with Krepis at his back. All three were covered in the thin blood of the chuul.

"I'm never eating lobster again," croaked Natrac.

Geth bared his teeth in grim humor and risked a glance up at the top of the mound. The clouds that had covered the sky flashed with distant heat lightning and against that fitful flickering, bulky figures struggled. Chuul raised their pincers and dolgaunts struck with tentacles. Above the battle, robes whipping in the wind, floated two more mind flayers. Geth caught a glimpse of dark shapes tumbling down the steep side of the mound as orcs managed to topple a chuul, only to be caught and stunned by the mental blast of one of the illithids.

"Where's Batul?" he spat over his shoulder at Krepis. "Why isn't he doing something?"

Lightning danced from the clouds in a bolt that wrapped around one of the floating mind flayers. The thin creature's limbs and tentacles snapped into sudden stiffness and it dropped out of the air like a wounded bird. The brilliant flare left an image imprinted on Geth's eyes: the silhouette of an old orc with his hunda stick raised to the sky.

"Batul doing something!" Krepis shouted above the thunder that rolled across the battlefield.

The lightning had barely given the hunters and dolgrims pause, but it gave Geth fresh hope. He thrust up the byeshk sword.

"Take it to them!" he roared—and charged.

One of the mind flayers had a particular streak of cruelty. When the illithids left Dandra, it turned her head so that she could see Virikhad's psicrystal gleaming in the dim light of laboratory. With the weird device of copper and bone clutching her head, Dandra felt like she had no will at all. She couldn't think, she couldn't move, she could barely call up memories from only moments before—not that there was much to remember. The laboratory was still. The only sound, apart from a brief, distant flurry of excitement and activity that came and went elsewhere in the mound, was her breathing.

Somehow she could still *feel*, though, maybe out of instinct like breathing or blinking her eyes. Emotions bubbled inside her, primal emotions, raw and pure. Fear. Rage. Uncluttered by thought, they burned her.

There was something familiar about that purity of emotion. Her mind drifted and flew back through her memories, back before her anger and her fear, back before Bull Hollow and that first trip Zarash'ak and even before Sharn. Back before she'd been a person to when she'd been a crystal, before she'd even developed a proper mind. Back to the time when all that she'd been was emotion, new and raw, eager and focused.

She hadn't been fear, then. She hadn't been rage. She had been determination.

She had been and always would be.

Light shone on the walls of the laboratory. Orange light, the glow of a proper flame, not the blue-green light of Dah'mir's strange torches. Dandra heard the whisper of quiet footsteps, heard someone murmur her name. The light came closer. It moved around the table and Ashi stepped into Dandra's field of vision. The big hunter carried a naked blade and a stick of wood that had burned through nearly half of its length. Dandra saw her spear strapped across her back. Ashi's face was pale, but strangely resolved. She moved back and Dandra felt the straps that bound her body being released. The hunter returned to her vision, bending down to look into her eyes.

"Dandra?" she asked again. Ashi's eyes flicked to the spindly device that the illithids had slid down over her head. She set down her sword and reached up to tug the device away.

Thought returned to fill Dandra's head with a rush of demands and concerns, but pure determination cut through all of them. She reached for her powers with an ease like nothing she'd known before and spun out a rippling web of *vayhatana*.

Ashi slammed back hard against the ground. She struggled desperately as Dandra sat up and glared down at her. "Let me go!" she spat. "I'm here to—"

Dandra squatted down and slapped her. "You're here to what?" she snapped. "Hunt me? I'm already here. Torment me? Let's wait for the mind flayers to come back. Murder my friends? I think Dah'mir's already done that!"

"No, you stupid outclanner!" snarled Ashi. "I'm here to rescue you!"

"Really? Why would you do that?" Dandra narrowed her eyes in concentration and Ashi's body rose from the floor, flying through the air to slam against the wall of the laboratory. The big woman grunted in pain. She blinked and focused her eyes on Dandra.

"I'd do it because Singe asked me to!" Ashi said. "While you were under Dah'mir's power, Singe helped me understand things about myself. I'm leaving the Bonetree clan. It was too late for me to save him, but—"

"Save him?"

Dandra's concentration faltered. The invisible bonds that held Ashi faded. Dandra reached to summon up the *vayhatana* again—until she realized that Ashi, although standing free, hadn't moved. The hunter looked at her, waiting.

"I hid that I knew you weren't Tetkashtai all the way from Zarash'ak," she said after a moment. "I'm sorry for what I did to you, Dandra. Singe has shown me that Dah'mir isn't what I thought he was. I want a new life and if you'll let me, I'll start it by making things right with you."

Dandra stared at her. "I . . ."

"Dandra," Ashi pleaded, "why else would I betray Dah'mir?"

The kalashtar clenched her teeth. "Start with this, then," she said. "You said it's too late to save Singe. Save him from what?"

"He's fighting Hruucan," Ashi answered. "Hruucan demanded it in revenge for the scars Singe inflicted on him." She grimaced. "He won't kill Singe—Dah'mir won't let him—but he'll cripple him. The Bonetree and all the children of Khyber are watching the fight. That's why I was able to get in here. The mound's empty!"

"It's empty because Dah'mir's preparing an ambush," Dandra told her. "Geth survived Dah'mir's attack in Zarash'ak and now he's bringing an orc raid here to rescue Singe and I. They're already in Bonetree territory but they're walking into a trap."

Ashi drew a sharp breath and her fists tightened. "There was no sign of a raid or an ambush laid when I entered the mound—but I heard fighting as I followed the tunnels. I thought it was some echo or ghost."

Dandra's throat tightened. "Light of il-Yannah." It had started. "How quickly can you get me back to the surface?"

"I marked the way." Ashi reached behind her back and pulled Dandra's spear free of a harness. "I kept it," she said. "A trophy at first, but now . . ." She held out the weapon.

Dandra took it. "Thank you," she said. Holding the spear brought some of her determination back to her. She looked around Dah'mir's laboratory, at the strange device with the blue-black shard in its heart, at Virikhad's violet crystal. Dandra walked over to the crystal and held her hand above it. She could feel the faint spark of Tetkashtai's old lover inside and for a moment a part of her itched to take up the crystal and make a connection with him. At the same time, though, she knew what even a short imprisonment had done to Tetkashtai and Medala. Virikhad had been locked inside his crystal without access to a body for far longer than either of them ever had. There was no telling how far he had fallen in his desperation.

"Dandra?" asked Ashi. She stood at the door of the laboratory.

"One moment." Dandra lifted her hand. No matter what his mental state might be, she couldn't leave Virikhad here. Steeling herself, she went over to the kalashtar's withered body and tugged a pouch from his belt, then used the head of her spear to tap the violet crystal into it. She looked up at the Dah'mir's strange device again.

She had tricked Tetkashtai into agreeing to return to Zarash'ak by hinting that perhaps there was a way to undo what Dah'mir had done to them. Now she was almost certain that there wasn't. She and Tetkashtai were trapped as surely as Virikhad. Why had Dah'mir created such a terrible device? She might still be able to find a way to force the truth from the green-eyed man, but there was one thing she was certain of—the device should *never* have existed.

She didn't have the strength or the time to destroy it, but maybe there was something she could do. Focusing her concentration on the dragonshard at the device's center, she spun *vayhatana* around it and wrenched the shard free of the brass and crystal that surrounded it. The laboratory had a high ceiling. Dandra lifted the shard all the way up—then brought it crashing down as hard as she could.

It hit the floor of the laboratory with a shattering impact that echoed through the chamber. Dandra stepped forward and examined the deep crack that now ran through its heart with a fierce satisfaction. Ashi stepped up beside her to stare down in amazement.

"Now," said Dandra, turning away from the ruined shard. "We can go."

Singe hurt. When Hruucan's tendrils had burrowed into him in Bull Hollow, it had seemed like the greatest agony of his life. When Medala's powers had wracked him, he had thought *that* was a threshold of suffering. But Hruucan's tendrils had only dug into his skin and Medala's powers, for all that they felt real enough, had only acted upon his mind. Now Singe *really* hurt.

He hit the ground again. As he struggled for breath, Hruucan's tentacles wrapped around his right calf and ripped through the fabric of his trousers to expose the soft flesh underneath. They dug in, making him scream—then they pulled, wrenching on his entire leg so hard that his scream broke. The crowd cheered. Singe kicked feebly at the tentacles with his free leg and Hruucan released him. For the moment.

The magical armor he had conjured was tough, but not impenetrable. Not all of the dolgaunt's blows pierced its protection, but more than enough had. His arms and legs were blistered from Hruucan's touch. His ribcage was sore and whenever he breathed deep a sharp pain burst inside him. His sides hurt where Hruucan's blows had driven deep to bruise tender organs. All of his joints ached. His left shoulder had been dislocated—then cruelly popped back into place. One eye was swollen badly, he could taste dust mingling with blood on his lips, and all he could hear out of one ear was a loud ringing.

Even through the pain though, Singe knew that there were three parts of him that Hruucan hadn't hurt badly—or at least not too badly. The dolgaunt hadn't hurt his legs. He could still walk and fight. The dolgaunt hadn't hurt his hands. He could still grip his rapier. And, except for the blow that still ached through his guts, the dolgaunt hadn't hurt his groin. He would still be able to father children for the Bonetree clan.

None of his carefully prepared magic had helped him. Hruucan either shattered his spells before he could cast them or dodged the flames with uncanny speed.

Singe forced himself up onto his hands and knees, then groped for his rapier in the dirt and stumbled to his feet once more. "Come on," he slurred at the waiting dolgaunt. "Give me another!"

Hruucan tensed, ready for another strike.

Before he could even move though, new shouts rose up from the crowd. For one brief, confused moment, Singe wondered if someone out there had finally started to cheer for him. Then it registered in this throbbing mind that the crowd was moving, turning away from the combatants in the ring to stare at something else. He lifted his aching head, trying to see beyond the glare of the high torches. Heat lightning had come to the night.

When it flashed he caught a glimpse of fighting up on the top of the mound.

Something was happening below as well. Dah'mir was standing and shouting so loudly that the sound of his voice shuddered in Singe's head. "The shifter! Bring the shifter to me!"

The crowd around the ring burst like a nest of baby spiders. Singe's head swam. A shifter? *The* shifter? Crazy hope soared inside him. Geth had come for them!

Lightning flashed in sudden brilliance, throwing the shape that moved in front of him into stark relief. Singe blinked as thunder rolled. Hruucan still stood in the ring, tentacles streaming and swaying.

"We're not done," the dolgaunt rasped.

He leaped into the air and his legs snapped out. Both feet hit Singe's aching chest, the dolgaunt's entire weight behind them. Singe flew back to slam into one of the towering torch poles. He slid onto the ground, legs sprawled. Darkness swirled around him, threatening to draw him down.

No, he told himself, fighting to resist that pull. *No! Not now!*

Somewhere lightning flashed again. Singe's head fell back against the pole, staring up at a sky that tossed in growing agitation—and at a long oil-soaked rag that had come loose from the torch above. It swayed back and forth in the wind, fat drops of flaming oil shaking off it and dripping down. Singe watched one splatter against his hand, the magic of his ring sucking the flame away before it burned him. A desperate plan formed in his head.

Hruucan looked at him for a moment longer, then turned away. Singe thrust himself to his feet and dove for the dolgaunt's back. Hruucan spun around, but Singe grabbed him and pulled him close. The writhing buds on Hruucan's skin reacted as if they had minds of their own, burrowing into Singe's flesh out of instinct alone. The wizard gasped and held on with one hand as he stretched the other out free. "Let's see you dodge this," he choked—and hissed a word of magic. A tiny, intense tongue of flame sprang into the palm of his free hand. Hruucan's horrid face tightened.

Singe tipped his hand and let the tiny flame fall.

Fire exploded around them. Hruucan tried to leap away from the flame, but Singe clung tight, holding him back. The dolgaunt's mouth opened to scream and fire rushed in. Singe closed his eyes, shutting out the sight of Hruucan's death. He couldn't shut out the feel of it though. The dolgaunt stiffened in his arms, writhing skin turning crisp and hard under his fingers. The buds that had burrowed into his flesh burst against him like a thousand tiny sparks.

Protected by his grandfather's ring, all Singe felt of the flames was a pleasant warmth. When that faded, he opened his eyes.

He held a blackened corpse, mouth frozen wide, tendrils and tentacles seared away. The wizard shuddered in horror and thrust it away. What had been Hruucan hit the scorched ground with a dry crunch and a spray of cinders. Singe swayed, suddenly weak, and sat down hard.

All around the ring, the swarming crowd had turned back, startled by the flames. Fire had consumed two of the torchpoles, but by the light of the remaining torches, Singe could see the pale faces of the Bonetree clan and a few startled dolgrims staring at him. Dah'mir had fallen silent. The distant sounds of fighting on the top of the mound went on, punctuated by another bolt of lightning and a high, unnatural squeal, but the fighting on the ground ended in a clash of metal, a familiar growl, and the thud of a falling body.

Geth leaped into the torchlight. Natrac and two other orcs were with him. The shifter spun, protecting the others as a dolgrim tried to take them from behind. A vicious-looking sword that Singe had never seen before flashed twilight-purple. In an instant, the dolgrim had one less arm and one more mouth, a jagged slash that opened across its belly. Another blow hacked deep into its deformed skull and it dropped. Geth wrenched the sword free and joined Natrac and the orcs in a cluster around Singe.

As Bonetree hunters and more dolgrims began to push in, forming a new and threatening crowd around a now much smaller ring, he spared a glance down at the wizard. "I had a feeling it was you in here," he growled.

"The fire?" asked Singe with a weak smile.

"The screaming." Geth glanced at the orcs. "Orshok, help him. Krepis, can you see what's happening on the mound?"

As the larger of the orcs tried to peer off above into the night, the other squatted down quickly, pulling a flask from a pouch. "A healing potion," he said to Singe, and the wizard realized with a start that he was the same orc who had helped them in Zarash'ak. The orc opened the flask. A smell like bitter tea mixed with over-ripe fruit stung Singe's nostrils. He twitched his head away out of reflex, but the motion sent a spasm of pain down his back. The orc grabbed his face and turned it back to him, forcing the flask against his lips. "Drink," he ordered.

The potion tasted as bad as it smelled, but as it worked its way down his throat, a cool sensation spread through his body that was utterly different from Fause's foul healing. The worst of his pain eased away, leaving him with only bruises and scrapes. Singe drew a deep breath.

"I'd enjoy that," said Natrac. "It could be your last." He thrust a long knife fastened where his missing hand should have been at a Bonetree hunter as she took a step closer. She bared her teeth and darted back.

The orc helped Singe to his feet. The wizard squeezed in between him and Geth. Together with Natrac and the second orc, they numbered five. He looked out at the massed hunters and dolgrims who clustered around them just out of sword reach, shifting and jostling for best position in the coming slaughter. "You healed me for *this*?" he asked.

"You're welcome," Geth grunted. "Where's Dandra?"

"In the mound. Unless—" His eyes darted across the crowd. He might have been wrong, but it seemed like one tall hunter was missing from the battle. Breath hissed between his teeth. "Ashi. Twelve moons, Ashi's gone for her!"

"Ashi?"

"Long story. She's changed sides. She's blood of Deneith, Geth!"

The shifter cursed. "So we don't know where Dandra is. Any spells handy?"

"A couple." Singe tried to gauge the effect his magical flames might produce. "I might be able to open us a path to the mound, but getting away again would be something else."

"We'll worry about that when we have to," said Geth. He hesitated, then added, "Singe, about Narath—if we get out of this, we'll talk. No more running."

Singe shot him sharp glance. "Deal," he said.

Geth looked at the two orcs and Natrac. "Ready?" They nodded. Geth looked to Singe. "Do it," he said. Singe drew a breath and spread his hand, calling the words of a spell to mind . . .

But before he could cast the spell, a ripple and a murmur spread through their enemies. The mass of bodies surrounding them was pulling back, a path opening through the ranks. A path that led directly toward the mound—and Dah'mir and Medala.

The pair was still on their platform, though they looked distinctly less calm than Singe had ever seen them. Dah'mir sat stiffly in his chair as yet another bolt of lightning flashed overhead. Medala crouched on her seat, flinching like the dog at the thunder. When she caught sight of Singe along the open path though, her hand snapped out to point at him. "You defy Dah'mir!" she shrieked. "You defy him! I'll turn your mind inside out! I'll feed you your own fears! I'll—"

"Medala!" snapped Dah'mir. "Enough! Sit down!" His green-eyed gaze snapped around and he glared at them. "Give me Tetkashtai. Give me the crystal."

Singe felt waves of charisma wash over him, Dah'mir's astounding and eerie presence beating against him. He wasn't sure why he was fighting the green-eyed man. If he'd had Dandra's crystal, he'd have given it up to him.

Geth just stood up straight, his eyes hard. "No," he said.

The denial seemed to break Dah'mir's spell over all of them. Singe blinked and shook his head as Dah'mir sat back sharply. His pale, beautiful face was contorted with incoherent rage. If his presence had been overwhelming before, it was now terrifying. Singe's legs shook. Medala let out a screech that was almost inhuman. Around them, the Bonetree hunters and even the dolgrims were trembling and falling back.

Dah'mir rose and stepped down from the platform, the black leather of his robes whispering around him. The aura of his presence surrounded him like twilight, dark and growing darker with every heartbeat. He seemed to loom over them all. Even Geth was pale. He raised his arms, crossing sword and gauntlet before him, ready for a fight that the expression on his face said he knew he wouldn't win.

"The crystal!" roared Dah'mir in a voice that rocked the night. *"Give it to me or—"*

His words died in the flash of lightning that fell down out of the sky, dropping on him in a twisting bolt so intense that the ground shook. All around the spot where Dah'mir had stood, hunters were thrown back. The platform on which he had sat was battered aside and Medala sent flying. Even fifteen paces away, the energy of the bolt stung Singe's arm as he flung it up to shield his eyes. At his side, Geth staggered back, then staggered again as thunder hammered them.

After an instant of stunned silence, Orshok threw up his arms and let out a whoop of triumph—a whoop that died as suddenly as the lightning had fallen.

Dah'mir was picking himself up from the ground. His fine robes were scorched and his pale face smudged, but his acid-green eyes were brighter than ever. He whirled like a striking serpent, shouting an arcane word as his fingers flicked at the night.

As if dawn had come early, daylight spread across the side of the mound to reveal a battered party of orcs—and the scattered bodies of chuul, dolgaunts, and even mind flayers. Near the top of the slope, stood an old white-haired orc, his staff still directed toward Dah'mir.

The moment froze.

Then a warrior among the orcs raised an axe over his head and screamed out a wild battle cry. The cry whipped through the orcs and abruptly they were pounding down the slopes in a howling, savage green wave.

The Bonetree hunters and dolgrims leaped to meet them without even a word from Dah'mir, horrid shrieks and wild screams rising into the air. More threw themselves wildly at Geth and

Singe's little band. From the corner of his eye, Singe saw Orshok spin a staff while Krepis met a dolgrim with a thrust from a spear. Natrac battled a Bonetree hunter, one of the bloodthirsty young men who had tried to challenge Ashi. Dolgrims leaped at Geth; the shifter threw one back with a thrust of his gauntlet, then cut down the other with a swing of his sword.

Singe just stared at Dah'mir's back, turned to them as he glared up at the old orc on the mound. There was a clear line between him and the green-eyed man. The wizard thrust out his hand and spat a word of magic.

Flames roared from his hand, two seething bolts that washed over Dah'mir's back and engulfed him utterly.

The fiery blast had even less effect than the lightning. Dah'mir whirled and the magical flames were snuffed out in the folds of his robe. Eyes filled with utter rage pierced Singe—then Dah'mir stiffened and his face twisted in anger. His hands clenched into fists, he threw back his head, and roared, *"Enough!"*

The flash of lightning lit the tunnel ahead. Thunder shook the stone-lined walls. "Il-Yannah!" Dandra gasped.

"We're close!" Ashi shouted. She raced forward. Dandra tightened her grip on her spear and darted after her.

It seemed as if the sun rose as they reached the mouth of the mound, a warm and magical light that flooded the tunnel and shone across a scene of chaos outside. Dandra caught a glimpse of a crowd of Bonetree hunters and dolgrims. Of Singe, Geth, Natrac, and two orcs standing at defense, weapons bristling.

Of Dah'mir standing, pointing up at the slope of the mound, green eyes blazing.

She froze at the sight of him.

His presence was as stunning and irresistible as ever, drawing her every thought to him in horrible fascination. All the way up through the tunnels of the mound, following the path that Ashi had marked, Dandra had tried to prepare herself for this moment, fortifying herself, telling herself that this time she would *not* succumb to his charm.

But there was no charm about Dah'mir now. Rage poured from him instead. He was furious and terrible, some ancient power, some predator of unbelievable madness and strength. Standing atop a toppled chair, Medala screamed and ranted as if animated by that madness. Dandra fought to pull back, to close her eyes and cut off the sight.

Ashi did it for her, dragging her back into the tunnel as cries of battle rage and the thunder of charging feet rolled down from above. Orcs streamed past the tunnel mouth in a tide of fury. Hunters and dolgrims surged forward to meet them. Violence swirled outside the mound—but Ashi's quick action had broken Dah'mir's hold on her. Dandra sucked in a heaving breath. Ashi released her. "Are you all right?"

"Dah'mir almost had me again." There was a frightening suspicion growing inside her. She could still hear Medala screaming in reflection of the insanity that shone in Dah'mir's eyes. "It's his madness," she breathed half to herself. "There's something about his madness . . ."

There was no time to follow the thought. The distinctive roar of flame rushed over the battlefield. Dandra gasped. "Singe!" Bracing herself against Dah'mir's power, she leaped back to the tunnel mouth in time to see the green-eyed man, his robes smoking, throw back his head and roar.

A roar that changed and grew deeper as Dah'mir's throat and chest swelled and stretched and . . . transformed.

"Light of il-Yannah!" she breathed in shock.

"Twelve bloody moons!" cursed Singe in awe. Geth could only stare, his gauntlet and the Dhakaani sword just weights on his arms.

The change began in Dah'mir's face. His cheeks swept back into his ears. His chin grew sharp and pointed as the tip of a knife, his entire lower face stretching out after it. His eyebrows rose and vanished as flat, sweeping horns rose from his head.

Clenched fists became knotted claws. Arms and legs shifted and changed. Black hair and robes of leather merged and became scaly hide as pale skin darkened and took on a sheen of copper that spread down Dah'mir's throat and belly. A thick tail thrust out of his back and he grew—and grew—*and grew*.

Acid-green eyes as big as lanterns narrowed. Massive legs flexed and thrust against the ground. Wings like coppery-black sails stretched from Dah'mir's side to beat the air.

Geth's lips peeled back to bare his teeth and he found his voice. "Tiger, Wolf, and Rat!" he snarled as the dragon leaped into the sky.

CHAPTER

17

Everywhere around them, the fury of battle gave way to panicked chaos. Orc raiders and Bonetree hunters alike fell back in awe at the sight of the terrible and majestic monster climbing into the night. With shouts of gut-deep fear, they reeled apart, fighting to scatter.

The dolgrims didn't flee. Wiry arms rose in triumph and gash-like mouths gibbered horrid glee as they surged forward to hack and thrust at raiders and one-time allies alike. There was an eager spark in their eyes that Geth would have sworn hadn't been there before, as if they had been freed to unleash the darkest bloodlusts of their twisted souls.

The shifter spun. Across the battlefield, the mouth of the mound gaped like a shadow under Dah'mir's magical light. Geth flung out his arm, pointing with the Dhakaani sword. "There!" he said. "We need to get in there! We need shelter!"

Natrac's eyes were wide, his pupils so large that barely a sliver of color showed around the black. "In there? Are you insane? We need to—"

The half-orc's words faltered as Dah'mir's wings dipped and his massive, shining body turned in an arc. On the other side of the churning battle, a knot of orcs was still fighting, caught up in mindless rage. Dah'mir's wedge-shaped head darted forward and his throat heaved.

Thin yellow bile burst from his jaws in a long, hot gout. It swept across the ground below like a line of foul rain. Where it fell, the ground smoked and trampled plants shriveled. Most of it, though, spattered against the fighting orcs and their dolgrim assailants, drenching them.

Flesh melted, eaten away by the dragon's acid. Huge red sores opened and spread. Skin sloughed from muscles and muscles fell away from bones. The orcs died squealing and writhing in the steaming mud. The dolgrims died too, but with excited screams that might almost have been praise for their dragon-lord.

Singe grabbed Natrac and dragged him toward the mound. In shock, the half-orc stumbled at first, then charged for the shelter of the mound's mouth. Orshok and Krepis needed no encouragement—they leaped forward like sprinters. Dolgrims closed in around them. Geth held the rear of their desperate flight, beating back the four-armed horrors with sword and gauntlet. He kept one eye on the sky. Dah'mir's bulk hampered his agility, but he more than made up for it in sheer strength. It took only a few beats of his massive wings to put the dragon high in the sky. He wheeled around the far side of the mound and began a wide turn for another pass over the battlefield.

A memory of Breek washed over Geth, a vision of Adolan's eagle soaring high into the air before plunging down in a devastating strike. His stomach clenched. He beat back a flurry of attacks from a dolgrim, then hammered his armored fist into the creature's face. The dolgrim staggered back with the bloody imprint of his knuckles stamped over a shattered cheek. Geth leaped after the others. He peered ahead, trying to keep them all on a path through melee and toward the mouth of the mound.

There was a figure in the shadows, tall and powerful with long, dark gold hair. Ashi, watching the flow of battle. Her eyes met briefly with Geth's, and he felt a twinge of astonishment as the hunter gave him a slight nod before glancing back as if speaking to someone hidden deeper in the tunnel. "She has her!" Geth said to Singe as the fighting pushed them together again. "Grandfather Rat, I think Ashi has Dandra! They're just inside the mound!"

"If they're smart, they'll stay there!" Singe wheezed.

Blood flecked the wizard's lips and his face had gone pale again. Orshok's potion hadn't healed all of his wounds. Geth didn't think Singe could go on fighting much longer. Dah'mir's return wasn't the only thing they were racing. He swept his arm into the air, urging the others forward. "Hurry!" he shouted. "To the mound!"

"Wait!" said Krepis. He pointed with his hunda stick. "There's Batul!"

Geth turned to follow the pointing stick. Surrounded by dolgrims, the old druid stood back to back with two Fat Tusk orcs. Geth bared his teeth, torn by a primal desire to seek shelter and the need to help an ally. He raised his sword and ordered, "Break them free!"

He led the charge across the battlefield—now nearly empty of everything but dolgrims, the dead, and the wounded. He whirled and darted, slashing at the dolgrims with the heavy sword, sweeping their attacks aside with his magewrought gauntlet. A spear reached under his arm and creased shifting-toughened skin. Geth roared and lashed out with a kick that sank into the dolgrim's gut and doubled it over, both mouths screeching in pain. An overhand blow cut deep into the deformed skull of another dolgrim—and they were through, standing beside Batul and his guardians and fighting back the rest of the dolgrims.

Geth threw a glance at the elderly orc. "Tell me you didn't expect this!"

"I didn't expect it!" Batul's hunda stick was smeared with gore and he was bleeding from a gash under his good eye. "A true dragon leading a cult of the Dragon Below . . . not even the wildest tales of Gatekeeper lore hint at something like this!" A dolgrim tried to break through the circle of Batul's protectors. The druid swung his hunda in a sharp blow that sent it hopping back, then fixed his eye on Geth. "There may be a way to escape Dah'mir—if you have the strength for it."

Something in Batul's voice lifted the hair on Geth's neck and arms. "What?"

"Gatekeeper magic and Dhakaani weapons together ended the Daelkyr War. Dah'mir isn't a creature of Xoriat or a creation of the daelkyr, but he carries their taint. I have Gatekeeper magic. You have a Dhakaani weapon."

The flow of battle surged and shifted, leaving them in the clear for a moment. Geth stared at Batul. "You want me to kill a dragon?"

"No." Batul's hands tightened on his hunda. "Nothing either of us can do could kill him. But we can wound him and give the others a chance to escape."

The shifter caught the omission in his words. "The others," he said, "but not us."

Batul nodded. For a moment, Geth's heart thundered in his chest, then he nodded in return—

—just as Singe shouted out *"Twelve moons! He's back!"* Geth's gaze snapped up to the sky.

Dah'mir's descent from the night came like a storm. He swooped in from the east, a dark and speeding mass in the cloud-shrouded moonlight. As he swept into the magical light that illuminated the battlefield, color seemed to explode across his scales—a lightning flash of dulled copper tinged with corroded black. Thunder clapped with the spread of his wings and rolled through the ground as he settled at the other end of the battlefield. His green eyes shone with rage and his blunt muzzle was open to expose huge teeth. Even the dolgrims scurried away from him, their cheers fading in fright.

An enormous, sharp-pointed tongue slipped out of Dah'mir's mouth and licked blood off the scales of his face. More blood stained his talons. Geth guessed that some of those orc raiders, maybe even some of the Bonetree hunters, who had fled the battlefield weren't fleeing any longer. The shifter dropped slowly into a defensive stance, sword and gauntlet raised together, as if an attempt at defense would do any good at all.

Alongside him, Singe, Natrac, Krepis, and Orshok raised their weapons as well. Geth glanced at Batul. The Gatekeeper had closed his eyes. Geth adjusted his grip on the Dhakaani sword, trying to settle his sweating palm around the hilt.

Singe's eyes were on Dah'mir. "What's he waiting for?" he asked.

"He's waiting," said Medala's harsh voice, "for me."

Battle-trained reflexes and nerves already on edge brought Geth snapping around. Medala stood like an iron pillar in the midst of the carnage of the battleground. Her body was rigid with rage, the veins and muscles of her thin neck standing out like cables. Her arms were stiff at her side, her eyes wide with an insane hatred.

As fast as his reflexes might have been, thought was faster. The crystalline tone of a chime seemingly so loud that it could have roused the dead shimmered through him—and all at once his chest squeezed tight, forcing the breath out of his lungs. Darkness swept around the edges of his vision and it was all Geth could do to gasp for air. The chime echoed in his mind, rolling on and on. Geth could see the others reeling around him as well. Krepis was clutching his throat. Batul sagged against his staff. Singe was on his knees, sucking in breath after wracking breath.

"You think you can escape?" spat Medala, her voice rising into a shriek. "You think you can find shelter from my master's wrath? There is none! Khyber waits below all things and the lords of Khyber count Dah'mir among their greatest servants! There will be no more defiance from you!"

Every word seemed to grate across the lingering echoes in Geth's mind. He could feel Adolan's collar cold around his neck, but unlike the protection the Gatekeeper stones had offered from the mental attack of the mind flayer or Dah'mir's commanding presence, the ancient magic seemed to falter before Medala's psionic power. Geth tried to heave himself up straight, to swing his sword at Medala, but all he could manage was a feeble stagger.

Medala's eyes flashed and agony crashed through him in another ringing chime. He fell against the ground and his next breath sucked in gritty soil.

In the darkness of the mound, Dandra pressed her back against the packed earth of the tunnel wall and listened to the noises of the battle outside. Cheers of triumph from dolgrims, terrible cries from people dying a horrible death.

"He spits acid!" said Ashi in shock. The big hunter stood closer to the tunnel mouth, motionless in the thin shadows, describing what was taking place outside. "Dandra, he spits acid!"

Dandra could hear the rage and fear that trembled in Ashi's voice. She squeezed her eyes shut, half-glad that she couldn't see what the hunter did, half-sick that she didn't even dare to look. Dah'mir's transformation hadn't diminished his fascinating, captivating presence at all—it might have even increased it. As the dragon had taken to the air, Dandra had felt his power tug on her. She'd hurled herself back into the shadows but she didn't dare look out on the battlefield again. "Singe?" she asked Ashi. "Geth? Are they still—?"

"They're alive and fighting," Ashi said. "They're coming this way—maybe trying to rescue you, maybe just looking for shelter!"

Dandra's eyes snapped open as new hope kindled in her heart. "Where's Dah'mir?"

Ashi leaned out of the mound mouth slightly. "I don't see him." She glanced back. "Dandra, Dah'mir's age, his power—the Bonetree thought they were gifts of the Dragon Below. We didn't know . . ."

"It doesn't matter now!" Dandra sprang away from the wall and up to the gaping mouth. The air outside was heavy with the smell of blood and battle, but compared to the air within the mound, it was sweet. She peered out cautiously. There was no sign of Dah'mir, but that could change at any moment. Across the battlefield, Geth, Singe, and their band of orcs had turned aside, going to the aid of an old orc who fought with surprising vitality in spite of his age.

Caught in the heat of battle, they didn't see Medala rise from the ground of the battlefield, fury gathered around her like a cloak.

"Il-Yannah!" Dandra gasped. She drew a sharp breath to call a warning—only to be whirled back into the tunnel before she could even form the words. Ashi hit the tunnel wall beside her.

"Dah'mir is back! He's landing!"

Helpless, Dandra swallowed her warning and pressed her

head back as enormous wings rattled the air and the weight of a dragon shook the ground. For a moment, silence settled over the battlefield and the mound.

Silence that was broken by the crystal chime of Medala's psionic power, as clear and loud to Dandra as if the other kalashtar had been standing right next to her. She clenched her spear so tight that the pale wood hurt her fingers. Outside, she could hear Medala threatening and cursing her friends. "Ashi, what's happening out there?"

"They can't breathe!" Ashi said. "They looked ready to defend themselves, but now they can't breathe!"

"It's Medala." Dandra bit her tongue in horror. Your friends are dying, she screamed at herself silently. Your friends are dying and you're *hiding!*

What choice did she have? Without Tetkashtai, she was no match for Medala. Even with Tetkashtai, Dah'mir's power could overwhelm her in moments, but if she could deal with the mad kalashtar, her friends might be able to escape the dragon. If only she had Tetkashtai's crystal, she would at least be able to use powers other than simple tricks of *vayhatana* . . .

Her eyes narrowed then sprang wide and she swallowed hard. "Ashi, I have an idea, but I need you to create a diversion."

"How?"

Dandra's jaw tightened. "Fight Medala. Resist her powers for as long as you can."

A savage grin twisted across Ashi's face. "That I can do. What will you do?"

Dandra reached to her belt and opened a pouch. Spinning a fine web of *vayhatana*, she reached inside and lifted out Virikhad's violet psicrystal with her thoughts alone. Even through that nebulous contact, it seemed that she could feel the spirit of the kalashtar trapped inside.

"I'm going to reunite old friends." She looked up. "Are you ready?"

Ashi raised her sword. "More than ready!" Fury flushed her face as she lunged out of the tunnel mouth. "For Ner, Medala! *For Ner!*"

Dandra drew a breath and followed her, tugging the violet crystal after her. Focus, she told herself. Send the crystal to Medala. Ignore everything else . . .

The instant she stepped into open air, that focus vanished.

Perhaps thirty paces away, Singe crouched on the ground, his entire body heaving as he fought for breath. Beside him, Geth writhed in the dirt, wracked by pain. Medala was whirling to face Ashi's unexpected attack, alarm written on her face. Ashi herself was leaping past dolgrims, sword held low and ready to strike.

Dah'mir's scaled, dark copper form towered over everything, green eyes staring down with a mad, hungry intensity—and those eyes darted to her. Dandra felt the dragon's smothering presence, but the only emotion that was reflected in his eyes was pure rage. Great jaws opened in a roar that shook the night, almost drowning out the chime of Medala's power.

Ashi—along with more than half a dozen dolgrims—staggered and froze as Medala turned her will against them.

The web of *vayhatana* that held Virikhad's crystal suspended disappeared along with Dandra's concentration. The crystal fell to the ground and for a moment all Dandra could do was stare at it.

"You!" shrieked Medala. She thrust out a hand, the chime of her power building. Dah'mir, a coppery juggernaut almost half as tall as the mound itself, lunged toward her. His horrible presence washed over her. Fear stabbed into Dandra's gut and nearly drove conscious thought from her mind.

Instinct and resolve took its place.

She had stood here nearly two months before with only one thought in mind: escape. And she had escaped. She had taken the long step, barely thinking as she had leaped hundreds of paces in a single stride.

She didn't need to go so far this time.

Dandra stepped forward, bending down as she moved. Her fingers snatched up the violet crystal—

—and Virikhad exploded in her mind like a howling gale, tearing across the landscape of her psyche. *Tetkashtai? Tetkashtai?*

Time froze, like a moment in a dream. The assault of Virikhad's mind on hers wrenched up memories of Sharn, of the passion that he and Tetkashtai had shared, of the passion that he had carried into his studies of dragonshards as well. Dandra felt his anguish at being trapped in the crystal. His violet light formed distorted images of the unchanging fastness of Dah'mir's strange laboratory, visions of his own body wasting away, his skull being opened and his brain devoured by the illithids.

Worse, Virikhad had loved freedom and movement as much as, if not even more, than Tetkashtai. He had been an intensely social being. So long in the crystal without power or true sensation had left him with only raw pain and loneliness.

But Dandra couldn't afford to give him what he needed. She let him wash over her, but gave him nothing to hold onto. She was a reed bending before his wind, offering no resistance. Her body continued to move, one leg following the other on a long step already put in motion. Her moving arm swung up again—

—to meet the fingers of Medala's outstretched hand. For one brief moment, both women touched the crystal. Somewhere beyond Virikhad's pain, Dandra could feel Medala's twisted mind and her surprise at the sudden contact, at thirty paces crossed in an instant.

Dandra cast the barest thread of a link into Virikhad's tortured light. *I'm sorry,* she said.

Before Medala could react, she let go of the crystal. Virikhad vanished from her mind. Dandra wrapped her hand around Medala's, forcing the gray-haired kalashtar's grasp tight around the violet crystal.

As Dah'mir's presence fell over her once more, Dandra heard Medala's wail like a distant echo.

The chime of Medala's power fell abruptly silent. Air flowed easily into Geth's lungs, the torturous pain passed like a memory, and for a moment all that the shifter wanted to do was lie on the cool dirt and breathe. The sound of woman's scream of anguish, however, brought him to his feet. *"Dandra!"* he said—then froze, the name still on his lips.

Less than four paces away, Dandra stood calmly, her eyes placid and fixed on Dah'mir. The dragon was a metallic stream of motion, caught in the act of leaping toward the mouth of the mound but at the same time skidding and twisting to stare in surprise at Dandra, like a house cat chasing a cricket. Everywhere, dolgrims were scattering with squeals of alarm. Between Dandra and Dah'mir, Ashi was rising unsteadily to her feet, just as Singe, Natrac and the orcs were doing around Geth.

The anguished scream was coming from Medala. The kalashtar stood behind Dandra, one arm outstretched and her fist clenched as if she held something in her grasp. Her eyes were wild. In the scant moments that Geth stared, they seemed to grow even wider. Her head snapped sharply from side to side. Her scream rose and cracked.

Silver-white light blazed around her, flaring up then snuffing itself out in less than a heartbeat. When it vanished, it took Medala with it.

Something, some dark pebble, fell to the ground where she had stood.

Dah'mir's huge, lithe form stiffened. *"No!"* he roared. *"Medala!"* Green eyes burned. Geth stumbled back from the sheer rage in the dragon's gaze. He heard Orshok cry out in fear. Dah'mir's scaly lips peeled back from his muzzle. "Khyber claim you all!" he snarled—and spat out a word that made Geth's ears ache. A greasy, clinging foulness—less than smoke but more than shadow—burst out of the air.

Geth shouted as it groped and slithered across his skin, sliding into his mouth and down his throat, making him gag. From the corner of his eye, though, he saw Batul snap a gnarled hand into the air and shout an angry word in response.

Nature answered his prayer in a blast of wind that tore across the battlefield, scouring away the foulness of Dah'mir's magic, and raising a cloud of stinging dust that brought renewed squeals out of the dolgrims. Geth's clothes flapped around him. Dandra, eyes fixed on Dah'mir, was caught by the wind and shoved to her knees. Singe yelled something and leaped for her, staggering in the gale.

Dah'mir roared again and recoiled, his wings folded tight against his body, his eyes squeezed tight against the wind.

"Geth!" said Batul. "Now!"

Gatekeeper magic and Dhakaani sword. Geth clenched his jaw tight. He darted to Singe where the wizard knelt with his arms around Dandra. "Run!" he said over the wind. "Get everyone away!"

"What?"

"Do it! Do it like Robrand gave the order himself!" Geth reached to his belt, tore free the pouch that contained Tetkashtai's crystal, and thrust it at him. "Give that to Dandra!"

He spun away and leaped for Dah'mir without looking back. He heard Singe call his name once, then the wizard began shouting commands at Natrac and the others. The shifter heard Batul shout something as well—another prayer, an invocation that throbbed with power.

The wind rose to a storm in answer. The grit it carried became painful, like a rain of needles. Geth reached deep and forced his tired body to shift once more. Renewed energy surged through him and the piercing pain of the wind eased as he plunged through it. Around him, though, the dolgrims that Dah'mir had commanded weren't so lucky. They screeched and tried to flee from the druid's magic, but it was as if nature held a special fury for the twisted aberrations. The creatures tried to flee, but the wind tore at their exposed skin, stripping it raw and bloody. They tumbled before nature's wrath like autumn leaves.

In Geth's hand, the Dhakaani sword began to glow with a dim twilight radiance, an ember fanned by the angry wind.

Geth pushed himself hard, racing with the storm. Dah'mir crouched back, hissing in frustration at the lancing wind that cut between his scales. Geth clenched his teeth. Batul was right, he thought—they had no hope of killing the dragon. If he was fast enough, though, maybe he could hold out against Dah'mir long enough to buy Singe, Dandra, and the others the time they need to escape.

He swept up the ancient sword and hurled himself forward. *"This is for Adolan, you bastard!"*

Eyes still closed tight, Dah'mir roared back at him—and lunged, not at the shifter, but up, toward the sky. His body uncoiled. His wings cracked open. Muscular hind legs strained and thrust against the ground . . .

Geth didn't hesitate for a moment. He threw himself into the air, leaping to meet the climbing dragon.

His body slammed into a foreleg as thick as a tree trunk and he grabbed onto the scaly limb as the ground whirled away beneath him. He was lifted out of the raging stream of Batul's magic, and the air that rushed against him was cool, not stinging. Overhead, Dah'mir's chest thrust and pushed. From his shoulders all the way along the length of his body and tail, his great wings swept the night. For a moment, Geth felt a rushing thrill at the experience— then Dah'mir shook his leg violently. Geth wrenched his head around, his hair whipping across his face, to look up. Dah'mir's neck stretched out straight as he flew, but the dragon had managed to twist his head around enough to look down at his own massive chest. One angry green eye fixed on Geth and went wide.

"Get off me!" Dah'mir roared. He shook his leg again, but Geth clung tight, trying not to slash himself with his own sword. Dah'mir flexed, folding both legs to scrape them together. Geth clenched his teeth against the wind that tore at his breath and thrust himself higher, beyond the dragon's awkward reach. Dah'mir roared again. His wings snapped out, his neck arched and his entire body rolled as he swept into a turn.

For a moment, the night sky, clouds breaking, swung below Geth. The Ring of Siberys flashed past in a shining arc, then Dah'mir righted himself and the Ring was replaced by moonlight reflected in water far below. The long loops of the river streaked by; the Bonetree mound, still lit by Dah'mir's magic, grew like a swelling boil.

"Cling then!" said Dah'mir over the wind. His legs folded close and his wings beat even harder, speeding him forward. "Cling like a flea and watch your friends die before me!"

A blue-black flash caught Geth's eye. One arm and both legs hugging the dragon's thick foreleg tight, he twisted his head and looked up at Dah'mir's massive chest, straining not much more than an arms length above him. Just as it had glittered against his leather robes as a man, a single Khyber dragonshard seemed set in Dah'mir's chest as a dragon. The scales surrounding it were gnarled and misshapen. Geth clenched his sharp teeth tight.

"Fleas bite, dragon!" he snarled.

He leaned out and swung his sword as hard as he could at the dragonshard and the twisted scales around it.

The Dhakaani blade flashed with a dull glow, as if nature's rage still clung to it, as if the Gatekeeper magic had breathed anger into the metal. Its jagged edge shattered the Khyber shard and bit deep into Dah'mir's flesh—deeper than Geth would have hoped or expected.

Black blood burst out of the dragon's chest, drenching Geth in a hot, steaming spray. Dah'mir twisted and crumpled in mid-air, the thunderous rhythm of his beating wings out of time. A grating howl louder than anything Geth had ever heard burst out of his jaws. The shifter caught a brief glimpse of a dark cloud bursting up from the banks of the river—the black herons of the Bonetree—before Dah'mir's wings stopped beating altogether and he tumbled out of the sky, plunging toward the rising herons.

Geth's guts pushed themselves up into his throat and he choked on a scream as he fell along with the dragon. He felt Dah'mir's leg wrenched away from him. Talons slashed at him, but fell short. Geth caught a glimpse of acid-green eyes, the bright light of madness in them dimmed by agony but still sharp and now tinged with hate as well.

They flickered—then shifter and dragon were plunging past the darting wings of the black herons. Greasy feathers surrounded Geth, obscuring even Dah'mir's writhing bulk.

A scant moment later he fell out of the whirling flock. He had only long enough to realize that he was falling alone before the water of the river slammed into him.

CHAPTER

18

A blaze of agony woke him, a fire that cut through the darkness and throbbed through his shoulders and torso. Hands held him tight, dragging on him. The sound of a dragon's roar echoed in his ears. He cried out and struggled, trying to defend himself.

The dragon's roar gave way to cursing. "Twelve moons! Someone get that sword away from him!"

Singe's voice, Geth realized. Then Dandra's. "Hold him out of the water and I'll lift him."

A moment later, a gentle pressure surrounded Geth's body. The hands that had held him let go and he rose slowly from water into air. His body turned. There was some pain but not as bad as it had been moments before. Geth's eyes flickered open.

He hung suspended in the air. Beside him, Singe, Ashi, and Dandra crouched in a wide, flat-bottomed boat. Dandra's gaze was focused on him. Her yellow-green psicrystal hung around her neck. Her fingers flickered and his dripping body slid sideways, then down into the boat. Hard wood pressed against his back and he coughed out a groan of pain.

Dandra bent over him. "Geth, can you hear me?"

Geth coughed again and water spattered out of his mouth, but he nodded. The air was gray with the light of early morning. "Where—?" he asked.

"On the river south of the ancestor mound," said Singe. "Lie still." He prodded Geth's torso gently. The shifter gasped and writhed at the touch. His arm snapped up—and the Dhakaani sword with it. His fingers were clenched around the weapon's hilt, wrapped so tight they were white and numb. Singe cursed, grabbing his arm and forcing it back down. "Careful!"

"Natrac? Batul?" asked Geth. His head was still reeling. Stringing more than a few words together hurt.

"Here," said Natrac's voice. There was a bump as another boat nudged up against theirs. Geth turned his head enough to see the hooked ends of hunda sticks slip over the sides of the boat, holding the two craft together. Orshok and Krepis peered over, then Batul pushed them aside. The old orc looked tired, though Geth thought maybe he looked worse.

"We're all here," said Dandra. Geth stared at her, then fixed his eye on Singe.

"Told you to run," he said thinly.

"We did at first. But after you took Dah'mir for a ride, there wasn't much point—the dolgrims and the Bonetree hunters were scattered." The wizard looked down at him. "Ashi led us to the Bonetree boats when we saw you fall."

"You and Dah'mir," said Batul. The druid's face was somber. "What did you do to him?"

"I hit him." Geth started to lift the Dhakaani sword again, but the strength seemed to have gone from his arm—from all of his limbs. A vague memory stirred inside him of plunging beneath the surface of the river, then splashing back to the surface and holding tight to a floating log as the river currents bore him through the night. "The sword . . . Gatekeeper magic and Dhakaani weapons. The sword wounded him."

Batul looked startled. "You brought Dah'mir down with one blow? That's more than Gatekeeper magic."

"There was a dragonshard in his chest—a weak spot in his scales."

"But one blow?" Batul stared at the sword in Geth's hand.

"We saw him disappear," said Singe. "How badly was he wounded?"

The last glimpse of madness and hatred in Dah'mir's eyes returned to Geth. A chill sank deep into his belly. "Not badly enough," he said.

❤

Banging on his cabin door and Karth's shouts dragged Vennet out of sleep. "Captain! *Captain!*"

It took a moment before Vennet realized that the big man's voice was tight with fear. Though they'd accepted Vennet's explanation of events in Zarash'ak, most of the crew had been on edge since leaving the City of Stilts. Vennet had even switched *Lightning on Water* over to a Sharn-Trolanport run, hoping that some time well away from the Shadow Marches would ease their tensions. Through it all, though, Karth had been one of the few solid, sensible members of the crew. If he was frightened of something . . .

Vennet sat up sharply in his bed. "What is it, Karth?"

"Birds, captain! Dozens of them!"

"What?" Vennet threw aside the bedclothes—and froze.

Dawn's pale glow glimmered through the shutters over the cabin's window. Thin lines of light fell across a tall black heron with shining, acid-green eyes that stood in the shadows of the cabin. Something black and wet dripped from its narrow chest to puddle on the floor directly over his hidden strong box and the two precious dragonshards it contained.

Vennet felt a cold sweat break out on his forehead.

"Captain d'Lyrandar," said the heron. "I have need of you now."

APPENDIX 1
GLOSSARY

Adar: A small nation on the continent of Sarlona. Homeland of the *kalashtar*.

Adar! Adar! Bhintava adarani!: An Adaran battlecry that translates to "Adar! Adar! Defend those who seek aid!"

Adolan: A druid of the Gatekeeper sect, protector of Bull Hollow and guardian of the Bull Hole.

Ashi: A hunter of the Bonetree clan, one of the clan's most capable trackers and fighters.

ashi: A dark gold reed. The inhabitants of the Shadow Marches use its starchy pith to make a type of bread.

Aundair: One of the original Five Nations of Galifar, Aundair houses the seat of the Arcane Congress and the University of Wyrnarn. Currently under the rule of Queen Aurala ir'Wyrnarn.

Azhani: The language shared by the human clans of the Shadow Marches.

Batul: An elder orc druid of the Gatekeeper sect and the spiritual leader of the Fat Tusk tribe. He is blind in one eye, but gifted with prophetic dreams.

Bear: A cultural hero figure among shifters based on one of the animal forms of their lycanthrope ancestors. Usually referred to as "Cousin," Bear embodies the attributes of strength and caution.

Blademarks: The mercenary's guild of *House Deneith*.

Boar: A cultural hero figure among shifters based on one of the animal forms of their lycanthrope ancestors. Usually referred to as "Cousin," Boar represents tremendous endurance, but also unrestrained and reckless enthusiasm.

Bonetree clan: A human barbarian clan of the Shadow Marches, worshipers of the Dragon Below. The heart of their territory is an enormous earthen mound built over generations. The Azhani term is *Drumasaz*.

Breek: An eagle, companion to Adolan.

Breff: A hunter of the Bonetree clan.

Bull Hollow: A hamlet on the far western edge of the Eldeen Reaches, just below the Shadowcrags.

byeshk: A rare metal, hard and dense with a purple sheen. Weapons made of byeshk are capable of inflicting great injuries on daelkyr and their creations.

chuul: Monstrous creatures larger than a man, resembling huge crayfish with four powerful legs and enormous claws. The tentacles surrounding a chuul's mouth are capable of paralyzing its prey.

crysteel: An alloy created from iron and a rare crystalline substance. Crysteel is used to make weapons favored by those skilled in psionics.

d'Deneith, Robrand: A dragonmarked heir of House Deneith, once leader of the Frostbrand company of the Blademarks, disgraced after the Massacre at Narath.

d'Deneith, Toller: A dragonmarked heir of House Deneith, nephew to Robrand d'Deneith, in training to become a commander of the Blademarks.

d'Lyrandar, Vennet: A dragonmarked half-elf of House Lyrandar, captain of *Lightning on Water*.

daelkyr: Powerful lords of Xoriat, the daelkyr are madness and corruption personified. After the Daelkyr War, surviving daelkyr on Eberron were bound in the depths of Khyber by Gatekeeper druids.

Daelkyr War: An invasion of Eberron by creatures from Xoriat, led by the daelkyr, approximately nine thousand years before the present. Centered around the Shadow Marches, it ended with the defeat of the daelkyr by the united forces of the orcs of the Shadow Marches and the hobgoblins of the Empire of Dhakaan, but left both races decimated.

dagga: An orc expression of affirmation commonly used by folk of Zarash'ak. A more intense version, *"Kuv dagga!"* is akin to swearing a minor oath.

Dah'mir: A priest of the Dragon Below and leader of the Bonetree clan, he has a strange power over kalashtar.

dahr: An Adaran expression for something or someone vile; pl. "dahri."

Dal: A hunter of the Bonetree clan

Dandra: A kalashtar, hunted by the Bonetree clan after being captured by Dah'mir. She wears a yellow-green psicrystal, wields a spear forged from crysteel, and specializes in whitefire, augmented by her skill with *vayhatana.*

Deneith, House: A dragonmark house bearing the Mark of Sentinel. House Deneith operates services offering various forms of protection, including the mercenary companies of the Blademarks and the law enforcement services of the Sentinel Marshals.

Dhakaani Empire: *see Empire of Dhakaan.*

dolgaunt: Horrid creatures created by the daelkyr from hobgoblins during the Daelkyr War, dolgaunts have long, powerful tentacles springing from their shoulders. They have no eyes but perceive their surroundings through sensitive cilia that cover their skin.

dolgrim: Foot soldiers in the armies of the daelkyr, dolgrims were created by the daelkyr from goblins. A dolgrim has four arms and two mouths and resembles two goblins crushed together.

Dragon Below, the: *see Khyber*

dragonmark: 1) A mark that appears on the surface of the skin and grants mystical powers to its bearer. 2) A slang term for the bearer of a dragonmark.

dragonshard: A form of mineral with mystical properties, said to be a shard of one of the great progenitor dragons. There are three different types of shard, each with different properties. A shard has no abilities in and of itself, but an artificer or wizard can use a shard to create an object with useful effects. *Siberys shards* fall from the sky and have the potential to enhance the power of dragonmarks. *Eberron shards* are found in the soil and enhance traditional magic. *Khyber shards* are found deep below the surface of the world and are used as a focus binding mystical energy.

Eberron: 1) The world. 2) A mythical dragon said to have formed the world from her body in primordial times and to have given birth to natural life. Also known as "The Dragon Between." See *Khyber, Siberys.*

Eldeen Reaches: Once this term was used to describe the vast stretches of woodland found on the west coast of Khorvaire, inhabited mostly by nomadic shifter tribes and druidic sects. In 958 YK the people of western Aundair broke ties with the Audairian crown and joined their lands to the Eldeen Reaches, vastly increasing the population of the nation and bringing it into the public eye. Inhabitants are known as Reachers. Among themselves, Reachers refer to their homeland as "the Eldeen."

Empire of Dhakaan: An ancient empire ruled by hobgoblins, the Empire of Dhakaan stretched across southern Khorvaire millennia before the arrival of humans. Dhakaan was weaked by the Daelkyr War and collapsed about six thousand years before the present.

Etta: A hunter of the Bonetree clan.

Fat Tusk: A tribe of orcs living in the Shadow Marches.

Fause: The leader of a Cult of the Dragon Below in Zarash'ak.

Frostbrand: A Blademarks company of House Deneith, commanded by Robrand d'Deneith, specializing in wilderness and winter operations. It was disbanded after the Massacre at Narath.

Gatekeepers: A sect of druids, originators of the druidic tradition in the Shadow Marches and the Eldeen Reaches. Originally formed to defend Eberron from invasion by Xoriat during the Daelkyr War, they watch over the seals that bind the daelkyr in Khyber.

Geth: A shifter veteran of the Last War, he served with the Frostbrand until the Massacre at Narath, then wandered Khorvaire before finding refuge in Bull Hollow. He wields a sword and a great-gauntlet, a magewrought gauntlet that is both shield and weapon.

Gig: A hunter of the Bonetree clan.

Hand-wit: A hunter of the Bonetree clan.

Hruucan: A dolgaunt appointed by Dah'mir to accompany the Bonetree hunters in their pursuit of Dandra.

illithid: An abomination from Xoriat, the plane of madness. An illithid is roughly the same size and shape as a human but possesses a squidlike head with tentacles arrayed around a fanged maw. Illithids feed on the brains of sentient creatures and possess the ability to paralyze or manipulate the minds of lesser creatures. Illithids are more commonly known as *mind flayers*.

il-Yannah: A word from the Quor tongue, translating to "the Great Light." This mystical force is the focus of the religion of the *kalashtar*.

Jhegesh Dol: A stretch of haunted swamp in the Shadow Marches, once the site of a daelkyr stronghold during the Daelkyr War.

kalashtar: The kalashtar are an offshoot of humanity. Stories say that the kalashtar are humans touched by spirits from another plane of existence and that they possess strange mental powers.

Karrnath: One of the original Five Nations of Galifar. Karrnath is a cold, grim land whose people are renowned for their martial prowess. The current ruler of Karrnath is King Kaius ir'Wynarn III.

Karth: A sailor on *Lightning on Water*.

kesh: a kalashtar term for the telepathic mindlink all kalashtar can create with other beings.

Khorvaire: One of the continents of Eberron.

Khyber: I) The underworld. 2) A mythical dragon, also known as "The Dragon Below." After killing Siberys, Khyber was imprisoned by Eberron and transformed into the underworld. Khyber is said to have given birth to a host of demons and other unnatural creatures. See *Eberron, Siberys*.

Kirla: A stable-owner in Yrlag

Appendix

Krepis: An orc of the Fat Tusk tribe and a druid of the Gatekeeper sect. A student of Batul.

Last War, the: This conflict began in 894 YK with the death of King Jarot ir'Wyrnarn, the last king of Galifar. Following Jarot's death, three of his five children refused to follow the ancient traditions of succession, and the kingdom split. The war lasted over a hundred years, and it took the utter destruction of Cyre to bring the other nations to the negotiating table. No one has admitted defeat, but no one wants to risk being the next victim of the Mourning. The chronicles are calling the conflict "the Last War," hoping that the bloodshed might have finally slaked humanity's thirst for battle. Only time will tell if this hope is in vain.

Lightning on Water: A House Lyrandar elemental galleon. Instead of sails, an elemental galleon uses a bound air elemental for propulsion.

long step: A kalashtar term for psionic teleportation.

Lyrandar, House: A dragonmarked house bearing the Mark of Storm. House Lyrandar has economic control of shipping in Khorvaire.

Medalashana: A kalashtar, once a companion of Tetkashtai and Virikhad, later renamed Medala by Dah'mir. She specializes in the art of telepathy.

Metrol: The capital of Cyre. Metrol was destroyed by the Mourning.

Mukur: A hunter of the Bonetree clan.

Narath: A river town in northern Karrnath, close to the coast of the Bitter Sea. Destroyed in 989 YK in the infamous Massacre at Narath.

Natrac: A half-orc of Zarash'ak, he specializes in helping tribespeople of the northern Shadow Marches move south to Zarash'ak in return for a period of indentured servitude.

Ner: The huntmaster of the Bonetree clan. The longest-lived huntmaster ever to lead the Bonetree hunters.

Orshok: A young orc druid of the Fat Tusk tribe and a student of Batul.

Pado: A hunter of the Bonetree clan.

Pandon: A merchant of Zarash'ak and a passenger on *Lightning on Water*.

psicrystal: A sentient crystal created by psions as a tool and companion. Each psicrystal is a unique reflection of the psion who created it.

psion: Someone who is skilled in the art of psionics, the power of the mind. Kalashtar are natural psions, able to manifest the telepathic link they call the *kesh*. Many go on to master greater skills.

Rat: A cultural hero figure among shifters based on one of the animal forms of their lycanthrope ancestors. Usually referred to as "Grandfather," he is depicted as a cunning and stealthy trickster. "Grandfather Rat!" is a common expression of frustration.

Sandar: An innkeeper in Bull Hollow.

Sarlona: One of the continents of Eberron. Humanity arose in Sarlona, and colonists from Sarlona established human civilization on Khorvaire.

Sentinel Marshals: The dragonmarked House Deneith is the primary source for mercenary soldiers and bodyguards in Khorvaire. The Sentinel Marshals are a specialized form of mercenary—bounty hunters empowered to enforce the laws of Galifar across Khorvaire. This right was granted by the King of Galifar, but when Galifar collapsed the rulers of the Five Nations agreed to let the Sentinel Marshals pursue their prey across all nations, to maintain a neutral lawkeeping force that would be respected throughout Khorvaire. See *House Deneith*.

Shadow Marches: A region of desolate swamps on the southwestern coast of Khorvaire. The Shadow Marches have a strange connection to Xoriat and were at the center of the Daelkyr War many millennia ago.

Shadowcrags: A rugged mountain chain that forms the western border of the Eldeen Reaches.

shifter: A humanoid race said to be descended from humans and lycanthropes. Shifters have a feral, bestial appearance and can briefly call on their lycanthropic heritage to draw animalistic characteristics to the fore.

Siberys: 1) The ring of stones that circle the world; seen as a shining band like clustered stars in the southern sky. 2) A mythical dragon, also called "The Dragon Above." Siberys is said to have been destroyed by Khyber. Some believe that the Ring of Siberys is the source of all magic.

Singe: An Aundairian wizard specializing in both fire magic and swordsmanship. A lieutenant in the Blademarks, he served with the Frostbrand company until the Massacre at Narath. His real name is Etan Bayard, but he prefers his nickname.

Sita: A hunter of the Bonetree clan.

Sovereign Host, the: a religion found across much of Khorvaire. The Lords of the Host are Arawai (god of agriculture), Aureon (god of law and knowledge), Balinor (god of beasts and the hunt), Boldrei (god of community and hearth), Dol Arrah (god of honor and sacrifice), Dol Dorn (god of strength at arms), Kol Korran (god of trade and wealth), Olladra (god of good fortune), and Onatar (god of artifice and the forge).

tak: a Reacher expression for "thank you;" "twice tak" is "thank you very much."

Temmen: A staff-fighter in Zarash'ak.

Tetkashtai: The presence that inhabits Dandra's psicrystal.

Thul: A stableboy in Bull Hollow.

Tiger: A cultural hero figure among shifters based on one of the animal forms of their lycanthrope ancestors. Tiger is noble being, a warrior of incomparable grace and speed. Unlike the other shifter culture-heroes, no relation is ever claimed to Tiger. "Tiger's blood!" is a common oath of anger.

vayhatana: A kalashtar term for psionic telekinesis. Literally translated, it means "ghost breath."

Veta: A barmaid in Bull Hollow.

Vvaraak: The black dragon who taught the first Gatekeepers and began the druidic tradition in western Khorvaire many thousands of years ago. She was also known as "the Scaled Apostate."

whitefire: A kalashtar term for flame produced with psionics.

Wolf: A cultural hero figure among shifters based on one of the animal forms of their lycanthrope ancestors. Wolf is wise, honorable, and knowledgeable in the ways of magic. She is often referred to as "Grandmother" and "Grandmother Wolf!" is a common expression of awe.

Xoriat: One of alternate planes, Xoriat is also known as the Realm of Madness. It is the home of the daelkyr and illithids, but has been held apart from Eberron since the end of the Daelkyr War thanks to the magic of the Gatekeepers.

Yrlag: A town on the Grithic River, the border between the Shadow Marches and the Eldeen Reaches. The westernmost port on southern Khorvaire, it is a barely civilized place and the trading center for much of this isolated region. Before humans arrived in Khorvaire, it was the westernmost outpost of the Empire of Dhakaan and the Dhakaani influence can still be seen in its oldest structure.

Zarash'ak: The capital of the Shadow Marches, often called the City of Stilts because of the architecture that raises it above the threat of floods.

APPENDIX 2
THE AZHANI LANGUAGE

AZHANI PRONUNCIATION GUIDE

Consonants are pronounced as they appear, except:

g always hard, as in *get*

ch always soft, as in *church*

zh as the z sound in *azure*

bh, vh, dh aspirated sound (a breathy version of the consonant)

Vowels are pronounced as:

a *cat*

e *bet*

i *seem*

o *so*

u *moon*

Vowels in sequence are pronounced individually as above, except:

ei the long vowel sound found in *shade*

eo long *a* combined with a long *o*

Except in conjugation 2 verbs, two identical vowel sounds are broken by a glottal stop: ' (tt in *mitten* is a glottal stop).

APPENDIX

AZHANI WORDS

a: one (number)

ahine: a scream of fright

ahris: to obey (takes conjugation 2)

ahron: a scream of rage

all: fire

ama: a woman

amot: five (number)

andgri'imo: downstream, literally translated, it means "where the river goes."

ano: a man

ashi: 1) a reed with a starchy pith used to make bread, 2) the bread made from the reed, 3) a deep gold-yellow, the color of both reed and bread. Probably a loanword from Orc.

aushen: to return to a place (takes conjugation 2)

az: a clan. As a suffix, it is appended to a name to formally indicate a clan ("Drumas" is the Bonetree, "Drumasaz" is the Bonetree clan)

azam: 1) a member of a clan, 2) a person. In the plural form, "azams" it means "others." By extension, the only people are those associated with a clan. All others are "duskav" or strangers.

bet: night

betch: darkness

bibis: a rabbit

bron: to be (takes conjugation 1). An older, archaic form of "to be."

brosh: divine magic, especially healing magic. Brosh is often translated as "body-magic" and is considered a very different thing from kint or "world-magic."

broshama/broshano: a skilled healer, often one with special knowledge or limited magical ability. Often woman, hence the common translation of the term as "herbwife."

che: the. Plural: ches

che ___ gri: this. Literally translated, it means "the thing here."

cheo: what

Daraskint: Eberron, the mystical Dragon Between. "Eberron" is also commonly used.

Darasvern: Siberys, the mystical Dragon Above. "Siberys" is also commonly used.

Darasvhir: Khyber, the mystical Dragon Below. "Khyber" is also commonly used.

do: to do (takes conjugation 1).

doke: will (conjugation 1; future tense is regular and is formed the same as the present tense; past tense "would" never varies and is always "tdoke").

dru: bone

duskav: stranger

e: and

each: zhir

eche: that. Plural: eches

egri: there

eva: three (number)

firgri'i: everywhere

gentis: depths

get: deep (adjective)

gri: here

gri'i: where

ha-: a marker of respect. Adding the prefix ha- to something implies respect and sets it above other things of its kinds.

harano: honor. Literally translated it means "a respected name."

hushen: to return from a place (takes conjugation 2)

itri: must

kint: arcane magic, but also any magic that is not obivously healing or defensive. Kint is opposed to brosh and is often refered to as "world-magic."

kintama/kintano: a wizard or hermit. Kintamas and kintanos are usually considered as dangerous, bad-tempered individuals who live as hermits.

klavit: to bring back (takes conjugation I)

kri: to be (takes conjugation 2; third person singular is irregular — "krii"). A relatively recent term for "to be."

kriazam: a changeling. Literally translated, it means "false person."

kto: than

mado: to need (takes conjugation I)

make: shall (conjugation I; future tense is regular and is formed the same as the present tense; past tense "should" never varies and is always "tmake")

mas: tree

mot: four (number)

pa-: more or very

pinde: to know (takes conjugation 2)

pret: can (conjugation I; past tense "could" never varies and is always "tpret")

rana: a shaman or priest

rano: a name

reis: tough. "Reis" is a condition rather than an adjective and a person is said to "have reis" rather than "be reis."

rond: fierce. "Rond" is a condition rather than an adjective and a person is said to "have rond" rather than "be rond."

shei: to hunt (takes conjugation I)

sheid: a hunter

shial: to pray (takes conjugation I)

sikint: a term used among the Bonetree to describe the psionics used by kalashtar. "Sikint" combines the "psi-" prefix with the Azhani word for magic.

Su: For/In the name of

sut: to follow or accompany (takes conjugation I)

ta: to have (takes conjugation I)

teith: blood

teithkint: a rare form of blood magic practiced among certain clans of the Az.

theth: I) silence. 2) silent (adjective).

va: two (number)

varda: a fight, specifically a fight between individuals. It's similar to "duel" in meaning but without formality. "Varda" can take place in the middle of mass combat.

vit: to bring (takes conjugation I)

zhan: to speak (takes conjugation I)

zhani: language

AZHANI EXPRESSIONS

Che Harana: "Revered", the title given by the Bonetree clan to Dah'mir. Literally translated it means "the honored priest."

Drumasaz: The Bonetree clan. Often referred to simply as "Drumas."

Khyberit gentis: "Khyber's depths" — an expression of frustration.

Kriid patheth. A sheia bibisas.: "Be very quiet. I'm hunting rabbits."

Rond betch: "Fierce darkness" — an expression of amazement or anger.

Rond e reis: A worthy adversary or a strong warrior is said to be characterized by "rond e reis" — they are fierce and tough.

Su Drumas! Su Darasvhir!: "For the Bonetree! For the Dragon Below!" — the pledge and battle cry of the Bonetree clan.

Varda su teith e harano: "A fight for blood and honor."

AZHANI PRONOUNS

first person (I)	a; objective (me) — at. "A" is often dropped in normal use ("A shei" and "Shei" both mean "I hunt.")
second person (you)	do; objective (you) — dod
third person masculine (he)	an; objective (him) — ano
third person feminine (she)	am; objective (her) — ama
first person plural inclusive (we)	has; objective (us) — hast. Azhani distinguishes between the inclusive first person plural (we — all of us) and the exclusive (we — us but not you).
first person plural exclusive (we)	as; objective (us) — ast
second person plural (you)	dos; objective (you) — doz
third person plural masculine (they)	ans; objective (them) — anas
third person plural femine (they)	ams; objective (them) — amas

OTHER PARTS OF SPEECH

plural	-s or -as after s ("sheid" — a hunter, "sheids" — hunters)
possessive	-it ("sheidit" — "hunter's"); also applied to pronouns ("ait" — mine, "doit" — yours)
distance	e- ("esheid" — a hunter over there)
negation	toch, applied to both nouns and verbs ("toch esheid" — not a hunter, "toch shei" — not hunting)
appearance	kri- ("krishei" — seems to hunt); sometimes applied to nouns to imply a fake, impersonation, or deception ("krisheid" — a false hunter)
imperatives	the subject pronoun is dropped in imperatives

AZHANI CONJUGATIONS

	Conjugation 1	Conjugation 2
First person singular	-a ("sheia" — I hunt)	no change to infinitive ("pinde" — I know)
Second person singular	-i ("shei'i" — you hunt)	-t or -d depending on voice quality of preceding phoneme ("pinded" — you know, but "ahrist" — you obey)
Third person singular masculine (or indeterminant gender)	-o ("sheio" — he hunts)	-(repetition of last vowel sound)r ("pindeer" — he knows, but "ahrisir" — he obeys
Third person singular feminine	-on ("sheion" — she hunts)	same as masculine. Conjugation 2 does not contain gender.
first person plural inclusive	-as ("sheias" — we all hunt)	-si ("pindesi" — we know)
first person plural exclusive	-az ("sheiaz" — we hunt, not you)	-zi ("pindezi" — we know, not you)
second person plural	-is ("shei'is" — you hunt)	-ti or -di depending on voice quality of preceding phoneme ("pindeti" — you know, but "ahristi" — you obey)
third person plural (regardless of gender)	-os ("sheios" — they hunt)	-(repetition of last vowel sound)r ("pindeeri" — they know)

Conjugation 1 covers virtually all Azhani verbs. **Conjugation 2** verbs tend to be newer and more esoteric in nature. The unusual nature of their conjugation, together with the way they break the otherwise constant rule that identical vowels sounds are broken with a glotal stop (*i.e.* "mado'o" but "pindeer") suggests a these verbs were adapted from some other source.

SOME AZHANI TENSES

past	t+ the appropriate conjugation I ending+ the conjugated verb ("a sheia" — I hunt; "a tasheia" — I hunted)
past imperfect	the infinitive verb with the conjugation of to do ("a shei doa" — I was hunting)
future	do-+ the infinitive verb with ke +conjugation of to be (archaic form) ("a doshie kebrona" — I will hunt)

ENTER THE NEW WORLD OF

THE
DREAMING DARK
TRILOGY

Written by Keith Baker
The winning voice of the DUNGEONS & DRAGONS® setting search

CITY OF TOWERS
Volume One

Hardened by the Last War, four soldiers have come to Sharn,
fabled City of Towers, capital of adventure. In a time of uneasy
peace, these hardened warriors must struggle to survive. And
then people start turning up dead. The heroes find themselves
in an adventure that will take them from the highest reaches of
power to the most sordid depths of the city of wonder, shadow,
and adventure.

THE SHATTERED LAND
Volume Two

The epic adventure continues as Daine and the remnants of
his company travel to the dark continent of Xen'drik on an
adventure that may kill them all.

AVAILABLE IN 2005!

ENTER THE EXCITING, NEW DUNGEONS AND DRAGONS® SETTING... THE WORLD OF

THE
WAR~TORN
TRILOGY

THE CRIMSON TALISMAN
Book One

Adrian Cole

Erethindel, the fabled Crimson Talisman. Long sought by the forces of darkness. Long guarded in secret by one family. But now the secret has been revealed, and only one young man can keep it safe. As the talisman's powers awaken within him, Erethindel tears at his soul.

THE ORB OF XORIAT
Book Two

Edward Bolme

The Last War is over, and it took all that Teron ever had. A monk trained for war, he is the last of his Order. Now he is on a quest to find a powerful weapon that might set the world at war again.

AVAILABLE IN 2005!

TWO NEW SERIES EMERGE FROM THE RAVAGED WASTES OF... THE WORLD OF

THE
LOST MARK
TRILOGY

MARKED FOR DEATH
Book One

Matt Forbeck

Twelve dragonmarks. Sigils of immense magical power. Born by scions of mighty Houses, used through the centuries to wield authority and shape wonders throughout the Eberron world. But there are only twelve marks. Until now. Matt Forbeck begins the terrifying saga of the thirteenth dragonmark . . . The Mark of Death.

THE
DRAGON BELOW
TRILOGY

THE BINDING STONE
Book One

Don Bassingthwaite

A chance rescue brings old rivals together with a strange ally in a mission of vengeance against powers of ancient madness and corruption. But in the haunted forests of the Eldeen Reaches, even the most stalwart hero can soon find himself prey to the hidden horrors within the untamed wilderness.

AVAILABLE IN 2005!

FROM *NEW YORK TIMES*
BEST-SELLING AUTHOR
R.A. SALVATORE

In taverns, around campfires, and in the loftiest council chambers of Faerûn, people whisper the tales of a lone dark elf who stumbled out of the merciless Underdark to the no less unforgiving wilderness of the World Above and carved a life for himself, then lived a legend...

THE LEGEND OF DRIZZT

For the first time in deluxe hardcover editions, all three volumes of the Dark Elf Trilogy take their rightful place at the beginning of one of the greatest fantasy epics of all time. Each title contains striking new cover art and portions of an all-new author interview, with the questions posed by none other than the readers themselves.

HOMELAND
Being born in Menzoberranzan means a hard life surrounded by evil.

EXILE
But the only thing worse is being driven from the city with hunters on your trail.

SOJOURN
Unless you can find your way out, never to return.

THIS IS WHERE YOUR STORY BEGINS

Create your own heroes and embark on epic tales
of adventure filled with monsters, magic, trouble,
and treasure with the **Dungeons & Dragons**®
roleplaying game. You'll find everything you need to
get started in the **D&D**® *Basic Game* and can take your game
to the next level with the **D&D** *Player's Handbook*™.

Pick them up at your favorite bookstore.

wizards.com/dnd